Blood Vows Book Two

The Betrayal

E. JAMIE

ISBN-13: 978-0-9920463-1-6

FOR THE LADIES AT FL

CHAPTER ONE

They landed in Galway Airport by Alessandro's private jet on the first of September, both equally happy to get away from their families. Andy, the bodyguard, was with them at Alessandro's insistence. Never mind that Bree pointed out they were in a whole other country.

"I'm taking no chances with my family," Alessandro told her. He sent Andy out ahead of them off the plane to make sure it was safe before letting them disembark.

Gianni, a quiet baby for the most part had not been thrilled during both takeoff and landing. Will however, was happy as a clam, having been allowed in the cockpit a few times with the pilot.

He'd announced that he was gonna be a pilot when he 'growed up'.

Bree had been to Dublin once when she was young and that had been fun, but Dublin was a bustling city while Galway was…not. At least not by comparison.

As they stepped off the plane, she could swear she heard crickets chirping…if Galway even had crickets. One thing it had a lot of though was rain. As Bree clutched Gianni to her breast, the rain whipped furiously at her face. Alessandro tried covering them with both his umbrella and jacket as they rushed into the airport.

"Wow, dat was rewwy wet, huh, mommy?" Will said wiping his damp face.

"I thought we'd have to start counting animals two by two,"

Bree joked, pulling the blanket off Gianni's face. His brown eyes blinked, startled at the bright airport lighting.

"Ye'llbetheDardano'sthen,won'tye?Jesus,MaryandJosephbutit'sc omin' downouttheresureaslikethegreatdelugeitself.Yercar'swaitin'foryetota keyoutotheSeaBreezeLodgebutmaybeyel'llbewantin'toheadovertoM urphy'sBarforapintandabitetoeatbeforeyelayyerheaddown?" The little bald came after them with the force of a hurricane, taking Alessandro's hand and shaking it vigorously, his blue eyes like little indigo raisins in his face.

"I'm sorry, what?" Alessandro asked making Bree bite back a smile.

The man's smile wavered slightly.

"Thanks, but I think we'll just go straight to our rooms at the Sea Breeze Lodge," Bree said.

He turned back to Alessandro. "OhEnglishareye? Takemyadviceladdie. Whileyerhereletyermissusdothetalkin'"

"Seriously, what?" Alessandro repeated.

"He said, welcome to Galway," Bree lied, nodding to the man, thanking him silently for the warning about the lack of warmth towards the English as she moved Alessandro towards their waiting car.

"Brianna!" Alessandro cried out. Bree jolted awake. She turned and saw Alessandro standing over Gianni's bassinet, a hand clamped over his mouth.

"What is it? What's wrong?" Bree asked coming up beside him, her heart racing. She looked down at Gianni who didn't seem to be in any kind of trouble, happily kicking away under his blanket.

"He smiled at me!" Alessandro burst with excitement.

"He what?" Bree asked, half excited, half irked that Alessandro had nearly caused her to have a heart attack.

"He smiled. His mouth it - I saw it. He actually smiled at me. Oh, it was the most beautiful thing in the world." He reached in and grabbed Gianni, lifting him into his arms.

Bree smiled widely, as touched by Alessandro's joy as she was by the knowledge that her little boy had smiled for the first time, though she was a bit sad that she had not been the recipient of that first grin. "What did you do to make him smile?"

"Ah…" Alessandro bit back a grin and cleared his throat. "I might've sung a song."

"Really? What song?"

"As his mother, I don't think I should repeat it for you," Alessandro said, his cheeks and the tips of his ears pink.

"Oh come on, Alessandro. The windows didn't break so you couldn't have done that bad a job."

"It's not my ability that I'm referring to," Alessandro replied.

Bree narrowed her eyes. "Just what were you singing to my son? And so help me if you say anything by Sir Mix-a-lot I'll castrate you,"

"Not quite," Alessandro said. "All right. But, remember you asked for it. Your cousin Max, taught it to me."

Bree crossed her arms over her breasts and waited.

> *"Now go wash your face and comb your hair, its dang near time to start*
> *but let me tell you 'fore we go, there's one that's got my heart*
> *don't chase that gal with the yeller hair and wears a dress of green*
> *that little gal belongs to me, I know she's past sixteen.*
> *Hey, I won't go huntin' with you Gianni but I'll go chasin' women*
> *so put your hounds back in the pens and quit your silly grinnin'*
> *the moon is right and I'm half tight, my life is just beginnin'*
> *I won't go huntin' with you Gianni but I'll go chasin' women.*
> *Now I'm headed for the general store when a silly thing I seen*
> *they make 'em in the city and it's called a magazine*
> *I turned to page thirty-two, huh, look at what I found*
> *them girls wear clothes that we ain't seen beneath them gingham gowns."*

Bree was torn between laughing out loud and smacking him

over his tousled head. Never mind that Gianni was making gurgling sounds and smacking his lips together and of course, grinning. "You're singing to him about porn?"

"Not exactly. I mean, what about the part about the girl with the yellow hair and green dress that stole my heart?"

"You made that part up because I was standing in front of you," Bree insisted.

"I did not," Alessandro insisted.

Bree didn't believe him, but her heart was too full at the smile on Gianni's face. "Yeah well, keep it up and the only one getting under my gingham gown will be this little guy," Bree extended her arms for the baby as she pulled down the strap of her nightgown.

"That might be a more valid threat if we were actually engaging in anything that I would miss as a result of punishment for my bawdy songs." Alessandro pointed out sitting on the bed behind her, sweeping her hair over one shoulder with his hand so that he could nuzzle her neck.

Bree sighed, her body warm and still slightly heavy with sleep. Gianni's lips suckled eagerly as his father's lips trailed slowly along bare skin.

"I have never wanted to be an infant more," Alessandro murmured, reaching up to cup her free breast.

"I'm certainly glad you're full grown," Bree pointed out.

"Mmmm," Alessandro agreed. "Full grown and aching,"

"Well, maybe we could do something about that later," Bree offered, her body humming and more than ready to get back to their regularly scheduled fucking program.

"Darling, don't dangle the dream like that and then take it away," Alessandro whispered in her ear. "I can barely stand waiting to get inside of you again,"

Bree's body grew flushed and damp. "Me neither," she admitted turning to look at him. He caught her mouth with his and slid his tongue along her teeth before she opened her mouth to meet his tongue with her own. Bree trembled with the need of way too long without him. His hand travelled down to press his fingers into her thigh. He nibbled her bottom lip as he pulled back with a smile.

"Oh why are you loitering here, pretty maid?
I am waiting for my true love, softly she said
Shall I be your true love and will you agree

Down by the green bushes to tarry with me?"

"Mmm, bushes? Really? How kinky," Bree said smiling and reaching down to stroke Gianni's cheek. His brown eyes fluttered before closing again, intent on his meal. "I'll see what I can do," she said, winking at Alessandro who laughed at her.

"We should go wake up Will and get downstairs for breakfast," Bree said when Gianni finally released her.

"Or we could stay in," Alessandro wiggled his eyebrows at her suggestively. "We could make our own coffee or tea."

"And Will?" Bree asked.

"Coffee will put some hair on his chest," Alessandro offered. She smacked his arm and scrambled off the bed placing Gianni back in his bassinet.

He was having none of that though and began to fuss and whimper.

"I know, I know. You miss mummy's breasts. I know just how you feel," Alessandro joked.

Bree looked out the window and gasped at the gorgeous sunrise. "Would you look at that?"

Alessandro followed her gaze and nodded. "New York sunrise doesn't quite cut it, does it?"

Bree made her way to the bathroom, stopping when she heard his voice.

"I like big butts and I cannot lie. You other brothers can't deny—"

Bree grabbed a sponge from inside the bathroom and threw it at his head before shutting the door.

They had lunch at Murphy's Pub. Will loved the green coloured soda; and the patrons adored him, teaching him all manner of naughty Irish songs, which he sang loudly as he skipped down the street after they left the pub. The bartender, a rather robust woman by the name of Morganna, Morgie for short, gave them directions to St. Malachy, Francesca's parish. Bree and Alessandro would be going there the next day.

"Are you sure I won't be struck by lightning?" Alessandro asked as they walked through Eyre Square, Will ahead of them, a sack of bread around his wrist. Alessandro had to remind him to break off pieces and not throw whole slices at the poor birds. Andy walked ahead of them, a walkie-talkie strapped around his waist and a gun in the pocket of his jacket.

"Mmm, good point. Maybe I should go alone," Bree joked.

"Not bloody likely," Alessandro replied pulling her close as she pushed Gianni in the stroller. "I'm not letting you out of my sight,"

"That sounds promising," Bree said with a smile.

They spent most of the day getting familiar with the city. The time flew by as every five minutes someone stopped them to fawn over the baby and Will inevitably would have to do something to shift attention to him. Usually, he'd break out into one of his newly acquired Irish songs, sending the people into howls of laughter. They marvelled at how much Gianni looked like Alessandro and Will they said, looked more like Bree.

Alessandro said nothing, but Bree could tell the reminder that Will wasn't biologically his had dampened his spirits.

He was silent all through dinner at one of restaurants close to the docks.

"Daddy, we go in da boats tomorrow?" Will asked, mesmerized by the sight of the large boats outside.

Alessandro nodded silently, distracted.

When they got back to the lodge, it was dark. Bree asked Andy if he wouldn't mind watching Will and the baby for about two hours. She had an idea that she thought might cheer him up but she couldn't be gone long. Gianni needed her close…er…needed her breasts close.

"Where are we going exactly?" Alessandro asked as Bree guided him through the streets, hoping she remembered where the exact spot was in the dark. It was secluded enough for what she had in mind.

"To find some green bushes," Bree replied, referring to his earlier song with a hand on his thigh.

He jumped in the driver's seat and stared at her, his eyes hungry in the dark. "Brianna, my naughty girl,"

"That's me," Bree whispered telling him to stop the car.

There were no streetlights as there was no street. Only the moonlight kept her from falling on her face as she took Alessandro's hand and led him to the high bushes, the scent of heather filled the air.

They were close to the water. She briefly wondered if Adriano and Francesca had ever come here to this exact spot. She felt an inexplicable pull to it for some reason and wondered if that was why.

Bree smiled up at him as she began pulling his shirt out from the waistband of his jeans. Her hands moved under his shirt, caressing warm, tight skin. "I've missed you," she whispered. "I've missed feeling you inside of me," Bree undid the buttons of his shirt, running kisses along the inches of slowly revealed skin.

"Ditto," Alessandro said hoarsely, using her expression.

He looked like hard, silver marble as she slid the fabric off his shoulders, the moon behind him making his skin gleam.

She got down to her knees and undid his jeans, pulling the material down off his hips, letting his erection free. Bree took him into her mouth, running her tongue along the tight, warm skin, feeling the soft drops of his arousal gather on her tongue. Her hands went to his behind, bringing him closer.

"Christ, Brianna. You look like some deliciously debauched angel down there," he growled, his fingers tightening in her hair.

She smiled up at him and sucked harder, her own body opening, clutching in anticipation of the shaft in her mouth driving deep into her pussy.

He swore and pulled her away from him. "Your turn, darling." His hands trembled with barely restrained passion as he guided her onto the ground.

The smell of earth, flowers and Alessandro filled her nostrils as he moved down. "You're like gold all over," he murmured, stroking her skin before moving down between her legs.

Bree trembled at his touch, looking up at the moon and stars above them. The sight before her blurred and then got sharper as Alessandro's mouth followed his fingers, stroking, piercing, and fucking her deeply. She was thankful it hadn't rained all day, though the air was cool.

Alessandro's body was warm and his touch on her thighs, spreading her wider, was like fire. She reached down and gripped his head. Begging, pleading…coming. As her body trembled and arched, rolling in powerful waves, Alessandro came up, covering her and pushed into her with one deep thrust.

Bree cried out, part pleasure and a slight sting of pain at her still slightly sore body. But she wanted, needed his cock like a wanderer long denied water.

"Are you all right?" Alessandro asked, sucking in his breath.

Bree nodded. "Don't stop," She dug her nails into his shoulders. "Oh God,"

He moved slowly, belying the violence etched on his face that told her he wanted to ram her into the ground, fuck her straight through the earth.

Bree wrapped her legs around his waist. "Oh I've missed you," she sighed into his ear, rolling her hips eagerly beneath him, ignoring the hard packed floor under her.

Alessandro brought his mouth down to her neck, sucking at her pulse, scratching her with his stubble. She writhed against him, wanting him deeper, harder.

Bree must have said the words aloud 'cause his grip on her hips tightened and he drove down more violently, shaking above her.

She trembled, her breasts growing heavy, the skin and nerves stretching and filling until before Bree could warn him, her breasts burst her milk between them. Alessandro gave a start of surprise and pulled back.

Bree felt a moment's embarrassment, not knowing how he would react. She doubted he'd ever slept with a woman who'd just given birth before.

"Wow," Alessandro murmured, he looked down at her in question. "Do you think our son would mind?" Before she could ask what he meant, Alessandro lowered his mouth to her breasts, licking, sucking, and drinking the silky sweet liquid.

"Oh God…Oh God…" Bree moaned, her body feeling as if it had been submerged in electricity.

His hips slowed their thrusts as he concentrated on her breasts.

She trembled at the foreign sensations. *He'd* never done this. Michael. There was something elemental, primal about Alessandro doing this to her.

Bree clutched tight around his cock, feeling the deep pulsing begin in her chest and rolling downward in breathtaking waves.

"Must save some for our son," Alessandro said coming back up to her mouth so she could taste the sweetness of her milk on his lips.

She raised her hips up to match his thrusts, which had renewed their driving fierceness.

"Oh Alessandro…I love you, I love you, I love you…" she panted in his ear as he fucked her in delicious deep thrusts.

Then he was flipping her over so that she was on top. His cock was buried even deeper now and Bree couldn't breathe for the frenzied sensations exploding through her.

"Come for me, darling," he growled and she could feel him swelling thicker inside of her with impending release. "Come with me."

Then she was. Bree arched back and cried out as she came, feeling him filling her with his orgasm and his very soul at the same time. She felt as if she was melting into him, merging, joining every single part of her body, every nerve ending, every vein and muscle with his until they were one pulsing, rolling, arching body. Her body tensed and bowed forward, her mouth in his hair as she collapsed against him, feeling his thick release pulsing into her. She panted, breathless against his face as he cradled her against his body, pulling her down onto him.

"Well, that was new," Alessandro, panted with a laugh.

They'd never come at the same time like that before. It had felt so…different, like their souls had been anchored somewhere outside of themselves, here in this place.

That's how Bree knew. Adriano and Francesca had made love here before.

She was sure of it, not with her brain. With her soul.

CHAPTER TWO

St. Malachy's church was a small but elegantly structured building. The outside showed the wear of the years with clean but weather-beaten wood and stone. The inside gleamed with shining black and white tiled floor and pews of shining dark brown wood. Two round trays of lit votive candles flanked the front of the altar. Stained glass windows in a simple pattern of lines and circles ran along the walls. Long burgundy carpet ran up the aisle, climbing up the few stairs to the altar.

"Mommy, look. Dat's da baby Jesus, right?" Will asked, running up the aisle to the eggshell white statue of the Madonna with the aforementioned 'Baby Jesus' in her arms. His small voice boomed in the empty chapel and Bree cringed, grateful that no one was around to be disturbed but not eager for the priest on duty to find them just yet.

"Shhh, Will. That's right."

"Ca' I have a cookie today?" Will asked.

'Cookie' was the Eucharist and ever since Will had seen her and the other O'Reileys go up to get communion, he'd been itching to get his turn. Never mind that Bree insisted to him that the host didn't taste like much. Once, she'd cheated and given him a little piece out of her mouth. He'd wanted more.

"You're too young still. You'll have your communion when you're eight."

"How many more days is dat? Is taking forever!" Will insisted. "I still only in da fours!"

"It'll come like that," Alessandro said, snapping his fingers.

Will raised his fingers and tried to mimic the act, scowling when he couldn't make the same popping sound. Alessandro bent down so he was eye level with Will and took his small hand in his, positioning the fingers appropriately. Didn't work.

"Can't do it," Will said annoyed. "My fingers is stupid,"

"Ah no worries, little Will. With some practice you'll be a pro in no time," Alessandro assured him. "Try this,"

Bree burst out laughing when Alessandro proceeded to pat his own head and rub his stomach at the same time.

"Ah you laugh, darling but it's quite a learned skill," Alessandro insisted, turning to look at her as he continued to pat his head.

"Look daddy! I can did it!" Will exclaimed with a squeal of delight. And Bree smiled because sure enough he was patting his head and rubbing his tummy at the same time.

She turned away from them to take in more of the church's décor and gave a little gasp at the small gold plaque by the font of holy water at the entrance. "Alessandro, look," She pushed Gianni's stroller closer to the plaque so she could read it.

Alessandro got to his feet and followed her. Bree's heart raced as she read the engraved words aloud. "In honor of Francesca O'Reiley. Nineteen twenty-seven to nineteen forty-nine."

"A tragedy it was," A male voice remarked behind them. Bree turned and saw a middle-aged man in a roman collar. His face was sad but kind with wide brown eyes. She immediately dismissed him as too young to have known Francesca or Adriano personally.

"Yes, it was. My name is Bree O'Reiley," she extended her hand to the priest, deciding on using her maiden name for convenience's sake. People might be more apt to open up to her if they knew she was personally connected to Francesca.

"Father Scott. Ah, a relation, are ye?" he asked.

Bree nodded. "She was my great aunt. I was hoping to learn some more about her."

"Oh, well, I wish I could help ye meself. But I wasn't born yet when our poor Francesca fell of that cliff,"

Fell. Right. Alessandro gave Bree a look that told her he was thinking the same thing. So that was the story that had been sold so that Francesca's reputation wouldn't be tarnished.

"They never found her body, ye know? 'Tis the reason there be no plot for her in the cemetery."

"Her priest was a Father Mallory. Do you know if he's still around?" Alessandro asked.

"Oh, afraid not. Father Mallory passed on just last year. The cancer was what he had. May the lord bless his soul."

Bree bit back a curse.

"But ye know, Sister Brannigan, the Mother Superior over at the convent is still alive and she might be able to help ye."

Bree smiled with a renewed burst of excitement. "Can you tell us how to get there?"

"Oh 'tis a mere skip and a jump from here, it is. Follow this same road and ye'll hit it in no time."

"Excuse me. Can I have a cookie?" Will asked, tugging on the man's robe.

Father Scott smiled as he went down on one knee. "And who might you be, young lad?"

"My name is William Donovan," Will extended his hand and Bree heard Alessandro snort behind her. "Dis is my little brudder Gianni but he don't do nuffin except sleep and eat my mommy,"

Bree covered her mouth in shock and could not look at the priest. It didn't help that Alessandro's snort had turned into full blown laughter.

Father Scott's cheeks went bright pink, but he gave Bree a sympathetic smile. "And it's a cookie, yer wantin'?"

"He wants the host, Father. I tried to explain to him that he's too young," Bree said.

"She say I too young for everyting!" Will exclaimed.

"Ah, well, let's see what we can do about that, shall we? Do ye know your Hail Mary's, young William?"

"Hail Mary full of cake!" Will said, confidently quoting the beginning of a joke Max had taught him back in New York.

The convent was in considerably better condition than St. Malachy's. It stood high atop a grassy hill. Only the black roof was visible from St. Malachy's. In front of them, flanking the road was an abundance of trees that practically hid the convent from view.

"A skip and a jump. Sure," Bree grumbled. Father Scott neglected to mention that the skipping and jumping would be taking place mostly up hill. And Alessandro had left the car back at the hotel. The weather was mild and sunny for early September and the weatherman had promised a break from the rain. Still, Bree brought the umbrella with her, just in case.

The path was well worn up to the convent but it was a hell of a climb. Gianni had awoken from his nap with a confused wail. Poor kid, probably wondering why the hell his world was now tilted. Alessandro reached in and grabbed him from the stroller.

Will was barely panting, clutching his bag of little round Eucharists and happily munching away. The priest had offered him a handful from the as of yet unblessed supply. Will had firmly announced that when he grew up he was gonna be a 'peest' too.

The mental image of one of her children becoming a priest had sent Bree into a fit of giggles that had lasted a good ten minutes, and even now, still made her smile. That would be the height of irony, she thought. The son of Bree O'Reiley, a man of the cloth.

"I'd say it's rather ingenious of the superiors up at the convent, wouldn't you?" Alessandro asked.

"What do you mean?" Bree asked looking up briefly before returning her gaze to the ground, looking out for stray branches or stones that might make her trip.

"Well, any sins the sisters commit on their errands down in the city, they can make up for in their climb back up. Exercise as penance," he said.

"Yeah, no kidding," Bree panted as they finally reached the top.

"How was that, Gianni?" Alessandro asked holding the baby up. "Enjoy your little trek?" The baby arched and closed one eye.

"I'll take that as a yes."

"So this is it," Bree remarked, looking at the simple white stone building, surrounded by grey, fortress-like stonewalls.

"I could make a chastity joke about breaching the walls but who knows who's listening on the other side, eh?" Alessandro cracked.

Bree shook her head and walked up to the black iron gate.

"Haloooo?" A disembodied, static voice made them jump. Then Alessandro pointed to the small speaker and keypad next to gate.

"And who says religion is outdated? Most likely to protect all the untouched treasures inside, no doubt."

Bree smacked his chest and shushed him. "Uh, hi. My name is Bree O'Reiley. I'm here to talk to the Mother Superior."

"Oooh, Mother Superior is having her nap right now but yer name is O'Reiley, did ye say?"

"That's right," Bree said. She turned to Alessandro and smiled.

"And you think your name is the only one with any power."

"No self-respecting Dardano would ever use his name to get into a convent," Alessandro pointed out.

"Come on in then and ye can have a cuppa while I get the Mother Superior up for ye," the woman offered through the speaker. With a click and a buzz, the iron gate unlocked and Bree pushed through.

"Where are we?" Will asked following behind Bree and the stroller.

"This is a convent, Will. Your great great Aunt Francesca used to visit and help the nuns here."

"It's a big house. Not as big as yours though," Will remarked reaching up and taking Alessandro's free hand. The impeccably manicured lawn and bushes of white roses and violets flanked the walk up to the building. The door swung open as they made their way up the stairs. A rosy cheeked, roly-poly of a woman smiled at them. "Haloo there, Ms. O'Reiley-Ooh, I beg yer pardon, Mrs. O'Reiley," she corrected as she took in Alessandro and the two children.

Bree looked at Alessandro who was none too happy be thought of as Mr. O'Reiley. "Just nod and smile. We want information from these people and I think they'd frown on knowing we're not married," she whispered.

"And so you couldn't say, Mrs. Dardano?" Alessandro scowled lowering his voice, as they got closer to the door.

"I don't think the Dardanos have the best track record here according to my grandfather," Bree reminded him.

They were led into the Mother Superior's office. The woman who'd met them at the door introduced herself as Sister McReady and poured them each a cup of tea after asking if they wanted sugar. She pursed her lips when Alessandro asked for milk in his tea. "I'll go get the Mother Superior."

"You just had to show you're English, didn't ya?" Bree cracked. "Milk in your tea."

"How come dat lady looked like a penguin?" Will asked.

"That's what nuns wear," Bree explained. Gianni began fussing in Alessandro's arms and Bree felt her breasts respond to his need. *Dammit.* What kind of first impression would they make if the nun walked in on Bree with her breast hanging out and a baby attached to it? She quickly undid her blouse "Here, give him to me quick. By some miracle maybe he'll be done before she gets here."

Thankfully, Sister Brannigan's age worked in Bree's favour. Gianni made quicker progress than the old nun. And he fell asleep mid-feeding. She was just doing up her last button when an old woman appeared in the doorway with Sister McReady at her side.

She took one look at Alessandro and Bree and placed a hand on her chest. "Jesus, Mary and Joseph. Francesca, lass. Is that you?"

And then she fainted.

"Holy shit!" Bree rushed to the fallen nun's side, ignoring Sister McReady's scowl of disapproval at her language.

"Mommy! You killed da penguin lady!" Will cried out in surprise.

Bree lightly slapped the old woman's face and felt a rush of relief when the Mother Superior stirred. The last thing she needed on her conscience was a dead nun.

The old woman's blue eyes opened and anger filled them when her gaze shifted to Alessandro. "You. You spawn of the devil. Why don't ye take yerself back where ye came from and leave our poor Francesca alone?"

"Oh, Mother Superior, yer confused is all. Come now. On yer feet, mum," Sister McReady said helping the old woman up.

"Uh, I'm sorry. Sister. Francesca was my great aunt. My name is Bree."

"Bree? Jaysus but it's a ridiculous resemblance it is," the old woman panted, holding her chest. "And you?" She asked turning to Alessandro. "Of course yer not Adriano Dardano, of course but I'll be a drunken fairy if yer not the spitting image of that demon of temptation, sent to corrupt our poor Francesca. Such a good girl she was," Sister Brannigan murmured, tears filling her eyes. "Such a good girl."

"Should we call a doctor?" Alessandro asked.

"Oh pfft!" the old nun insisted. "Just a wee loss of breath, me lad. Nothing at all. At my age, it keeps things exciting, it does,"

"What can you tell us about my great aunt and Adriano Dardano?" Bree asked.

Sister Brannigan lifted her gaze to Sister McReady and asked her to leave them alone. Once the younger nun left, the old woman shook her head. "I saw it the first time she mentioned his name to me. It was as if a light had been switched on inside of her. A light I'd only seen when she spoke of her devotion to our Lord."

Bree sat back and listened, imagining two such opposite things provoking a similar reaction like that.

"He'd come to Ireland to visit his friend. Our poor Gavin's cousin, the Shaunessy boy."

"They met at St Malachy's, right?" Bree asked. "He'd been injured."

"Aye. At the annual church social. One of our boys got a wee bit too deep in his cups, forgot his manners with Frankie and Adriano intervened. Well, before you knew it, tempers were up and fists started flying. Cracked in the head by a bottle, Adriano was, not that it damaged the part of him that could plot and plan that poor girl's downfall."

"You don't sound like a fan," Alessandro replied wryly.

Sister Brannigan scowled at him. "Francesca was a wee innocent of seventeen, for all her sinful bravado. And yer Adriano Dardano had no business tangling with the likes of her as she was promised to our Gavin. I could see how that devil's show of heroism put the stars in her eyes. Though to hear Francesca tell it, she had it all under control,"

"Just because she was young doesn't mean she was some naïve little twit who didn't know her own mind," Bree said, insulted on her great aunt's behalf.

"Aye, she knew her own mind and no one could tell Francesca any different. From the time they were children, everyone in the village knew that she and Gavin were meant for each other. That was her path in life,"

"God forbid she should change her mind," Alessandro said.

"'Twasn't she that changed it. Mr. Dardano," the nun spat, her blue eyes fiery with irritation.

Bree turned back and urged Alessandro to keep his mouth shut.

"Forgive me, darling but it's hardly fair to expect me to just listen here as my grandfather's name is dragged through the mud. Francesca was free to make her own choice, or should have been."

"Her choice was to give her heart to Gavin. She was happy. At peace. And then *he* came along and muddied it all up for her. Though I'll give you that, young Mr. Dardano. She was free to make her own choices and when she came to me, asking my advice, I reminded her of her promises, but that she also shouldn't lead poor Gavin on if her feelings had genuinely changed. My heart was heavy about it." The woman sighed. "I met him just the once, yer grandfather. Like I said, spittin image of ye, he was and much of the same gift fer gab as ye have. Strong minded. Could charm the wool off a sheep yer grand da could." She struggled to her feet. "Got to move around a bit or the old bones lock up on me and then it's a trial and a half gettin' back up again."

Bree held her breath as she watched the woman shuffle around the room, her thick black habit making a soft swishing sound as she moved.

"How come you have to wear dat big coat inside?" Will asked, popping another communion wafer in his mouth. "Ain't you hot?"

Sister Branningan blinked and stared at him. "What is that yer eatin' there, young man? Jaysus! Is that the body of Christ, yer snackin' away on?"

"Noooooooo!" Will screamed when she reached for the bag of wafers. He clutched it tight to his chest. "My cookies! Da peest gimmie dem!"

Bree cringed and got to her feet. "Father Scott gave him some from the unblessed supply,"

The old woman shook her head but eased away from Will who continued to eye her suspiciously and keep a death grip on his bag.

"Aye well, that Father Scott is an odd one. As are all these new priests with their new ideas. Do ye know they don't read the mass in Latin anymore? A travesty it is."

At the commotion, Gianni awaked and began to cry. Bree rushed over to him and lifted him up out of the stroller.

"It's okay, sweetie. Mommy's here. Shh..." Bree rubbed his back soothingly.

"And if he isn't a lovely wee baby, ye have there," Sister Branningan remarked with a smile. "Would ye mind?" she asked, extending her hands.

Bree eased Gianni into the nun's arms. The old woman's face softened considerably as Gianni quieted down, one tiny hand reaching out to grab the thick crucifix around her neck. "Ah there we are then. Nice and peaceful aren't we now?"

"Did you think her heart would have turned back to Gavin if Adriano left?" Bree asked.

Sister Brannigan looked up blankly. "Who?"

Bree bit back a whimper of impatience. "Francesca,"

"Oh," Sister Brannigan's eyes widened. "Why, Frankie's been dead for o'r fifty years now, child."

Bree looked back at Alessandro in confusion. "Sister, we're here to talk about Francesca and Adriano, remember?"

The old woman's eyes cleared and she nodded. "Ah yes. Yes of course, ye are. That Adriano Dardano. He should have known better. He should have known to leave poor Francesca alone. Love does make ye take leave of yer senses though, doesn't it?"

"No kidding," Bree remarked out loud without meaning to. She felt Alessandro's eyes on her but didn't turn around.

"So for all your hatred of the man, you do believe he loved her?" Alessandro asked.

"I hardly hated him. I don't hate anyone, young man. God does not allow for any such emotion when serving him. I pitied your grand da, I did. Ye'd have to be blind or stupid not to see how much he loved our Francesca. But she wasn't meant for him."

She ran a long, wrinkled finger down Gianni's cheek. "Aye, 'twas a miserable situation over all. But none paid more dearly than our Francesca. None more dearly than her."

CHAPTER THREE

Bree woke to the feeling of Alessandro's hand creeping across her ribcage. Higher. The window was partially opened and the sound of the water drifted into the bedroom, along with the faint sounds of the boats. His fingers curved under one breast, molding the full curve, heavy with milk. She sighed and burrowed closer to his warmth. The morning was chilly but the cool air felt good against her face.

Sister Brannigan had assured them they could come back. But today was Will's birthday and the past would have to wait as they celebrated the future.

Alessandro's hand drifted to the strap of her nightgown, easing it down with slow but purposeful intent. Bree's body immediately responded, her behind pushing back in welcome against his arousal. She sighed when his mouth came down along the skin of her shoulder.

They heard a small whimper from the bassinet. Alessandro's hand stilled and Bree froze. *No…nononono.* She pleaded silently, her eyes squeezing shut. Then nothing. She heard Alessandro give a grateful sigh as his hand continued its exploration. His thumb caressed her nipple, making it pucker. Bree sucked in her breath and took Alessandro's other hand, easing it between her legs.

Another, more insistent whimper.

Bree followed it with a whimper of her own, pushing Alessandro's fingers more tightly against her damp center. "It's okay," she whispered. "Just give it a minute. Maybe he'll go back to sleep,"

Quiet.

Alessandro's fingers continued. Bree turned towards him and smiled at the sleepy hunger in his gaze. She eased onto him, running her mouth along the hard muscles of his chest, sprinkled with a light dusting of dark hair. His fingers went into her hair, rubbing her scalp as he guided her upwards to his mouth. Her hips rocked slowly against the morning evidence of his desire. His mouth claimed her with a greedy grunt and his tongue teased the curves of her mouth.

Another whimper that grew steadily into a full-blown wail. Bree fell against Alessandro with a sad laugh of defeat.

"He knows. I swear he knows I want to fuck his mother. Bloody hell," Alessandro swore. "And now I have to watch that lucky bugger sucking on your breasts. Sorry. I love you, but that's more than I can bear this morning," He spanked her behind and moved her off of him.

"Awww," Bree commiserated, climbing out of the bed to pick up a crying Gianni. Her body a full wet mess of aroused nerves. "Rain check?"

Alessandro rolled his eyes. "Only if I can drag you into the nearest coat closet."

"Deal," Bree promised.

Alessandro opened the door and nearly tripped over an excited Will.

"Is my birthday today! I'm dis many, see?" He held up all five fingers as he bounced on the balls of his feet.

"You are? Why I completely forgot," Alessandro lied, reaching down and picking Will up into his arms.

"Well, you have to 'member now! 'Cause you have to get me a pesent and cake."

Bree came out, a happily sucking Gianni at her breast, discreetly hidden by her nightgown. Alessandro scowled at her. "You evil temptress," he said, reaching over and kissing her cheek. He dropped a kiss on Gianni's forehead. "You lucky bugger. I'm gonna take a shower and then we can go down for breakfast. Lots to do today. Apparently it's some kind of special occasion." Alessandro shrugged with a teasing smile, motioning his eyes toward Will.

"Daddy! It's my birthday!" Will repeated. "Mommy guess what?" he turned and smiled at Bree.

"What?" Bree asked indulgently.

"Did you 'member it was my birthday?" Will asked. "I want a chocwate cake."

"Oh is it today? Are you sure?" Bree asked.

"Yes, I'm sure! You told me when I wokeded up dat it would be my birthday. Well, now I wokeded up!"

"Well, what do you know? You are awake now. That must mean we have to have a party."

Will jumped up and down excitedly. "Dat's true! Did you get my pesent already?"

Bree had found a hilarious bike/wagon thing that Will could sit in and peddle his way down the road while bubbles came out the end. He'd seen it in a store a few days earlier and the shopkeeper had let him ride around on it.

Alessandro had gotten him a small brown Irish Jack Russell puppy. While Bree agreed it was the cutest thing ever and was touched that Morgie at the pub was willing to sell one of her litter of three, she worried what Will's reaction would be. Considering what her son had seen Arturo do to the poor dog, she didn't want him to be reminded of something so awful.

"Do you think he's forgotten?" Alessandro had asked her as the lay in bed the night before.

"I don't want him to have that kind of a memory forever. He's too little to have that in the back of his innocent mind."

"I know you don't," Alessandro had said, pulling her closer and kissing her head. "Will is a strong, resilient boy. He's a happy child, despite what he's seen. I want him to have something positive to replace the memory of that dead dog. Not that it will completely, but it will help him think of something happy when he thinks of a dog."

"Are you sure?" Bree asked uncertainly.

"No. But I want you to allow me to try," Alessandro admitted.

And so Alessandro had gotten the dog. It had been staying at Murphy's Bar for the past few days where the party would be held.

Bree got Gianni dressed, meanwhile fielding questions from Will who was trying to discover what his presents were. After putting Gianni in the car seat and setting it by the door, so they could leave straight after breakfast. Bree ducked back into the bathroom and found Alessandro leaning over the sink, a towel around his waist as he finished shaving.

He cocked an eyebrow as she brought her arms around his waist and pressed her mouth to his back. He smelled of delicious, spicy after-shave. "Think we have time for a quickie?" Bree asked looking down at her watch. They had ten minutes before breakfast.

Alessandro reached around and grabbed her, placing her up onto the sink and dropping his towel. His erection sprang thick and ready between them.

An insistent knock had them darting apart.

"Mommy, Gianni stinks. I tink he went poopy diaper,"

Bree bit into Alessandro's shoulder as they both gave muted screams of frustration.

"It's gonna be one long fucking day," Alessandro groaned.

"SURPRISE!" Everyone in the pub came out of their respective hiding places.

Will nearly fell out of Bree's arms with a startled squeal of excitement.

Gianni, jolted by the sudden noise began to cry. Alessandro reached into the stroller and pulled him out to comfort him.

"Is a supise party fo me!" Will clapped in delight. "'Cause is my birthday!"

"That's right, wee Will," Morgie said, coming out holding a big blue balloon.

"Did you know I'm dis many?" Will asked holding up his hand, fingers spread wide.

"All of five? Oh by Saint Brigit, ye'll be an old man soon," Morgie joked.

Alessandro had arranged for the pub to close for Will's private party, inviting most of the locals that they had become familiar with over the past few days to bring their children.

"Where's my cake?" Will asked, urging Bree to let him down.

"That's coming later," Bree told him as Gianni quieted down in Alessandro's arms as his father stroked his back and bounced him gently.

"Where's my pesents?" Will asked.

"Later," Bree repeated.

Will looked back at his mother, his lips pursed in such a perfect mimic of Irish disapproval that Bree almost laughed out loud.

"For now, little William, why don't you head on over with the other wee boys and girls and play," Morgie offered with a hand to Will's back, guiding him towards the small crowd of children at the back of the pub.

"Oooh and let me have a look at this wee darling," Morgie extended her arms for Gianni and Alessandro didn't even try to deny her. Gianni reached up to grab a fistful of her red hair. But Morgie, being a curvy mother of seven, was well versed in dodging little fingers and easily took his hand before he could get a good grasp.

"Come on then, Dardano. Sit yerself down and have a pint," Morgie's husband, Thomas insisted, slapping a hearty hand against Alessandro's back. Bree watched Alessandro quickly scan the room and nod to Andy at the back of the pub in silent undeniable order. *Keep an eye out.* Bree sighed. Even here, in Ireland, they couldn't let their guard down.

"Oy, English!" A voice called out behind them. "I'm finally remembering where it is I've heard yer name before." Bree and Alessandro turned to see a tall, lanky middle-aged man limping up to them. Geordie had lost his leg in the gulf war back in '91. While he wasn't a fan of the English by any stretch of the imagination, Alessandro had endeared himself to many of the locals, Geordie included, by buying a round of beers for everyone. They dubbed Alessandro 'all right, for a Sassenach," They had nicknamed him 'English".

"'Twas me father-in-law reminded me of it, he did. I'm sittin with him last night after our dinner, havin' a bit of a smoke outside-"

"Is the stupid blighter still, smokin'? After the doctor be telling him not to?" Morgie asked. "I swear, that old man hasn't got the sense God gave a goat, he doesn't."

"Aye and what that eejit doctor be about?" Michael Kinnean, a black Irish man, which Bree had tried to disguise her surprise over the first time she met him, piped up. "A sad day it is when a man works his whole long life and he can't be having a smoke from his pipe on his own bleedin' porch. 'Tis a disgrace, I tell ye, the way doctors who wouldn't know their arse from their elbow are trying to take away the wee pleasures in life, just so they can line their own pockets."

"Ah, Geordie, you were saying?" Bree jumped in before the whole crowd began philosophising.

"Oh, aye. You're right. Right. Now, as I was sayin'. There I was, sittin' on me porch, telling him about the Englishman who's polluted our midst. No offence ye understand, when he starts in again on the fight at St Malachy's all those years ago and he knew a Dardano back then but he was an Italian."

"Yes, my grandfather Adriano was from Italy. I grew up in London," Alessandro explained.

"Ohhh, so ye're an Italian, ye are? That explains it then. 'Tis not the English blood that runs through yer veins. Just yer funny accent."

Alessandro bit his lip and Bree could see him trying not laugh. *His* funny accent. *Right.*

"Oh, did ye know young Rosie McKinnon is marrying an Italian?" Morgie spoke up. "And not even a Catholic one at that? One of that science religion with its nonsense about spaceships and they like. Her poor parents are about ready to keel over from the shame of it."

"My grandfather?" Alessandro urged trying to swing the conversation back.

"Oy, yes. Cracked him on the head our Finn did. Oh mind ye, it was an accident of course. Me father in law's a kind a soul as ye'll ever meet. But he was swept into the fray that started when that n'er do well Patrick Leeny disrespected Ms O'Reiley back then. The Leeny boy had your grandda held back by his hooligan friends. Poor Finn tries to swing his bottle of ale at Patrick but the blighter moved at the last minute and it caught yer grandfather on the side of the head and down he goes like a sack of potatoes, the poor soul. If it wasn't for the lass Francesca's quick work with a needle and thread to patch up the poor boy, it'd be the undertaker who'd have been tuckin' him in that night."

"Aye and from what I hear, a right job that lass did, 'tuckin' him in indeed, if ye get me meaning," Gertie Riley piped up with a snort.

Bree scowled at the young blond woman. Morgie clucked her tongue and motioned towards Bree in warning.

"Mind yer tongue ye stupid bird. And I'll not have ye speakin ill of the dead in front of the poor woman's great niece."

"No, that's all right," Bree, said not sure she wanted Gertie's version of anything, but desperate for any more info on Adriano and Francesca. "I want to hear what happened.

"I'm only telling what me sainted mother's sister told her." Then Gertie smiled and stepped closer so that the side of her breast brushed Alessandro's elbow.

"Though, I can't really fault the poor sister for being taken in by such a charmer as yer grandfather,"

Alessandro looked down and cocked an eyebrow at Gertie's none too subtle attempt at flirtation.

Bree gritted her teeth and reminded herself that it's not nice to kill someone on your son's birthday.

How could she even think what she's thinking? Alessandro wondered silently as he watched Brianna glare pure murder at the misguided Gertie smiling up at him. Alessandro cocked an amused eyebrow and gave her a polite smile when he noticed the look on Brianna's face. Didn't she know that if it weren't for all these people, Alessandro would drag her onto the bar and fuck her madly? As it was, his body had maintained its state of semi arousal for most of the morning and into this late afternoon. He was half-tempted to drag her into the nearest closet.

And she was jealous. Alessandro wanted to laugh at the ridiculous notion. While he could still appreciate the beauty of young Gertie on an aesthetic level, Brianna really had ruined him for other women. If anything, the fact that she had carried his son in her body, given birth to his child, made his primal need and want of her all that more intense. Alessandro considered himself sophisticated and well-schooled in the ways of women and how to seduce them. With Brianna, he just wanted. Her strength, her heart, her passion, her courage, all coupled with a body that kept him hard as a rock for more time than was surely healthy, created the only woman he would ever love. Ever.

If the sainted Francesca had even a smidge of the fire Brianna did, he could understand how his grandfather had fallen. And, if Bernardo was to be believed, how that love had destroyed his grandfather.

Bernardo was a very big believer in fate. Alessandro had always fashioned himself much more pragmatic. And then came Brianna. He believed in forever because of her.

He gently moved away from Gertie, giving her a polite smile as he walked up to Brianna.

After they had asked Geordie if they could meet with his father in law, Kevin and a few of the other men had taken up their instruments and set up on the small stage in front of the few tables. As they finished a lively song, they switched to an Irish ballad that Alessandro didn't recognize but that made Brianna smile.

"My grandma and grandpa dance to this song every year on their anniversary," she explained.

"Well then." Alessandro bowed in front of her and extended his hand.

Brianna looked at him skeptically but took his arm. "A waltz, I can do,"

He led her to the crowd of other dancers as the musicians played "The Galway Shawl". Keely O'Neil added her beautiful voice to the music as Alessandro moved with Brianna around the small area.

He pulled her a little closer than a waltz dictated but no one said anything. She smiled up at him, well aware of what he was doing.

"You know you're just making it worse," she said.

"Be glad I don't push up your dress right here and now," Alessandro whispered, making her laugh. When the song ended, he dropped a kiss on her mouth, hearing a few people sigh and *awww* behind them.

There was a very pregnant woman whose name Alessandro couldn't remember standing next to one of the tables.

"What on earth?" He asked, as they moved towards her, watching one of the older women swing what looked like a ring on a chain in front of her belly.

"Oh that," Brianna said with a giggle. "They're trying to find out the sex of the baby. Ruthie Morrissey is the local gypsy."

"They're trying to what?" Alessandro asked. Gypsies. Really. He tried not to roll his eyes as Brianna pulled him towards the spectacle. "Come on."

As Alessandro watched, Bree explained what was happening.

"If it swings back and forth, that means she's gonna have a girl. If it goes in a circle, she's gonna have a boy."

"Oh, quite. Well, for our next baby I'll make sure to tell Alex Winters we won't be needing his services."

She looked at him in surprise at the mention of another baby, but Alessandro wrapped an arm around her and pretended to focus his attention back on the ring test. He had to believe she had moved past her fear of his name and her family. Their relationship was so perfect here in Ireland, everything he wanted it to be with the exception of her agreeing to marry him. He hadn't asked her again. He didn't want to upset what they had. He didn't like feeling like a coward and feeling like Brianna held his future in her hands, but the alternative was pushing too hard and having her walls come back up.

He'd do anything he had to so that didn't happen.

Ruthie's test divined that the woman was giving birth to a baby boy. The crowd of women clapped and Alessandro pretended to be suitably impressed as well.

"How about ye tell our Bree's fortune?" Genie Dorsey asked.

"Oh, I don't know," Brianna protested.

"Ye can find out if yer wee Gianni and Will might be getting a sibling,"

Brianna turned to Alessandro with a suspicious glance.

Alessandro shrugged innocently.

Brianna took the seat Genie vacated in front of Ruthie.

"Ye can have some tea and I'll read yer tea leaves. How about a palm readin' in the meantime, lovey?"

"Sure. Why not?" Brianna said extended her hand across the table as Genie went to order the tea for her.

"All right then. Let's have a lookie, here. Oh my."

"What? Is she going to meet a tall, dark and handsome stranger?" Alessandro scoffed.

Brianna reached back and smacked his stomach with her free hand.

"Joke all ye want but Ruthie hasn't been wrong yet. All though there was that whole Michael Dwyer debacle which put the poor man in a wheelchair." Gertie said coming up to their table.

Alessandro watched Bree's shoulder's stiffen at the other woman's presence.

"Aye, but that was hardly her fault. She only said Megan Forsythe was havin' a baby before the year was out. Never mind that her Michael was going to be in Dublin when the wee bun was put in the oven," Genie explained coming back.

"As I was saying," Ruthie said determinedly steering them back to the task at hand. "Ye've had quite a life haven't ye, lovey?"

Brianna snorted. "Can't say it's been boring,"

"Mmmm, and ye've had yer share of heart ache, I can see."

"Who hasn't?" Alessandro asked.

"Shut up," Brianna insisted poking him with her free finger.

"Ye've been married before?"

Ruthie asked and Brianna startled in surprise.

"Uh…yes,"

Ruthie clucked sympathetically. "Sorry for your loss, lovey."

And it was Alessandro's turn to be surprised. How did she know Michael died?

"Oh this is rather odd. I see two other marriages for ye. But the line isn't broken. It's veers off and then turns back in on itself. Very odd. Can't say as I've ever seen that before."

"Two other marriages?" Alessandro asked not liking the sound of that by any means.

"Aye. Three marriages I'm seeing. But her heart line is strong and crosses through that line." She turned back to Brianna. "That's one soul mate for ya, lovey."

Three marriages. What the hell did that mean, exactly? Bree's hand trembled in Ruthie's.

"Ah don't ye worry, lovey. Everything will turn out as well it should." Again, she lifted knowing eyes up to Alessandro.

She felt a little uneasy at the assumption that the second marriage was going to be to Alessandro. She was just getting used to the idea of them together and she could imagine living with him back in New York. Together. As a couple. But marriage? To a Dardano?

But in your heart, his name doesn't matter to you and you know it.

No. But it matters to my family.

But you know full well that he is nothing like Bernardo. Alessandro is a good man. You need to live your life for you. Not your family.

But what about Michael? The Dardanos killed him.

One Dardano killed him. Bernardo.

How can I connect myself to him, be a part of his family?

Alessandro is willing to be a part of yours, knowing they hate him.

"Who's the third marriage?" Bree asked, silently willing the back and forth of her mental torment to stop.

"Aye well, that yer hand doesn't tell me. But I do see another child for ye. 'Tis three children ye'll be mother to."

"Another child?" Bree asked. That part made her happy.

Though it did nothing to answer her questions and only created more. But she did want to try and have a girl someday.

With Alessandro.

Shut up.

You love him

What if that's not enough?

If you have love, you can work through anything else.

"I think we should do the cake now," Bree said taking her hand back before the damned gypsy could come up with more to send her mind spinning.

Alessandro didn't look all that thrilled and Bree forced a smile as she followed him to the kitchen to get the cake.

"Come on, Alessandro. You don't really believe in this stuff anyway so why let it upset you?"

"Who says I'm upset? I'm not upset. I wouldn't call it upset, no. More like perturbed. Confused. Intrigued. Not upset by any means," he insisted pulling the box out of the refrigerator.

"Right. And if you hadn't said 'upset' four times. I'd believe you," Bree cracked.

Alessandro dropped a kiss on the crown of her head. "I'm not up-" then he narrowed his eyes at her and smiled. "Disturbed by the ramblings of some Irish gypsy. I see a bright shiny future for us. Together and that's something we will make happen together. Not something we'll leave up to fate."

"So you don't believe in fate?" Bree asked following him back to the party.

He stopped and turned to her. "Well, it's rather hard not to after hearing how Francesca and Adriano met. They met when he was injured. You and I met after a car accident. It's kind of hard to dismiss, don't you think?"

"Yeah," Bree agreed, wrapping an arm around his waist. "That part got to me a little too. Do you get the feeling we were meant to be here? Like maybe there's something in Francesca and Adriano's story that we're missing?"

Alessandro nodded as he placed the number 5 candle in the center of the chocolate cake and lit it. "It's an odd feeling, like an itch you can't quite get to." Then he gave her a devilish smile. "Though I have a more prominent itch right now and it's been driving me mad all day, darling," He leaned down and kissed her.

"Mmm, ditto. But I promise to make it worth your while

tonight." Bree forced herself to pull away.

"I don't think I can wait that long, Sunshine," Alessandro said, a hand moving down her back over the curve of her behind.

"What do you suggest? A quickie in the closet?"

"It's an idea," Alessandro offered.

Bree smacked his chest and walked towards the swinging door.

"What?" he asked behind her. "I'm not kidding."

Morgie and Genie quieted the children and brought them to the center of the room while Alessandro and Bree came out with the cake and everyone began their chorus of 'Happy Birthday'.

"Now make a wish and blow the candle," Bree urged, stroking Will's back.

"I wish for Alessandro to live wif us forever and ever and not go away anymore," he said aloud then blew out the candle.

Bree closed her eyes and clamped a hand over her mouth as a wave of mixed emotions barrelled through her. Sadness, longing and embarrassment. That was her wish too. She just wished she had the courage to make that happen.

The guests grew quiet and looked at Alessandro and Bree curiously. Alessandro forced a small laugh.

"You're not supposed to say your wish out loud Will or it won't come true. Now, shall we cut the cake?"

As they served the guests their pieces of cake, Alessandro came back to Bree and pulled her close to him, her back against his chest.

"I'm never leaving you again. I couldn't survive it," he said huskily into her hair.

Bree shivered against him. She forced herself to turn and smile at him. "Have some cake," she pinched off a piece and fed it to him.

He took her fingers into his mouth, his eyes flaring with the need that hummed between them. It seemed to be growing with every passing minute and Bree wasn't sure they could hold out much longer.

"Do you think they'd miss us if we left for a little while? I'm going crazy, darling. Believe me, this wouldn't take long at all." Alessandro groaned.

"Seeing as it's our son's party. Uh, yeah," she joked, but her own voice was shaky.

"God, I need a distraction," Alessandro sighed. "You're too

fucking beautiful for words and I'm too fucking hard,"

His words sent her arousal through the roof.

"Let's just get through the presents and then we'll see what we can do," Bree whispered licking the taste of his mouth and the chocolate off her fingers.

"You're a little tease, you know?" Alessandro said, pushing his erection against her hip.

"No. A tease wouldn't follow through on her promise. I will definitely follow through," Bree whispered, turning around and very carefully, very secretly pressing her behind against his erection.

CHAPTER FOUR

Will let out a shriek of pleasure when he opened up Bree's little bubble bike/wagon. "Dis from da store! I 'member mommy! I 'member!" He gasped and jumped up and down.

"So I guess you like it?" Bree asked unnecessarily, smiling.

He climbed over the box and wrapping paper and threw his arms around her, Gianni between them. "Oh I love you mommy. Is da bestest pesent ever in da whole entire world!" He gave her a big wet (still smudged with chocolate icing) kiss on her cheek and Bree's eyes misted. He pulled back.

"Where Alessandro go? I wanna him to see my wagon!"

"He went to get your other present. The one he got for you," Bree replied with a little beat of trepidation. She hoped this didn't backfire in Alessandro's face.

"What is it?" Will asked eagerly.

"I'm not gonna tell you, kiddo. It's a surprise."

"But I gonna be nice and when Gianni big, I let him pay wif my wagon."

"Well that's very nice of you, Will. But I'm still not gonna tell you."

Will sighed dramatically. "Okay. I just open anudder one," He turned to the other gifts and grabbed one into his lap.

A minute later, Bree saw Alessandro coming out from behind the back of the bar with a wicker basket. He smiled at her, but she could tell that for all his assurances that this was the right thing to do, he was nervous too.

A bark turned Will's attention from the remote control car Morgie and her husband had got for him. He stared at the basket and jumped when he saw the tiny brown fluffy head peering out of it.

Bree bit her lip and waited. He didn't jump up or run screaming towards Alessandro in excitement or away from Alessandro in fear.

"Dat's a doggie?" he asked slowly. Bree saw his little hands shaking around the remote control.

Alessandro set the wicker basket down in front of Will, going down on one knee. The small dog looked around and set his gaze on Will with a loud yippy bark.

A few of the other kids let out excited exclamations but Will stayed put.

Bree took a deep uneasy breath, her heart hurting for both her little boy and for Alessandro, who so wanted Will to like his present.

"Is da doggie for me?" Will asked, blinking and Bree could see the tears coming to his eyes.

Oh no.

"If you want him," Alessandro replied.

Will raised a hand to the puppy and with trembling fingers he moved to pat the dog's head. The puppy moved his head upwards and licked the palm of Will's hand. Will jumped, startled, and then gave a bright smile that had Bree sagging back in her chair with relief.

He got up from the floor and ran to Alessandro, throwing his arms around him and burying his face in Alessandro's neck. Bree was close enough that she could hear Will whisper, "I happy you my daddy,"

Bree gasped and choked on a sob. Alessandro's eyes were red as he looked over Will's head at her.

The puppy barked again and Will turned back to it, his cheeks damp as he sat down in front of Alessandro. "C' I hold him?"

"Of course. He's yours," Alessandro insisted.

"What his name?" Will asked as Alessandro eased the dog onto his lap.

"Well what do you want to name him?" Bree asked, wiping her eyes.

The puppy settled his head comfortably on Will's thigh.

"I don' had a doggie before. My oder daddy was gonna buy me

one but he no have time before he had to go in hev'n. I don' know. Was' a good name for a doggie?"

"Well it's an Irish Jack terrier, so, how about, Jack?" Alessandro offered.

Will lifted the dog and turned it to face him. "I don tink he look like a Jack."

The dog's brown eyes blinked.

"Luke. I tink dat's better for a doggie,"

"I think Luke is a perfect name," Bree said.

The puppy reached out and licked Will's nose.

"He likes it!" Will exclaimed excited.

Bree noticed Alessandro seemed to get quieter as the afternoon wore on. He stood at the bar, drinking a beer.

Gertie was standing next to him, practically rubbing up against him.

Bree ground her teeth and grabbed a drink of lemonade off the table. She 'pretended' to bump into the little skank, dumping her lemonade down the young woman's back. Bree opened her mouth to apologize and then decided a more direct approach was needed. As Gertie stared at her in annoyance and pulled on her damp blouse, Bree smiled. "Maybe now you'll get the hint. Get your little skanky mitts off the man I love. Got it, Gert?"

Morgie burst out laughing behind the bar as Gertie stomped off. "There's no denying yer Irish, lovey. No denyin' at all."

Alessandro gave a small smile.

"You okay?" she asked rubbing his back.

"Sure, though I admit, that little confrontation with poor Gertie was rather arousing." He admitted. "Not that it helped the fact that I can barely walk without embarrassing myself as it is."

Bree looked down and tried not to laugh at his obvious discomfort. "I've never been so glad to be a woman,"

"I hold you entirely to blame," Alessandro said, narrowing his eyes at her.

Bree wrapped her arms around his neck. "Well, I sure as hell hope so." Then she leaned in and whispered in his ear. "Now about that closet,"

Gianni was safely asleep behind the bar while Morgie worked and Will was safely entertained with Luke and the children. Alessandro and Bree made sure they weren't seen sneaking into the closet that was next to the staircase, which led to the few bordering apartments.

As soon as they closed the door. Alessandro grabbed her.

"Fucking God," he gasped taking her mouth with hungry ferocity. His hands moved to her thighs, lifting her dress and cupping her damp center.

"Oh please…" Bree panted rolling her hips so that she rubbed against his fingers. Her hands wound into his hair, pulling him closer, wanting to devour him.

He seemed to be of like mind. His fingers pushed past her damp panties and into her center, making Bree whimper.

"I can't…I can't wait," Bree shivered, hovering on the razor's edge of her orgasm. She pulled at his belt buckle and undid his pants as his fingers rubbed her damp clutching walls with deep penetrating thrusts. His mouth moved down to her neck as Bree pushed against his fingers and arched back, her head hitting the wall as her orgasm slammed into her. "Fuck me…" Bree moaned, wanting, needing more.

Alessandro grabbed her and lifted her off the floor. "Yes…yes…" Bree begged, pressing her fingers into his shoulders as he dug his fingers into her hips and settled her down on his shaft, filling her completely.

"Fuckin' hell," Alessandro panted pinning her to the wall and pushing into her repeatedly.

The door suddenly opened and there was a gasp of surprise. Alessandro and Bree froze.

Bree buried her face in Alessandro's chest.

"Well…I…just came to get me Thomas's boots," Morgie said.

Alessandro said nothing, his breath hard and ragged over Bree's head.

"Just don't pay me no mind at all," Morgie insisted and then shut the door behind them.

Bree reached over and placed a hand over Alessandro's on the steering wheel. He looked at her. "Mmm?" he asked, moving his hand off the steering wheel so he could link his fingers with hers

"Nothing. Just thinking," Bree said.

He gave her a grin that told her what he hoped she'd been thinking about.

"And den Gianni, when you get bigger, I gonna take you to da- Aw! JesusmarriedJoseph! Mommy, look what Gianni did!"

Bree turned at her son's misunderstanding of the very Irish expression and out of the corner of her eye she saw Alessandro laughing. She spotted Gianni's spit up on his clothes and dug in to the baby bag for some wipes. She handed them to Will.

"Oh ew! Dat's gross, mommy. I no touching it,"

"Clean him up, kiddo. 'Fraid being a big brother's not just about teaching him how to play ball and ride a bike."

"I tink you jus' like making up rules," Will grumbled dabbing at the mess.

"It's one of my few joys as your mother," Bree cracked.

"I get no joys," Will said.

Luke decided to pipe up then.

"See? You hurt his feelings," Bree said.

"Aw, I'm sowwy Luke. You gimme some joys," Will said, leaning over and patting the small dog's head. "What about you, daddy? You got some joys?"

Alessandro reached for Bree's hand again. "Many of them, young Will."

They were just back from dinner with Geordie's father in law, the infamous bottle wielding Finn, who had told them the full story of Adriano's injury.

"The poor man had two of Patrick's boys holding him, outnumbered so I tried to help him by bashing Patrick and sad to say I missed. Down your grand da goes like a sack of potatoes before I realized what I done. A nice enough man from what I knew of him. Bought me a genuine Italian leather wallet from him." And then he proceeded to show it to Alessandro, who held it with a quiet reverence.

"I'm thinking ye should have it. Seein' as ye be his relation."

Alessandro had tried to protest but Finn insisted. "The least I could do after konking him on the head like I did."

There was a note from the Mother Superior waiting for them back at the inn. Sister Brannigan wanted to meet with them the following day.

"It's back to the convent we go. We should be sure and bring some smelling salts this time," Alessandro joked.

"That girl didn't have a moment's peace from the day Adriano Dardano set foot in Galway and started chasing her." Sister Brannigan said, as she led them around the convent garden.

"Nice of Francesca to stay still for him to catch her then wasn't it?" Alessandro remarked dryly.

"Mmph," the nun responded.

"My grandfather loved Francesca," Alessandro insisted.

"Far be it from me to speak ill of the dead. But let's call a spade a spade, hmm? Your grandfather was a charmer. Now perhaps he didn't realize just how naïve our Francesca was and how besotted with him she was."

"Mmm, very generous of you," Alessandro grumbled.

"I will say that on the times he brought some food he had made with Francesca up to the convent, it was clear he had a wonderful talent in the kitchen. Now mind ye, the Italian food was a bit rich for my taste but still, rather good."

"I'm sure my grandfather's resting easier in his grave now that the holy sister has complimented his cooking," Alessandro whispered in Bree's ear making, her laugh out loud and Sister Brannigan turn to her in question.

Bree rubbed her eyes trying to see in the darkness. She could make out Alessandro on his knees leaning over the bassinet.

"What are you doing?" Bree asked, yawning as she moved closer to him.

"Just watching him," Alessandro whispered. "He's so quiet, it's unnerving. I mean, when I go on planes or in shopping malls, there are always these screaming babies. Gianni…I just need to look at him sometimes and touch him to make sure he's still alive. Rather silly, I know," Alessandro said sheepishly.

"Not so silly. And trust me, let him miss a feeding or not get his diaper changed when he wants and he won't be so quiet," Bree joked but she did marvel at how Gianni was wide awake and just kicking and occasionally gurgling away, but otherwise, he simply stared up at his father.

"I wonder what he's thinking," Alessandro said.

"He's thinking that it's the middle of the night. What are these weird big people doing staring at me?" Bree joked, wrapping an arm around his chest and pressing her mouth against his back. "My mom said when I was a baby I was a terror. Maybe you were quiet when you were a baby 'cause Will was a terror too, believe me."

"Sometimes I can't believe Gianni's mine. I feel like I missed out with Will and that makes me sad. Then I look at Gianni and it feels like a second chance."

"You really do love him don't you?" Bree said, her heart filling with emotion.

"Of course, he's my son," Alessandro said, taking her hand and pressing it against his chest.

"I mean Will," Bree explained.

"So do I," Alessandro replied.

Bree kissed his back again, and pressing her cheek to it she gave voice to what she didn't have the courage to before. "I love you."

Alessandro turned in surprise. He leaned over and switched on the lamp. His brown eyes were full and shining with hope and he could barely keep the smile off his face. "I'm sorry, but you could repeat that?"

Bree smiled, her eyes burning. She wrapped her arms around his neck and pressed her forehead to his. "I said, I love you, Alessandro Dardano,"

"Oh good," Alessandro smiled. He reached over and shut off the lamp. "Night, Night, Gianni." He laid her down on the bed and lifted up her nightgown.

CHAPTER FIVE

Sister Brannigan died two days later. She suffered a heart attack and while the doctors had done what they could, the old woman had just been too weakened to recover. While most of her few effects were left with the convent, she did leave a small bag to Bree, insisting that Sister Rose hand it to her personally. She was to meet Sister Rose at an old folk's home outside of the city as the nun was going to be busy most of the day, running errands.

"Hallo there! Mrs. O'Reiley. Come along, come along," Sister Rose said waving to her as she came out of one of the rooms.

Alessandro had elected to stay behind with the children this visit. Most likely because Murphy's was airing a rugby game and he didn't want to miss it to spend time in the presence of any more nuns.

"Let me take a moment off me feet. Will ye have a cuppa?" Sister Rose asked, shuffling to the open kitchen area and pulling the coffee pot out of the machine.

"How is Dr. McNeil this morning, Sister?" A small cherub faced nurse asked. She had a wild mess of red curls surrounding her face and Bree guessed her to be around the same age as herself. The nurse opened up a small box on the table and Bree realized what the vanilla smell was. Some white glazed vanilla donuts. "Help yerself, mum,"

Bree offered her thanks and set a donut on a napkin, taking a sip of her coffee first.

"Oh he thinks he's Michael Collins this morning, but otherwise, sweet as sugar," Sister Rose explained. She looked over at Bree and shook her head sadly. "'Tis a terrible thing when your mind goes even though the rest of you is good as gold. I pray to the good Lord every day he leaves me my senses before he calls me home. Like our Mother Superior, may the good lord rest her. Oh, and ye'll be comin' to the funeral surely?"

"I wasn't sure if we'd be allowed to," Bree said, "I thought it would just be the nuns at the convent."

"Oh, pfft! We don't hold to that here in Galway. Sister Brannigan helped many a soul in her lifetime. "'Tis only natural that they come to help her soul pass over as well. Father Scott will be sayin' a special mass for her tomorrow and then this Sunday will be the funeral. Laying her to rest on the convent grounds."

"Oh, then sure, we'll be there. Actually, I wanted to talk to you about that. I'd like to see Francesca's grave if that would be all right."

"Oh, well, and sure as ye could if there was one."

"What do you mean?" Bree asked, her eyes widening as she took a bite of the donut. It was beyond delicious and still a bit warm. The vanilla sugar topping melted heavenly on her tongue. She made a sound of appreciation.

"Ah that's our Rory Davis, owns the bakery in the village and makes the journey every morning, he does, up to sell his fresh pastries and the like. Ye'll find nowhere better than Rory's Place," the nurse, who introduced herself as Marie, explained.

"No kidding," Bree agreed. She would definitely take Alessandro and the boys there for breakfast at least once before they left. "Now, about Francesca's grave?"

"Aye, well, we couldn't very well bury her in the convent now could we?" Sister Rose pointed out.

"But I thought the official word was that she 'fell'," Bree asked, making her air quotes around the last word.

"Sure enough, but ye can't very well bury a person when there's nothing to bury now can ye?" Sister Rose reminded her.

"Oh! So her body was never found?" Bree asked uneasily. God, how awful. First to be so despondent that you jumped to your death…but then to just have your body wash out into the sea. A shudder went down her back as Bree imagined the fish and other sea creatures having at that poor girl's body when she should have been laid to rest in the land she so loved.

"'Fraid not. Washed away it was and the sea is not one to give back easily. But we had a service for her just the same. Ye've seen the plaque at St. Malachy's?"

"Yeah. We saw it. That's so sad," Bree said.

Marie rose from the table, having to get back to work.

"The whole affair was a sad one. But now, back to the matter at hand." Sister Rose pulled out a Ziploc bag and handed it to Bree. "The Mother Superior wanted ye to have this."

Bree took the bag and opened it, spilling the contents on the table. A locket, two letters; one was unaddressed and the other had a return address in London. "I don't…understand. What is this stuff? Francesca's?" She ran her finger over the silver locket, the cover was slightly dented so it took some effort to get it open, but when she did her heart did a slight jump at the face that greeted her. Not Alessandro, but so close. Adriano.

"She didn't keep the locket with her when she jum-died?" Bree corrected quickly. She lifted the letter. It was to a cemetery in London. "What this for?" She lifted the yellowed paper out of the addressed envelope and scanned it quickly. It was from the curator at The Sacred Angels Cemetery, thanking Sister Brannigan for her financial contribution to the care of plot number 777.

She pulled out the second letter from the blank envelope and her mouth fell open. Her eyes scanned the first few words and then skipped to the closing salutation. A shiver went through her and she quickly stopped reading. It was from Adriano. It didn't feel right to read it without Alessandro. With superhuman will she forced herself to bank her curiosity and stick the letter back into the envelope for now. She looked at Sister Rose in question.

The woman shook her head. "I just know that Mother Superior wanted ye to have these things."

Bree stared at the items and the simple silver chain around her finger.

Why? The question stayed with her as she paced around the inn, waiting for Alessandro and the boys. Why wouldn't she keep Adriano's locket around her neck.

Who was in plot 777 in London and why was it important? Whose address was this? Bree wondered, staring at the slip of paper.

Her curiosity was most definitely peaked.

Andy burst into the room. He, along with Morgie's husband, Thomas, who was sporting a bruised jaw, were holding a bleeding Alessandro between them.

Andy set down Gianni's bassinet as Will rushed into the room.

"My God, what happened?"

"Alessandro got hitted a lot! But he hitted back a lot too! Oh wow, mommy. It lotsa, lotsa fun! Like a movie!" Will exclaimed excited.

They set Alessandro on the floor.

"Oh he'll be all right," Thomas assured her. "Just a few too many pints is all,"

"What?" Bree asked kneeling down next to him.

Alessandro opened one eye and then gasped, "Why Brianna! Helloooo, darling!"

"You're drunk?" Bree asked in disbelief.

Alessandro scowled. "Of course not," But then he curled into a fetal position and burst out laughing.

"Oh dear. I think something's wrong with the room," Alessandro said, staring up at the ceiling from his position on the floor, "It seems to be moving, Brianna. How interesting! We don't have to pay extra do we?"

"Are you serious?" Bree snapped. "You actually got drunk and in a fight while you were supposed to be watching Will and Gianni?"

"A little bit, I'm afraid," Alessandro nodded smiling like a moron. "But if it's any constitution…er…no, not the right word…confraglation…constipation! Ah that's it. If it's any constipation, it was a very short fight."

Bree turned around and kicked Alessandro in the ass. "Get up, you idiot!"

"Owww!" Alessandro cried out and stared up at her in surprise, "You just kicked my bum!"

"Mommy! Is nod his fault. Da mean men started it. Dey said he was a lemon and dat he no my real daddy," Will explained.

Bree turned to Thomas in confusion.

"A limey, mum. Though the rest of it's true enough. Said to his face that the wee lad looks nothing like him at all and Mr. Alessandro has no shame like his grandda didn't and he probably seduced ye from yer husband the way Adriano seduced our Francesca from poor Gavin."

Bree bit back a curse and leaned down so she was face to bloody face with Alessandro.

He smiled at her. "Say it again,"

"Say what?" Bree asked wearily.

"Say you love me 'gain."

"You know you're gonna give me grey hair, right?"

"Oh certainly," Alessandro said, "But that's all right love, you'll still be very very pretty to me." He raised a hand to cup her face and she saw that his knuckles were bleeding.

She jumped when he bellowed/sang, "Yooouuu arrre soooo beeeaauuuttifuull to meeeeee."

"Oh no, no Alessandro. How about we try for some nice quiet?" Bree pleaded, wincing at the loud off key rendition. She struggled to get him back on his feet.

"If ye don't mind me saying, love. Ye'll get naught but gibberish out of him tonight so I'd hold off on the lectures until tomorrow. Like as he'll be feeling, a sound talking to will have more of the desired painful effect," Thomas suggested.

"Daddy, pease stop singing. You nod vewy good," Will said, plugging his ears with his fingers.

"Oh, Will. You know daddy loves you, right?" Alessandro asked, "Come take a nap with daddy,"

"Daddy! Dat's da floor!"

"Would you help me get him on the couch?" Bree asked Thomas.

"I beg your pardon but I wanna stay right where I am. On the foor. Floor. Oh Oh Oh Oh I wish I was back home in Derry. Oh Oh Oh Oh I wish I was back home in Derry. I cursed them to hell as our bow fought the swell. Our ship danced like a moth in the firelights. White horses rode high as the devil passed by. Taking souls to Hades by twilight!" Alessandro bellowed.

"Fine. God. Anything to stop that god awful racket," Thomas winced, leaning down and grabbing Alessandro by the arm. "You are gonna have quite the headache in the morning."

"I'm going to make a good sharp axe. Shining steel tempered in the fire. We'll chop you down like an old dead tree. Dirty old town, dirty old town!" Alessandro sang.

They managed to get him on the couch, where he promptly fell to one side, his face planted in the sofa cushion. "Ow," he said, his voice muffled.

Thomas made his way to the door and smiled at her in sympathy. "I wish you luck with him, love. Try not to shred him too badly in the morning."

“Fare thee well to Doneen, fare thee well for a while and to all the kind people I'm leaving behind. To the streams and the meadows where late I have been and the high rocky slopes round the cliffs of Doneen!”

Bree closed the door and stormed back to Alessandro. “Oh sweet Jesus, shut up!” Bree burst. She grabbed a throw pillow and smacked his body with it. “Shut up! Shut up!”

Alessandro blinked and looked up at her. “Darling, I sense you’re upset.”

Before she could punch him in his already bruised face, she went to the bathroom and grabbed some water and a small towel.

“All we need now is to get charged extra to repair the blood you’re dripping on the couch.”

She sat next to him and he smiled at her. “I think you like me,”

His hand went to her thigh and he squeezed it suggestively.

“Are you kidding me?” Bree asked.

“I’m hurt, darling. I think any medicinal professional would subscribe sex. Lots and lots of sex.”

“Do you?” Bree scowled, trying not to smile in return of that stupidly charming grin. His dark hair was in utter disarray, falling into his eyes boyishly. Or eye, Bree thought, seeing as he could only get the one open.

“Oh I do,” Alessandro nodded.

“Alessandro?” Bree purred leaning over him.

“Mmm?”

“You’re sleeping on the couch.”

“But I don wanna sleep I wanna fuck. A lot.”

“Alessandro!” Bree cried out looking at Will.

Alessandro looked up at Will. “Shhh!” He put a finger to his lips.

“Goodnight Alessandro,” Bree stormed into the bedroom and grabbed an extra blanket.

“But Briiiiaaaannnnaaaa! I wanna have seeeeex! Don’t you?” he asked struggling to sit up and look at her over the backrest. “I know you like it. We’re really good at it, you know?”

She threw the blanket at his head.

“Mommy, wha’s ‘fuck’?”

Bree closed her eyes. Oh Alessandro was soooo gonna get it in the morning.

Will picked up Gianni's bassinet and dragged him into Bree and Alessandro's room. "Come on Gianni. Daddy wanna do fuck to mommy."

Bree stared down at her sleeping beloved. Her loud enough to saw logs, snoring beloved. He'd somehow made it off the couch and was sleeping on the small black coffee table in front of it. His 6'4 frame was curled inward so that his jean-clad ass was sticking up in the air. Will sometimes slept that way too. It was a lot cuter on the five year old, but Bree conceded that maybe that was because she'd never been as furious with Will as she was with Alessandro right now.

She'd slept like crap. Turns out she was too used to Alessandro sleeping next to her now and his absence made her wake up every few hours, which only made her angrier at him. Not to mention all the terrible scenarios his negligence had 'caused to play through her mind most of the night.

Drunk. In a bar. With her babies.

Fighting. Outside a bar. With her babies.

Gianni had woken up her up early and after feeding him she settled him back down in his bassinet and came out to see that the crying hadn't disturbed his father in the least.

She stared down at him in disbelief. Will came out rubbing his eyes.

"Mommy is-"

Bree raised a finger to her lips. She had a much more appropriate method of waking for her beloved this morning.

"Why daddy on da table?" Will whispered.

Bree grabbed the coffee pot out of the machine. It was empty. Too bad. She would have liked dumping it over his hung-over head. No matter.

She clenched the handle tight and banged it into the side of the coffee table repeatedly. Alessandro came awake with a start, lost his balance and fell off the table, landing at her feet. Bree continued to slam the coffee pot against the wood, the loud thunking sounds pleasantly appearing to split Alessandro's skull.

He grabbed his head and cried out. "Owwwww! Fuckin' hell!"

Bree went on banging, making Alessandro groan in obvious

agony. "I'm up! For the love of God, woman, I'm up!"

"Ohhh, are you?" Bree asked, leaning over him. "Maybe I should make sure." She gave a few more whacks of the coffee pot against the table.

"Oh you sadistic little bitch," Alessandro swore, his features contorted in pain.

"Mommy, stop dat! Daddy's got owwies," Will insisted patting Alessandro's head, which made Alessandro cringe.

"Good. Daddy deserves a lot of owwies for what he did last night," Bree seethed.

"What I did?" Alessandro asked blankly.

Bree glared at him and raised the coffee pot, ready to crash it over his head.

"Oh, no nonono! I remember. I…think." He raised his hands in defense.

"Do you?" Bree asked, setting the coffee pot down.

"I remember being at Murphy's and, oh, my team won," Alessandro said smiling up at Bree. His smile faded. "But you don't care about that. We were drinking in celebration. Quite a lot of drinking occurred, I admit. And then…well, do you think I could have some coffee and aspirin? My head is in a rather high level of agony right now."

"Oh really?" Bree asked, she raised the coffee pot and then slammed it down repeatedly on the coffee table.

"Owwwwwww!" Alessandro covered his head with his arms.

His cry almost blotted out Gianni's, who was none too happy to be awakened by the racket.

"What? Why are you so upset?" Alessandro asked.

"'Cause mommy din' wanna do fuck with you," Will explained.

Alessandro turned his head in surprise so quickly that he whimpered and closed his eyes. "Will, where did you learn that word?"

"Where do you think?" Bree asked, crossing her arms over her chest.

Alessandro rubbed a hand through his hair, the effort to remember obviously doing nothing to ease his pain.

She stormed to the bedroom and picked up Gianni who, if a nearly two month old could scowl, was scowling at her for his rude awakening.

She came back to see Will sliding the coffee pot back into the machine.

"But you say da word," Will pointed out as Alessandro was trying to explain why 'fuck' was not a good word to add to the little boy's growing vocabulary.

"Yes and I shouldn't say it either," Alessandro said, he looked up hopefully at Bree.

She glared back at him. If he thought that was gonna earn him points!

"Please, Brianna. Just tell me what I did because in my condition I'm lucky I can remember my own name. So either put me out of my misery or forgive me for whatever it is I- oh," Alessandro suddenly said, his gaze moving off of her slightly.

"Ah, the light bulb finally comes on," Bree sneered.

"Oh hang on a moment. I didn't do anything wrong here," Alessandro insisted.

Bree cocked her head in disbelief. "Excuse me?" She could barely get the words out, so complete was her fury.

"The children were never in any danger. I made sure of that. They were being watched while, forgive me, I took a moment to enjoy myself," he said.

Bree looked around. "Where did that goddamned pot go?"

Alessandro rubbed his temples. "Now, yes I got into a fight with some jerks who were probably goading me into one for their own amusement but I would never have taken them on if I wasn't absolutely certain that Will and Gianni weren't being well taken care of."

"That's not even the point!" Bree burst. "You got drunk while you were supposed to be watching them. You got into a fight, while you were supposed to be watching them!"

"But mommy! Dat nod his fault. Da bad men were mean and laughing at daddy,"

"Will, go to your room," Bree ordered.

"No!" Will shot back.

"Right now," Bree seethed.

"Fuck!" Will swore, storming to his room.

"Will!" Both Alessandro and Bree scolded at the same time. Alessandro winced and climbed back onto the couch as Bree went to Will.

"We already told you that's a bad word."

"Yeah, but you say lots a tings. You say Alessandro my daddy now but when oder peoples say dat he's nod and he get mad, you get mad at him! Dat's worse den me saying words."

"In. Your. Room. Now," Bree demanded.

Will loudly slammed the door, letting her know what he thought of her trying to boss him around.

Alessandro groaned in pain and Bree turned to deal with her other 'child'. "Alessandro, where in that teeny pea sized thing you call a brain do you think it's okay to drink and get into bar fights while you're supposed to be taking care of your kids? Now I understand you're new to this whole parenting thing but-"

"Oh no you don't. You're not going to throw my inexperience in my face here. You know that I would do, and have done, anything to protect what is mine. And that includes not putting up with any attacks on your honor or that of ours as a family. I did nothing wrong here."

"Oh is that so?" Bree asked.

"Quite so. And if you expect me to apologize for defending you and our children, Sunshine, you've got a long wait ahead of you," Alessandro growled at her.

"Well, then I hope you find a very comfy spot on that coffee table tonight because until you can see the error of your ways, that is where you are going to be sleeping!"

Alessandro stared at her. "You're not serious."

"Quite serious, Sunshine," Bree glared back.

CHAPTER SIX

Bree came awake when she felt the bed dip. She groaned in dismay, thinking that Will was trying to climb into bed with her. But no. The occupant was significantly larger.

"What do you think you're doing?" She snapped, watching Alessandro pull back the covers and pull his legs in under the blankets.

"I'm going to sleep, darling. I don't think any amorous advances would be welcome tonight seeing as you're in a bit of a snit, so 'night, darling."

"Get out of this bed, right now or so help me, I will do something to you that will severely compromise your ability to father any more children."

"Ah, so you admit that there will be more children for us?" He gave her a small smile.

Bree came up on her elbows and narrowed her eyes. "Alessandro, go back to your coffee table."

"No."

"What do you mean, no? I'm furious with you. I don't want to sleep with you, now get out,"

"Let me put it another way, Sunshine," he reached over and tapped her nose playfully. "Not bloody hardly. I am paying for this room and that includes this bed."

"Fine. Then I'll go somewhere else," Bree said, kicking the blanket off of her.

Alessandro reached out a long leg and hooked it around one of hers, trapping her. "If you don't want me to tie you to this bed, you'll stay where you are. And you know how much I'd enjoy that."

"Dammit, Alessandro would you stop fooling around? I'm pissed at you!" Bree insisted.

"Yes. I get that, so you're staying in the bed 'cause if I let you push me away, you'll push me straight out of your heart again because that's what you do," Alessandro shot back.

Bree stared at him. "What are you talking about?"

"I finally got you to admit your feelings for me, I'm not about to start from the bottom again and fight to get back into your heart. It's just not going to happen, Brianna-"

"Alessandro. Alessandro, stop! I'm mad at you but…but that doesn't change how I feel about you."

Alessandro blinked in confusion. "But…you said that-"

Bree shook her head in disbelief. Did he really think she could turn her feelings off that easily? "We had a fight…unless you apologize, we're still having it, but that has nothing to do with our relationship. I love you, okay? That's a done deal. Believe me, I tried to fight it but it is what it is. Couples fight. I mean, haven't you ever fought with a girlfriend?"

Alessandro cleared his throat uncomfortable and his cheeks became pink. "I've um... never actually had one."

Bree was sure she had heard wrong. "No, I asked if you'd ever fought with a girlfriend."

"I know. That's never quite been an issue seeing as I never...had anything steady enough to call a relationship."

Bree leaned her cheek on her fist, observing this strange creature. "How is that possible?" Then she winced. "Oh don't tell me. It's a 'wham bam, thank you ma'am thing right?"

Alessandro scowled. "I prefer to think of it as more like passing ships. Enjoyable but with no need for anything permanent."

Bree did not like to think of how many ships Alessandro had passed on his voyage to her so she decided another tactic was in order. "What about your father? I mean, as much as I hate Bernardo and would hardly nominate him for any father of the year awards, you two must fight, right? But yet you still love him and…" She paused to roll her eyes. "I'm assuming he acts like he still loves you."

"Well, it's never really been an issue," Alessandro admitted with a shrug. "I've never disobeyed my father. Anything he asked me to do I did. I mean, that's what a loyal son does." He swallowed hard and couldn't meet her gaze all of a sudden.

Bree knew it was insane but she almost felt sorry for Alessandro. For all her screw-ups her family, deep down, loved her. Even if it wasn't always the kind of accepting love she dreamed of and some days it was really hard to remember. If she needed them, they'd be there for her.

Unconditional love was a foreign concept to this man. Bree's heart softened a little, and despite her intention to stay furious with him, she leaned over and placed a small kiss on his cheek.

"I love you. There's nothing you could do to change that. But I'm still pissed at you, so I'm not sleeping with you until you admit what you did was incredibly stupid."

Alessandro set his jaw. "And I'm not apologizing for something I'm not in the least bit remorseful for. The children were fine and those men were insulting both me and us as a family. It is not in my makeup to allow people to besmirch not only my name, but those of the people I love. Consider the fact that I left those men alive. I call that growth."

Bree shook her head, "You would."

"So I say we're at an impasse, darling, and as angry as you are I don't think you can hold out without me inside of you for too long." He leaned in close, running a tantalizing finger across her chin. "I mean, you remember what happened the last time we went too long without making love, don't you, my darling?"

Bree remembered only too well and so did her body, which throbbed with arousal at the memory. Bastard. She smiled at him and took his finger, guiding it to her mouth. She sucked slowly for an instant, watching his eyes flare. "Mmm, I bet you'll break before I will Alessandro. You'll come to me, flowers in hand begging me to accept your apology."

"Oh there will be begging, Sunshine," Alessandro said, leaning in to whisper in her ear, his breath hot against her skin, "But it won't be coming from me."

Bree nearly came right there but this was a matter of principal so she used every ounce of willpower to pull away and turn off the lamp. "Well, if you refuse to leave my bed, I guess there's nothing I can do about it. Sweet dreams, Alessandro."

"Same to you, darling," Alessandro said.

And Bree could hear the amusement in his voice. Oh, he was

gonna enjoy torturing her. *Ditto, you son of bitch. Fucking ditto.*

"Evening, Sunshine," Brianna taunted, using his expression as she stared up at Alessandro.

His eyes widened as he took in the sight before him. She was sitting in the bathtub amid a cloud of bubbles, their son Gianni securely in her arms. Her golden hair was piled up on top of her head in soft, tempting locks and her skin was damp and glistening. He could see the tops of her ample breasts, peeking just above the bubbles. Gianni's baby seat rested next to the tub.

"I…you…" Alessandro explained and he saw her blue eyes flicker triumphantly.

"Seeeee," Gianni uttered through a spit bubble. He looked at Alessandro and gave him a gummy grin, which did little to distract Alessandro from the other naked creature in the tub. Gianni smacked his tiny fist in the bubbles making them poof up. "Heee,"

"Oh, you know what. Now that you're here, maybe you can hang on to him while I shave my legs? I don't want to take him out to put him in the baby seat yet. He likes the water."

"You want me to stand here and watch you shave your legs?" Alessandro croaked. *Oh God*, he'd hoped a few hours spent with a bunch of big, burly Irish men would take the edge off the rampant desire for this woman that seemed only to be growing with every passing day of her stupid ultimatum.

They agreed with him, Brianna was being much too unreasonable and it was a point of pride for him as a man not to apologize for his actions.

But just the visual she painted in his head and he could feel himself growing hard again.

"'Course not," Brianna pointed out, "You're going to have to kneel next to the tub if you're going to hold him." Her eyes moved down to his groin and she gave a small smile as she handed Gianni over to him.

"Blrrrpeep," Gianni remarked and Alessandro liked to think his son was commiserating with him.

Pride, Dardano, Pride!

And then one shapely leg came up out of the water and propped itself right next to him.

Fuckin' hell.

"So, how was your evening?" Brianna asked casually as she

soaped her leg.

"Quite well," Alessandro replied, trying to focus on Gianni and not the leg at his side with its little pink-toenailed feet. He flicked a little bit of the warm water in Gianni's face playfully with his free hand. The baby jerked and blinked but giggled at him. "Thomas and Morgie are having an anniversary party tomorrow and they've invited us."

"No kidding? How long have they been married again? Twenty-five years I think, right? That's silver if I remember right. That was nice of them. Hmm…I wonder what I'll wear?"

You could go naked. I'd like that. Then I could just bend you over right before they cut the cake and fuck your delicious brains out, darling. Alessandro simply smiled.

"I think I'll go shopping tomorrow. Care to come with?"

Only if I can fuck you in the change room. Stop it, Alessandro!

"Sounds like fun," Alessandro said.

"Hmm, no sarcasm?" Brianna asked, revealing more and more smooth touchable skin with every pass of her razor.

Fuck. When she lay next to him tonight, she'd be all smooth and he'd be in hell, imaging those legs wrapped around his waist, or up against his chest as he plowed into her.

"Will's asleep?" Alessandro asked, trying to take his brain off his damned cock. But the blood seemed to be pooling there traitorously and it was a wonder he was still able to form coherent thoughts. He'd be spouting monosyllables soon.

His fingers itched to touch that damp, smooth skin.

Gianni giggled as if amused by the torment his father was in. Alessandro flicked him with water again.

"Yep. He spent the last few hours spinning around the living room pretending to be a helicopter and also explaining why it wasn't fair that he had to have cooked carrots instead of ice cream with his dinner. He went into this whole spiel about how he'll only grow bigger if he's happy and how carrots only make him sad and that makes him cry and wastes water 'cause he cries. And since people can't live without water, carrots are bad for him, and not good. I think he's going to be a lawyer," Brianna explained, her eyes dancing with amusement.

Her smiling eyes got him as aroused as her body did. Maybe more because those eyes captured his heart as well as his cock.

"Ouch, damn!" Brianna jerked and a thin prickle of blood

appeared on her knee where the razor had cut her.

Alessandro liked to think she wasn't as calm as she appeared to be and that was why she'd nicked herself. He lifted Gianni up out of the water and placed him on the towel in his baby seat. Alessandro reached over with his free hand and pulled out some tissue, dabbing lightly on her knee. Brianna jumped slightly at the touch of his fingers and Alessandro risked a further exploration up her thigh. The bubbles had dissipated a bit and he could see her pussy under the water. His cock leapt in his pants.

Her eyes were watching him, but she didn't stop him at first. She was trembling a little.

"Alessandro…" she whispered.

Beg me. Beg me to touch your pussy. Beg me to fuck you and put us both out of our misery.

"Stop," Brianna pleaded. "This isn't fair."

"I'm hard as a fucking rock, Brianna. That's not fair," Alessandro said, his fingers traveled over to her pussy and Brianna whimpered as he ran one long finger down over her folds.

Gianni was apparently on mommy's side because he chose that moment to pee an impressive arc that hit Alessandro's shirt.

Bree looked up in surprise when Alessandro walked into the bedroom as she was snapping the garter in place, attaching it to the black sheer nylon stocking. At the open mouth look on his face, Bree straightened and smiled, her stomach fluttering at the lust in his eyes. He shut the door behind him.

"Hello there, Alessandro," she said with a lightness she did not feel. God, laying next to him every night was getting harder and harder, pun intended. Every morning she woke up to find he had turned to her in his sleep, wrapping on arm around her, his cock hard and thick against her bottom. It was all she could do not to rub her ass against him like a cat in heat. One week and she was ready to throw him down and push herself down on him. Was that normal? Bree wondered.

Some couples didn't have sex as often as they liked because of work or kids and stress. Some couples didn't need to have sex often, but with Alessandro she was like a sex starved nympho. She wanted him all the time. Her passion for him was absolutely insatiable and if anything, knowing that Alessandro was even more insatiable than she was, made her want him even more. Knowing that he desired her that much, would enjoy nothing more than to keep her on her back 24/7 made her pussy throb like she didn't think was possible.

And he didn't even have to touch her. God knew he was sexy as sin and only had to look at her to set her aflame, but it was the things he did as much as the way he looked that made her want him so much. The power and danger he emanated struck a dark chord in her, aroused her lust, but so did his sweetness, the gentleness that he tempered his power with when it came to those he loved.

He'd fallen asleep on the couch watching a movie with Will the night before and the sight of him, with Will gathered in his lap like her son thought that was the safest place on earth, had made her insides leap with desire.

"When did you buy that?" Alessandro asked, his voice tight.

"When you took Will to the shop's bathroom," Bree explained. She needed to close her legs because, oh God, the look in his eyes was making her so wet. He looked like a barely restrained panther, ready to pounce.

He was already dressed and had decided not to shave. Bree was convinced it was because he knew she loved the dark stubble. He had to know that every time she saw that stubble she remembered his head between her legs, the stubble deliciously scraping her tender inner thighs as he tongue fucked her. Even now, the memory was making her so close to climax, she had to clench her fists to stop shaking.

"You're not wearing any…" Alessandro whispered.

"Panties? Bree asked, trying with all her might to give him an amused smile. "I figured I'd go commando tonight. I was going to whisper it in your ear later but, ta-da!" She raised an arm up dramatically. She could torture him just as badly and if anything that turned her on even more.

He pounced. With a primal growl he grabbed her, pushed her against the wall and kissed her, thrusting his tongue in her mouth and his fingers hard into her pussy.

He pumped his fingers fast and deep. Her orgasm shot through her instantly with the force of a detonated bomb. She bit his lip in her attempt to stifle a scream. In the next second he stepped away from her and Bree had to grab onto the wall or she'd fall down. She stared at him, uncomprehending.

Alessandro was visibly shaking and his lip was glistening with a smear of blood but he looked over at the bed and saw the pale yellow dress that she had chosen to wear and with frustrating nonchalance said, "Nice dress." He licked his finger, smiled at her and left.

Bree stood there, trembling. Her orgasm, instead of sating her, made her all the more aroused because she wanted his cock fucking her, not his fingers. She wanted that beautiful cock ramming her mindlessly as only he knew how.

Bastard.

The party was lovely, but inwardly, Bree was in hell. She made sure Alessandro was suffering too though; 'accidentally' brushing her hand against his cock and bending over often in Alessandro's line of vision.

But then, when they were eating, his hand was on her thigh, stroking lightly and moving higher, but instead of a reproduction of their dinner with Addleworth, his fingers stayed frustratingly away from her pussy.

Maybe she was being unreasonable.

"Well, of course ye are," Ruthie explained and Bree was not surprised that most of them knew about her ultimatum. "If yer gonna punish him, makes no sense to me to do it with somethin' that'll be making ye suffer as much as him."

"But he's wrong," Bree insisted, though her anger over that had certainly abated over the past few days.

"Aye, a bit hot headed he was but lovey, he made sure those kids were well watched over before he gave those eejits what for. Wouldn't ye say he suffered enough?" Morgie asked.

The next day was the last straw. It was an oddly warm day for the first of October. Indian Summer. They were at the pub and a few of the local men, Alessandro included, were helping Thomas expand the pub's kitchen by adding a separate pantry.

There were shirtless men walking around, of which, Alessandro was also one and the only one Bree could not take her eyes off of. As Thomas and the men worked, Bree helped Morgie during the busy lunch crowd, taking breaks whenever Gianni needed to be fed, to enjoy the outside view.

Alessandro wore jeans that hung low on his hips and hugged his ass illegally, and as Bree watched him hammer a nail into a piece of wood, her body was getting wetter and wetter. Every pound of his hammer was like a thrust into her body. Sweat was glistening on his hard muscled body and Bree was dying to dig her nails into those muscles again.

Yep, she was being unreasonable.

He looked at her, dark eyes burning with lust as she handed him a beer.

"I was thinking…" Bree said, her voice hoarse. She had to clear it before she could continue.

"Oh?" he asked, his voice dripping over her like honey.

She was punishing herself really and if she forced herself to look at it from his side, without the haze of stubbornness and fury, he did make sure the kids were watched before he went out and fought with those guys. If he was truly irresponsible, he wouldn't have cared where the kids were and left them alone.

But he shouldn't have gotten drunk in the first place!

Stupid, yes. But hadn't he suffered enough? God she was so damned horny.

"I was thinking maybe I've been overreacting,"

"Re-" he cleared his throat, his eyes widening a little, "Really?"

"Yeah. So…um, I'm thinking, maybe we could…uh…ask Morgie to watch the boys tonight."

He walked up to her so that his damp chest was right in her face and it was all she could do not to lean forward and lick him. "I do believe you're forgetting something, darling."

Bree blinked in confusion.

He leaned his face closer to her so that his breath was hot against her face. "Beg me,"

Bree grit her teeth but, *oh God*…her body was practically humming with need. "Please take me home," she whispered.

"And?" Alessandro urged, his voice rough.

"Make love to me," she said, "Please take me home and make love to me."

"Oh no, darling. I'm going to take you home but I'm not going to make love to you. I'm going to fuck you. I'm going to fuck your beautiful stubborn body so goddamned hard."

They didn't wait until they got home. Alessandro turned to her and his eyes seemed to sear her skin with the passion in them. He kept his eyes on her as he turned off the ignition and growled, "Get in the back seat. Now."

Bree didn't hesitate. She climbed back and pulled him against her, ignoring that she was partially off the leather seat when he grabbed her and pulled at her panties. He got them to her upper thighs and was unbuttoning his jeans. Bree was frantic, pushing them off his ass along with his boxers.

"Hurry. Hurry!" Bree panted, her body humming with greedy fire.

One hard thrust into her and Bree was pushed into the car door. "Oh God. Yes!" She cried.

He didn't give her a moment to catch her breath or re-acquaint herself with the thick, punishing cock in her body.

One thrust was all it took to have her coming, her pussy slick and dripping as he pounded into her, the bands of her panties cutting into her skin, but she didn't care. She moved with him, frantic, desperate.

It took him less than a minute and then he was coming too, his cock swelling almost impossibly inside of her as he spent himself.

He fell against her like dead weight. Bree undulated her hips a little, wanting to keep the sensation of his cock inside of her just a little bit longer.

"Sorry about that," he murmured sheepishly as he moved off of her. "Quicker than I had intended."

"I couldn't wait either," Bree admitted. Her blood was racing in her veins and she was still breathing quickly as they took their seats and pulled back onto the street.

"But I think I'll make you wait again," Alessandro said, giving her an evil, pure Dardano smile.

Her insides quickened and Bree had to shift on the seat a bit. "What do you mean?"

"Lift up your dress," Alessandro said, keeping his eyes on the road.

Bree rolled her eyes and pulled the hem of her dress up to her thighs.

"Higher," he ordered.

Bree's stomach tightened nervously. "Alessandro, what are you talking about? People might see."

"We're moving. Who's going to see us?" Alessandro pointed out. "You made me suffer, darling. Now it's your turn. Lift up your dress to your stomach and spread your legs wide."

Bree blinked in surprise but there was a rush of excitement in her that wanted to do as he ordered. "What? And you think I haven't suffered?"

"Well, this whole thing was your idea after all," Alessandro pointed out.

"Yes, and I already caved and begged so what more-"

"Oh no, my love," Alessandro said, sparing her a heated, dangerous glance. "You have not begun to beg. You will pay for denying me all these nights."

Bree narrowed her eyes at him, about to tell him where to shove it…when she remembered that was actually the point, really. She loved him, wanted him and wanted to explore everything with him. She wasn't a shy woman by any stretch of the imagination but Alessandro pushed her boundaries and if anything, that made her bond with him all the more strongly. Nothing felt wrong with him. Nothing. Funny how he was trying to order her, command her and yet as she obeyed, spreading her legs open, Bree felt deep in her soul that she'd never felt more free.

She moaned when his fingers touched her pussy. Bree met his gaze as he slid one finger inside of her. "Oh God…" she sighed, letting her head fall back against the head rest. She moved her hips closer, wanting more.

Alessandros had his bottom lip between his teeth and his breath was short as he tried to focus on the road. "Don't come yet. Not until I say, understand?"

"Oh, I don't think I can sto-"

"Ah, not until I say," Alessandro ordered moving his finger slowly inside of her. They came to a red light, another car next to them.

Bree tried to move and cover herself quickly but Alessandro wouldn't let her.

"It's all right, darling. It's dark. They can't see you. But how fucking hot would it be if they could? Could you imagine it? The looks on their faces as they watched your face, knowing my fingers were inside of you."

Bree shook at the shocking image. She dared not look and see if the people in the other car could see her. "Oh Alessandro…please. Please let me…"

He inserted a second finger as they began to drive again and picked up the thrusting pace of his hand.

When she got too close, he slowed down, then picked up the pace again until she was going crazy.

She could barely walk as Alessandro opened the door to their rooms. Alessandro picked Bree up and carried her into the bedroom.

“God, I’ve missed you. So much,” He buried his face in her neck and Bree clutched him close.

He set her down on the bed and smiled at her. “You know what I want now?”

“Uh, yeah?” Bree asked, her body aching with the need to come.

“I want you to go get that garter, and put it on,”

Bree looked up at him in surprise. “I thought the object of this game was to get me to take clothes off,”

“I want you to put that garter on, and then I want to tie you to this bed and do very, very wicked things to you. First with my mouth, then with my hands, and then if I think you deserve it, with my cock, my love. How does that sound?” He leaned down and whispered in her ear, "Now you can come."

CHAPTER SEVEN

Bree came. She grabbed the blanket in both fists and squeezed her eyes shut as the explosions went off in her pussy at his verbal fucking.

When she opened her eyes again, he was grinning at her.

"I swear, someday I'm going to win and I'm going to make you pay."

Alessandro's grin widened. "I'm quite looking forward to that day. Now the garter," he reminded her.

"Be prepared to get very, very hard, you smug bastard," Bree said getting up from the bed.

Alessandro grabbed her hand and put it over the bulge in his jeans. "Mission accomplished, Sunshine. Oh, and wear the nylons too. But no knickers."

"They're called panties," Bree scowled. He smacked her behind as she went to change.

When she came out in nothing but the garter and stockings, she was rewarded with the naked lust in his eyes.

"Christ, but you're so exquisite it actually almost hurts to look at you," Alessandro whispered.

Bree gave him a small smile. Then she felt a little shiver of anticipation as she saw the various silk ties in his hands.

"Do you trust me?" Alessandro asked as he pushed her back onto the bed.

"Yes," Bree admitted, letting him take her arms and tie them to the iron railings, followed by her legs.

"Good, now prepare to take your punishment, darling," He

moved his head down her stomach and Bree was very glad that he still hadn't shaved.

Bree sucked in her breath and her nerves screamed in utter bliss as Alessandro's mouth met her pussy. His stubbly cheeks tickled her soft thighs in contrast with the dampness of his mouth. His hands held her hips, his thumbs running over her skin as he tickled her with the flicking of his tongue. He knew just when to pull her clitoris into his mouth and suck her and just when to back off, drawing her higher and higher. Her body was tight as a bowstring, ready to snap.

"Beg me, darling. Beg me to let you come now," Alessandro said. He ran his tongue up her soaked folds in one long lick before pulling her ass up in his hands, as much as he could in her restrained position.

Bree shivered, knowing he was readying himself to send her over the edge. "Please. Oh please, Alessandro. Make me come…make me come." Bree closed her eyes in anticipation.

"Watch me," Alessandro ordered, lightly pinching the swollen nub of flesh at her center.

Bree cried out at the delicious sensation and opened her eyes, lowering her chin to watch him.

And then his tongue thrust into the wet heat of her pussy, plunging, ramming deep into her. His head moved purposely and Bree was shaking, arching beneath him. The restraints heightened her sensations because she had nothing to turn to so she could ease the relentless thrusting.

He devoured her like a starving animal. He feasted on her.

"Oh…Oh…Oh! God!" Bree cried as her nerves exploded and his touch gentled, easing her back down. Oh God. She fell against the mattress, trying to catch her breath as tiny aftershocks popped under skin. "Oh Alessandro…You're going to kill me."

"And miss out on making love to you for the rest of my life? Not a very good plan if you ask me," Alessandro joked.

Rest of my life. Bree smiled, the idea no longer scaring her. She wanted no future without this man. Ruthie's prophecy pricked the back of her mind and she felt a beat of unease. Three marriages but one soul mate. Bree watched Alessandro pull his t-shirt off, appreciating the pure, muscled beauty of him. This was her soul mate. This man knew the darkest parts of her soul and loved them, accepted them. This was the man she wanted to grow old with, whose arms she wanted to drift off in every night until the day they never woke up again.

When he was naked, he leaned over her and positioned herself between her legs. Bree's legs instinctively tried to wrap around his waist but the ties wouldn't let her. She gave a whimper of frustration and undulated against him.

He took his cock and rubbed it against the soaked lips of her core. "Would you like me to fuck you, my love?"

Bree's eyes drifted as he rubbed the head in circles on her clitoris. "Oh yes."

With his free hand, her ran his fingers over the sheer nylons covering her legs and the exposed skin of her thighs. "Would you like me to shove my cock in you, darling?" He rubbed the opening of her pussy.

"Please…Alessandro…I beg you. I'm begging-" Her breath left her as he thrust his shaft into her in one smooth, deep thrust.

Bree cried out his name as he moved inside of her with hard, punishing strokes. Her fingers itched to touch him, to dig her nails into his shoulders and feel the tension in his muscles as his body reared into her with the force and passion of a delicious conquering animal.

"Like this, darling?" Alessandro asked, meeting her mouth as his hips pumped hard between her thighs.

"Oh yes! Oh God, Alessandro. So good. Fuck… so good…"

"Did you dream of me fucking you when you were punishing me?" Alessandro growled.

Bree whimpered, trying to move with him.

"Did you touch yourself, thrust your fingers in this beautiful body and imagine it was me?"

"Oh yes…yes." The friction of his hard body was too delicious inside of her. Bree had no words for the way this man made her feel. He angled his hips, hitting an almost painfully sensitive spot inside her pussy and Bree was pulling against the restraints like a desperate animal. "Oh. Oh Don't stop! Oh my God. Oh my God. I'm gonna come, Alessandro! I'm gonna come so fucking hard. Don't ever stop."

He stopped his movements. "Then say you were wrong." Alessandro looked down from above her, his body glistening with sweat.

"What?" Bree asked, trembling. Oh sweet God, if he made even the smallest movement she was gonna come like a freight train.

"Say you were wrong," he demanded, "Wrong to deny me. You were wrong to shut me out and keep me from fucking you anytime I wanted. Tell me that you'll never hate me for doing what I have to do for our family."

Her pride stung and she glared at him. She felt him grown thicker in her pussy. Her pussy clenched him tight, hungry, not caring about her pride, wanting only what it wanted and that was to be fucked hard and deep. "Yes," she panted, "Yes, I was wrong."

He smiled and pulled out of her. When she was about to scream her fury at him, he reached over and undid the ties around her arms. She winced at the uncomfortable muscles.

"I need your hands on me. I've missed feeling your hands on me so fucking much, Brianna." And then he was thrusting back into her and Bree was wrapping her arms tight around him, digging her nails into his damp back as he sent her hurtling into another orgasm.

"Promise me. Promise me that you'll never shut me out again," Alessandro said, his words coming out more like a plea than an order and Bree felt her own beat of victory. His movements were getting rougher, more uneven and the bruising kisses told her he was desperately close to coming.

"Never. I promise," Bree sighed, meeting his gaze. "I'll never shut you out again. I love you, Alessandro. I love you." She met his mouth, taking in his harsh breathing, feeling his racing heart against hers.

And then he was coming. Bree buried her face against his damp neck, licking the hot flushed skin and feeling the quick beat of his pulse against her tongue.

He fell against her in blissful exhaustion and Bree cradled her beautiful tormentor against her breasts.

When he could manage to move, he undid the ties around her ankles and drew her against his chest, cuddling against her back.

"I'm sorry too," he said, nuzzling the back of her neck.

Bree looked back at him and kissed him briefly.

"I shouldn't have gotten drunk with the boys in my care. I'll never do that again."

She reached down and took his hand that was caressing her breasts. "Thank you for saying so."

They were quiet for a few minutes.

"Alessandro?"

"Hmm?" he asked, his breath caressing the top of her head.

"You remember that thing that you asked me when we were in your father's house?"

"Darling, right now I can't even remember my own name."

"About marrying me."

He went very still behind her. "Yes?"

"Well," Bree tightened her fingers around his. "When we get back to New York, will you ask me again?"

Alessandro kissed the top of her head. "Deal, my love." And she could hear in his voice how happy she'd made him.

It echoed the happiness she felt herself.

She loves me. She'll forgive me if I tell her.

I'll lose her. She'll never understand why I followed Bernardo's order. Why I helped my father frame her brother in law.

Marry her now. Here. In Ireland. Then she'll be yours forever.

And you'll never know if you can truly trust her with your heart because you'll be entering this marriage with a lie.

Who cares? You'll have her! That's all that matters.

No. Having her whole heart, her whole trust, her acceptance. That matters.

More than living your life with her?

Yes.

More than her carrying your name?

Yes.

More than her carrying your future children?

Y...yes.

You are a disgrace to the Dardano name.

Alessandro jumped on the couch at the sound of his father's voice in his head.

"You okay?" Brianna asked, her feet nudging his stomach as they sat on the couch.

"Brianna…" Alessandro opened his mouth but the words wouldn't come. Fear kept them locked tight in his throat.

Gianni whimpered, coming awake.

"Oops. Boobie duty calls." Brianna pulled her feet up off up Alessandro's lap and stood up.

"Mommy's boobies are coming, Gianni," Will said. He lay on the floor in front of the TV, watching cartoons.

She came back, Gianni happily sucking at her breast.

I can't lose her.

If she finds out from anyone but you, you'll never get her back.

"Mommy. I got a question," Will said, pulling his attention away from the TV set. "Does my bobbies have milk too?"

"Nope. Only girls. Well, scratch that, only mommies," Brianna explained sitting back down on the couch.

"But what about da cows?" Will asked.

Brianna met Alessandro's amused gaze. "The cows?"

"Yeah. We went to da farm wif my oder daddy and we saw dem take da milk from da cows. Is dat da same milk dat's in mommies' boobies? Mommy's nod a cow,"

"Well, thank you for that," she said dryly. "No. It's not the same milk. The cow's milk is what comes in the bags and the cartons. What you put in your cereal."

"Oh dat's good. 'Cause I don' wanna drink milk from boobies.

"The milk from mommies is only for babies, and you certainly enjoyed it when you were a baby."

"Ew. Dat's gwoss, mommy! I tink you just teasing me."

"Nope, cross my heart. Gianni's still a baby so he can't eat hard food, only mommy's milk. You were a baby once too."

"But I don' remember da taste. Did I like it?"

"You bet," Brianna insisted.

"Kind of sweet, I'd say," Alessandro replied, smiling when Brianna glared at him, her beautiful face turning red.

"Wow, you member when you were a baby, daddy? Dat must have been even longer den when I was a baby 'cause you so big!"

"Your...uh, memory gets better as you get older," Alessandro explained quickly as Brianna reached between them and pinched his thigh.

Alessandro's arm tightened around Brianna, her head on his chest, her back to him as she fed their baby. *Is it wrong? Is it wrong to keep my mouth shut so that I can hold her like this forever?*

"Oh, before Gianni woke up, you wanted to say something?" Brianna turned her head to face him.

"I...um..."

Tell her. Tell her now and let her prove to you that what you have is strong enough to defy anything.

"I was thinking. Why don't we get married here?"

Oh Alessandro.

Her smile faded a little.

"Mommy and daddy are gonna get mawied?" Will asked, whipping around, his face beaming at them.

"I only thought, maybe it would be romantic. You know? Ireland? Here where Adriano and Francesca first met and fell in love. We could get that priest from St. Malachy's to do it."

Brianna reached over and took his hand. "I want to do it in New York. I want my family to be there when I stand up next to you. And more importantly we need to do it in New York. For me."

Alessandro shook his head. "I don't understand."

"You told me once that I was too afraid to love you openly, in the real world. I want to prove to you that I'm not. Do you get what I mean? I want us to go back to New York, be with our families again, live our lives day to day and show everyone that what we have is real. That we're not living in some fantasy land. I want you to see that I'm not afraid to love you openly."

Tell her now, you stupid wanker. Look at what she is willing to do for you. She's willing to stand up in front of her whole family and love you.

"We gonna get mawied?" Will repeated.

"Well, young William, yes, we are. We're getting married when we get home," Alessandro said, squeezing Brianna's fingers as he watched that smile light up her face.

"Can we go home tomowo?"

Yes, take her tonight on the first flight back to New York and run straight to St. Luke's.

They sat at a table in one of the cafes that lined the harbour, appreciating the rare stint of warm October weather as Will and Luke ran on the boardwalk and the grass, Andy keeping a watchful eye.

Alessandro returned to the table after making his phone call.

"What did your guy in London say?" Bree asked.

"Well, your plot 777 has been tended for the past fifty years by the late Sister Brannigan. Or that's what anyone who checks out the story is supposed to believe. Now, he doesn't know who's in the grave yet but it turns out someone has been using Sister Brannigan's name to hide the fact that the real person sending the money to care for that grave lives somewhere in Naples."

"Naples?" Bree asked, "And this person is still writing the checks?"

"Well, no, Sister Brannigan was the one putting her name on the checks to the cemetery. Someone else was making the deposits into her personal account."

"But now that she's gone?"

"I suppose the Neapolitan benefactor will have to find someone else if he wants to remain anonymous."

Bree snorted, "For a second I thought maybe it might be Bernardo."

"Well, why not? I mean, a little bank fraud isn't likely to keep my father up at night," Alessandro said.

"But he's in New York," Bree reminded him.

"Geography, darling?" Alessandro asked amused.

"You say that with such pride it scares me," Bree said rolling her eyes.

"I love you too," Alessandro smiled. "But no. If he was, why let us go off on this whole journey?"

"It's Bernardo. If there's something I've learned about your father it's that the rules of logic don't apply to him. Or any other kind of rules," Bree added, "Maybe this is all some kind of big elaborate plan and we're gonna go home and find out he's been keeping Francesca and Adriano frozen in his basement in one of those sci-fi freezers that they say you can buy and use to come back to life in a hundred years."

Alessandro shook his head at her, not impressed with her sense of humour.

CHAPTER EIGHT

"Are you cold?" Bree asked, looking back at Alessandro as they lay in bed. The warm weather seemed to be leaving them, the beginnings of a rain storm taking its place.

"What?" Alessandro asked startled.

"You're shivering. What's going on with you, hmm?" She smiled and turned her body around so she was facing him. "Need some help warming up?" She pressed her mouth to his chest, making her way south.

Alessandro stopped her and gathered her into his arms so she was almost on his lap. He held her tight, almost too tightly, and Bree felt a beat of alarm.

"What is it, Alessandro?" She asked, rubbing his arms.

"I love you," he murmured, kissing her.

"I know," she said when he pulled back.

He shook his head. "Forgive me," He gave her a rueful smile. "I was just remembering how I felt when you…didn't…when we were apart."

Bree nodded in understanding. "Well, that was in the past, okay? We are never gonna be apart again." She lifted her chin and brushed a kiss on his lips. "You're it for me, Alessandro. You're the man I want to spend the rest of my life with."

She saw his eyes glisten and smiled at the show of emotion. "You're the man I want to raise our children with. You're the man I want to grow old and lumpy with."

At that he gave a shaky laugh, sniffling.

Bree let her hand trail down beneath the blanket. "You're the man I want to make love with every day of my life until our old bones creak louder than the bed springs."

Alessandro burst out laughing and Bree wrapped her arms around his neck. "Don't think about the past anymore. Let's move forward and let's be happy."

Alessandro cocked an eyebrow. "Is that an order, young lady?"

"Yes, Sir. From this second on, you're not allowed to think about how much we hurt each other and how stupid you were-"

"How stupid I-"

"Ah!" Bree pressed her fingers against his lips. "How stupid we both were."

"And what would the punishment be for disobeying such an order?" Alessandro asked, his fingers trailing down her back.

"Oh it would be very bad," Bree assured him playfully.

"Very?" Alessandro asked, his eyes lit with amusement.

"Oh yes. Brutal. Vicious even."

"Oh that does sound terrible," Alessandro agreed.

"There might even be whips," Bree warned.

"Oh dear," Alessandro smiled.

A knock on the bedroom door interrupted their play.

"Mommy?" A small voice asked through the door.

Bree reached over and grabbed her robe. "Come on in, sweetie."

"I don' like da tunder,"

"Come on, Will," Alessandro said, motioning him to the bed. He and Bree made room for the little boy. "You want to know a little secret?" He lowered his head to Will. "I don't like thunder very much either."

Will gasped. "You a-scared of da tunderstorms?"

"Yep," Alessandro admitted as he winked at Bree.

"But you a growed up."

"Well grownups are scared of things too," Alessandro pointed out.

"Like what?" Will asked.

"Some of us don't like thunder storms, some of us are scared of rats or big purple dinosaurs," that he directed at Bree who lightly slapped the side of his head, mocking her about her dislike of Barney, the children's show.

"But mostly, I'm scared of anything happening to you, or

Gianni, or your mother."

"But you gonna protet us 'cause you my daddy. C' I axe you a question?"

"Sure thing, Question Box," Alessandro said.

"When we go home. You gonna live wif us, right?"

"That's right," Alessandro said, smiling at Bree.

"You pomish?"

"Cross my heart, hope to die, stick a needle in my eye," Alessandro joked.

"Good," Will said.

After Will drifted off to sleep, they finally settled down to read Adriano's letter together.

"This letter isn't to Francesca," Alessandro said, scanning the contents quickly.

"No." Bree replied with a shiver as she watched his face grow more serious with each passing second.

"It's his curse, Brianna. It's his curse against all the O'Reileys." Alessandro met her gaze and then cleared his throat and began to read.

"My heart is broken. Why, my love? Why? It would kill me, but I would have respected her wishes and stayed away. It would be small consolation but surely better than this…agony. At least I would have the small comfort of knowing she was here, walking the earth and we were sleeping under the same sky. When I looked up at the moon, I would know she was seeing the very same one.

And I will not lie. I held out hope. Hope that someday, she would get over the grief of losing her betrothed and turn to me again. My love for her was too strong.

I have no need of happiness now. What good is it to feel a racing pulse, a full heart, passion that steals the very breath from your body when what is left is a crippling misery that makes your very soul that once sang, wish for death?

But I do not blame her. My angel. She has committed a mortal sin by ending her life but surely God has not damned her for the sin that was mine. Surely he has plucked her from damnation to live with him in heaven.

I am not certain I believe in God anymore. Or at least, not in the merciful, loving God my Francesca had believed in.

I do not even blame young Joe, who was only stupidly following his father's teachings about right and wrong and truth and lies. Seeing no room for the frailties of the human heart. He is a young boy. What does he know of love and feelings that could make you want to gladly denounce all you hold true to be with your heart's greatest desire.

My blame remains on him. Her father. I have never felt such murder in my heart as he spewed his hatred and righteous indignation at my beloved, poisoning her against me, making her feel no better than a whore. My angel. My Francesca. How that bastardo sullied what was good and pure and it is him I blame for her death.

For a moment, one brief blissful moment, when we spoke in the church after Gavin's funeral I had hoped, prayed, that there was still a chance.

She was tearful, frightened, wary of me, with good reason but I held her in my arms, begged her not to throw away what we were to each other to placate a dead man, that we must live for each other and not for those around us. A second chance was there, in her eyes, in her hands as she held me, my body, my heart. We were to slip away the next morning but she needed to gather her things, things too precious to her to leave behind.

I shall curse my weakness for eternity for giving her that time. I waited for her. Waited for my angel who never came back.

I know it was her father who intercepted her. Peter O'Reiley. How I curse that name. It was as if he took her from me a second time.

His morality was more important than his daughter's happiness and oh, how happy we would have been.

He has damned me to an eternity of cold, unfeeling existence.

And I damn him. Damn him. Curse him. It is only my love for my angel that keeps me from killing the man who took my heart from me. That, she would not forgive, and when she looks down on me from heaven, I want her to feel love, not hatred.

So I curse him. May he never know peace and may his daughter's death eat away at him until he dies, knowing it was HE that killed her.

May no O'Reiley ever know peace for the cruelty of their sanctimonious blood. I shall make my son my revenge. I cannot imagine touching another woman after knowing heaven, but I shall move forward, if only to satisfy this thirst for vengeance that burns within me. There must be more. More Dardanos to make sure that the O'Reileys pay. My vengeance will begin with my son.

He will be my instrument of vengeance against the O'Reileys. May the violence of my agony be rained down on all of them. When I am gone from this earth, he and his descendants will carry out the path of my violence and pain, down, down until every last O'Reiley and their cold righteous hearts are wiped from the face of the earth.

There will only be one measure of mercy I show them, for the sake of my love for Francesca. If they make right the sins of their ancestor Peter O'Reiley. If a Dardano and a O'Reiley are united in love and allowed to have that love flourish as mine was not, then I shall rest. Then my vengeance shall rest.

Only then will I find my peace. Only then will my soul be at rest.

Until then, like my Francesca, my heart is stilled, my soul is ripped away.

I am nothing. I am lost.

I am dead."

Bree shivered as Alessandro finished reading, his face pale. "We did it, Alessandro!"

"Did it?" Alessandro asked.

"The vendetta is over because of us! We're going to be together just like Adriano wanted." Bree wrapped her arms around Alessandro, careful not to wake Will. "We'll go back to New York and show this to Bernardo and he will have to back off of my family for good. This is awesome, Alessandro!"

"You're right," Alessandro agreed carefully.

"What is with you? Why aren't you happier?" Bree asked.

"I am. I'm relieved, darling. I just…this letter just breaks my heart. It's hard to be happy after reading about such pain and knowing that he lived the rest of his life this way."

Bree nodded solemnly. "You're right. It is awful and a part of me grieves that my great aunt Francesca and your grandfather were deprived of the loves of their lives but I'm just so happy that we get to fix this for them. We're going to go home, be married and live the rest of our lives together."

They would go home, be married and Alessandro suggested a honeymoon in London to discover the significance of the things in Sister Brannigan's bag.

It was hard saying good-bye to Morgie and Thomas and the rest of the Galway residents they had become close to. Ruthie gave her a good luck Celtic charm to wear around her neck. It was a small gold pendant in the shape of a hand with tiny lines over it like a real miniature palm.

"Oh great, so you never forget that you're going to marry someone else after me," Alessandro murmured scowling.

"Now that's not what I said at all, love," Ruthie pointed out patting his shoulder, startling him with the knowledge that she had heard him when his voice was almost inaudible.

They promised to call Morgie when they got settled back home.

They walked off the plane and were just entering the airport terminal when out of nowhere, Bree's uncle Jack and her father appeared and made their way toward them.

"What the-?" Bree asked, unease shooting through her. "Daddy, what are you doing here? Did something happen to mom?"

She gave a start of surprise when her uncle Jack surreptitiously pushed a gun in Alessandro's side.

"You're going to come with us, and you're not going to make a scene."

"Wait, what?" Bree asked, watching as her uncle and father pushed them towards the airport exit.

Andy stepped forward and Alessandro quickly shook his head. He glared at Jack. "Put that damn thing away, I won't fight you and I don't want you to scare the children."

"Hold on! There's… there's some mistake. Hang on!" Bree shouted.

Her father ignored her and began pulling Alessandro away. "I said HANG ON!" Bree screamed. Heads turned their way.

"Brianna, don't make a scene," Alessandro insisted with a pleading look toward Will who had stopped his stride behind them and was now looking at the grownups questioningly.

"What the hell is this?" Bree hissed.

"Your boyfriend here had Charlie arrested for drug trafficking. Planted coke on one of our ships." Jack explained.

Bree shook her head. "That's ridiculous! He had nothing- dammit, wait!" Bree pleaded as Jack pulled Alessandro away.

It suddenly occurred to Bree that beyond telling her not to make a scene Alessandro hadn't said a word in his defence. He wasn't fighting against them, he wasn't yelling at them to let him go.

And he wasn't looking at Bree. He was looking down at the floor and his eyes were closed.

"He…um…Alessandro?' Bree asked. "Alessandro, look at me."

"Brianna…" his voice was low and broken. He didn't raise his eyes.

Oh no. Please God, not again.

"Look at me," Bree begged, she placed a hand on his face and lifted his head. Alessandro's eyes were red. "You tell them. Tell them that it was all Bernardo, please. Tell them that you had nothing to do with what happened to my brother in law."

"All right, let's go," Jack said pulling. "We're going to have a little discussion at the house."

"I said, wait!" Bree snapped.

"My daddy no go nowhere. We go home now?" Will asked, picking up on the unease looking up at Alessandro.

She saw Alessandro shudder and then his image blurred because tears had filled her eyes.

There had to be some mistake. This was just some nightmare and she would wake up in Alessandro's arms. Happy. Oh God, they'd been so happy.

A lie. Had it been a lie? Had he played her for a complete fool yet again? And now, what, was she supposed to just let Alessandro leave with her father and uncle, knowing what would happen when they got him alone in the basement. Was she going to let them met out the punishment that others who had gone against the O'Reileys had faced?

They were quiet as they walked into her parents' house. Angela and Bree's sister Beth came forward and her mother asked Will if he wanted to come help her bake some cookies. Bree could see the knowledge in her mother's eyes. She was well aware what was about to happen.

Will looked back at Alessandro, his gaze uneasy as if picking up on the tension among them all but unsure of its 'cause.

"Yeah, that sounds like fun," Bree said, forcing a smile for her son's sake. "You and Gianni go with grandma and auntie Beth." She swallowed hard as Will took his grandmother's hand and crossed the living room toward the kitchen.

Bree whirled on her father. "Daddy, please don't do this-"

“Bree, stop it,” John insisted. "You know what has to be done."

"There has to be some other explanation." This she directed at Alessandro who closed his eyes.

"We don't deal in drugs. We never have and this scum has sullied our name and put an innocent man in prison. Do you have any idea what it is going to take to set Charlie free and that's assuming we can!" her uncle snapped.

“I want to talk to him alone.”

“Out of the question,” John said. “I don’t want this man anywhere near you again. Did you not hear what he did?”

"I want to hear it from his own mouth."

"No." Her father ordered her to stay upstairs and made his way to the door that led to the basement stairs with Alessandro and her uncle.

"Daddy, please! I'm not going to let you kill him! Promise me you won't," she whispered, tears filling her eyes.

John looked at her for a long time and then slammed the door in her face.

You never went into the basement. That was the rule ingrained in Brianna and her brother and cousins ever since they were children. It was only after they entered their teens that it began to dawn on them the business their family was in. They thought it was cool, initially. Dangerous. Sexy. Just like the movies. Then people they loved would get caught in the crossfire, and the cold reality would set in.

The room was soundproof and spare. She had sneaked down once on a dare. It wasn't like the basements of her school friends with their man caves or laundry rooms. There were no windows. There was a table, chair, and that was it. The room reeked of fear and violence. After seeing it that one time, she was happy to stay away.

John came upstairs after a while and Brianna bit her lip, to keep from crying out at the splatters on his shirt. "You can see him." He held the door open for her.

She hesitated. It was what she had wanted but now she was afraid to see what condition Alessandro was in. She also feared hearing him say her father was right. She forced herself to make her way down the stairs.

Alessandro was sitting in the chair, his white linen shirt damp with sweat and blood. His hair was damp. There was a bruise growing on the side of his jaw and one eye was swelling shut. His lip was split open and the blood was trickling onto his chin. His good eye looked so hopeless when it met hers and Bree felt fresh tears spring to her eyes.

She shrugged and spread out her arms helplessly. "I don't know why I'm here." She placed her hands on her hips and looked down at the floor, trying to get a hold of her wrecked emotions. "It's true isn't it? What they're saying about you. You did it, right?"

"Yes," Alessandro replied, his voice full of such self-loathing that Bree's heart broke all over again.

Bree gaze went to the table, with its array of weapons spread on top. She didn't see them bring any down, so she briefly wondered where in this room they were kept.

"How are the boys?" Alessandro asked.

"They're still in the kitchen." She took a shaky breath. "I guess the dumbest question I could ask right now would be 'why didn't you tell me?' But I know why."

Alessandro said nothing, just looked up at her as if he was trying not to shatter.

"You didn't trust me."

"Brianna-"

Bree shook her head. "No, I get it. I wouldn't have told me either. I mean, that's what you and I do, right? We keep secrets from each other. We betray each other. We hurt each other." She took a deep, shaky breath, blinking back tears.

"That's not true, darling. You changed me. You make me a better man. Our love-"

"Is not enough," Bree said, wanting to scream at him, wanting to fall into his arms, unable to do anything but stand there. "How dumb was I to think that if we just gave into our feelings for each other and allowed ourselves to be happy then everything else would be perfect?"

"It can. Oh it can, my love. Please. I know you're hurt right now and I don't blame you. I should have told you what I had done but I was so afraid I'd lose you. I tried. I tried so many times."

"I know you did," Bree said. She reached into her purse and pulled out a tissue and cleaned his chin. "I sat upstairs thinking about our trip and I could actually pick out the instances when it felt like you were trying to tell me something important."

"Would it have mattered?" Alessandro asked. "If I had told you then-"

"As opposed to having you carted away by my family? Yeah," Bree snapped then lowered her head. "But you didn't and I have to deal with that now. Our sons have to deal with that. We can't keep doing this to them, Alessandro."

"What can I do to make this better? Tell me what you need for me to do to fix this."

"You cut ties with Bernardo," Bree decided, knowing damned well that he would do no such thing, which only broke her heart that much more.

Alessandro stiffened. "I can't turn my back on my father, Brianna."

"He's the one that made you do this. I…don't even care all that much about what he did to Charlie…How selfish is that? It's what Bernardo's done to you that I can't accept."

"My father loves me. He's been there-"

"To turn you into his puppet, Alessandro." Then she raised her hand and shook her head, stepping away. "This is exactly why you and I are not gonna work. No matter how much we love each other. Our loyalties to our families are going to keep us hurting each other, lying to each other."

"You're angry with me. That's why you're saying these things," Alessandro insisted.

"No. I'm not mad at you. I'm not," Bree assured him. "I love you."

"Brianna, listen to me. We cannot let our families affect how we feel about each other. Have you learned nothing from Francesca and Adriano's story?"

"Of course I did but Alessandro, your father makes you into this…evil person who thinks the rules don't apply to him. The lives we live, the world we live in, there are rules. Your father doesn't care and he's teaching you not to care about those rules either! Don't you see? The reason we were so happy in Ireland was because you could be your own man, away from Bernardo."

"So I'm evil now?" Alessandro scowled.

"No! No, that's not…goddammit," Bree wiped the tears that escaped down her cheeks. "I'm so scared, Alessandro."

"I know," Alessandro replied.

"I'm afraid of what my father still might do to you and I'm

afraid of what Bernardo is grooming you to be."

"You were ready to accept Bernardo as a part of my life when you agreed to marry me. Are you saying you can't do that anymore?"

"I don't know," Bree replied. "I don't know what the right thing to do here is."

"I knew this was going to happen. You told me that I was a different person in Ireland, well you were a different person too. You were unafraid. You believed in our love. You trusted me-"

"And you lied to me," Bree reminded him curtly, "You can't pin this on me being afraid or on my family."

"Can't I?"

"No, Alessandro!"

"Well, you tell me, when was I supposed to tell you the truth, darling? When you were determined to hate me? When we were at my father's mansion? In Ireland when I held you in my arms and you looked at me and told me that the past didn't matter? That all that mattered was out future? You tell me, Brianna, when would have been the right time to destroy your faith in me?"

"I DON'T KNOW!" she screamed at him, then broke down sobbing. "This is all so damned fucked up, Alessandro!"

Alessandro's eyes softened. "I know. Just please, don't make any decisions until they let me go and we can talk about this."

Bree shook her head. "Are you sure they will? I can try and save you but there's no point in anything else, Alessandro. We can't get married because I'm always gonna be wondering what Bernardo is making you do now, what you're keeping from me. As long as he has control of you, we can't have a future. I was living in some fantasy to think otherwise. It's him or me, Alessandro. Choose."

"It's me or the O'Reileys, Brianna. You choose," Alessandro shot back.

Bree gave him a sad smile. "I did choose, Alessandro. And then I found out that you were lying to me."

Alessandro looked crestfallen and Bree wanted to burst out crying again. "I'd better go. I…I won't let my father kill you. When you're back home, I'll bring Will and Gianni to see you."

"Oh I get visitation rights. How kind of you," Alessandro sneered.

"You had more, Alessandro. But Bernardo was more important to you, and as long as he is, you and I have no future." Bree turned to walk away.

"Brianna, don't do this. Brianna!"

She kept walking away, her heart breaking with every step.

"BRIANNAAAAA!"

CHAPTER NINE

She met her father in the living room. "I'm begging you not to kill him."

Her father scowled at her. "This man is our sworn enemy. He has-"

"I know who he is and I know what he's done. I also know he is Gianni's father, and in our hearts, he is Will's father. Will loves him."

"And you," Jack snorted.

She glared at her uncle. "This is not about me."

He was silent, but his disbelief was there in his eyes.

Bree turned back to her father. "He did what he did on the order of his father. Even though I despise Bernardo, we all know that family is everything. It doesn't make it forgivable, but it does make it understandable. I'm begging you for Will's sake. Don't make him lose another father."

"She could be pregnant with his child," Beth said softly, coming out of the kitchen.

Bree gave a start. They hadn't been trying to conceive but it wasn't outside of the realm of possibility. She grabbed on to the lie. "I am."

Her father's mouth fell open and her uncle swore.

She met her sister's gaze in gratitude. "That's right. I found out in Ireland that, yes, I'm pregnant again."

Beth gave her a tiny nod, acknowledging the lie.

"Son of a…" Her father clenched his fists.

"Don't leave this baby without a father, Daddy. Please."

John looked from her to her sister. "Untie the son of bitch and toss him on the street."

"Can I help you?" The ferret-faced butler asked, his German accent thick with disapproval.

"Is Hannibal Lecter in?" Bree asked pushing pasting him into the foyer of the Dardano mansion.

"Uh, excuse me, Miss but you cannot simply barge in-"

"Oh but it looks like I am. Get over it, Ralphie," Bree said rushing into the living room where Bernardo sat with Alessandro.

"My name is Rafe. Sir, I tried to stop her but-"

"Don't worry about it, Rafe. Brianna, what a surprise," Bernardo greeted

"Yes, darling what are you doing here?" Alessandro asked.

She threw Adriano's letter at Bernardo. The old man caught it against his chest.

"Alessandro already told me about this. This is nothing new."

"Oh good, so then you're familiar with that last part there."

"Is there a point to your ranting, young lady?" Bernardo asked, impatient.

"I'll do it," Bree spat her heart racing with both rage and fear over what she was about to do. Was it the right decision? Would her family understand? Would it even work or was she setting herself for a disaster of epic proportions? Would her children end up paying the ultimate price?

"Do it?" Bernardo asked.

"If you agree to end this vendetta against my family, no more threats, no more violence, no more deaths, I'll fulfill the terms of Adriano's curse. I'll marry Alessandro."

Alessandro sucked in his breath behind her. His face was still a mass of bruises, but he was alive at least and she focused on that.

"Brianna, what are you saying? Are you saying you changed your mind?"

"That depends on your father. Odd, how everything comes back to him, isn't it?" Bree asked bitterly.

"You agree to marry my son. To become a Dardano?"

Bree shuddered at that. "I despise you. I hate you more than I've ever hated anyone and that is a pretty long list, but I love my family, and I love your son."

Alessandro placed a hand on her shoulder and she was so angry that she was pushed to this point that she jerked away from him.

"So if protecting them means making a deal with you, then fine. But you hold up your end of the bargain. You stop all violence against my family. It stops today."

"All that matters to me is my son's happiness-"

Bree snorted at that but otherwise didn't comment. If his son's happiness mattered to him at all he wouldn't be trying to make Alessandro into a carbon copy of himself. But that was all right, Bree thought, she'd bide her time, give Bernardo what he wanted and meanwhile, do all she could to undermine his influence on Alessandro. If she had to make a deal with the devil to save the man she loved, so be it.

"Well, I think this calls for a celebration! Brava! Come Alessandro, Brianna, stay for dinner. We have a wedding to plan."

"Hang on. Wait a second, there is not going to be any 'wedding'," Bree insisted.

"Brianna, you just said that you agreed to my grandfather's terms," Alessandro reminded her as Bernardo stopped behind his chair next to the dining table.

"I agreed to marry you. We'll go to city hall and sign the pa-"

"Bah! No! Out of the question. My son will not be married like some peasant. He is a Dardano. This marriage will be done with all the proper celebration that he deserves. In a church under the eyes of God."

"Are you serious? You, the anti-Christ?"

"All right that's enough!" Alessandro shouted in frustration. "Both of you just stop. This is not the way to solve anything."

"Alessandro, this will be your wedding. Are you telling me that you'd be happy just going to some office and signing papers?" Bernardo asked.

"No, but Father, this is a decision that Brianna and I need to make on our own."

"Alessandro-"

"Father, let it go!" Alessandro insisted.

Bree narrowed her eyes at Bernardo and smiled, though it faded when Alessandro turned to her.

"Brianna, you read my grandfather's words, they clearly say that a Dardano and a O'Reiley must be joined in the eyes of God. That means in a church."

"Alessandro-," Bree protested but Alessandro took her hands in his and she felt a shiver of a very different kind at his touch as he pulled her away from his father.

"I love you. I know that you doubt that at times but I do. If we do this, I want to do it right, not just for us, but for them, for Francesca and Adriano. We can really finally put their souls at peace. I want to marry you and that means in the eyes of God, not just legally."

"Alessandro, you can't seriously be asking-"

"I am. Because when we say our vows, I want them to mean more than just words on paper. I want them to come from our souls, darling, from our hearts. What do you say, eh? I want to marry you in the truest sense of the word, in St. Luke's."

Bree stopped him. "Alessandro, I'm just doing this to save my family." Which wasn't completely true, she was doing it in hopes of saving him as well and knowing that, what was this small concession?

"But if we're going to be married, if we're going to say vows, we're going to mean them, Brianna. This will be a real marriage or there will be no marriage," Alessandro insisted, stiffening.

"Fine," Bree agreed. "St. Luke's it is." And if she was lucky, lightning would not set the whole church on fire.

"How could you?" Angela asked, her eyes blazing with hurt and disgust.

"I had to, mom. I did it for us," Bree pleaded with her for understanding.

"Oh please, you did it for you," Carrie insisted.

Bree glared at her. "How dare you-"

"Give me a break Bree, you have always been in love with Alessandro despite the fact that he's a Dardano. Never mind that he was probably in on Michael's death as well."

"No. He had nothing to do with Michael's death. He promised-," Bree began but Carrie snorted in disbelief.

"Bree, not even you can possibly be that gullible. He's a Dardano. He's evil. For once can you stop being selfish and think about the danger you're putting your children in."

"Oh gullible. You wanna talk gullible? Why don't we ask Colin about that, huh?" Bree snapped. Carrie, the good sister, the sainted O'Reiley against which all future O'Reileys would be measured against, was knocking boots with someone other than the sainted Colin Neally, her husband.

Alessandro had been particularly gleeful when he imparted that little tidbit after she let him take Gianni for a doctor's visit by himself. He'd seen them making out in the lounge. Bree had wanted to rush over to Carrie and shove that news down her sanctimonious little throat, but Alessandro insisted that Bree hold onto her info until the best moment.

"And when would that be exactly?" Bree had asked fuming. Her whole family treated her like some misguided, prodigal daughter, fighting to be worthy of their forgiveness for falling in love with the enemy. And here was their precious Carrie…

"When it's to your advantage, darling. Trust me," Alessandro had assured her.

"Well, sure. I mean, who else would I trust when it comes to deceit and blackmail?" Bree had told him.

"Flattery, darling, will get you everywhere," Alessandro had whispered cupping her breast as she stood at the kitchen counter.

Carrie blinked guiltily. "What are you talking about?"

"Oh please. Spare me the St. Carrie act because I am sick of it," Bree turned and grabbed Will, prepared to walk out of the pub.

"Sweetie, wait. Don't leave, please. We just want what's best for you," her father assured her.

"What's best for me is to have my family there on my wedding day, but I suppose that's too much to ask from the morally superior O'Reileys," Bree sniffled, her eyes burning. Dammit, she promised herself that she wouldn't cry.

"Look, I don't think you get just how evil these men are. Bree, look what they did to Charlie," her aunt Keira said.

"If I do this, there will be no more danger. Everyone I love will be safe. That's the deal. Bernardo promised-"

"You can't believe any promises that man makes, Bree. Baby girl, you're smarter than this," Angela said. "I know you want to believe that Alessandro is a good man-"

"Alessandro is a good man. You don't know that because none of you even bothered to get past his last name but I know him. I do, and I love him, that's all that matters."

"Honey, you can't change a man and you'll only hurt yourself if you try," Angela reminded her.

"Oh mom-" Bree squeezed her eyes shut. "I am ending this

vendetta between our families. It's what Adriano wanted and you know what, I understand how Francesca felt because Great Grandpa Pete was just plain wrong in how he treated her. His disapproval caused Francesca to kill herself. Well I'm not making her mistake. I know that it's too much to ask for you guys to accept me but I don't regret the decision I'm making. I'm doing this for our family and I'm doing it for Alessandro because I know he loves me. And I know that I can pull him out from under Bernardo's influence-"

"I am not willing to sacrifice my daughter to save Bernardo's son," Angela snapped.

"I mean, this is so typical of you, Bree. Every time I think you've changed you prove me wrong," Carrie said.

"Well, you've certainly changed haven't you?" Bree shot back, sick of her sister's holier than thou attitude.

"I don't know what you're trying-"

"You've certainly fallen off your pedestal, huh. I wonder if Colin knows that his golden girl is nothing more than a two faced adulterous little bitch."

"Bree!" Angela gasped as the others stared in stunned silence.

Carrie had gone white faced, her blue eyes wide.

"Bree, we're begging you. Don't do this. Don't turn your back on your family like this," Keira pleaded.

"Forget it, Aunt Keira. Bree doesn't care if she destroys her family," Carrie said.

"Oh you want to take shots at how I feel about family? You're hardly the expert. I mean were you thinking about family when you were knocking boots with Alex Winters in the hospital lounge?" Bree yelled at her.

"You bitch," Carrie hissed, red faced.

"Bree, that was completely uncalled for. Now you apologize," Angela demanded.

Bree shook her head, her tears filling her eyes. "Right. 'Cause everything is my fault, right mom? Well, don't worry. As of today, you don't have to worry about me any longer. In a few hours, I won't be an O'Reiley anymore. I'll be a Dardano."

Angela rushed ahead and grabbed her before Bree could turn and grab Will and Gianni to leave.

"No, Bree. No! Don't do this. I will not sacrifice my daughter to those monsters. I will not allow it!" she said, her eyes wide and desperate.

"Mom, if you're not gonna stand by me on my wedding day, then we have nothing more to say to each other."

Meggie and Beth were the only people who would stand next to Bree on her wedding day. Apart from that, she had no one. The bosses who were loyal to her family, because her parent's disapproval was well known, stayed away. The families who were loyal to the Dardanos were there along with Alessandro's aunt Roxanna, her daughter Tina and Tina's husband, Carlo. Kevin Hadley was pulling best man duty.

"Thank you so much for being here with me," Bree said as Meggie helped her put up her hair.

"Like I'd be anywhere else," Meggie said. There was a knock on the door to the bridal dressing room where they were making some last minute preparations.

"Don't tell me that's Alessandro. He can't see me,"

Meggie went to answer the door and then gasped in surprise. "Guess who?"

Bree covered her mouth and cried out as her brother Brian poked his head into the room.

"Somebody getting married?" he asked with a wide smile.

"Oh my God! Brian!" Bree threw her arms around her brother and buried her face in his chest.

"Oh, Bree, your makeup!" Meggie scolded pulling her way.

"I don't care," Bree sniffled through her tears. "What are you doing here? I thought you said you wouldn't be able to make it?"

"Well, as much as I hate being grateful to a Dardano, your fiancé seems to have some pull with my boss over at the paper. He pulled me from my assignment in Zimbabwe for a few days. I've got enough photos that they can run the story and let me know if they need me for anything else. In the meantime, I'm all yours."

"Alessandro did this?" Bree asked, her heart warming.

"Yeah, and if it wasn't for Will assuring me that Alessandro was a good guy I would have figured it was some kind of Dardano set up."

"What? Will knew too?" Bree asked. "I'm amazed he didn't spill the beans. Did you know too?" She asked Meggie.

The woman shook her head.

"So you're marrying a Dardano. Can I ask which of your

marbles you lost exactly?"

"Don't you start. I'm doing this for our family. Never mind that they don't seem to care and just chalk it up to Bree being a screw up again."

"Come on, Bree. You have to admit out of all the insane things you've done-"

"Can we not take that trip down memory lane?" Bree insisted. "Look, if you're really here for me then that means more to me than you know but if you're just gonna tow the O'Reiley line then you can go,"

Brian raised his hands in surrender. "No, that's not why I'm here. I want to give you away today, if you'll let me."

"Mmm, well. I guess since you're already all dressed up," Bree noticed, taking in his polished, handsome appearance in the tuxedo.

"I mean, I shined my shoes and everything," Brian pointed out smiling.

"Oh well then, that just cinches it. You have to walk me down the aisle," Bree joked reaching up and hugging him again. "Oh, thank you so much for being here, even if this isn't exactly the wedding of my dreams. Bernardo promised he would leave the O'Reileys alone if I married Alessandro."

"I see," Brian remarked, though his face looked like he hardly understood at all. "So you don't actually love Alessandro, is that it?"

"No," Bree insisted. "I mean, yes. I mean no, it's not that I don't love him. That's not the point. I do love him. He's…I can't seem to make anyone understand but there's something so good and loving in Alessandro. Almost…innocent about him. The way he loves me and the boys. I've never been loved by anyone the way Alessandro loves me."

"Innocent. A Dardano?" Brian asked with obvious skepticism.

"You know what?" Bree threw up her hands in frustration.

"I'm sorry, I'm sorry! The important thing is that he loves you and you love him."

"He does and I do. Now I just have to get him the hell away from his father and everything will turn out perfectly."

"Wait what does that mean? What are you planning, Bree?" Brian asked.

"Nothing. I swear," Bree assured him, putting on her most

innocent face.

Brian cocked a light eyebrow, obviously knowing his sister too well.

"Mommy, you see da supise?" Will asked knocking on the door as he yelled through it.

Brian pulled open the door while Meggie reapplied Bree's makeup.

"Yes, you sneaky boy. How did you keep such a big secret?" Bree asked impressed.

"I's a good seaky boy," Will explained smiling. "Da fat man say w'as taking you so long?"

"Oh is Bernardo in a rush?" Bree sneered she took an extra-long time to check herself once more in the mirror.

"All right, you. Let's get the show on the road, already," Meggie insisted.

She was trembling. She noticed because Brian's arm was shaking as she held it.

"You know you don't have to do this right?" Brian pointed out.

"Yes, I do. But I just have to remember that I love Alessandro. We can deal with anything as long as we focus on that."

"All I want is for you to be happy," Brian leaned over and kissed the top of her head.

The organ music began, making Bree jump as the doors swung open.

She gave Alessandro a small smile and scowled at Bernardo. Before she could even think about giving into her fears and changing her mind, Meggie was taking her seat next to Beth and Alessandro was stepping forward to take her from Brian. Her brother whispered something in Alessandro's ear that made Alessandro clench his jaw before focusing back on her.

"Dearly beloved, we are gathered in the sight of God to join Brianna O'Reiley and Alessandro Dardano in holy matrimony."

Bree's hands felt cold in Alessandro's and he rubbed the back of her hands with his thumbs as the priest went on. When he got to the part about any objections, Bree figured it was a good thing that her family wasn't there because the reply to that would have been pretty deafening.

Then she realized it was time for the vows. *You can do this. You can make these promises because you love him.* Alessandro gave her fingers a little squeeze. "I, Brianna, take you, Alessandro, to be my beloved husband, to have and to hold you, to honour you, to treasure you, to be at your side in sorrow and in joy, in the good times, and in the bad, and to love and cherish you always. I promise you this from my heart, for all the days of my life."

Her eyes burned as she focused on Alessandro as he repeated the words, his voice choked with emotion.

When Will ran up excitedly with the rings he nearly knocked Alessandro over in his exuberance as he handed them to him.

There was writing inside both bands. *My Beloved.* He slowly slipped the ring on her finger and she felt a shiver go down her back.

She truly belonged to him now. It was a heady feeling.

Bree slipped the ring on his finger and repeated the words, "With this ring, I thee wed." There. He officially belonged to her now. Her eyes moved to Bernardo and she couldn't help the surge of triumph. *He's mine now. He belongs to me now. Not you.*

"By the power vested in me, I now pronounce you husband and wife. Ladies and gentlemen, let me introduce to you Mr. and Mrs. Alessandro and Brianna Dardano."

Brianna Dardano. *Good God.* She started when Bernardo burst out in applause. She lifted her eyes to the ceiling but focused back on Alessandro and the priest told him to kiss the bride.

He leaned forward and cupped her face, smiling as he captured her mouth with his own.

The world disappeared in a sweet blissful haze as Alessandro kissed her. A kiss of promise for what was in store for tonight. God she couldn't wait. She'd missed him so much.

In the next instant, three loud shots thundered through St. Luke's and Alessandro was falling against her, blood soaking the back of his tuxedo.

Bree caught him and her heart was screaming, though on the outside, she couldn't seem to make a sound.

The church exploded in a cacophy of noise as people rushed out and the men drew their guns and ran to find the threat.

"Daaaadddyyyy!" Will shrieked but then his voice was muffled as Brian covered the little boy with his body at the sound of more gun shots.

Gianni, awakened by the commotion began to shriek as Meggie pulled him close to her body and lay against the seat of the pew.

Bree fell to the altar, breaking Alessandro's fall as his blood pumped out against her cradling hands. The world around her seemed to sharpen from the adrenaline, shock and pure terror coursing through her.

Alessandro struggled to stay conscious, his face white as his hand lifted to her cheek.

"Alessandro! Stay with me. Please, look at me. Keep your eyes on me. It's okay. It's okay," Bree promised, the words tumbling from her mouth automatically, having no real meaning.

"Dammit, call for an ambulance!" Bernardo's boomed through the church as he rushed to Alessandro's other side, stroking his son's head.

The priest jumped fearfully. "Of course." He ran down the aisle, Brian and Kevin close behind him.

"Where are you going?" Meggie asked.

"To see if they're still back there," Brian growled, fury evident in his voice.

They. The shooter. Someone had shot Alessandro. Stood back, aimed a gun and intended to kill him. Bree fought back a surge of vomit. No! They wouldn't take Alessandro from her. She would NOT lose him now. "Alessandro!" Bree shook him as his eyes rolled back in his head. He blinked and tried to meet her gaze but the effort was too much and his eyes fluttered closed. "No!" Bree pleaded, her tears falling on him. "Please, Alessandro. Please! Come back. Oh God."

Then someone was pulling her away from him and Bree was struggling out of their grasp.

"Let us take him," a paramedic said; his voice soft. "Let us help him."

Bree watched as they lifted Alessandro onto the gurney. "Careful. Please. Be careful with him."

"You'd better save my son," Bernardo growled. His voice full of anger and desperation. Bree briefly wondered if she looked as pale as he did.

"We'll do what we can, sir," one of the men replied as they set about their work.

Then Alessandro spoke…his voice so faint and weak she almost missed it. His hand was moving up, searching. "Br…Brnna, Brianna," he whispered.

Bree rushed forwards and grabbed his hand, noting distantly

that hers was covered in blood. His blood. His life, pouring out of him. "I'm here. I'm here Alessandro and I'm not going anywhere."

"Tell Gianni…Tell Will…I love…" he grimaced in a spasm of pain.

"Shut up," Bree snapped, fear mixing with fury at him, at God for taking him away from her. "I'm not telling them anything. You are going to be fine, dammit. I am not letting you go, you hear me, you Dardano? I am not letting you die and that is the end of this."

He gave her a weak smile. "God…love you…so much." Then his eyes drifted shut again and the paramedics pulled him away.

"Where daddy going? Don' take my daddy! Don' take my daddy away!" Will cried and Bree reached out and grabbed him as he tried to follow the gurney.

"It's okay," Bree promised holding on to her little boy. She turned him around and got down on her knees to meet his gaze. "Sweetie, I promise you, daddy will be fine. They're just gonna take him to the hospital to make him all better." *Please God.*

"Da bad man did it! Da bad man here mommy! Da bad man gon' kill ebbebody!" Will shrieked and Bree pulled him towards her.

"No honey. Nobody is gonna hurt you. I swear." She got to her feet when she saw Brian coming back.

He slowly shook his head. Whoever the shooter was — Arturo? God help me — he was gone.

"I have to get to the hospital," Bree said rushing forward to take Gianni, who was still crying.

"No, first you have to sit down and take a minute," Meggie insisted shaking her head.

She let Meggie guide her to the chair. Brian took the handkerchief out of the pocket of his tuxedo jacket and handed it to her.

Behind her she could hear Bernardo yelling at a policeman who had been sent to investigate the scene. The cop quickly had enough of Bernardo's ranting and promised that a detective would meet them at the hospital to investigate further. Right, Bree thought with a surge of bitterness. They'd probably give the shooter a medal.

Bernardo dropped beside her on the pew, deflated, a man defeated. "If I find out an O'Reiley is behind this. You can say goodbye to hope of a peaceful existence, my dear. If my son dies, no O'Reiley in the world will be safe. Do you hear me?"

Bree shook her head. "I married him. That was the deal. You keep up your end of the bargain as I did mine."

"That's right. You are his wife now and you will act like it or by God-"

"Don't you dare," Bree hissed. "Don't you threaten me. I just watched the man I love being carted out of here barely alive because of you,"

"Me?" Bernardo asked.

"Oh who do you think did it, Bernardo? Arturo. Your sick creation. You must be so proud. You raised a real sicko."

Murder blazed in his eyes but Bree was too terrified about losing Alessandro to care. "You will fulfill your duty as his wife. My son loves you so you will go to the hospital and you will make him fight to live. You will give him the will to come back to us or so help me-"

"You know what? Can we save the death threats for some other time? A man is fighting for his life and I need to get my sister to the hospital," Brian snapped, pulling Bree to her feet. "Come on, Bree. We'll go in my car."

"We go see Daddy now?" Will asked, tears falling down his cheeks.

"Yeah, come on big guy. Let's go see daddy. I bet he misses you and is just sitting in his bed wondering what's taking everybody so long," Meggie said, picking Will up and following Bree, her sister Beth, Gianni and Brian out of the church.

CHAPTER TEN

"Your husband is in critical condition, Mrs. Dardano. We're waiting for him to stabilize before we can operate," the doctor explained.

Critical. Operate. Bree trembled as she took a step back, coming up against Brian, who wrapped an arm around her.

"The bullet entered his left kidney, causing severe internal bleeding. We have to be careful when we go in to retrieve the bullet that we don't cause further tearing."

Internal bleeding…tearing.

"You save my son. I don't care what it takes, what it costs," Bernardo said as Uncle Jack entered the emergency room, followed by most of the other O'Reileys.

"Oh my God, when I heard there'd been a shooting at the church. Oh baby, thank God you're all right!" Angela rushed towards Bree and Beth, pulling them both into her arms.

Bree pulled away from her. "I can't do this now," she said unable to deal with her mother's inconsistent affection and her husband's fight for his life at the same time.

"Sweetie, please tell me you'll stop this insanity now," Angela pleaded. "Please tell me you'll stay away from the Dardanos now.

"Oh, God. I really cannot do this right now. Mom, my husband is in there, with a bullet in his back. I am not about to abandon him!"

"Oh well, we really shouldn't expect any less shouldn't we?" Carrie said.

Bree noticed briefly that Colin wasn't with her. She didn't have time to gloat about it before Carrie went ahead with her diatribe. "You've just had bullets rained down on not only your head but those of your children. How typical, Bree, really,"

That was it. Terror and emotional exhaustion made Bree snap and she attacked Carrie, sending her older sister sprawling to the floor as Bree punched, scratched and pulled at her hair. She attacked like a crazed animal, about to lose one of the only things she cared about in the whole world.

"Okay, that's enough," Brian insisted pulling Bree off of Carrie. "That's it!" her brother shouted in her ear as Bree tried to break free.

Bree panted as Carrie got to her feet with Kevin's help, wiping the blood off her busted lip.

"What the hell is going on here?" Tina demanded, stepping away from Alex and Carlo who now wore a white doctor's coat, having changed out of his tuxedo.

"Nothing. Just a little misunderstanding isn't it?" Brian asked easing his grip off of Bree.

"Right," Bree hissed through her teeth, "Get out of here."

"Bree," Angela protested. "We only-"

"I said GET OUT! All of you. You don't give a damn about Alessandro and you're just here to rub my nose in how you are so much more superior than me. Well, you know what? That's fine. I don't want to be an O'Reiley anymore. Alessandro is my family. My babies are my family. I'm a Dardano now so you either accept it or you can all stay the hell away from me from now on," Bree said.

"Bree you don't mean that," her father insisted.

"Daddy, if you're asking me to turn my back on the man I love, yes, I do." Bree assured him, tears running down her face.

"Well," John said taking a step back, pain evident on his face. "Then you're not the woman I thought you were."

"I never was daddy," Bree said through her tears. "You just didn't want to accept me any other way."

She fell into Brian's arms sobbing as her family left and must have drifted off because she was jolted awake by Bernardo's bellowing.

"What do you mean you still can't operate? This is my son we are talking about!"

"We've managed to stop the bleeding but it's still too dangerous to try and remove the bullet."

"So what, you're just gonna wait for him to die?" Bree asked getting to her feet.

"We're waiting twenty-four hours. If he hasn't stabilized we'll need authorization to operate-"

"Yes, of course. You have my permission," Bernardo insisted.

"Uh, actually, we'll need his wife to authorize the surgery," Carlo said, sympathetic green eyes moving to Bree.

"Sure. Anything you have to do, please," Bree begged, closing her eyes.

"Thank you, Mrs. Dardano," the doctor nodded, giving her a look that told her he was glad to be dealing with her and not Bernardo.

"Can I see him now?" Bree asked.

"I wan' see daddy too!" Will demanded, rushing away from Meggie.

"Just one at a time right now," Carlo said.

"No!" Will snapped. "I go see my daddy now! He my daddy, nod yours!"

"Honey, I'll bring you in a little while okay?" Bree said, running her hand over Will's hair.

Will scowled but agreed. "You promise?"

"Sure do," Bree assured him.

"Don't worry kiddo. How about we go get you something to eat, huh?" Brian asked, lifting Will up onto his shoulders.

Bree mouthed her gratitude to her brother and then went to Alessandro's room in the ICU. Her legs nearly gave way as she saw just how many tubes he was hooked up to.

She walked slowly towards him, taking in how he looked so eerily still. "Okay you," she said, her voice choked. "We have to have a talk. I know you're a Dardano, but a wedding reception in the ICU? Not so classy." She lowered her head, her attempt at levity falling flat under the weight of her heartbreak. She blinked back her tears and cupped his face. "You listen to me, okay? You are not leaving me. You're not allowed. You're going to fight, understand? Alessandro, I will not bury another husband. Do you hear me? I refuse to grieve for you. That is not even an option because you are my life." She kissed his forehead, the beeping of the heart monitor and the respirators the only sounds in the room. "Funny huh? I spent so much time pushing you away and here I am begging you to stay. Not just for me, but for our boys. Will's already lost one father, don't you leave him too. And Gianni…don't you dare leave him nothing but stories about some man in a picture frame."

Bree took his hand, rubbing his ring finger. "Please, Alessandro. Fight. I won't survive without you. I won't." She kissed his palm. "We've fought too hard for you to just give up when we're finally going to be happy. Dammit Alessandro, you owe me! You owe me a life, a happy life together. So don't you dare die on me. Don't you leave me to deal with that son of a bitch father of yours by myself." She covered her mouth with her free hand to stifle her sobs. She leaned down and kissed his still mouth. "I love you…I love you so much…" Her tears fell on his face as she rested her forehead against his.

He was in surgery, and Bree didn't know what to do with herself. It was encouraging to hear Alex tell her that Alessandro had stabilized but then she realized that meant they were going to cut him open and throw him right back into the danger.

Meggie had stayed with her most of the night after she assured Beth that she should go home and get some sleep. Gianni wouldn't stop crying, Bree asked the doctor if they could give her baby something for the teething pain and it had effectively put Gianni to sleep. Meggie followed soon after, nearly falling out of her chair and Bree sent her home as well. Brian would drive her and then he promised to return. Bree told him he didn't have to and her older brother told her not to argue with him.

Bernardo hadn't slept in two days and it was starting to show on the old man's face. Bree tried to not feel sympathy over his obvious worry about his son, but she couldn't help wondering, what kind of man kills with such ease and cares nothing for turning his son into a killer as well and yet is so wrecked by the thought of losing him?

Bree held a sleeping Will closer to her and when Brian returned, she asked her brother if he could watch him for a little while. She needed to get out of the damned waiting room.

Bree hadn't intended to go to the hospital chapel again but found herself there for the third time in two days. It was empty at that hour and dimly lit. Bree sat in the front pew and looked up at the large crucifix that hung over the altar. She didn't know what to pray for anymore.

Beyond, *Save him*, nothing really registered in her sleep deprived brain. Meggie had brought her some new clothes, taking the bloody white dress. Bree didn't ask what she had done with it but she hoped Meggie had burned the fucking thing. She could never look at the dress again without thinking of the shooting. Serves her right, Bree thought. Talk about bad luck. She really did destroy everything she touched didn't she? First Michael, now Alessandro. Bree closed her heavy, exhausted eyes.

He had pulled through the operation and for the first time, the doctors sounded genuinely optimistic. But they'd know more when Alessandro woke up.

And there was still a risk of infection, that set in two days later.

She should have known better than to get her hopes up, but Bree kept a brave face for Will who kept asking her when Alessandro was gonna open his eyes.

The infection was spreading and the doctors no longer smiled when they saw her. They stayed determined, but there was no hope in their eyes or their voices. If it spread to his heart or his brain…Bernardo cut them off at that point, promising murder if they didn't save his son.

Bree woke from a short, fitful nap, her head on Brian's shoulder as Will sat on the floor in front of them, next to Alessandro's bed.

"Mornin'," Brian said rubbing her shoulder.

"How long that time?" Bree asked.

"A whole half hour," Brian remarked dryly.

Bree sighed. She supposed it was better than the ten-minute snatches of sleep she was used to getting lately.

"Mommy, lookit my picture!" Will announced turning around and handing her what he had been working on. It was a large head with spikey hair, a wide smile and big round eyes. Stick arms were spread out. *For dadi. Luf u dis much* was written underneath.

The image swam before Bree's tear-filled gaze.

"Can you put it up der for me?" Will asked pointing to the wall above Alessandro's bed.

"This is awesome dude," Brian said as Bree taped it to the wall.

"You tink daddy like it?" Will asked.

"Oh I know he'll love it and it'll be just the thing to wake him up, you just watch," Bree promised.

"I hope so. I miss him lots. You don' tink…" Will pressed his lips tight together and turned away.

"What?" Bree asked.

Will played with the edge of Alessandro's blanket. "You don' tink he go up in hev'n like my other daddy, right?"

"No!" Bree snapped making Will jump and his eyes water. Bree forced herself to use a softer tone. "Sorry sweetie. No, I promise you, Alessandro is not going to die."

Brian gave her a look of warning but Bree ignored him. Alessandro dying was not an option. But Will did give her an idea.

The next day, she asked Brian and Beth to watch Will and Gianni as she needed to get out of the hospital for at least an hour.

Bree sat on the bench in the chilly November air and stared at the familiar tombstone of her first husband.

It was blustery cold but Bree ignored the wind that whipped at her hair and focused on her dead husband's name.

Andy respectfully stayed near the iron gate a few yards away. She'd wanted to come alone but he was having none of it. "If Alessandro wakes up and has a coronary after learning you went off on your own, how will you feel? You'll have two deaths on your head."

"Two?" Bree had asked.

"You bet. His, and mine when he kills me."

It was kinda disconcerting having a stranger know her so well.

Bree took a deep breath, wincing at the cold air that pierced her nose. She wasn't sure how coming here would help but she just knew she needed to talk to Michael. "You know, it's a lot easier to argue with you like this," she remarked with a small smile. "When I think of how many more of our fights I'd have won…" her words broke on a sob. "Oh God Michael, I need your help. I need you to put a word in up there or something because I can't lose him. I can't." She wiped her damp cheeks, certain that if she left the tears on her skin, they'd turn to ice.

"I thought I wouldn't survive losing you, but he helped me. Alessandro helped me put myself back together. I can't go through losing him. There's gotta be some kind of rule of tact I'm breaking here, asking my dead husband to help my new husband live, but you know me, I was never that big on tact."

She stuck her hands in the pockets of her coat, feeling the cold metal of her wedding ring against her skin. "You know, he's a

Dardano anyway so I'm sure you won't have to twist God's arm much to send him back." She shook her head. "He's a good man. Really. More than a little misguided in his loyalty to his father but I think I love him even more for that. Don't hate me for that, I beg you. He's such a good father to Will and oh God, Michael, I don't think our little boy can survive losing another father. He's been through so much this year. And it's not like we can count on my family to help us through any of it. They think Alessandro is the anti-Christ," she added with a little laugh, "Will asked me if Alessandro was going to go to heaven like you did. I don't know what I'll do if Alessandro dies. I love him so much even when I want to throttle him. Sound familiar? But God, I know we could be happy if we were just given a chance, you know? I could pull him out from his father's influence and we could actually have a life. Our baby deserves to know his father. Will deserves to have Alessandro raise him if you can't and dammit…" Bree closed her eyes as the tears dripped off her chin. "I deserve to be happy. I deserve to be loved and have a family and grow old with someone who adores me as much as Alessandro does. Everybody else gets that. They get married and have babies and live in houses with picket fences and grow old surrounded by their families…why not me?"

"I'm not even sure I believe in heaven really, but I can't shake the feeling that you're…somewhere and that you can hear me. If you can, I beg you, help Alessandro find his way back to us."

Bree got back to the hospital to find Bernardo Dardano smiling, and not in his usual evil, creepy way.

"Mommy! Guess what? Daddy's eye-fiction go away!" Will exclaimed beaming.

"His…?" Bree looked over at Brian and Beth for translation.

"The infection is starting to clear up and his fever has gone down," Bernardo said, his voice animated for the first time in weeks. "And where have you been?"

Bree bit back the urge to tell him it was none of his business and concentrate on the fact that Alessandro was beginning to recover. Thank God…Thank you, Michael. She fell into the chair as relief washed over her. Her sister sat down and hugged her. "He's going to be just fine. It's only a matter of time before he's awake and back to his obnoxious, chauvinistic self."

"Daddy gonna wake up soon, right, mommy?" Will asked. "And den he see my picture!"

"Can we see him now?" Bree asked getting to her feet and calling out to Alex as he passed by.

Now that Alessandro was out of the woods, Alex didn't bother hiding his irritation with her over what she had done to Carrie. She saw him take a deep breath. "Sure," he snapped.

Right, like she was the one who had anything to feel guilty about. But Bree pushed thoughts of Alex away and almost skipped into Alessandro's room.

"He still sleeping," Will said with disappointment and Brian and Beth followed them in with a sleeping Gianni.

"Yep kiddo. He's pretty tired 'cause he's fought so hard to come back to you. He'll be awake in no time," Brian promised.

Bree smiled at her brother in gratitude.

Her siblings stayed with her for another hour before he took Will and Gianni back to Bree's apartment for some rest and to visit Luke who was staying at a dog daycare for the time being.

Bree sat back and felt giddy as she watched Alessandro sleep. He was coming back to her.

She spent the next morning reading from the newspaper for him, hoping her voice would wake him. When that didn't do it, Bree smiled and leaned close to him on the pillow.

"Okay you, if that didn't do it, I might just have to break into song."

"Good God, no," an exhausted voice spoke, making Bree's heart stop as she saw Alessandro's face screw up in a grimace of either pain or disgust, she didn't care which. "Anything but that."

Bree held her breath for a panicked second until she realized how exhausted he must be, but oh she wanted to see his eyes again. Those beautiful eyes the color of dark caramel, that she feared she'd never see again.

"Come on lazy ass," Bree whispered, her voice shaky as she laid her head against his.

"Mmm….plan to be…very lazy when…out of here. First…wedding night," he gave her a weak smile and then went under again.

Bree just stared at him, tears of gratitude and joy pouring down her face.

He woke up again a few hours later. "Love you," he murmured.

"Felt you here…whole time…fighting…love you."

"Daddy," Will poked Alessandro's foot. "Wake up daddy. Time to go home now."

Alessandro grimaced and opened his eyes. "Will…" he gave the little boy a small, tired smile.

"Hi daddy! Guess what, Gianni have a toof and I growed a whole centy-peter since da last time. Gianni only growed a half a centy-peter. The doctor checked me. I's bigger. And unco Brian say he gonna by a sail boat and I can ride it wif him and is it true we go live in da fat man's house. All togedder like in da country where dey talk funny?"

Bree scowled at that little bit. Bernardo insisted they move into the mansion as soon as Alessandro was ready. *We'll just see about that.* She focused on the brighter side of things.

"Missed you…very much…Young William. How's Gianni?" he asked.

"Unco Brian bing him later. Did you see my picture?" Will asked pointing up behind him above the bed.

Alessandro tried to follow Will's finger but grimaced in pain.

"Here, I'll bring it down for you." Bree pulled the picture down and handed it to Alessandro who smiled as he read the words and saw the comical head.

"You like it?" Will asked climbing up beside him on the bed.

"Wait Will, don't-," Bree protested but Alessandro raised his hand.

" 's all right. I love…picture very much. Love you even…more."

"Maybe we should let you rest for a little while."

"No he rest lots already. Now he play wif me and den we go home," Will insisted resting his head on Alessandro's chest.

Bree grimaced, not sure if he was hurting Alessandro or not. The man didn't let on.

"I don't mind," Alessandro assured her. He leaned down and kissed the top of Will's head.

"I had the most bizarre dreams while I was out," Alessandro explained the next day. "My grandfather Adriano was in this park feeding birds and I was sitting next to him and he was telling me all about family loyalty and how I shouldn't let it blind me to what was right in front of me. Then I looked at the birds and Will and Gianni were playing together. Then in another dream, I saw you and you were telling me all about Michael and how you loved him. Then I was back in the park and instead of my grandfather next to me, it was Michael and he was telling me that if I ever hurt you, I'd have to answer to him and that God didn't want me until I became a better man. Then there you were again. Except we were in this house…in Italy and you were having a baby that I knew somehow would be a baby girl and Francesca was there and she was hitting me over the head with a baguette and telling me to get away from her because I was a Dardano."

Bree tried not laugh at that mental image. Her eyes filled with tears at the mention of his dream about Michael.

Alessandro's face suddenly became very serious. "The last one I remember, it was you on that cliff, instead of Francesca."

Bree shivered at that mental image. "Did I jump?"

He closed his eyes briefly and then met her gaze. "I pushed you."

CHAPTER ELEVEN

"I still don't understand why we can't live back in my apartment," Bree grumbled as she watched the movers bring her things into the Dardano mansion one month later. God she hated this creepy place. When the old fart died she was *so* redecorating.

"Because Brianna, there simply is not enough room for all four of us in your apartment. My grandfather's terms were very specific. We need to be a family and my father is my family just as much as you are," Alessandro reminded her.

"Blah blah blah," Bree grumbled, but she didn't argue too much. *Pick your battles.* That had to be the new strategy here. Bernardo thought he would have more power over his son if he lived here, well, she'd be here too and she most definitely would not allow that to happen. *Keep your enemies close.*

"Welcome Mr. Dardano," Rafe said after letting them in.

Bree glared at him, waiting to be acknowledged.

"Mrs. Dardano," he added with considerably less enthusiasm, if it was possible. The butler was definitely not happy to have them here.

"I is Mr. Dardano too," Will explained, sticking out his hand to the butler who stared at him.

Rafe grunted and turned away.

Will looked up at Bree. "I no like him. He nod polite."

"No, he's not. Let's just ignore him."

"An' he look like a turtle,"

Bree bit back a smile of agreement.

"Home sweet home, Gianni," Alessandro said, smiling down at the baby who looked around and sneezed.

"Uh, looks like Gianni is allergic to the place. Let's go," Bree said but followed Alessandro into the foyer.

"Ah there is my boy! Come, come, we shall have dinner soon. Are you hungry Giovanni? I bet you are."

"It's Gianni," Bree stubbornly corrected.

Bernardo reached for the baby, which Alessandro eased into his arms, as she watched uncomfortably.

"Can we go swmming, like da last time?" Will asked running in and jumping on the couch.

"Sure, soon," Alessandro promised.

"Are you sure you're ready for that?" Bree asked. "I don't want you to over exert yourself too soon."

"Relax darling, I'm not training for a triathlon. I don't plan to over exert myself," then he leaned in and whispered, "I plan to take things nice and slow."

Bree shivered with the understanding that he wasn't talking about swimming at all.

"I'm not letting you carry me to the bed, Alessandro," Bree insisted as she pushed Alessandro towards the footboard, a rectangular shaped board with a mix of maple and oak wood, intricately carved. Four long dark oak posts flanked each corner of the bed, the crown of which was a gorgeous arched headboard with same two toned color as the foot board, elegant without being ostentatious. Two gold — Bree wouldn't be surprised if they were real gold — lamps with beige satin lamp shades rested on night tables in the same style as the bed. The floor was smooth oak and was covered with a grey rug.

The bed linens were an inviting mix of gold and off white and Bree knew without touching them that the sheets were satin.

She wasn't overly fond of the green curtains, though she liked the white molded windows and doorway. Her favourite part of the bedroom though had to be the ensuite bathroom.

A shower with glass door and a gleaming white claw foot tub that on closer inspection was also a Jacuzzi. Gold fixtures and a full length gold framed mirror on the wall next to the door. The countertop was a mix of white and peach marble, as was the tiled floor.

"Really Brianna, you must allow me to fulfill my long held fantasy of carrying my wife over the threshold and making wild debauched love to her," Alessandro insisted with a devilish smile before he took her hand and kissed it.

"Hmm, well, Alessandro, in this fantasy did you happen to be recovering from a gunshot wound?" Bree asked, pulling her hand away.

Alessandro gave her a look of impatience.

"That's what I thought. No carrying. You're getting into this bed and so am I and then we can…well, no debauchery just yet," Bree replied with a wink.

"My wife is a bossy shrew," Alessandro remarked good-naturedly and began pulling off his clothes.

"The sooner you learn that the better," Bree said pulling off the grey sweater dress she wore.

"Brianna. I wanted our wedding night to be romantic," Alessandro insisted, pushing back the covers, stopping to give Bree a heated look that told her he appreciated her quick discarding of clothing.

Bree climbed into the bed and wrapped her arms around him, clad now only in a satin baby blue teddy.

"Now why did you not tell me you were wearing that? My day would have been quite brighter."

"Because you're insatiable and if I told you what I had on underneath the dress we never would have made it here without you tearing your stitches."

"I'm insatiable? *I* am?" Alessandro asked cocking an eyebrow as he ran his warm hands along the satin material covering her body.

"Alessandro. You're alive. I can touch you, look into your eyes and hear your arrogant English voice. We're gonna spend the rest of our lives together, that's plenty romantic for me." Bree pressed her mouth against him. He tasted of coffee and peppermint.

He nibbled slightly on her lower lip before pulling away. "Darling, that sounds lovely, but my wedding night fantasy was more along the lines of fucking you into the mattress."

Bree smacked his shoulder. "Patience, Dardano. Tonight we take things slow, the mattress fucking will come in time. Now, get on your back and let me put my hands on you and assure myself that you're real."

Alessandro sighed but did as she ordered.

"Now if you feel anything-"

"I certainly hope so or we have a very big problem," Alessandro joked.

She smacked his chest. "If you feel any pain you let me know and we'll stop."

"Says the woman who's smacked me twice in the past five minutes," Alessandro said, but his eyes were shining with amusement.

Bree sighed, resting her head on her hand and just staring into those eyes.

"What?" Alessandro asked.

"I'm just afraid to stop looking at you because I'm afraid this is a dream and you're still unconscious in the hospital."

Alessandro took her hand and placed in over his heart. "Feel that? I'm right here and I'm not going anywhere."

Bree shivered a little and moved her hand downward. Brushing a kiss on his chest, she tasted the warmt skin, feelt the soft dark body hair beneath her tongue. She watched the swell of his cock rising in his boxers and ran her finger along the waistband of the dark blue material. She listened to him suck in his breath as she motioned to for him to move so she could pull them down.

His cock sprang free and eager and she looked up at him with a grin of amusement. She ran a short dark red finger nail along the warm tight skin, stopping to run her thumb along the swollen head. "Oh baby, I've missed you."

"God," Alessandro sighed as she wrapped her fingers around the base of his cock and began to stroke him slowly.

"Good?" Bree asked, watching him bite his lip.

"Oh yes," Alessandro moaned.

She lowered her mouth to the head of his cock, wrapping her lips around the dark head. Her body grew wet at the taste of him and Bree wondered if she herself was gonna be able to be gentle when she took this beautiful cock into her body. "Better?"

"Mmmmm," was all Alessandro could manage to get out before she took more of the hot length into her mouth.

"Are you in any pain?" Bree stopped briefly to ask him.

"Oh yes, put me out of my misery, darling," Alessandro begged, moving his hips restlessly.

Bree grabbed the sac at the base of his cock gently and squeezed as she ran her tongue along the length of his cock before taking all of him into her mouth.

"Oh God…Brianna…yeah…Oh yes…"

Bree sucked his cock eagerly, feeling him swell thicker as his voice grew more desperate. She stroked him in time with the motion of her mouth until she was sure he was seconds away from coming, then she concentrated on the head, tightening her lips around the swollen, slick crown.

With a cry of bliss, Alessandro grabbed the back of her head and Bree felt the thrill of satisfaction, of Alessandro spending himself in her mouth.

"Are you all right?" Bree asked, stretching herself above Alessandro. She rested her hands on his chest.

"Quite," he said with a satisfied smile. "I have the woman I love to the point of stupidity in my bed, as my wife no less, my son is asleep is in the nursery and my other son is asleep in what in his words is 'a big boy bed'. I say a hole in my kidney was a small price to pay for that."

"Don't even joke about that," Bree shivered kissing him. "Whoever did this is gonna pay-"

"Let's table that discussion for another time, eh?" Alessandro asked, running his fingers down her spine. "I have more pleasant things occupying my mind at the moment."

"Deal," Bree agreed sighing as Alessandro ran his mouth down the curve of her ear to her neck. She felt his hand come around to her waist and travel upwards to cup her breast. Her mouth opened over his as his thumb stroked her nipple to a very aroused peak, shifting her off him a bit so he could repay the other in kind.

His tongue ran along her teeth before stroking hers, getting her drunk on the heat and taste of his mouth. Her body opened eagerly, anxious to have him fill her. Then, as if reading her mind, his fingers were there sliding along her slick center, rubbing her clitoris ever so gently. She moaned into his mouth and spread her thighs open a little bit more in invitation.

"I love you," Alessandro whispered and her eyes fluttered open to find him gazing up at her as he pushed a long finger inside of her.

"Love you too," Bree moaned, moving her mouth down his jaw to his neck, her breath hitching with emotion as she felt the beat of his pulse against her tongue, the pulse that had been so close to being stilled forever.

He pushed a second finger into her and pumped slowly, urging her higher and higher towards her orgasm. She was trembling, clutching his fingers as her belly tightened with delicious tension.

"Come here," Alessandro murmured with a smile as he pulled his fingers out and she whimpered with disappointment. He grabbed her hips and pulled her higher above him. "Kneel over me. I want to taste you."

Just that mental image was enough to send her that much closer so that when she settled her pussy over his mouth it took just the merest brush of the tip of his tongue against her clitoris to send her hurtling over the edge. Bree grabbed the headboard and cried out as her body exploded with intense fire. She bucked with the force of it and Alessandro gripped her thighs to steady her, licking her with more determination after she came down from her high, eager to send her towards the pinnacle again.

"Oh God…Alessandro…Yes…Oh…push your tongue…" And before she could get the words out he was fucking her with his tongue. The man knew her so well that he knew almost exactly what she wanted before she even asked him.

She was desperate and gasping as he made love to her with his mouth, her hips moving eagerly and then sparks exploded behind her eyes as she cried out his name and came with a trembling fury against his mouth.

"Oh Alessandro…" Bree sighed, little aftershocks popping off under her skin. Her nerves were sated but her pussy was still clutching and greedy, needing to be filled by the deliciously muscled hard body beneath her. "I need you inside of me. Now." She moved down his body and reached for his cock. He grabbed her behind and settled her over his shaft, once again erect and wanting. "If you're in any pain-"

But Alessandro cut her off with his kiss. "Ride me, my beautiful Brianna." He pulled her down, filling her with every thick hot inch of him until she was saddled completely against her stallion of a husband. His eyes flared with animalistic hunger, as if he could read her mind.

"Fuuuuuccck," she moaned ecstatic at the delicious hard friction of his cock in her pussy and at this angle he was rubbing against her clitoris as well, sending her nerves rolling.

"Come here," he panted, cupping the back of her head, sliding his fingers into her hair and pulling her down to meet his mouth.

"Love you…always. Forever," Alessandro pumped up and Bree's desire fogged brain registered that it was costing him, no matter if he pretended otherwise.

"Alessandro," Bree moaned, meaning to back off but Alessandro thrust his tongue into her mouth and pumped his cock up inside of her twice more before he cried out her name in orgasm. She followed him over in a more subdued but still intense wave of electricity.

And when she pulled back, she could see the pain etched on his face.

"Alessandro," Bree sighed, moving off of him.

"Brianna. I was not going to be denied my wedding night with my wife. We'd waited long enough," he said stubbornly.

"I love you so much, you stupid Brit." Bree leaned her head over his heart, grateful for the pounding against her ear. "But you've had a major operation. You're still healing so you need to accept that your body is not at a hundred percent."

"Luckily, I have come prepared for such an eventuality," Alessandro said, making her lift her head in curiosity. "In one of the smaller pieces of luggage," he explained motioning towards the black leather bags along the wall.

She got out of the bed, shooting him a smile when he groaned in appreciation. When she found the right bag, she unzipped it and he told her to look under his shirts and ties. "You have too many ti-Oh!" Bree clamped a hand over her mouth in amused shock. "Mr. Dardano! What is this and where did you get it?" She pulled the flesh colored vibrator out from under the ties and held it up.

"That, my beloved wife, is back up and as to where I got it, well, there's a very upscale sex shop in Paris with quite an array of interesting items. Remind me to take you there soon."

Bree rolled her eyes, no way was she going to a sex shop with her horny husband. "Why would you even imagine that I would-"

"Oh well, after a particular delicious dream while I was in the hospital recovery from my poor gunshot wound and since then, it was all I could think about. You wouldn't want to deny a man his dying wish would you?" Alessandro affected a laughable pout.

"You're not dying anymore," Bree reminded him.

"Really darling, you're hardly a prude. You are a modern beautiful woman. Like you've never used one?" Alessandro teased.

Bree narrowed her eyes at him and climbed back onto the bed.

"That is beside the point."

"The point is I would find it utterly debauched and delicious to fuck my wife with this vibrator very hard until I am recovered enough to do it myself," Alessandro said. "Come now, darling. We both know you're going to love this."

CHAPTER TWELVE

Alessandro took a breast into his mouth as he ran the tip of the vibrator along the curve of the other breast. The low hum sounded underneath the panting of Bree's breath.

"Open your eyes," Alessandro asked, running the instrument over the nipple.

Bree jumped beneath him and bit her bottom lip but kept her eyes open; her own sensations heightened by the stark lust in his eyes.

Every pass of the vibrator along her skin was like a trail of electricity and when he slid the toy down along her lower abdomen, her pussy contracted hungrily. His fingers followed the path of the vibrator so that the shivers of electricity didn't end.

He teased around her mound, over the rounded bone but didn't slide it along her wet folds.

His tongue ran along the seam of her lips and Bree opened her mouth, eager for his kiss. He took her whimper with a groan of triumph. Laying his hand flat on her stomach he let the tip of the vibrator dance just an inch away from her clitoris so Bree had merely to shift her hips to have the shaft meet the over-sensitized nub. But Bree stayed put, the anticipation of when he'd finally touch her there making his kiss, his fingers just that much more arousing.

Alessandro moved his mouth to her ear, biting lightly on the lobe, making her pussy seep a little with trembling desire. Then with slight sucking movements he moved down her neck to the other breast, taking the nipple into his mouth and biting it with a little more force. Not enough to hurt beyond a slight sting, but enough to make her cry out with need. But then he'd sooth it with his tongue.

And do it again.

Occasionally, he'd return to her mouth as if drawn back there by a needy magnetic pull.

As he slid the vibrator up along her pubic bone before diving down again, Bree was trembling, torn between begging him to fill her or staying in this dizzying limbo of delicious anticipation.

Her fingers tightened in his hair before sliding down to dig into the hard muscle of his shoulders. She raised her knees on either side of his strong body, a silent plea. She'd wait willingly for him to heal, knowing that once he did, his virility would, as always, take her breath away, but for now the teasing naughtiness of the sex toy and exploring this new facet of their relationship would be an eager substitute.

"Fuck me…" Bree sighed, imagining what it would be like when he was fully healed. *Oh God, he'd kill her,* Bree was sure. His talent for fucking was shockingly unparalleled. He was the most erotic mix of control and wildness Bree had ever known.

He smiled against her mouth and slid down her body until his face was a few inches away from her slick pussy. "Here?" Alessandro asked; his breath hot against the folds.

Bree gasped, the heat caressing her pussy like a teasing touch. "Yes…please shove it in me…fuck me."

"Mmm? Hard and fast or slow and gentle, darling?" Alessandro asked, the heat of his mouth made her cry out as her nerves pulsed, making her pussy throb desperately.

"Hard…fast. Fuck me har-" — *sob* — "-d!" Bree screamed as he thrust the vibrator in one deep hard move. She was so wet that the thick toy met no resistant at all. And then once he pushed it in, her pussy grabbed it like a starving child, shaking at the delicious fullness of the hard veined tool.

"Good?" Alessandro asked with a wicked smile.

"Oh God, yes. More. Fuck me more," Bree pleaded, her hips begging him along with her voice.

He moved the vibrator in a circular motion and angled it so that the vibrations hit her clitoris occasionally, sending fresh explosions bursting through her veins.

"Oh Alessandro…please…don't stop. Oh my God!" Bree cried. As she got closer to orgasm, Alessandro would back off, thrusting hard and deep so that her orgasm was teased from deep inside of the walls of her pussy as opposed to her clitoris.

Her skin was damp with sweat as he alternated his focus away from and toward her clitoris.

His hand made up for the temporary deficiency of his injured body and he pounded the vibrator hard and fast until she was grabbing the sheets, grabbing his hair, digging her nails into his shoulders and all the while begging for more, begging for him to never stop.

He kissed her stomach, trailing his lips down until his mouth was just there over her clitoris and Bree couldn't breathe in anticipation of what he was going to do next.

He gave her a knowing smile before slowing the thrusts of his hand and closing his mouth over her clitoris.

She bowed upwards and cried out his name as her orgasm shot through her with mind numbing power.

He nibbled lightly on her clitoris, flicking it with his tongue as he pumped the vibrator faster, angling it so that as he moved to the side and recaptured her pulsing nub between his teeth he could pump harder, deeper and pull another orgasm from the clutching, desperate walls of her pussy.

"Oh God…Oh God…I can't," Bree begged, feeling the rolling churning sensations ebbing and flowing in her blood. She shook her head from side to side as he fucked her and sucked her, drawing her swollen nub tight into his mouth. She bore down, looking for relief, looking for more, wanting the torment to never ever stop.

Her hands went up to the headboard, wishing it had bars, her nails scraped against the wood as her body became a wild craving thing.

"Come for me again, my delicious creature," Alessandro purred against her pussy before sucking her clitoris into his mouth again.

"Ohhhhh, please!" Bree begged. "Don't stop…don't stop…" She could feel the tight coil begin to throb in the pit of her stomach and knew he would give her no mercy until she came again…and maybe not even then.

She bit her lower lip and whimpered as he rubbed the vibrator around inside of her causing devastating friction in her walls. His teeth and his tongue made the sharper sensations war with the deeper pulling throb of the orgasm slithering from her lower belly outward.

The coil tightened to an almost painful degree and then Bree felt an all-encompassing explosion go off in her belly followed by a sharp stab of blinding release as what felt like two joint orgasms made her entire universe still and then fall in a screaming rush.

Alessandro brought her down slowly, pulling the vibrator out once her pussy stopped spasming and she could breathe and open her eyes again.

"Oh God," Bree sighed, still shaking as Alessandro moved up behind her and pulled her into his arms, "Oh my God."

He gave a soft laugh.

She panted and pressed a kiss to the dark hairs on his chest. "We're definitely doing that again."

"Mmm. Darling, you haven't seen anything yet," Alessandro promised, his fingers brushing the curve of her behind as he kissed the top of her damp head.

And Bree swore she came again, just a little.

"I don' tink he likes squash," Will remarked watching Gianni's lips smack around the orange mush and his little body recoil. "I tink he like my pudding better." He dipped his finger in his bowl and lifted it to Gianni's mouth before Bree could protest.

Gianni blinked as Will pushed the sweet pudding past his lips. His tiny tongue darted out and his eyes followed Will's finger back to the bowl.

"Don't you dare," Bree said, holding Will's wrist down.

"But he like it better," Will insisted.

"Yes, but the squash is better for him. You can give him some of your pudding later."

"I nod gonna save it fo' later. I eat it now," Will reminded her.

"Well, you could always save some for Gianni," Alessandro pointed out, popping the last bite of steak into his mouth.

Will stared at his pudding and then at Gianni who was pumping his fists at his brother's desert. "I don' tink I'm gonna do dat." He proceeded to grab another spoonful.

"Bahhhhhhhhhhhhhhhhhhhhhhh!" Gianni burst in frustration, seeing that his brother was eating what he clearly thought was meant for him.

"Sorry Gianni. Eat yo' yucky sqash."

As Bree spooned more squash into Gianni's mouth, Gianni took great pleasure in spiting it out again.

"Perhaps it is too early to take him off the bottle?" Bernardo asked.

Bree glared at him and forced herself not to grab her spoon and fling squash at her father in law's head. "No. It's not," she assured him forcing a smile.

"It's just that he doesn't seem to be enjoying it and my rug seems to be taking the brunt of it."

"It's a vegetable, Father. There is not a child alive who would enjoy something that looks like that," Alessandro pointed out.

"Thank you," Bree said dryly.

"You're welcome, dear. I'm sure I hated vegetables as a child." He looked to his father for confirmation.

"I wouldn't know," Bernardo shrugged

"Do you have a mommy, daddy?" Will asked picking up on the conversation.

That's my boy. Bree pretended to turn her attention back to Gianni.

"Of course," Alessandro said, a slight edge to his voice.

"Where she go?" Will asked.

Gianni pushed the bowl of squash away with a wide swipe of his hand, knocking it over so that much of it was smeared on Bernardo's expensive pretentious carpet.

That's my boy, Bree repeated.

"She died when I was young," Alessandro said.

"Rafe! Get the maid in here to clean up this mess," Bernardo barked.

Gianni jumped in his high chair. "Mummmggheee baaah!" He whimpered.

"Do you mind not scaring my son? I know it's hard for you but try," Bree insisted. She turned back to Gianni. "Okay, you win. But not chocolate pudding. You're getting fruit. Hey Ralphie," Bree called out, knowing it would irritate the ferret faced butler that she was still mangling his name. "Could you get the cook to mash up some bananas for me?"

"It's Rafe. And of course, Mrs. Dardano," he said grudgingly.

"My mum died a long time ago," Alessandro explained and Bree watched him, noting his discomfort with the topic.

"Oh dat's too bad. You must miss her lots," Will remarked.

She noted the sad flicker in Alessandro's eyes and her heart broke for him. *Damn Bernardo.*

Rafe returned a few minutes later with the mashed bananas that Gianni eyed with great skepticism. "Will that be all?"

"Your little boy is very happy, Mrs. Dardano," Dr. Sheri Graham assured her as Will chased another child up and down the hallway.

Bree felt a little pang, watching him and wishing that Gianni was older so that he and Will could run around together. She rubbed the back of her baby's head, making him smile at her.

"He told me he doesn't have nightmares anymore about the 'bad man' and I don't think he will be experiencing anymore bed wetting."

"That's such a relief. His happiness is the most important thing to me."

"Does he ever talk about his father to you? I mean Michael?" Dr. Graham asked, her eyes kind but Bree could tell she clearly had something on her mind.

"Not lately, apart from the time Alessandro was in the hospital and he asked me if Alessandro was going to go to heaven like his father did."

Sheri nodded. "Well, he's been asking me questions about Michael. Now, don't get me wrong, they're perfectly normal questions for someone who's been through what he has and now has a new father figure, but…"

"But…?" Bree urged.

"He told me that he dreams about his father a lot."

Bree leaned against the wall, her chest tight. "Yeah, he mentioned it a few times to me but…a lot?"

"Children aren't that familiar with guilt as a concept until they get to be around Will's age and I think that's just what he's been experiencing. It's a foreign emotion to him."

"He asked me sometimes if I thought Michael would be mad at him for wanting Alessandro to be his father. I thought he'd gotten over that."

"Oh please, don't worry."

"What can I say to help him get over that?" Bree asked.

"Actually, I think it would be better if he talked with Alessandro about Michael. I mean, up until this point, I'm sure you have been the one to answer all his questions about his father-"

"But Alessandro never knew Michael. He died before we met so I don't see how Alessandro could answer any of his questions."

"Maybe not, but it's more about cementing their relationship so that Will can see that it's okay to love Alessandro more than Michael."

"He said that?' Bree asked trying to push down the feeling of betrayal.

Sheri nodded. "Please don't take this personally. Will is very young and it's only normal as he grows that he finds himself more attached to the father figure in his life now than one he was only has a few memories of."

Bree grit her teeth, cursing Bernardo for taking away Michael's right to raise his child.

Oh she'd make that son of a bitch pay somehow, Bree swore.

"He doesn't dare mention this to you because he's afraid you'll get mad at him. And there's something else."

Bree forced her attention back to the shrink, and back to the fact that her priority had to be Will right now, not her desire for revenge.

"He's afraid that now that Gianni is here that Alessandro might love the baby more because he's Gianni's real daddy."

Bree scowled. Alessandro gave no indication that he loved Gianni more than Will, but the fact that her little boy was worried about this broke her heart. "Okay, so what do I do or what can Alessandro do for that matter?"

"I think it would be a good idea if Will and Alessandro spent some time together without you."

Bree blinked. Well, she knew she could trust Alessandro with Will and knew that they adored each other so that shouldn't be a problem. So why was the idea…*Brianna O'Reiley Donovan Dardano, are you jealous of your son's relationship with his father?* "I think that's a great idea." She forced herself to smile.

"Mommy, dis Mickey. Can he come home wif us and play?" Will asked, the little blond boy trailing behind him. Both boys were flushed with exertion.

The idea of Rafe's horrified face at two five year olds running around and screaming made Bree smile but she forced herself to say no, though she did have an idea that would be even better.

Alex cornered her right before she was going to make an

appointment at the nurse's station to see him.

"Bree, I'm going to be referring you to Carlo from now on," Alex informed her. "I think in light of recent events it would be a conflict of interest for me to continue to be your doctor."

"Is that right?" Bree asked leaning her elbow on the counter and raising an eyebrow.

"Yes, I wouldn't feel comfortable about it considering what you did to Carrie."

"Aw, that's nice," Bree smiled sarcastically, staring up at his smug self-righteous face. "Nice to know this place has such moral upstanding doctors."

"Yes, so I will be referring you to him from now on," Alex said, clenching his jaw.

"Great," Bree said, fighting not to roll her eyes.

"Have a good afternoon," he said curtly and turned to walk away.

Don't do it. Don't do it, Bree. The evil Bree won though. "You too, Dr. Home Wrecker."

Alex's step faltered but he didn't turn around.

"Gappy!" Will exclaimed rushing towards John who had just exited the elevator.

Bree's stomach tightened nervously as her father scooped Will up into his arms.

"Your sister just confessed to me about your little pregnancy ruse." He pinned her with an accusatory glare. "Be very grateful you are now married to that man, Bree."

She swallowed. "Yeah, well… False alarm I guess."

John exhaled in exasperation. She was well used to the sound. "How are you doing?" he asked her softly.

Bree blinked the burning from her eyes. "Fine."

"Have you spoken to your mother lately?" He asked.

"I think you know the answer to that," Bree replied, pushing the stroller back and forth as Gianni began to whimper.

"Bree, when are you going to-"

"Daddy, don't start. You guys were the ones who pushed me out," she said, watching her father set Will back on the floor.

"Young lady that was your deci-"

"You know what, daddy. I really don't want to keep rehashing this with you. You either accept that Alessandro is a part of my life or we have nothing more to say to each other. Not that I expect that to ever happen in my life time."

CHAPTER THIRTEEN

He loves me more, Alessandro thought as Will climbed on one of the snow banks, his small hand tucked safely in Alessandro's. He tried not to gloat over the fact but it was quite hard. He didn't think it was possible to feel as full of joy as when Brianna told him that she loved him, but this morning, when she confessed what Dr. Graham had told her, Alessandro's heart felt as if it was going to burst out of his chest. Will loved him more than Michael, his biological father. Alessandro glanced warily up at the sky fearing if there really was a heaven Michael Donovan was just waiting for the right moment to send a lightning bolt shooting down. He figured it'd be best to keep Will close, just in case.

"Daddy, c' I have iceceem?" Will asked.

"Ice cream? Good God, Will, it's the middle of December. Which reminds me, what do you want for Christmas?" Alessandro asked as they walked through the snow-covered park.

"I 'till have to do my list," Will explained.

"Ah, well. Would you like to give me a hint?"

"It be a long list," he informed him.

"Oh I have no doubt," Alessandro said smiling.

" 'kay. C' I have a horsie?"

"Is that a hint?" Alessandro asked, watching the little puffs of breath coming out of Will's mouth.

"No, horsie," Will repeated.

"Well, you know you can ride any of the horses in our stables any time you want."

"Mommy say I too little," Will said with a stubborn scowl. "I don tink so 'cause I see little people on horsies on da TV all da time."

"You're quite right, young William."

" 'sides. Is nod da same. Those are your daddy's horsies. I wants one of my own."

"How about if I let you pick one of our horses for your very own?"

Will gave him a bright smile. "I tink dat's a very good idea. Wha' should I name it?"

Alessandro watched as Luke burrowed his nose in the snow and then shook his small body. "Well, that depends on whether you want a male or a female horse."

"Mmm. I tink I want a boy horsie. Girl horsies have babies and dat's too much trouble."

Alessandro bit back a laugh. "Male horse it is then. Let's see. My favourite horse's name is Abbott."

"A But?" Will asked laughing.

"Abbott," Alessandro corrected.

"Chimney," Will suddenly decided, stopping.

Alessandro blinked in confusion. "I'm sorry, did you say 'Chimney'?"

"It make sense," Will assured him. "Santa come down da chimney and he is my pesent, right? So his name be Chimney."

"I agree. Quite logical," Alessandro nodded.

"Well, dat one ting on my list. Der be more."

"Duly noted," he said. He followed Will's gaze to a father who was helping his kids build a snowman.

"How would you like to raid the kitchen later for a carrot and some dates? We can build a snowman right on the front lawn. Scare the crap out of Rafe when he looks out the window."

"No, dat's okay," Will said, his voice taking on a sad quality that immediately put Alessandro on the alert.

"How come?" Alessandro asked.

Will shrugged and ran ahead to chase Luke for a little bit.

"Did you and your daddy build snowmen together?" Alessandro asked leaning down and scratching Luke's ears. He grabbed Luke's leash and pulled him towards a bench so that Will had no choice but to follow.

"You my daddy," Will pointed out.

"Yes but Michael was your daddy too. You know, in a few days it'll be the anniversary of the day he died. It's okay if you're sad about that."

"I nod sad," Will said.

"I know your mother misses him very much," Alessandro said, pushing down the small flare of jealousy at that.

"She do?" Will asked.

"Sure. It's only natural. She loved him very much."

"But she say she loves you," Will said, climbing up onto the bench.

Alessandro smiled at the small victory. If Will was ready to listen maybe he could help. "Yes, but that doesn't mean she didn't love Michael."

"And you no mad at her?"

"Not at all," Alessandro said. Jealous, maybe, but he recognized the irrationality of that emotion even as he acknowledged it.

"He say is okay if you my daddy," Will said.

"In your dreams?" Alessandro asked carefully. He watched Will pick at his coat as he swung his small legs back and forth.

"Uh huh,"

"Well, I'm sure that's true. Your daddy would want you to be happy."

"But den he be mad at me sumtines 'cause…"

"Because…?" Alessandro pressed gently.

"I'm cold. We go home now?" Will asked moving to slide off the bench but Alessandro stopped him.

"Will, I'm your daddy now, right?" Alessandro asked.

Will nodded.

"Then I'd like it very much if you could tell me if something was bothering you."

"Sumtines, he be mad at me 'cause I say I don' want you to go in hev'n wif him."

"Ah, so this happened when I was in the hospital."

Will nodded. "I tolded him dat I loved you 'cause you were my new daddy and I deemed he got mad at me 'cause I love you more den him."

Alessandro felt his eyes well up at the sweet admission and tried to not gloat again. "Sometimes, when bad things happen, they spill over into our dreams. I'm sure you were very scared when I was shot, right?"

"A lot," Will nodded, leaning his head against the arm of Alessandro's coat.

"Well, sometimes, when we're scared, our dreams get screwed up. You ever hear that funny saying that you shouldn't have spicy food before you go to bed?"

Will nodded and Alessandro rubbed the side of his face with a gloved hand.

"Well that's 'cause it'll give you some very strange dreams. I dreamed a lot when I was shot too. I dreamt of Michael."

Will lifted his head in surprise.

"That's right. And he told me that I better take very good care of you."

"He wasn't mad?" he asked in a small voice.

"Not at all. See? I think 'cause you were scared, that made your dreams go all confused."

"Dat makes sense…but…"

"But you still feel bad?" Alessandro guessed. "You shouldn't. It makes me very happy to know that you love me."

"But I forget lots from my other daddy now."

"That's only natural because you're growing up. I don't remember a lot from my childhood. I don't remember a lot about my…" Alessandro stopped, an uncomfortable tightening in the pit of his stomach. He cleared his throat and forced himself to finish the thought for Will's sake, "mother."

"Did she go in heaven too?" Will asked.

"Yeah and then Bernardo raised me and as much as I must have loved my mummy, I spent more time with Bernardo so it's only natural I would be close to my father."

"But I spend more time wif my oder daddy."

"Not really. You were a baby first and you don't really remember anything from that time."

"So you no tink your mummy be mad?"

"I think she'd be happy that I had someone who loved me so much to take care of me."

"Dat make sense. So is…is okay dat I love you more?"

Alessandro took a deep shaky breath and blinked the tears back. "It's more than okay."

Will climbed up on his knees and hugged Alessandro. "Good. Now can we go get iceceem?"

"Ice cream? Dude, it's freezing," a voice said behind them.

Alessandro turned to see Brian coming towards them.

"Unco Bwian!" Will said excited.

"Hey, Little Man. Your daddy there is just the man I wanted to see," Brian said in a tone of voice that had Alessandro's insides clenching with dread that he was about to be treated to another O'Reiley sermon.

"Will, you wanna go play with Luke for a little while?" Alessandro suggested, leaning down and kissing the top of his head.

"I nod a dummy, you know? You wanna talk. But Unco Bwian, you no yell at my daddy, 'kay? I haf good ears," Will warned climbing down off the bench and taking Luke's leash from Alessandro. He let go of it and let the dog run, kicking up snow.

"That kid is too smart," Brian said shaking his head.

"He's all Brianna," Alessandro said with a laugh. Then he straightened and cocked his head. "Though I suppose you knew Michael so you'd know if Will was more like him or his mother."

"Oh trust me, he's all Bree," Brian said with a snort. "You're good with him."

"I love him more than life itself," Alessandro admitted.

"Even though he's not yours?" Brian countered.

"He's mine," Alessandro said firmly.

"Mmm. So, imagine my surprise when I get a call from the HR guy at Dardano Enterprises offering me a position with your company, at the recommendation of Mr. Alessandro Dardano himself."

"I've seen your work. You're an incredible photographer. We could use someone like you," Alessandro insisted.

"Right. And the real reason?" Brian pressed, cocking an eyebrow.

Alessandro found himself smiling despite himself. "Don't shit a shitter, eh, ol' boy?"

"Exactly."

"Bree needs more O'Reileys on her side."

"Because of you," Brian stated.

Alessandro would have been offended if it had been said in accusation but Brian's tone was one of simple fact. "Because of me."

"Believe me, Bree is the queen of denial. There is no one better at lying to herself. She loves you, genuinely."

"As I love her."

"I want to say that that's all that matters but I stopped believing in fairy tales a long time ago."

Alessandro noted the hint of sadness and knew the reason was the woman Alessandro had read about in Brian's past. He thought it wise not to mention his own liaisons with Rebecca Malford at the moment.

"You're a Dardano."

"Last time I checked, yes," Alessandro nodded preparing himself.

"Your family is my family's sworn enemy. I'm supposed to believe that all of that is out the window because you and Bree have decided to play house?"

"It has on the Dardanos' side, but then again, it was never the Dardanos who started this feud in the first place."

"Right, Bree wrote me about the whole Francesca, Adriano thing. That's a hell of a kick in the head. But I suppose a lot of feuds start that way."

"Brianna wants peace between our families, as do I. If the O'Reileys refuse to acknowledge that, well, my heart breaks for her, but Brianna is putting the family she has now first and that means me and the children."

"Awfully convenient for you," Brian pointed out. "But being your wife also puts a hell of a target on her back and I'm not just talking about Arturo. The Dardanos have a long history of enemies. Longer than the O'Reileys."

"Being a Dardano also provides her with the best protection money can buy. She will never be in any danger as long as I'm alive. Not her, and not the boys."

"Says the guy with a hole in his kidney," Brian pointed out.

Alessandro grit his teeth. "That was a shot aimed directly at me. Brianna was never in any danger."

"And you know this how?" Brian asked.

"If it had been Arturo, he would have taken out everyone in that church, not just me."

"So what's the situation there? Any leads on your crazy brother?"

"He's not in New York. Smart man. He's laying low. But his men are still around."

"So Bree and my nephews are still in danger," Brian said.

"They are safest with me in the Dardano mansion."

"I hope so. Because I promise you, if any more harm comes to my sister or her children-"

"You don't even have to finish that threat, Brian, because if anything happened to Brianna or the boys I'd put a gun in my own mouth. But not after I made whoever was responsible pay. I promise you that."

He could tell the vehemence of his words took Brian aback.

"I'm not sure if that was meant to reassure or scare the shit out of me. But…I believe you when you say you love her."

"So you'll stay in New York?" Alessandro pressed.

Brian sighed. "This place holds a lot of bad memories for me."

A burst of Will's laughter carried over to them and they saw him on the ground with Luke jumping around over him.

"But my family is here and it's time to make some new ones."

"Come back to the house and we can celebrate your new position," Alessandro placed a hand on Brian's back in congratulations. "Come on, Will. Time to go."

"We go for iceceem now?" Will asked running back towards them, a wet, flushed but very happy mess, Luke bouncing and yipping behind him.

"You're not gonna let that go, huh?" Brian asked.

"O' course nod. I like iceceem."

"Well, how about when we get home I give you some gelato?" Alessandro asked taking Will's hand.

"W'as dat?"

"It's Italian ice cream."

Will gasped. "I know! Dat's a whole udder countwy. Like Eyeland. We gonna go Italian too?"

"Not this time. But we can go someday if you like," Alessandro suggested.

"Yay!" Will exclaimed. "And can we go to Disneyland too?"

"Sure," Alessandro said sharing a look of amusement with Brian.

"And SeaWord?"

"Mmmhmm."

"And Seasme Steet?"

"Hello Mudda…Hello Fadda…something, something…in Granada…,"

Gianni's little body curled in on itself as he shrieked with giggles. Bree wished she knew more of the silly song but her baby didn't seem to mind, nor did he seem to mind that Bree wouldn't be winning any American Idol contests any time soon. Bree leaned over Gianni, on his blanket on the couch. He looked up with an expectant smile, brown eyes shining back at her. Bree took a deep breath and began again. "Hello Mudda…"

The doorbell rang, interrupting her ridiculous serenade and Gianni gave a squeal that was a mix of glee and irritation at having the song interrupted.

Before Rafe could announce who it was, she heard Will's busy voice saying something about a…cat?

Her very wet child burst into the living room. "Mommy! We's gonna eat gato!"

"Isn't that 'cat' in Italian?" Bree asked as Gianni let out a squeal and extended his arms towards Alessandro. Bree transferred him over.

"He means gelato," Alessandro explained. "You want some gelato, Gianni? Hmm? You want some yummy gelato?"

"Mmmmmm," Gianni agreed reaching down and stuffing the lapel of Alessandro's coat into his mouth.

"Brian, you wanna stay for dinner. Balance out the Dardano-ness?" Bree asked.

"Actually, I had already invited him. We're going to celebrate your brother's decision to stay in New York," Alessandro announced.

Bree stared at her brother, joy making her shriek and throw herself into the arms of her sibling. "Oh my God, that's amazing! You're really staying?"

"Yep, I start work at Dardano Enterprises this Monday," Brian said.

Bree pulled away, her stomach plummeting. "I'm sorry, did you just say Dardano Enterprises?"

"Now, Brianna-" Alessandro warned.

"As in, where Rebecca works? Rebecca who stomped all over your heart? Nonononono. Uh uh, no!" Bree snapped shaking her finger at both men.

"Nonononoommnnnoommhph," Gianni echoed moving his head from side to side.

"He'll be working for me, not Rebecca," Alessandro promised.

"Oh shut up, that's just semantics. Brian, I don't want you working with that-"

"Easy," Alessandro cautioned moving his eyes meaningfully down towards Will.

"Woman," Bree amended.

"Do you want me to stay in New York?" Brian asked.

Bree huffed. "Well yeah, but…but…"

Brian wrapped an arm around her. "Then this job will allow me to do that. Trust me, Rebecca is not gonna be an issue."

"Right, where have I heard that before?" Bree threw a dark look at Alessandro who leaned in and kissed her cheek.

"I'm going to get cleaned up before risking the cook's ire and venturing into the kitchen."

"Yeah, you chicken. Take Drippy here with you or no ice cream for anybody," Bree promised pushing Will towards Alessandro, "Give me my nice, dry son back." Alessandro handed Gianni back to her.

"He loves those kids a lot," Brian remarked as Bree moved back to the couch.

"And they love him," Bree said.

"And you?" Brian pressed.

"Well, I hope my kids love me," Bree joked.

"Bree," Brian said.

"Yes, I love Alessandro. Yes I married him to end the vendetta but I love him more than I thought it was possible to love any man. Does that answer your question or do I have to threaten to tell you about our sex life if you don't quit grilling me?"

"Ew no!" Brian took a step back and raised his hands in surrender. "I just want to make sure that you're really happy and that you're not sacrificing yourself because of this whole Francesca, Adriano thing."

Bree sighed and leaned back against the couch, Gianni biting his fist as his head rested against her chest. "Okay, no, if it wasn't for the vendetta I wouldn't have married Alessandro yet. We were going through a hard time because of Alessandro's loyalty to his father. I didn't think I could deal with it but then…" Bree looked around to make sure no one would hear her and lowered her voice. "I figured if I ever wanted to get Alessandro away from Bernardo's evil influence, the way to do it was not to leave him."

"Oh, Bree," Brian groaned dropping his head into his hand.

"No, no, really. This is gonna work. It can't miss, Brian. I'm here, living with Alessandro in the same house as Bernardo so I can minimize that bastard's hold on him. Eventually, Alessandro will see that Bernardo is just trying to control him and his loyalties won't be divided anymore," Bree explained confidently.

"As opposed to you trying to control Alessandro?" Brian countered.

Bree scowled. "I'm doing no such thing. I'm saving the man I love from that monster, doing what I have to do to save my family."

"Mmm, and what happens when you 'save'," Brian crooked his fingers over the word. "Alessandro from his father? You think Bernardo is just gonna wave and wish you well. You're insane if you think you can go up against Bernardo."

"No, Bernardo won't do anything 'cause he's following his father's last wishes with my marriage to his son. Now that I've done that, the violence stops."

"I'm begging you, don't do this. God, now I'm relieved I'm staying in New York so I can keep you from doing something you'll-"

Bree bent closer to the coffee table when she saw what looked like brochures on it. "What is this?" she asked distantly. She clenched her teeth as she flipped through the pages. Boarding school brochures. "Oh hell no."

She leapt out of her seat on the sofa, murder on her mind.

Brian grabbed her arm. "Bree, take it easy. You don't know exactly what Bernardo has in mind-"

"The hell I don't. Bernardo!" She stormed out to the foyer and screamed up the stairs.

Rafe came out from the kitchen. "What seems to be the problem, Mrs. Dardano?"

"Where is your boss? Bernardo! You get your evil butt down here!"

"Bree. You have to calm down," Brian said.

"Bernardo is taking a nap. Maybe I could help?"

"Oh okay, you want to explain to me what the hell this is?" Bree asked smacking the brochures against his skinny chest.

"These are brochures," Rafe said.

"Really?" Bree asked sarcastically. "Bernardo!"

"What on earth is that damned racket?" Bernardo demanded

appearing at the top of the stairs.

"Mommy, why you scweeming?" Will asked appearing next to Bernardo. He jumped a little when he realized who was next to him. "Oh. Hi." Though Bernardo had never been mean to him, neither was he warm to Will and the little boy quickly picked up on the man's ambivalence towards him.

Bernardo stormed down the stairs. "What are you going on about?"

"This! This is what I'm going on about. How dare you? How dare you even thinking of putting my children in a boarding school?"

"Father!" Alessandro said stunned as he walked down the stairs towards them.

"That's right. If your father thinks he can just ship my kids off to another country-"

"Darling, calm down," Alessandro said resting a hand on Bree's shoulder.

Bree smacked his hand away. "Don't tell me to calm down. He wants to send my children to some snotty British boarding school!"

"The school is in Switzerland," Rafe interrupted.

"Shut up, Ralphie," Bree insisted bouncing Gianni lightly.

"I don't know what you're complaining about. Gianni will be attending one of the best schools in the world."

"No, no. Gianni will be going to school here, in America. In New York, close to his family."

"Young lady, my grandson will be having the best education befitting a Dardano. He will not be attending some common grade school with snot nosed brats. He will be raised in the manner best to equip him to join the Dardano empire when he is of age."

Bree gasped and had to remind herself that she was holding Gianni. "Alessandro, for the love of-"

"Father, I think you should have discussed with us first."

"What's to discuss? The boy is a Dardano." Bernardo turned into the living room.

"Half a Dardano," Bree shot back. "Alessandro, help me out here."

"What about Will?" Alessandro asked.

"What?" Bree demanded.

"Well, Father, you seemed to have Gianni's future all planned out what about his brother?"

"That's not helping!" Bree insisted slapping Alessandro's shoulder.

"No, you're right. Of course." Then he turned to his Bernardo. "I'm just insulted that you're not thinking about William as well."

"Uh, I don wanna go boring school," Will piped up.

"Will is not going to be a part of the Dardano empire when he comes of age," Bernardo insisted.

"And neither is Gianni. I don't want my son having anything to do with your family's side of the 'business'."

"Just listen to me, all right? Gianni's education is our responsibility. Mine and Brianna's. I'm sure we can find a perfectly good school for him here in the city."

"Bah! Don't be ridiculous. I will not have my grandson raised in New York like some commoner. Is that really all you want for your son? Don't you want him to have the advantages you did, Alessandro? Just look at the man you are now. Worthy of the name Dardano. You have power, stature and a sophistication only the very best education could provide. You loved the school you went to."

"I did, yes but I hated it as well because I was away from you. I don't want to see my sons only on holidays and vacations. No, Gianni will be going to school here in New York and then when he's older, Brianna and I will discuss what is best for his education. For both him and William," Alessandro announced firmly and Bree wanted to do a little dance of glee.

Gianni let out a giggle and Bree had to stifle a snort at his timing.

"Now, if this discussion is over, Will and I have a date with some gelato. Gianni, you want some too?" Alessandro picked Gianni up from Bree's arms and turned towards the kitchen. Brian followed them and before Bree move she turned to Bernardo and couldn't resist a smug grin of triumph.

CHAPTER FOURTEEN

He wasn't asleep. Bree could feel him shifting around on the bed. She lifted her head and turned to him. "What's up, Squirmy?"

"My wound is itching," he explained.

"That's good. It means you're healing," she leaned over and kissed his shoulder.

"Yes, but that doesn't help me with this blasted itch."

She sat up and switched on the lamp. "Alright, let's have a look."

Alessandro rolled onto his stomach as Bree peeled back the bandage. She sucked in her breath as she looked at the evidence that she had almost lost him. The skin was red and shiny, but the hole was healing, the skin drawn back together. She leaned down and kissed the area around it. Bree felt him tighten beneath her. "I love you," she whispered.

"Love you too," he murmured. "I'd love you even more if you massage that bit above my…right there."

Bree dug her fingers into the area right above his wound. He gave a sigh of pleasure.

"And because of this damned thing I haven't been able to work out so my muscles are all tight."

"Mmm, looks good from where I'm sitting," Bree assured him, biting his shoulder blade.

Alessandro gave a forlorn sigh. "And I'm too decrepit to fuck my wife the way I want. Darling, I think you should just bury me now. Trade me in for a younger model. I won't hold it personally," he lied.

"Never," she promised, "In fact. I have an idea that I think will get you back to your old self in no time." She slipped out of the bed and wrapped her robe around her. "But you're gonna have to lead the way because the last time…well, you blindfolded me."

"Good?" Bree asked digging her fingers into Alessandro's shoulders. The water in the grotto was warm and bubbling, caressing their skin.

"Hmmhmm…" he sighed. His fingers trailed down her spine and his legs brushed against hers. "This was a very, very good idea."

"I thought so," Bree smiled, brushing her lips across his. Their lower bodies swayed, coming against each other every once in a while. She ran her fingers down his chest, feeling the strong steady beat of his heart. She shivered, thinking of when he laid collapsed in her arms, his blood pouring out.

She wrapped her arms around him. "I was so scared, Alessandro," she admitted burying her face in his damp neck, "I was afraid it was happening all over again, that I was losing another man I loved, that my sons were going to lose another father."

"I felt you," Alessandro said, pulling back to push a lock of her damp hair behind her ear, "I felt your love, your courage." He lowered his head and kissed her sweetly, drawing a soft moan from her.

"If you were gonna die on me, I was gonna fight like hell to keep that from happening. I'd fight the devil himself for you, Alessandro Dardano," Bree vowed, let him think what he would, she knew she meant Bernardo.

"Well, rest assured, I'll be loving you even in hell," Alessandro promised, sliding his hands along her waist up to cup her bare breasts.

Her breath hitched as the sizzle of sensation shimmied through her skin. "Well then I'd follow you into hell."

He cupped her bottom and pressed it against his naked erection.

Bree sucked in her breath and slowly rocked her hips against him in invitation.

He groaned into her ear as he rubbed the warm head of his cock against her center.

Bree wrapped her legs around his waist. "Yes," she urged.

He pushed into her slowly so she could feel every hard inch joining his body to hers. "My soul…Soul of mine. I think I loved you from the moment I saw you."

Bree gasped at the words. "You knew? Even then, that first night?"

"I did," He admitted, pumping slowly, "It…mmm…startled me how strongly I felt for you just that night. Never…never felt like that for…God…another woman."

Bree rocked her hips greedily, controlling the speed so that Alessandro didn't have to make too much of an effort and possibly hurt himself. The purpose of bringing him down here was to relax him, ease his discomfort. "It was the sa…same for me," she said. "Oh God." she lowered her mouth to his shoulder, biting gently as his cock angled against a particularly sweet spot inside of her. "Never felt for anyone, what I felt…feel for you. You terrified me. I terrified me," she said brushing her lips up along his neck, his jaw.

He captured her mouth and slid his tongue along hers, making her go dizzy with the taste of him.

"Oh God…." Bree arched back, feeling her orgasm tickle her senses and hover just there, out of her reach, but soon…soon.

Alessandro's mouth captured a breast and Bree grabbed his head to anchor her as the back of her head hit the water, the surface caressing her ears. "My love…my soul…my beautiful…beautiful…Brianna," Alessandro sighed bringing her back up. Before he captured her mouth again he whispered, "my wife."

She nibbled his bottom lip and smiled. "Mine…mine…mine…mine."

His fingers slid between them caressing her belly before dipping lower to the swollen bundle of nerves just above where they were joined. "Ohhhhh," she nibbled his earlobe as he pressed his finger against his clitoris, he massaged it slowly. No rush.

"Oh yes…Oh…that's good." She shivered against him and met his gaze as she worked her hips eager for the explosion of not only her body, but of her soul that only this man could give her.

"Fuck," he sighed, his breath hot against her face as his cock swelled with upcoming release. He quickened the movement of his fingers and Bree's breath came out in uneven desperate puffs as she worked against him, with him.

And then there it was. Together they exploded, her eyes fluttering closed as she trembled, just like his. She felt every pulse and surge of his cock into her as her walls pulsed around him.

And then she opened her eyes, just as he did and he was caressing her face as they shivered with aftershocks. "I love you so much," she whispered, searching his face, memorizing it in case tomorrow, or the next day, or the day after that she lost him.

They dressed quietly and made their way back to the bedroom. She climbed in next to him and faced him, his arm lying securely over her waist, and he pressed his mouth to her forehead. "Better?" she asked him.

"Much," Alessandro smiled and as he drifted off to sleep. Bree stayed awake a few minutes more, watching him.

"I'll fight the devil himself for you," she repeated.

She only hoped that when she did, Alessandro would be fighting alongside her too.

Bree woke to something tickling her nose. She smacked the offending object away and tried to slide back into comfortable oblivion. There it was again, only this time, it was followed by a familiar voice in her ear.

"Good morning, Sunshine," Alessandro whispered, dragging the satiny soft object across the tip of her nose.

Curiosity made her open her eyes. A rose. A blue rose.

"I figured a single rose was safer than a dozen considering the massacre of the last blue roses I gave you," he smiled sheepishly. "Happy birthday, darling."

Bree blinked and tried to remember what day it was. The fifteenth apparently. She groaned and pulled the blankets back over her head. She was officially thirty today.

"Come on now, up we go," Alessandro pulled the blankets off her face and grabbed her arm, bringing her up.

"For my birthday, I want sleep," she groaned. Gianni had suffered through a painful night as another tooth was starting to come in and thus his parents had suffered as well.

"Nope, we've got a long day ahead of us. Let's go."

"Why?" Bree yawned.

"Because thirty years ago you were born and my life as I knew it would never be the same," Alessandro explained, nuzzling her neck.

"We never celebrate my birthday until Christmas, seeing as it's so close to it," Bree explained.

"Oh no, that won't do at all. Nope. We're celebrating it today. And to begin…" he handed her a small blue box.

Bree felt a little thrill go through her as she recognized the Tiffany box. "We're really celebrating today?"

"Of course," Alessandro replied.

She gave a small squeal of delight and opened the box. Her hand went to her mouth. "Oh wow." A small circle dotted with diamonds, with a slightly larger diamond inside hung on a thin silver chain.

"I kept wanting to get something bigger but every time I looked at the bigger stones they just didn't seem to fit you."

"No. This is perfect. Absolutely perfect," Bree assured running her finger over the diamonds. She took his face in her hands and kissed him. "I love it. Thank you." She lifted her hair and turned her back to him, presenting her neck.

He undid the clasp of the necklace the gypsy Ruthie had given her and slipped his necklace around her neck. Then he pressed his mouth to her skin and slid a hand around to her breast.

Bree purred and turned around wrapping her arms around him. As he lowered her to the pillows a very insistent knock brought any amorous plans to a screeching halt.

"Mommy. It's yo birthday!" Will shouted through the door.

Bree groaned as Alessandro got up to answer the door. Her son ran in and threw himself against the bed. "Hi! Wan' yo present now?"

"How about breakfast first?" Bree asked sliding out of the bed and wrapping the belt of her robe tighter around her middle.

"Okie. We haf' cake now?" He asked.

"Nope, breakfast as in cereal and fruit," Bree insisted.

"Well. I guess dat's better den Gianni's mush."

"Very true," Alessandro agreed.

Will's gift to her was a picture of him holding Gianni in a silver picture frame. It looked like a professional shot and Bree looked at Alessandro in question.

"A few days ago," he explained.

"Good morning, Brianna," Bernardo said coming to the table and handing her a gift wrapped box.

Bree took it and looked up at her father in law with blatant skepticism. "Uh…Um, thanks?" She turned the rectangular box over in her hand. She lifted it to her ear and shook it.

"Brianna," Alessandro scolded lightly.

"What? I'm just checking," Bree said with a smile. She opened the box and looked up at him in confusion. There were two envelopes inside. One was marked William Donovan and the other Gianni Dardano.

She opened the envelopes and her mouth fell open. In each were bonds for five hundred thousand dollars.

"They're to be held in trust for both of them for their education and to get them started in their chosen careers. Whatever they may be," Bernardo conceded.

"Father," Alessandro smiled reaching over Bree's head to hug his father. "This is wonderful, thank you for doing this."

She wanted to be gracious but inside Bree wanted to punch something. She'd been hoping the first chink in Alessandro's bond with his father had begun to develop but now this. Bernardo had very effectively ruined her victory. She cleared her throat and forced herself to smile. "Thank you." You bastard.

When Bree blew out the candles on her cake that afternoon she wished for one thing. Dear God, help me break Alessandro free from Bernardo. Help me pull him away from his father.

As Bree pulled the candles out Gianni, who was on Alessandro's, lap smacked his hand into the cake. He pulled it back with a gasp of surprise and brought the cream to his fingers. His mouth worked eagerly around his fingers sucking on the icing and he gave a squeal and delight and while Alessandro reached for a napkin Gianni dared a second smack of his hand into the cake and laughed as he brought the mess into his mouth and onto most of his face as well.

"I thought we might begin planning your wedding reception since we had to postpone it. How about this weekend?" Bernardo asked as Alessandro tried to clean up a squirming Gianni who wanted to go for his third visit to sugar town.

"Three days? There is no way we can plan a reception in so short a time." A jolt of horror shot through her as she realized that in three days it would be the eighteenth. The anniversary of Michael's death. "Oh no. No!" she shouted at him. "Are you nuts?"

Bernardo pretended to not know why she was objecting, or at

least that's what it looked like to Bree.

"Another date would be better, Father," Alessandro pointed out shaking his head.

So they decided on a Christmas Eve reception.

Brian came by later that evening. He brought Bree her gift, a ruby and gold bracelet.

"It's beautiful. Thank you." Bree hugged her brother.

"I want you to know that I told the family that I think they're making a huge mistake cutting you out. That you were doing everything you could to make sure that there would be no more violence between the Dardanos and the O'Reileys and that they should be supporting you and helping you instead of coming down on you all the time."

"Brian, thank you so much for doing that for me."

"They'll come around," he promised.

Bree wasn't nearly so sure.

"Can we go tobogganing?" Will asked jumping onto the couch and digging his head into one of the throw pillows, leaving Bree to direct her reply to his little butt.

"It's time for bed, kiddo."

Will gasped and whirled around with impressive speed. "Nooooo! I nod sleepy."

"That's because you had enough cake to fuel a rocket," Alessandro remarked wryly as he bounced a freshly bathed Gianni on his knee.

"No, Gianni had mo' cake den me," Will insisted.

"No, Gianni wore more cake than you. There's a difference," Bree said.

"Can you say daddy, Gianni? Daddy? Daaaddy"

"Eeeee," Gianni echoed.

"Daaa—" Alessandro urged.

"Aaaahhh," Gianni repeated.

"Deeee," Alessandro pressed.

"Eeemmmoonghhhe pooom,"

"That's pretty close," Alessandro joked.

"Gianni, you wanna go tobogganing, right?" Will asked.

"Heeeee," Gianni giggled at his older brother.

"Dat mean yes," Will informed his parents.

"What do you say?" Bree asked, turning back to Alessandro.

"I can't say as I've ever been tobogganing," Alessandro admitted.

"Ever?" Bree asked surprised.

"Oh dat's sad, daddy!" Will exclaimed. He slid off the couch. "Now we haf to go. Peeese?"

"Maybe it'll wear you out enough to burn up all that sugar," Bree said getting to her feet.

"Uh, what do I need?" Alessandro asked. "I don't have one of those…metal sheet things."

"A toboggan?" Bree asked. "No problem. I've got a few boxes in the basement. I think I put the toboggans in there too. It'll be fun. You wanna get Gianni's snow suit on?"

"We won't have to go far. We have some pretty decent hills on the Dardano property." Alessandro got up off the couch, holding Gianni up but his armpits. "Can you say 'toboggan', Gianni?"

"Right. He can't say 'daddy' but 'toboggan' should be no problem," Bree said with a snort.

"Bbbbnnng," Gianni replied.

Alessandro cocked a smug eyebrow at Bree. "See? My son is a genius."

"Sure. Why don't you get Baby Einstein dressed?"

Alessandro was right. The Dardano property stretched out a fair bit and there was an impressive hill just a few minutes away from the house.

The moon made the white snow gleam like silver and while there was a bite in the air, it was a comparatively warm night.

Bree held Will securely in front of her as they went down first, the whoosh of air bit into her skin and Will's squeal of delight pierced her ears.

Gianni wiggled in his father's arms excited by the spectacle and Alessandro's eyes were soft as he watched the two of them.

"Yo' turn, daddy!" Will insisted, grabbing the edge of Alessandro's coat.

"All right," he passed Gianni to Bree and let Will lead him around to the top of the hill.

"Say goodbye to those designer pants, Dardano!" Bree shouted up at him.

He pulled Will in front of him as they sat on the metal curved sheet. Alessandro gave Bree a little salute and then went shooting down. He and Will toppled over when they reached the bottom, but both were laughing so Bree was assured that there were no broken bones.

"Bloody hell!" Alessandro exclaimed, getting to his feet, his dark hair sticking up and his brown eyes smiling. "It's like skiing on your arse!" he laughed.

"Pretty much, yeah," Bree agreed. " 'kay, my turn again," she handed Gianni towards Alessandro who shook his head.

"Oh no. I'm definitely doing that again. Come on, Will." Before Bree could protest, Alessandro stepped out of her reach and grabbed Will's hand, running to the top of the hill again.

"Hey, you cheater!" Bree yelled.

"I'm a Dardano, darling. We're a sneaky, sleazy bunch!"

When they made it down a second time Bree reached up and brushed the snow out of his hair. "Let's not forget slimy."

Alessandro grinned. He leaned in and kissed her cheek. "Now let me take Gianni down." He reached for the baby.

"Down the hill? Oh I don't think so."

"Come now, Brianna. He'll love it." Alessandro insisted.

As if to prove his point, Gianni stretched his arms out towards his father.

"I stayed upright that last time. Nothing to worry about at all."

"Right. Sure," Bree replied skeptically but she handed her son over. "If you break my baby, you owe me another one!" she shouted.

Alessandro turned back and winked at her. "It would be my pleasure."

Gianni shrieked the whole way down but true to his word, Alessandro held him securely. When they reached the bottom, Gianni's lower lips quivered as if the shock had worn off and he was about to start crying. But he seemed to change his mind at the last minute and squealed in laughter.

"See? That was fun, wasn't it, Gianni?" Alessandro asked, bouncing the baby who reached down and grabbed a fist full of snow and brought it to his mouth.

"Heeee," he giggled.

"Now you and mommy go," Will insisted.

"Oh, I don't know. One of us should stay with the baby," Bree said though she really did want to slide down with him.

"I stay wif da baby."

"Just put him in the baby seat," Alessandro said.

"Are you sure? Maybe we should call it a night. I don't want you to over exert yourself. You're still healing."

"I feel just fine, thank you." He leaned in and whispered, "And I plan to show you how healed I am very, very soon."

"Come on, mommy! Go down wif daddy." Will insisted.

Alessandro wiggled his eyebrows suggestively at Bree, making her roll her eyes at her husband's dirty mind.

Gianni was none too happy to be snapped into the baby seat and angrily let his parents know it by screaming. But Will sat next to him on the snow and entertained him for a few minutes.

Bree took a seat in front of Alessandro, settling herself between his thighs.

"You can't tell but you feel very good against me, love," Alessandro whispered, nuzzling her neck.

Bree flushed and smacked his thigh. "Onward Jeeves,"

Bree closed her eyes and with Alessandro's arms securely around her, went over the edge with him. The world spun by in a dizzying blur and when they fell over this time, Alessandro landed on top of her laughing, but grew serious as he brushed the snow off her face and her hair off her forehead. "I love you, darling. Happy Birthday."

Bree lifted her mouth to his and kissed him. "Thank you for the best birthday ever."

CHAPTER FIFTEEN

“Good God,” Alessandro whispered coming out of the bathroom.

Bree caught his gaze in the mirror as she put on her earrings. Freshwater gold pearl and diamond drops that Alessandro had given her that morning as an early Christmas present. She went a little breathless herself, taking in his tall, gorgeous form in his tuxedo. “Ditto.”

He moved towards her and lifted a hand into her hair, falling down over her shoulders in blonde waves. She’d pinned up one side and curled the ends.

His mouth went to her shoulder and his other hand drifted across the front of her belly, the tips of his fingers resting just against her lower abdomen. The moist heat of his mouth against her skin made Bree shiver and when she took a step back against him, she couldn’t miss the growing evidence of his intent.

“Oh no. No you don’t,” Bree warned turning and shaking her head.

“Consider it an early Christmas present,” Alessandro said, capturing her breast with one hand, lifting the warm weight through the gold satin of the dress.

“No, Alessandro. Come on. We don’t have time and-”

“Oh darling, you underestimate my desire for my wife. This won’t take long.” He reached around to grab her behind and press her against the insistent bulge in his pants.

“Stop that, you horn dog! We have a house full of guests downstairs,” Bree reminded him, even as her own body was warming to the unmistakable desire in his eyes.

"You know, I was thinking-" Alessandro whispered, capturing her mouth.

Crap, she'd have to do her lipstick again, Bree thought distantly even as her arms were winding around Alessandro's neck. "No kidding."

"About that night we used the toy. I'd like to go shopping with you for something." His fingers were inching the floor length dress up along her calves, higher still to her thighs.

"Would you?" Bree teased, though she was curious.

"Mmm. Something I think you would enjoy very very much."

"Oh? And what about you? Or is this a sacrifice for you for my pleasure?"

"Oh no, darling." He slid his hand into the low neckline of her dress, searching out her breast with his warm hand.

Bree shivered at the contact of his skin against hers. They really didn't have time and they were all dressed up…She moaned as his thumb slid across her nipple.

"Believe me, I get plenty of pleasure watching you come." He pinched the nipple and Bree's eyes fluttered closed.

"God you're nuts," she murmured arching her head back as his mouth slid down over her collar bone.

"Feeling you come around my fingers, hearing you scream my name…your nails in my back…"

A sneaky hand was making its way under her dress to her panties. "Your gorgeous legs wrapped around my waist as I fuck you and those delicious cries you make when you're begging me to never stop because you know it's so good between us."

"Alessandro…we should go down-"

"Oh I agree." He smiled, mischievous brown eyes lifting to hers.

"Downstairs," she corrected.

"I like my meaning better," and with that he went down on his knees.

"No!" Bree hissed even as her body was screaming YES!

"Stop arguing with me, darling." His fingers slid past her panties and Bree whimpered as he pulled them down. He lifted the dress and told her to hold it against her as his fingers stroked her. "You're so lovely and wet for me. This won't take long at all." His thumb rubbed her clitoris as he eased two long fingers into her pussy.

"Oh God!" Bree cried out bucking her hips hungrily.

"Good?" he asked needlessly.

"Oh God!" she repeated.

"I thought so," Alessandro said smugly as he pumped his fingers.

It took all of two minutes and she was coming.

"So beautiful," he murmured as she trembled.

Before she came off her high, Alessandro's mouth followed his fingers.

"Oooooh," Bree whimpered. "We can't…we can't…People…down…Oh God…Oh God…"

He sucked her clitoris into his mouth flicking at it purposefully as Bree bit her fist and struggled to hold on to something as her legs shook. Her gold heels dug into the carpet.

"Tonight," Alessandro promised. "I'm gonna fuck you while you're wearing these heels."

"You're not…ready…" Bree reminded him as he took a moment to thrust his tongue up into her core. He used the tongue like a stiff cock and fucked her with it. His damp fingers gripped her thighs, holding her open for him as his tongue thrust back and forth, lapping up her juices as he sent her keening towards another orgasm.

"Oh, I am," Alessandro promised. "I'm all better, love, and tonight. I'm gonna show you just how much better."

"Don't…hurt…Oh God…yourself. Oh Alessandro!" Bree sucked in her breath as her orgasm slammed into her.

"God, Brianna," Alessandro groaned getting to his feet, his erection straining against his zipper. "What you fucking do to me, woman. Watching you bent over the vanity like that, getting ready, your dress stretched over your ass the way it was. It's all I can do not to throw you on the bed now and ram you like an animal until neither one of us can walk. It's been hell for me, not loving you as much as I wanted to, as hard as I wanted to."

"Gentle or hard, you drive me out of my mind. Because it's you." Bree assured him and was almost coming again at his words. "Fuck me now," she urged into his neck as her hands went down to his pants, freeing his cock.

The thick shaft filled her hand and Bree wrapped her fingers around him, stroking slowly and loving the desperate sounds he made. It made her feel powerful to know she could bring him to the brink like he did to her. His breath was hot against her face, he smelled of toothpaste and sex and Bree wondered briefly if the guests downstairs would be able to tell what they had done, even after they fixed themselves again.

"Oh God…I can't wait until tonight, Brianna. I need this…inside you, now." He gripped her hips and pushed her against the wall. "Wrap your legs around me."

"Are you sure?" Bree shivered even as her legs followed his order. The head of his cock brushed against her wet folds. "I don't want to hurt-OH GOD!" Bree screamed as he drove into her.

"Answer your question?" Alessandro asked tightly.

"Oh Alessandro…" Bree sighed as he began rocking his hips against her, driving his cock in short, thick jabs.

"Brianna…darling…" he growled pumping slowly. His mouth found hers again as he thrust deep into her, pressing his fingers into her hips. He guided her back and forth against him.

Bree bit into his tuxedo jacket as his cock drove into her, the friction sending her higher and higher towards the edge. His tongue met hers, sending her mind spinning with the drugging taste of his kiss, combined with the devastating movements of his body.

"Love you…God….I love you, Brianna…Never get enough…of you. You drive me…insane. Bloody…crazy." He ground his hips against her, trapping her between his hard muscled body and the wall.

"Yes…Oh yes…Don't stop…Love you…Love you, Alessandro…" She bucked her hips against him. She distantly wondered if she was hurting him but his mouth was stealing all rational thought from her and all she wanted was this man, her husband, inside of her body, her soul, forever. His hands were everywhere, holding her up, on her breasts, between their bodies on her clitoris until they were coming against each other. His cock swelled inside of her and Bree felt him release deep and hot inside of her as his mouth went to her shoulder and she felt the sting of his teeth in her skin as he jerked with the force of his orgasm. Her muscles clutched his cock greedily until she had milked him completely with the force of her own orgasm and when he slowly withdrew from him, Bree was missing him already.

"Well," Alessandro sighed laughing as they cleaned themselves up. "That should take the edge off."

"Did you bite me?" Bree asked stunned as she saw the teeth marks on her shoulder, visible beneath the gold strap of her dress. People would quite clearly see the marks until they faded.

"Darling, I can't tell you what it does to me to see my mark on you. Be glad we just had sex or I'd push the dress up over your head again."

"I suppose it's better we gave into it now as opposed to you throwing me onto the seafood buffet," Bree joked.

"Ladies and gentlemen, let us welcome my son and his new wife, Mr. and Mrs. Alessandro Dardano," Bernardo announced while Alessandro and Bree paused in the doorway.

"At least you have a name. I'm just Mrs. Dardano," Bree said rolling her eyes.

"There are a few women here who would kill to be Mrs. Dardano, you know?" Alessandro pointed out.

"Really? Where are they?" Bree asked scanning the room for young, beautiful sluts.

"Jealous, darling?" Alessandro asked lifting her hand to his mouth.

"Hardly," Bree lied. She lifted her mouth to his ear, " I'll just mention to them that you have a thing for your wife naked and wearing gold 'fuck me' heels and that none of them could ever drive you as crazy as I do."

She patted his cheek lovingly and pulled him with her to the center of the Dardano ballroom. The string quartet began an instrumental version of 'Can't Help Falling In Love With You'.

He gathered her into his arms and smiled down at her.

She heard a few people sigh as they watched them.

"And for the record, if anyone is jealous here it's every man in this room."

"Is that so?" Bree asked, blushing at the compliment.

"Oh definitely because all women pale in comparison to you." His fingers tightened around hers.

"You know, you've got me already. You don't need to keep laying it on," Bree reminded him, rolling her eyes but smiling.

"I mean every word, Brianna," Alessandro promised leaning his forehead against hers.

Bree shivered and bit her lip as she met his gaze.

"I don't think I've ever been this happy, darling. Ever,"

Alessandro admitted.

"Me neither," she replied in a small voice. It was true. How Alessandro made her feel was so different from anything she'd ever felt before.

"You and our boys. You're the family I've always wanted."

Bree swallowed the lump of emotion in her throat at his sweet declaration.

When the dance ended, they reluctantly parted to greet the guests.

When Bree got closer, she saw Will pulling at his little bow tie and Gianni in the baby seat, dressed in a little tuxedo, gnawing on his fist.

"Mommy! When we gonna have a party dat I don' haf to wear these slippy shoes?" Will asked looking down at the offending footwear.

"Try heels," Bree tossed back. "You look so handsome, Will."

"I look like daddy," Will said pulling his shoulders back proudly.

"You sure do and Gianni, come here to mommy. I knew you would look too adorable for words in your little baby tux." When she pulled him up out of his baby seat the guests close by all 'awwwed.', getting the attention of the other guests who joined in the fawning.

Will stepped in front of Bree and repeated, "I look like daddy."

"Yes you do," Alessandro said, coming away from a few men he was talking to in the corner.

"Well, don't you two just look like you belong on a wedding cake," a familiar Texan voice said behind them.

"Mr. Addleworth! I'm so glad you could make it," Bree said.

"Put your money where your mouth is, gorgeous." Addleworth extended his hand to her and led her to the dance floor after she passed Gianni back to the nanny. "So, how come I wasn't invited to the wedding?"

"Uh…" Bree stammered uncomfortably. "It was a really small wedding… just…family." She nearly choked on the word.

"I forgive you on the condition that you allow me to offer you a room in one of my hotels in Vegas for your honeymoon."

"Ah…we haven't really had time for a honeymoon."

"I insist. My treat. I won't take no for an answer," Addleworth insisted.

"I can see that."

"Can I have my wife back?" Alessandro asked coming up behind them.

"Well, I don't know about that there, Alessandro, my boy. This wifey here of yours is a mighty tempting creature."

"I'm well aware of that," Alessandro said, running a hand down Bree's back and dropping his chin on her shoulder.

"Fine, fine, but only if I can have her back later," Addleworth said. "I want to use her to promote one of my hotels. This face. This body. Woooooweeee!"

"Oh God," Bree snorted closing her eyes and turning eagerly into Alessandro's arms. "That guy is one of a kind."

"He knows a good thing when he sees one," Alessandro smiled at her.

She wrapped her arms around his neck. "What a coincidence, so do I."

"She is exquisite, Alessandro," the man next to him remarked as they both watched Brianna across the room. She had Gianni on her hip and a glass of champagne in her free hand as she talked with Fernando Maggiore, a young Italian count.

She smiled at him when Alessandro knew the man had the sense of humor of a slab of plywood. But she humoured him because Alessandro mentioned that he was looking to join in on the young count's import/export interests in Naples.

His wife was a very smart woman, Alessandro thought with a burst of pride. He turned to the man next to him, a Boston senator in Bernardo's pocket and Alessandro felt a beat of irritation over how exactly the man was looking at Brianna.

Only he had the right to look at his wife that way. Alessandro grit his teeth and tried to extract himself from the Senator's company before he shoved the man's teeth down his throat.

"She will be a very valuable asset to the Dardano empire. A powerful man needs a beautiful woman like her by his side," Bernardo said coming up next to them.

Alessandro turned to his father with a grateful smile.

"Of course," the senator agreed. "And you're very lucky to have two sons to carry on the powerful Dardano legacy."

Alessandro pressed his lips together imagining Brianna's reaction to that statement. The senator went on and Alessandro caught enough to just smile and throw in a comment or two as he watched Brianna. He saw that while she smiled at the Count, the smile she gave Gianni as the baby fiddled with her necklace was warmer, genuine and it made Alessandro feel an answering warmth in his chest.

And then she looked over at him and her smile pierced his heart. She turned Gianni around to face him and raised the baby's fist in greeting.

His father was saying something and Alessandro forced himself to tear his gaze away from the woman he loved. Out of the corner of his eye he saw her greet Meggie and Hadley.

"Come. There is something I want to give you in private," Bernardo said.

"I'll go get Brianna," Alessandro said but his father touched his arm.

"I'd rather you come alone."

He looked at his father curiously but followed Bernardo into his study. Alessandro looked down at the folder Bernardo handed to him. It had Gianni's name on it. He felt a mix of excitement and dread as he flipped through the documents. "You're giving him a third of everything."

"Yes," Bernardo agreed.

"All the Dardano holdings, all our interests. And…good God father," Alessandro blinked reading on. "On your passing, we're to divide your shares between us? I'm assuming you didn't show this to Brianna?"

"No, I did not think she would appreciate it in the manner it was intended."

Alessandro had to agree with him there. "But, Father, I'm sure she knows that Gianni will have a share in the Dardano empire as soon as he's of age but a third, a half?"

"He is family, and before you even mention it, there is a percentage set aside for Will when he comes of age if he decides his loyalty remains with the Dardano family."

If he decides not to take revenge for his father's murder.

Alessandro felt a shudder go down his back as he imagined that day. How would Will look at him? Would he forgive Alessandro for his loyalty to Bernardo, even knowing that Bernardo had killed Michael?

"If Gianni decides to split his shares with Will then the two of them can make those arrangements when the day comes," Bernardo said.

But Alessandro was still in the future, fearing that the boy he loved would someday come to hate him for being the son of the man who killed his father, for staying loyal to Bernardo and for raising Will in the same house.

You knew! You knew and did nothing! I hate you!

Alessandro closed his eyes and placed his shaking hands behind his back.

They walked back to the party and Brianna gave him a curious look as she walked towards him. She placed a hand on his arm and looked up at him in concern.

"Are you okay? You look kind of pale."

He cupped her face in his hands and kissed her, taking comfort in her immediate response.

There was a smattering of applause and a few whistles around them. But when they pulled apart Brianna was looking at him with eyes that knew something was bothering him.

Before she could ask though, Bernardo asked for everyone's attention.

"I would like to make a toast to my son and his new bride. I could not ask for a more loyal and wonderful son. He has been a joy to me all these years and it does my heart good to know that he has found true happiness with a woman who is truly worthy of him," Bernardo said.

"Who? Me? A lowly O'Reiley?" Brianna whispered to Alessandro.

"I wish you both a lifetime of happiness and a fruitful future."

"Is that hint for me to breed more Dardano heirs?" Brianna asked with a snort.

"Shush," Alessandro insisted with a smile.

The guests applauded the end of his toast and Alessandro moved out from behind Brianna to take his place. "I suppose that's my cue," he said smiling at them as he stood in front of them. He took a glass of champagne and turned to Brianna. Brian stepped up next to her, holding Gianni, Will standing next to them.

"Being a Dardano, speeches seem to be a requirement but I have to say that when I look at my wife, words fail me. To say I love her seems woefully inadequate. She is an incomparable woman. Exquisite, strong, but with a heart that is so warm. I am who I am because of her. I am alive today because of the strength of her love for me," Alessandro took a deep breath, his heart swelling with emotion. "I didn't think it was possible that I could love her more than I did the first time we met. Now, every day I watch her with our children, feel how she has changed my life, made me a better man, I love her more and more." He raised his glass to her and smiled at the tears he saw in her eyes, knowing they were happy tears.

Brianna pressed her lips to his as she took her turn. "Okay. I guess it's my turn now." She took a deep breath and met Alessandro's gaze. "A year ago today, I was at the lowest point in my life that I think I've ever been. And then I met a man who filled my heart with a joy I didn't think was possible. He became my friend. No questions asked. He became my love, loving me faults and all, and a few of you know just how numerous those are," she said and a few people chuckled in response. "You say I changed you." She turned to Alessandro. "Well, the same goes for me. You have given me the greatest gifts, Alessandro. Not just someone who loves me without judgement, but you've given me our beautiful son Gianni, and you're someone I am proud to have be a father to Will. I love you."

Alessandro blinked the tears back from his eyes and felt Will slip a small hand into his. "Daddy, we haf cake now?"

CHAPTER SIXTEEN

"Alone at last!" Alessandro exclaimed exuberantly as he picked Bree up and propped her on his shoulder.

Bree squealed and smacked his back. "Put me down! That is NOT how you carry someone over the threshold and besides, we've been married for a while now."

"Oh, many apologies, darling," he said closing the door behind him. "I can't seem to control myself with you."

Bree laughed and pinched his behind.

"Hey!" Alessandro protested, smacking hers. "Behave yourself."

"Says the man who is treating me like a sack of potatoes, put me down!" Bree demanded, giggling.

"Very well," he threw her on the bed.

"I think you're drunk," Bree said.

"Oh well then I shall have to endeavour to do my best to prove you wrong," Alessandro said running his hands up her thighs.

He followed his fingers with his lips making Bree shiver as the moist heat made its way up the smooth skin of her thighs.

She pushed her dress up and prepared to take it off but Alessandro stopped her.

"Not just yet, love," he whispered smiling up at her. He pressed a hand on her stomach to push her down on her back.

"Are you sure you're not tired?" Bree asked biting her lip and hoping to hell he said no. God she wanted him so bad she ached…everywhere. Watching him tonight, wheeling and dealing with some of the most powerful men in the country, charming their wives who looked at Alessandro like he was the main course and they wanted to devour him gave Bree a surge of possessive pride. She would remember earlier, when he had taken her passionately before they arrived downstairs, how much he wanted her, always, and she'd smile.

Then she'd feel his eyes on her, those hungry, beautiful eyes that darkened possessively when any man tried to charm her with what they thought was irresistible sensuality.

As if, Bree thought with a snort. If only they knew that while they were pouring it on, she was remembering the feel of her husband, the man she loved, thrusting powerfully inside of her just hours before.

"Stop asking me that," Alessandro insisted biting the inside of her thigh and making her breath hitch and her core grow slick.

"I just don't want you to hurt yourself," Bree assured him, running her fingers through his hair. "I kind of like you, you know?"

"Darling, I promise I feel wonderful. Wonderful and insanely aroused. God, I hated all those men fawning over my wife. They all wanted you, you know?"

He ran a finger along her damp center. Bree sucked in her breath and trembled.

"Ditto with all those bimbos undressing you with their eyes," she tossed back.

"Jealous, darling?" Alessandro asked smugly, nuzzling her mound with his lips.

Bree tightened her fingers in the sheets. "Yes. I wanted to gouge their eyes out. What about you, huh? I saw how you were looking at those men I was talking to. Were you jealous?"

"Oh yes," Alessandro replied, thrusting a finger into her.

Bree cried out and arched back, her head falling on the pillow. "Oh God."

"I wanted to kill them for looking at you, touching you, wanting you," Alessandro growled darkly as he pumped his middle finger inside of her.

The violence of his words should have frightened her but Bree spread her thighs wider, accepting his love in all its forms. "Oh yeah?" She urged, lifting her head and flashing her eyes at him. "Why?"

He pushed in a second finger, stretching her. "Because you're mine, darling." He flicked his tongue across her swollen numb, making her legs tense. "Every beautiful, wet inch of you is mine." He pumped slowly and ground the heel of his hand against her clitoris, making her whimper. And just when she was hovering on the edge, he pulled out his fingers and replaced them with his tongue.

"Ohhhh, fuuuccck," Bree cried out, her fingers tight in his hair. "God…oh God…you're good at that."

"All night I couldn't get the taste of you out of my memory. The feel of this beautiful body around me." He fucked her with his tongue slowly, making her writhe on the sheets. "It was all I could do not to drag you into some secret room and throw you on the floor."

That mental image pushed her over the edge and she came with a blissful cry against his mouth.

"Okay, now you can take off the dress," Alessandro smiled smugly. He made his way up her body and captured a breast in his mouth as she pulled the dress off. He winked at her. "But keep the heels on."

Oh right, Bree thought with a giggle. She ran her fingers along the nape of his neck. "Get on your back, Dardano." She sighed as he flicked his tongue over a nipple. "I want you in my mouth."

His dark eyes flared with approval and he pulled back and undressed in front of her. She ran her eyes over every bit of exposed skin. When he was completely naked Bree circled his magnificent cock with her fingers and pulled him into her mouth.

He let out a low needy growl and let her move him onto his back. Bree felt the throbbing return to her pussy as she sucked her husband's shaft, playing lightly with his sac. "Oh God…Brianna…Brianna…"

Bree looked up at him and lifted her mouth briefly. "How many women tonight wished they could be right where I am right now, with this beautiful naked body in front of them? To have you in their mouths. But you don't want them, do you?" She purred, running her tongue up along the swollen shaft. "You only want me. My mouth, sucking you. Isn't that right?" She sucked the head lightly, running her tongue along the tight skin that was slick with her mouth and the tiniest bit of his juices.

"Yes…Oh…fuck, yes!" Alessandro groaned as she lowered her mouth over his whole length, sucking him eagerly. His fingers drifted down to her breasts, pinching her nipples as her mouth devoured him.

She sucked him harder as she felt him getting close to his release. He swelled in her mouth and his movements became desperate. And then there he was, spilling into her mouth and Bree's pussy was clutching and releasing wanting him there again, dying to be filled the way only he could fill her.

"Bloody hell," he gasped, resting against the bed, his hand cradling the back of her neck. With his other hand, he slipped his fingers between her legs smiling when he felt how wet she was.

Bree wiggled her hips against the feel of his fingers, biting her lip in hungry invitation.

"Hmmm, do you want me here, darling?"

"Oh yes," Bree replied, shivering.

He stroked her slowly. "Does my exquisite wife want to be fucked?" He ran the tip of one finger teasingly around the opening.

"God yes," Bree pleaded, pushing her hips down a little to take his finger into her.

"How badly?" Alessandro asked, lifting his head to take one breast into his mouth.

Bree cried out and arched. "Bad…oh…so fucking bad."

"Does she want to be fucked hard?" Alessandro asked, biting her nipple just on the razor's edge of pain.

"Yes…fuck me hard," Bree begged, knowing what this delicious man was capable of.

"Does she want to be fucked like the beautiful, sexual, hungry animal that she is?"

Bree's eyes drifted closed, the desire thundering in her veins. She couldn't reply with anything more than a whimper.

"Get on your knees and turn around darling," Alessandro ordered.

Bree turned away from him and gripped the head board eagerly.

"Were you thinking about this, tonight? Waiting for the second that I could bend you over and ram into you like we both wanted? Could you see in my eyes that that was what I wanted? Every time I caught your eyes, this was what I wanted?"

She felt the head of his cock rubbing against her soaked folds and Bree was shaking as her nails gripped the headboard. "Oh yes, Alessandro. Take me now. Like this. Fuck me now."

He thrust into her from behind in one smooth stroke, making

them both cry out.

Bree arched back, coming up against his chest. "Oh fuck!"

He pulled out slowly and thrust home again, making her tremble with bursts of fiery sensation.

"Good?" Alessandro growled into her ear.

"More…" Bree begged. "More…"

He quickened his movements and Bree could feel his hand against her lower back before he gripped her hips to thrust deep and fast.

Bree held on to the head board as he fucked her, sending her crashing over an orgasm. "Don't stop. Oh my God…Don't stop,"

And he didn't. He alternated his pace, slow, then fast but he rammed into her, determined to make her come again and again.

"Oh God…so good, Brianna. So good," he groaned into her ear as his fingers pressed into the skin over her hips.

He fucked her. Took her, dominated her and oh God, how she loved it.

She could feel the damp heat of his skin against her back and she wondered distantly if he was going too hard. If he would suffer for his exertion later but oh God, he didn't stop and didn't sound like he was in pain and he was pushing her too close to the end again for her to stop him. Her blood was roaring in her ears and her pussy was tightening, clutching around him greedily.

And then he stopped and pulled out of her. Before she could object he pushed her onto her back and spread her legs, holding her ankles, he propped her heels against his chest thrust back into her.

Bree screamed at the deep penetration and arched her head into the pillow. His eyes were hungry, predatory over her as he thrust into her again and again, his face was flushed, his hard muscled body was glistening with sweat and Bree was coming as much from the unspeakable beauty of her husband in his animal, primal glory as the friction of his cock sawing hard in her pussy. He spread her legs, hooked them over his forearms and spread her wider…wider…opening her up to his brutal thrusts.

"Oh God…Alessandro….I can't….I can't again…" she moaned helplessly even as she felt the familiar tightening again deep in her belly.

He smiled at her, like a beast about to devour his prey and leaned over her, making his cock come right up against her clitoris as he pounded into her. "Yes you can, my darling. Come for me again…come with me again….again….again," he repeated, spreading her wide and meeting her mouth with his own as he rammed in once, twice, three times more.

They screamed their final orgasm into each other's mouths and Bree went mindless as she felt the breaking of skin and the metallic taste of blood…hers? His? She dug her nails into his ass and pulled his bucking body deep into her as the explosions rocketed through her blood.

"Oh God…" she panted when he collapsed on top of her, his sweaty body slick against hers. "Oh my God…"

Alessandro said nothing, Bree didn't think he could and she couldn't think anything more coherent than "Oh God…" as they both drifted off to sleep naked and damp, wrapped up in each other, body and soul.

They were woken up by a distraught Rafe who was beside himself with panic. Alessandro gripped the old man's arms and tried to get him to calm down. Haltingly, he managed to explain that Bernardo was having chest pains and was curled up on the floor.

Bree covered her mouth as Alessandro ran to his father's room and for a second she was glad he was gone because then he wouldn't have seen the mixed emotions on her face.

Yes, she hoped the old man died!

No, for Alessandro's sake she hoped Bernardo would be all right.

Shame, hope, panic churned through her as they followed the ambulance in their car.

The heart attack was mild, but they wanted to keep the old man in the hospital for a few days for observation. Alessandro hugged her and she could feel him sag in relief against her. She buried her face in his chest and swallowed down the feeling of shame at her disappointment. Her husband wanted to stay but Carlo assured him Bernardo would fine and that they should go home and rest.

Bree stared down at Bernardo's still form. The monitor was the only sound in the room apart from his deep breathing. Alessandro had gone down to the cafeteria with Will and Gianni to grab something to eat before they left for home. Bree lied and told him that she wanted to check in with Tina and her mother Roxanna for a few minutes before they left.

Even unconscious, the son of a bitch was formidable and Bree felt nervous around him.

"Why don't you do everyone a favour and just die already?" Bree said.

No response.

Bree sneered and shook her head, turning to leave.

"You could always smother me with a pillow," a groggy voice said behind her, making her heart nearly stop.

Bree whirled around wide-eyed and met Bernardo's dark gaze. She forced herself to shrug and crossed her arms.

"Do you think Alessandro would forgive you for murdering his father?" Bernardo asked.

They both knew the answer to that.

"I never understood my father's fascination with Francesca O'Reiley. Most of the O'Reiley women are weak. No fire. They are slaves to what is expected of them and lack the courage to go after what they want." Bernardo chuckled. The action made him grimace in pain. "But you, oh I knew you were the perfect woman for my boy. That right there. That is the fire I speak of. You, my girl, are worthy of the Dardano name."

"And so is that why you killed Michael?" Bree asked, her eyes blazing fire as her fists shook at her sides.

"When I saw how much you resembled Francesca's spirit, I knew it was what my father wanted. Finally I could fulfil his wish. His soul would be at rest."

"Michael…" she pressed.

"A necessary loss. I wish it could have been avoided."

Bree shook her head. "What kind of world do you live in where people are so easily dispensable to you? We're just chess pieces to be moved about all for the sake of some vow you made to a broken-hearted man."

"Brianna, you should know by now how important my family is to me. Anything or anyone that threatens that is very easily squashed."

"And Arturo? How will you deal with that threat knowing he's your creation?"

Bernardo scowled. "Arturo let the need for power poison his mind. His ambition became more important than the family."

"Mmm, programming go a little wonky, did it?" Bree asked

dryly. "You turned Arturo into what he became."

Bernardo smiled as if amused by her, which only got Bree more incensed.

"If you think I'm gonna let you do the same to Alessandro, you are sorely mistaken."

The smile disappeared. "Alessandro is nothing like Arturo. He is my heir. The future leader of the Dardano Empire."

"An accident of birth. Alessandro is a good man. He is loving and kind and warm and I will not let you turn him into some psychotic, power hungry murderer."

"My darling Brianna. I only want the best for Alessandro. That is all I have ever wanted. It is why I allowed him to marry you."

"Allowed?" Bree cocked an eyebrow. "I married Alessandro to end this stupid vendetta. I married Alessandro because I love him."

"Ask yourself, my girl, if I had objected to this marriage, would Alessandro have disobeyed me?"

Bree blinked, her stomach tightening uneasily. She remembered Alessandro's earlier words to her. Bernardo had wanted him to marry an O'Reiley but he had, not knowing that she was one, said to her that he didn't think he could have given her up. What did that mean? Alessandro would have kept her on the side? Like some mistress? That had to mean he loved her enough to keep her despite his father's wishes, didn't it? Did it? "You keep claiming that you love your son, if that is true then you want him to be happy."

"That is all I've ever wanted for him," Bernardo assured her.

Bree shook her head, unsure. "I have to believe you love him. I mean, I saw how you were when he was shot. I have to believe it's not just about having an heir for your great Dardano legacy."

"Young lady, my son, my grandson, they mean more to me than my own life."

"And if Alessandro decided that he wanted nothing more to do with the Dardano Empire? If he decided to be nothing more than a regular business man? Would you still love him then?" Bree asked.

"Alessandro will never turn his back on his legacy. The sooner you accept that, the happier your marriage will be."

"My marriage is fine, thank you," Bree insisted curtly.

"Brava. Then we can go on as a happy family, can we not?" Bernardo challenged.

"That's all I want," Bree lied.

Bernardo smiled at her, seeing the lie in her eyes. "Then we are in agreement."

New Years was a quiet affair. Bernardo was still recovering, though now at home and Bree was counting down the days until she and Alessandro could have some time alone. They would finally have their honeymoon.

In Paris. The city of love and romance. She wasn't sure who was looking forward to it more, her or Alessandro. Though she knew he was feeling guilty about it and she had to force herself to be gentle in her reminders that there really was nothing Alessandro could do for his father. Bernardo had Rafe and the other staff to cater to his every whim and Bree even assisted him sometimes, helping Bernardo reach things if it hurt him to stretch. It grated on her nerves but she tried to think long term. She couldn't antagonize Bernardo and look good in her husband's eyes at the same time. So if she felt like running Bernardo's head through a meat grinder most of the time, she kept it to herself.

And Bernardo could tell. It amused him to have her playing the happy daughter-in-law, and he seemed to be doing everything he could to push her just that little bit closer to the edge.

"More coffee, Bernardo?" Bree asked, holding the coffeepot over his porcelain mug, imagining it was his head.

Alessandro and Will were both staring at her with identical expressions of confusion.

Gianni was more succinct in his opinion and blew a raspberry, then dissolved in giggles, as he hit the edge of his bowl of mashed bananas with the spoon.

"Yes, Brianna, thank you," Bernardo replied with a smile that only she could tell was mocking.

"Bah! Bah! Bah. Meeeeeppppppoo. Deeemmee. Oh nnoooo. Ad den mufdit," Gianni said, sticking his hand into the bananas and showing them to his father, with commentary.

"Nicely done," Alessandro said dryly, rubbing Gianni's hand clean with a napkin.

"Noooooo!" Gianni objected apparently. He stuck his hand into the bananas once again. "Keddy Poof Donwannna Mippieeee. Badana. Mufditoo. Mufdit!"

Again, the hand was lifted to Alessandro for inspection.

"He wants you to eat it, daddy," Will explained.

"Does he now? Well, how do you translate, 'not in this lifetime' into baby language, young William?" Alessandro asked.

Gianni reached out and touched the body of the coffee pot with his dirty hand, drawing his fingers back at the obvious heat.

"Gianni!" Bree called out, too late.

Gianni grimaced and stared at his fingers. "Mmm, nooo. Owmm." He stuck the stung fingers into his mouth and squeezed his eyes shut. But didn't cry.

"That's my strong boy," Bernardo said with shining approval.

Gianni opened one eye and whimpered, continuing to suck on his fingers in what Bree liked to think was a muted 'fuck you'. That's my boy.

"But I wanna go too!" Will complained as Bree pulled him out of the tub. Alessandro quickly wrapped the towel around him and began rubbing him dry.

They had given their young nannyVanessa the next few days off so that they could spend as much time alone with Will and Gianni before they left for their honeymoon.

"I like honey!" Will pointed out.

"That's just what you call it when mummies and daddies go on their trip after they get married," Alessandro explained.

"We're only going for two weeks. That's fourteen sleeps," Bree explained, refilling the tub with warm water and more bubbles for Gianni who was clapping his hands in excitement.

"But dat's nod fair. What you gonna do all those days wif out us? You be bored."

Alessandro met Bree's gaze and winked at her. "I'm sure we'll find something to do even though we're going to miss you very very very very much," he said, proceeding to tickle Will, who buckled and squealed in delight.

"We have fries here! You don't have to go French land," Will grumbled later as Alessandro dressed him in his pajamas.

"Mummy and daddy just need some alone time, Will."

"You alone when Gianni and I go sleep," Will explained.

"Not quite the same," Bree snorted.

"Deeee. Mufdit," Gianni said scooping up bubbles and holding them up to Alessandro.

"Little one, I didn't eat it when it was bananas, what makes you think I'll eat soap?" Alessandro asked.

"Mmmmm. Oood," Gianni insisted.

"No is nod. Soap is bad," Will said. "And so is Frenchies."

"We're in agreement there," Alessandro said with a chuckle.

Gianni smacked his hand down in the water, sending a cloud of bubbles up into the air. "Meeee. Mufdit," he said, seeing as he had no luck with Alessandro, he'd try his hand at Bree.

"Only if daddy 'mufdit's' first," Bree smiled saucily at Alessandro.

"Well, that was fun," Alessandro said sarcastically when they finally got both boys to bed, Will insisting that France was not going to be any fun and that when he 'growed' up he was never going on any 'honey-moons'.

"Will did have a good point though," Alessandro said, rubbing Bree's shoulders as she kicked off her slippers.

"Mmm?" Bree asked, yawning.

"I mean, what will we do all by ourselves for fourteen whole days?"

"And thirteen long nights," Bree smiled, lifting her hand behind her to caress his cheek. "You're right. We should maybe plan an itinerary or something."

Alessandro picked her up and carried her to the bed. "Yes, we should pencil in time to see the museums…cathedrals…" He ran his mouth along her neck as his hands came up to cup her breasts over her nightgown.

"Or we could just stay in our hotel and make love all week," Bree purred, flipping him over onto his back.

"I think I'm going to need a more detailed plan," Alessandro said with a smile, caressing her spine with his fingers.

"Mmm, well let me give you a little preview," she said, running her lips down his chest…and still lower.

CHAPTER SEVENTEEN

"A pleasure, mademoiselle," the assistant said taking Bree's hand, and bringing it to his mouth.

"Uh, I think it's 'Madame'," she corrected. She moved the emerald green satin gown to her right arm so she could raise her left hand to make sure he saw her wedding ring.

"Oui, c'est mon épouse ainsi gardons nos mains à nous-mêmes ou à moi les enlèvera, comprennent?" Alessandro said coming into the studio.

The assistant to Operandi, who was showcasing a few of the latest collections and, as a personal favour to Alessandro, allowing Brianna a first pick, scowled but took a step back and nodded curtly before leaving them alone.

She tried not to be impressed at all the 'names' Alessandro knew but that was a little hard to do when she was holding a gown in her arms that cost more than her first car. "What did you say to that poor man?" Bree asked, holding the gown up against her and looking in the mirror. "I'm not so good with the French but it sounded like something about broken fingers?"

Alessandro wrapped and arm around her waist and nuzzled her neck from behind. "You're going to look absolutely breathtaking in that."

"Hmm, nice dodge of the subject there," Bree said, running her fingers over his across her stomach.

"Yes, I thought so," Alessandro grinned, tugging lightly on one of her diamond drop earrings with his teeth. "Now, I'm starving.

Can we go?"

"Something light. Remember we have that dinner tonight. And no, I still have to look at shoes."

Alessandro groaned and turned away from her, taking a seat on a long white leather bench.

Bree looked over the more than fifty pairs the assistant had left for her. Her eyes fell on a pair of shiny black leather high heels, open toe with a small, flat, black leather bow across the front. "Oh. Major bingo!" she exclaimed, picking them up. She turned to Alessandro and held them up expectantly.

He shrugged. "My only interest in those shoes would be if you were to wear them tonight while the rest of you is blissfully naked in our bed."

Bree blushed and shook her head. "Is that all you ever thing about?"

"Certainly not, but you said we couldn't eat yet."

Bree snorted and slipped on the shoe. She changed back into the dress and the heel of the shoe was just enough to have the bottom of the dress lightly graze the floor. She placed her foot on the bench next to Alessandro. "What do you think, seriously?" Bree pressed.

"Hmm, try raising it a bit more," Alessandro said.

Bree brought the hem up over her ankle.

"'Bit more," Alessandro urged.

Bree pulled the dress up along her calf.

"Not quite sure, yet, darling. Perhaps a bit more?" Alessandro grinned devilishly at her as Bree caught on.

She looked quickly towards the doorway and smiled down at her husband as she lifted the dress up onto her thigh.

Alessandro's mouth went to her leg and ran up along the skin making her shiver and she forced herself to stop him before they gave the staff here at the studio a free show.

"Okay, now we can eat," Bree said, pushing the dress down.

"Ah, Merci," Alessandro winked, smacking her bottom as she picked up her own clothes from the floor.

"I think tomorrow we should visit the vineyard," Alessandro said as they sat inside a café."It's too bad it's winter. I would take you to this beach outside of the city and we could go swimming naked."

"Right," Bree said, skeptically. She took a sip of her iced tea and placed the glass down as she moved closer to Alessandro. "It's one thing to be naked with you, but I'm not so much into the exhibitionism, honey."

"You should try it, really. It's wonderfully freeing," he assured her.

Bree snorted. "Sure…freeing to watching dozens of French women fawning over my naked husband. Not so much."

"Well, we could always go to my family's small villa. The beach there is ours. Private property." Alessandro winked at her. "How about that, sweetheart?" He nudged her under the table with his foot. "This summer?"

"I'm making no promises," Bree said but the idea did sound scandalously appealing.

"That reminds me. There's somewhere I want to take you before we get ready for dinner," Alessandro said, his desire filled eyes glittering with promise.

"You're not serious?" Bree asked halting in the middle of the sidewalk, staring up at the sign on the door.

"Really, darling. Where's your spirit of adventure?" Alessandro asked placing a hand on the small of her back and urging her towards the door.

"In the bedroom, where it belongs," Bree shot back, her cheeks pink from more than the cold air.

"I do believe a short while back we agreed it would be fun to go into one of these together."

"I was hopped up on endorphins after we'd just had sex. I can hardly be held responsible for anything that came out of my mouth at the time."

"Oh come on. It'll be fun. Besides, you're in a foreign country. You don't have to worry about being recognized here." Alessandro opened the door and came up against Bree so that she had no choice but to walk through.

"Ah Monsieur Dardano! How lovely to see you again." A smartly dressed woman came up to Alessandro with a bright smile.

Bree turned around and cocked an eyebrow at her husband.

He smiled sheepishly at her. "I said nothing about myself. Dardano Enterprises has done a few campa—"

"I didn't ask," Bree said raising a hand but enjoying the blush in her husband's cheeks. "Liar."

"How may we help you?"

Bree figured that was rather obvious but said nothing.

"My wife, Brianna and I will just have a look around for a few minutes. Brianna, this is Claudette, the proprietor of this lovely establishment…and the brothel upstairs," he added in a whisper in her ear.

Bree's eyes automatically went to the velvet curtain that Alessandro silently hinted hid a staircase. "Oh really?" she asked looking back meaningfully at her husband.

"Uh…what I mean is…it's rather common knowledge that…um…" Alessandro stammered.

Claudette winked at Bree and extended her hand, which Bree took with an answering smile. "Please, have a glass of wine, take your time and if you have any questions just let me know."

Alessandro handed Bree a glass of wine that he had poured from a silver tray on the glass counter.

Bree took the wine with a giggle of surprise. "Only in Paris." She walked over and looked at the items underneath the counter. Small gold shaped vibrators, which Alessandro explained, were of the anal variety.

"And is that real gold?" Bree asked in surprise.

"Quite," Alessandro nodded. "And those are real diamonds as well." He pointed to what looked like a large hoop earring dotted with diamonds, but with no visible clasp and considering where they were, Bree guessed there was another use for the ring.

"Ouch!" she exclaimed softly.

"Well, the part that rests against the man's actual skin has a rubber coating," Alessandro told her.

"My, how fancy," she said with a wide grin. "Though I can just imagine coming up against that with my mouth and the diamonds blinding me."

Alessandro chuckled with her and then pointed to what looked like a necklace of rather large pearls. "Those are genuine jade."

"Ohhh, I know what those are," Bree said with a nod. The small balls went up inside and she shivered imagining how fun they would be to play with. "That could be fun but…" she looked at the price tag of over two hundred dollars. "Holy shit."

"Don't worry about the price. They're well worth it and it's the price that adds to the luxury of it really."

She looked at a catalogue on the table, and saw what appeared to be sex dolls. Pamela Anderson, Marilyn Monroe, various porn stars and even a 'customized' option. "Customized?" Bree asked out loud.

Alessandro laughed behind her. "Well, let's say you or I have to go away on business and won't be seeing each other for any length of time. They would make a cast of…well…you."

"Shut up," Bree exclaimed in disbelief.

"I kid you not, darling."

"That's kind of…perversely romantic I guess." She smiled and took another sip of her wine.

She nearly choked when she turned and saw an easily over fifteen inch long glass dildo propped on an elegant ivory engraved stand like a piece of art. "Is that glass?" she asked rushing over to it.

"Uh, crystal, I think."

"Holy crap," she whispered. "And it's all…um…realistic looking, apart from the rather ambitious length. Do people actually buy the glass ones…or…oh, sorry, crystal? That sounds kind of uncomfortable."

Alessandro shrugged and lifted the price tag. "At one thousand dollars, I think it'd be more of an object d'art than for actual use. But hey, you'd never have to worry about performance issues."

Bree wrapped an arm around Alessandro's waist. "I think I'll take my flesh and blood man, thank you."

He smiled and kissed the crown of her head but she was sliding out from under his arms quickly as another object caught her attention. "What on earth…?"

A female mannequin stood in the corner with straps around her thighs and what looked like a tiny vibrator pressed against between her legs. "That's not a…uh…what do you call them…strap-ons, right?"

"No. Much too small I'd say. The little vibrator is for the woman's pleasure."

"But how does it work?" Bree asked. She looked at the name of the toy that was in a package of to the side. "The Butterfly…Hmm." All of a sudden the toy came to life, buzzing and flicking against the fake folds.

Bree took a stunned step back, coming up against Alessandro. They turned around and saw Claudette holding up what looked like a small remote control.

"Ohhhh," Bree said in sudden understanding, her own core fluttered in response. "Kind of loud though, isn't it?"

"Oh, non, ma chere. That's just because the mannequin is plastic. Against the human body it is completely silent and undetectable," the woman explained.

"I think that could be quite promising, don't you?" Alessandro asked, his breath hot against Bree's ear, and her folds grew slick in agreement.

He fingered the wireless remote control in his pocket just the…tiniest…little…bit.

Brianna whirled around and her beautiful blue eyes flashed with irritation, even as the heat in her cheeks flared. "Stop that." She shoved at his chest but the corner or her mouth lifted in a way that he knew she wasn't truly cross with him.

"Just checking to see if it works," Alessandro smiled as they exited their suite at the Ritz with its inviting apricot walls.

"It works," Brianna assured him, a little breathless.

They sat in the limo on the way to the accursed business dinner Bernardo suggested they attend with a few of his associates. Alessandro kept one hand on her knee, inching it up ever so slightly every few seconds as he pressed the button on the remote and watched Brianna bite her lower lip and her eyes flutter.

"I don't think this was such a good idea," she sighed, her hips moving restlessly.

Alessandro and his cock disagreed vehemently. He leaned over and inhaled the soft scent of her perfume, and got aroused as he whispered in her ear. "I can never get over how damned beautiful you are, and that you're mine. You belong to me."

He watched her shoulders pull back a little in indignation at the proprietary statement and her blue eyes met his with the intent to protest but she shuddered then and the words seemed to catch in her throat. She dug her nails into the soft white leather of the seat and Alessandro smiled at the mental image of her riding his cock just a few weeks ago in her new car. He wanted to watch her come now, and again and again as the night wore on and he wanted to be the only one who knew it. He wanted to be the only one who knew she had the vibrator buried deep inside her pussy, straps, black as midnight around her creamy white thighs and he was the one who controlled if she came or not. With just a flick of his fingers, more or less and she was making a soft whimpering sound.

It had been her idea to wear it tonight. She thought it would be sexy as hell, but now he could see the vulnerability of her situation was beginning to get to her.

Alessandro kept his hand on her under the table, his fingers venturing to the black straps every once in a while and stroking them, pulling ever so gently so that Brianna's eyes would flutter shut and he could feel her thigh muscles tense, just as they did when he pumped deep and hard into her just last night. Those beautiful smooth thighs had cradled him, damp as they took each other again and again.

His fingers slid along her skin, winking at her as he felt the dampness of her arousal.

"Would you like to dance, darling?"

Brianna stared at him, wide-eyed, her mouth wet and red though she had since worked through her lipstick by the passion-incurred gnawing by her teeth. She leaned in to him. "I don't think I can…I'm so…close, Alessandro," she whispered, taking a deep breath.

"I'll hold you," he assured her, wanting to feel her come against him, feel the beautiful shuddering of her body. "They won't be able to tell."

Her eyes were glazed with desire as they swayed to the music. Alessandro had one hand around her, pressing her tight against him, effectively hiding his erection from other eyes as well as her reaction. His other hand was in his pocket, pressing the button on the control again…again…again.

"Oh God…" Brianna whispered. Her nails dug into his suit jacket and he felt the heaving of her breasts against his chest as she breathed heavily. "Don't stop…Oh Alessandro…I'm gonna come…"

"More?" Alessandro growled in her ear.

"Oh yes…" Brianna pleaded, her face buried in his chest.

He pressed the button again, stroked it lovingly, imagining it was her clitoris as pressed the speed higher…higher, feeling each shudder of Brianna's impending release against him.

"Fuck…" she moaned, desperate and low. Her hips were restrained in her movements, an innocent contrast to the greedy upward driving motions of last night as she met each of his downward thrusts, wanting more, begging for more.

"Are you going to come, darling?" Alessandro asked, kissing the side of her face.

"So close. More…I want more…" she whispered.

"You'll have whatever your greedy heart desires," Alessandro promised, pressing the button in his pocket again.

Brianna swallowed a whimper and Alessandro felt her go rigid against him.

"Come, my beautiful wife," Alessandro whispered in her ear as his arm tightened around her, feeling her body shake and keeping her upright. He pressed the button still more and Alessandro saw her teeth grab the edge of his jacket's lapel and her hips came up against the swollen bulge in his pants. "I need your mouth. Right now. Right fucking now." He pulled her off the dance floor. Alessandro's fingers were tight around her wrist as Brianna bid the business men goodbye and they rushed outside to the limo.

Giving the driver directions back to the hotel, the closed the black divider and Alessandro undid his pants, keeping a hold on the remote in his pocket.

Brianna's mouth closed over him and a burst of warm tight heat made Alessandro's vision cloud.

"Oh yes…Just like…fuck…like that. Suck me…suck me…" He pumped his hips against her face, his fingers shaking against the remote control.

"Give me your hand," Brianna said before sucking him into her mouth again.

Alessandro offered her his hand and Brianna spread her thighs, pulling him under her dress. "Feel that?" she asked, licking the head of his cock.

Her thighs were wet, hot, but not as hot as her pussy. His fingers pushed against the steaming, damp skin of her clitoris, feeling the vibrator in her pussy. "Make me come again," Brianna urged, her eyes smiling up at him with delicious challenge.

With one hand on her clitoris, and the other hand on the remote, Alessandro brought her up slowly, stroking, pressing, watching her eyes glaze over and her breath hitch desperately as she sucked him. Her tongue and her lips, along with her fingers moved together in delicious synchronization until Alessandro was throwing his head back and driving up deep into her mouth and trying not to cry out his release.

And then he devoted himself to making her come once more

before they reached the hotel.

CHAPTER EIGHTEEN

They hadn't made it to the bed. Bree woke to the feel of her husband's warm skin beneath her cheek. She was sprawled over him and the white bedspread with pale silver roses covered them both. She imagined one of them must have pulled it off the bed last night but she couldn't recall if it had been her or Alessandro. She moved her legs and felt his limbs entwined with hers. Her thigh came up against the warm, thick heat of his cock and she heard him groan at the contact as his body came to life beneath hers. His fingers trailed upwards along her bare back and Bree nuzzled his chest before lifting her head and giving him a sleep smile. "Good morning."

"Quite," he agreed with a lazy grin. His fingers moved up into her hair and he pulled her closer to his mouth, kissing her slowly.

She moaned a little as her muscles protested the night on the carpeted floor, which even as lush as the pale yellow carpet was, was still the floor. But she was still too ridiculously happy to move and rubbed against him, loving the feel of his coarse hair tickling her smooth skin. Bree moved over him; meeting his tongue with her own. His morning stubble scraped her skin. God she loved the contrast of their bodies. He was hard and rough where she was soft and smooth. She slid her lips over to his cheek, tickling the stubble with her tongue before sliding her mouth down to his neck. She could still smell the faint hint of his cologne along with the smell of their sex that still clung to his skin like animalistic musk.

She dropped kisses along the broad expanse of his chest flicking at his nipples with her tongue, smiling when she heard his breath hitch. His fingers drew lazy patterns in her scalp as she slid further down his body, making him groan as her mouth moved along the skin of his stomach, following the line of fine dark hair until it grew coarser. The warm heat of his cock was just an inch away, and Bree made to take him in her hand.

Only to be halted in her intention by a knock on the door.

"Bloody hell!" Alessandro groaned in disappointment.

"That's probably breakfast," Bree said rolling off of him.

Alessandro stood, naked and semi aroused and she laid back and enjoyed the visual image before he slipped on his boxers and took his wallet out of his pants.

Bree arched, trying to stretch out her muscles and Alessandro gave her a dirty look as if she was displaying herself to him on purpose. Well, maybe she was a little.

Even though he blocked her from the hotel attendant's gaze with his body in the doorway, Bree was sure to cover herself with the blanket. Alessandro turned around, pulling in the tray with him and his eyes flared hungrily as he looked down at her.

"You look like a beautiful debauched angel," he said, his voice rough with desire.

"And you're what, the demon that's corrupted me?" Bree asked raising an eyebrow and letting the blanket fall down to her waist, baring her to him.

"It's my life's work, you know?" Alessandro grinned, going down on to his knees and leaning over her.

Bree placed a hand on his chest, halting him. "Is that coffee, I smell?" she asked. "The debauched angel is kind of hungry." She bit her lip and smiled up at his frustrated face.

Alessandro took a piece of croissant and held it up to her lips. "Now you tell me if that cardboard they make in America can even compare to this."

Bree opened her mouth as he slipped his finger and the pastry inside. She moaned with pleasure as the buttery flakiness all but melted on her tongue. "Oh my God. That is…orgasmic."

They remained on the carpet, both now covered in nothing but the blanket as the snow fell outside their open window. Bree looked over at a small ceramic jar with what looked like a porcelain spoon in it.

"What's in there?" Bree asked picking it up. On closer inspection she saw it was honey, with the little tool to drizzle it. "Hmmm."

"Let me pour you some tea." Alessandro lifted the teapot and Bree stilled his hand.

"Or maybe not," she said with a knowing smile. "I do believe I'm still hungry."

Alessandro's eyes glinted with aroused understanding. "Are you now? Maybe I should see if they have something else on the menu."

"Not necessary," Bree said, picking up the tool and playing with the honey. She lifted it to Alessandro's lips and ran the round grooved head across them. "I know exactly what I want." She placed a hand on his broad shoulder and guided him down to the carpet.

"Do you?" Alessandro asked, staring up at her.

"Mmhmm. I want something sweet." She leaned down and kissed him, licking at the honey on his lips before drizzling more in a figure eight on his chest. Bree trailed her tongue down along the sticky substance, nipping lightly at the skin. "Something I can really sink my teeth into." She spread some honey over his nipple before scraping it with her teeth, making Alessandro hiss beneath her. She trailed the honey down across his stomach, watching the muscles flex in anticipation of her mouth. "Something that will fill me up."

His cock was fully aroused now, jutting up and begging for her attention. Bree met his gaze and drizzled the honey over his cock, watching it slide over the head down the long thick member to its base. "Something hard and delicious."

"That very desperately wants you back, believe me," Alessandro joked, his voice trembling.

"Hmm…you think you can satisfy my craving?" Bree asked, licking at the sweet head of his cock.

"You tell me," he groaned as she took all of him into her mouth.

She licked him completely clean.

And then licked him completely clean again.

"Now. I believe it's your wifely duty to feed your husband." Alessandro breathlessly kissed her as he took the small honey jar and eased Bree onto her back.

A few minutes later, Alessandro suggested they take advantage of the Jacuzzi to clean off.

Bree melted against him as the warm water bubbled all around them. "I love you," she sighed, catching his earlobe with her teeth.

Alessandro groaned, his hands moving to her behind. "Say that again, darling." His lips ran along her jaw and he lifted his hand to catch a stray lock of her hair that had come loose from the clip in her hair. He wrapped it around his finger and Bree met his gaze, dropping a kiss on the tip of his nose.

"I love you…so much I feel dizzy with it." God, what she wouldn't give for them to stay like this forever, for them to gather their boys and just live here in this sweet bubble always.

"I'm drunk on you, darling. From the very first moment I clapped eyes on you, I've been utterly intoxicated."

"Mmmm, ditto," she said, going up on her knees so she could reach down between them and take his cock in her hand. "Ready to go again?" she asked, running the tip of her tongue along the seam of his lips.

Alessandro growled and caught her mouth in a deep, passionate kiss that told her all she needed to know.

She shivered as she rubbed her folds with the head of his cock gently. She met his eyes, watching them flare hungrily as she took every hot inch of him into her body. Bree exhaled at the blissful joining.

"Oh yes…" Alessandro moaned into her mouth before moving his hands back down to her ass to guide her.

Bree took his arms and pulled them back between them. She smiled at him and placed his hands over her breasts. "I'm running the show this time, Mr. Brit."

"Oh really?" Alessandro asked, thrusting upwards, making her gasp.

Bree smacked his shoulder. "Be nice."

"What if I don't want to be nice?" Alessandro asked, kneading her breasts. He pinched her nipples and Bree whimpered. "What if I want to be very, very naughty?"

She rolled her hips tauntingly, biting her lip at the delicious friction of his cock against her walls. "Haven't you heard that saying, nice guys finish last? I mean, you wouldn't want to finish first, would you?"

Alessandro laughed. "Very good point, darling." He nipped at her shoulder. "Very well. I await your command, milady."

"Oooh, milady. I like that," Bree said, moaning at the familiar tightening in her belly. "Your lady wants you to take her breast in your mouth and suck her."

Alessandro smiled and took a nipple into his mouth, sucking ever so gently. He looked up at her. "Like that, darling?"

Bree shivered rocking her hips faster, her mind blurring with the promise of the oncoming explosion. "More. Harder."

Alessandro sucked first on one nipple then the other with more pressure, scraping them lightly with his teeth.

"Oh yes…like that," Bree breathed, cradling his head, driving her fingers through his damp hair. Her blood was racing through her veins, her entire soul quickening as she hovered right there on the edge. "Touch me. Take your hand and stroke me…now…now…"

"Do you want me to stroke your pussy, milady?" Alessandro teased, flicking her nipple with his tongue between his teeth.

"Yes. Do it…"

"I'm sorry, but I want to make sure. I think I need to hear milady utter the words," Alessandro taunted dotting kisses along her collarbone.

Bree moved her hips greedily, squeezing his cock inside of her. She gazed down at him and breathed quick and hot against his face as her orgasm teased the edges of her nerve endings. "Take your fingers and stroke my pussy. Now."

"Yes, milady." Alessandro smiled at her. He pressed his fingers against her clitoris and rubbed slowly.

Bree whimpered, beginning to tremble. "Harder…oh, don't stop…Good…so good." She bit into his shoulder as her hips rose and fell, impaling herself over and over on his thick shaft as he applied more pressure against her clitoris and rubbed faster.

"Is milady going to come now?" he asked, taking her scream into his mouth as Bree exploded over him.

Bree arched against him as she went over the edge, bucking over him as her orgasm stole her breath.

She fell against him, burying her face in his damp neck. Bree rolled her hips and whimpered at the sharp burst of sensation. He was still hard as steel inside of her.

"If I may make a suggestion, darling?" Alessandro purred in her ear.

"Oh anything," Bree breathed lazily. She floated in the dreamy haze of pleasure, pliable and willing to go wherever he led now. She rubbed her cheek against his damp stubble and her pussy clenched hungrily. Oh she'd have that stubble rubbing against her thighs soon, she promised herself. In fact, she didn't think she'd want him to shave until they got back home.

"I would very much like to fuck milady's ass while the jets shoot against her beautiful pussy."

His words made a fresh burst of nerves throb through her walls and Bree gasped with the force of a tiny after shock. "Oh God, yes."

Turning around, Bree eased back against Alessandro's chest and eased herself down over his cock again, this time into her ass. He felt harder and even bigger now. The feel of the jets against her folds was too much and Bree eased back. "Not yet," she whimpered.

He covered her pussy with his hand, careful not to stroke her still too sensitive skin. "Tell me when," he breathed into her ear. With his free hand, he cupped one of her breasts, sending little pops of sensation as he tweaked her nipples gently. He pumped his hips upwards slowly.

Bree moaned, loving the feeling of his ravaging her gently, yet powerfully, feeling the delicious throb of his cock inside of her, of his breath against her neck and her name falling off his lips. The climb began again, deep in her abdomen with an insistent sweet pang and her clitoris was begging for attention yet again. She could feel him swell inside of her with his own impending release.

"Oh…okay…" she moaned bucking against him, pleading.

"Now?" he asked, his voice rough with restraint.

"Yes…yes…" Bree pleaded, her voice breaking.

He eased his hand away slowly and Bree was grateful because it drew out the delicious feeling without swamping her with too much too soon. The jet in front of her tickled its way up as Alessandro eased his fingers away and then it was pounding against her pussy and Bree threw her head back as her orgasm raced through her blood with punishing quickness. Her ass clenched

Alessandro's cock with tight convulsions as her body throbbed with her orgasm. Alessandro pushed up, up, getting deeper inside of her, pumping hard as the jets shot against her pussy. Part of her wanted to back away from the almost painful pressure but the darker part of herself kept her still, directly in its path, bearing against it eagerly, going mindless with sharp pleasure as Alessandro pumped his cock into her faster, faster. He came, deep and thick, stretching her beautifully. She came yet again, an almost painful explosion that had her screaming his name as her body seized and bucked over him.

She fell back against him, feeling his harsh breathing against her as his orgasm drained him as well.

"Alright…Now it's my turn, darling," he panted in her ear, gripping her hair with delicious intent. "We're going to spend the rest of the day in bed…and you're going to follow my every command."

"And in Life's noisiest hour,
There whispers still the ceaseless Love of Thee,
The heart's Self-solace and soliloquy.
You mould my hopes, you fashion me within;
And to the leading Love-throb in the Heart Thro' all my Being, thro' my pulse's beat;
You lie in all my many Thoughts, like Light,
Like the fair light of Dawn, or summer Eve
On rippling Stream, or cloud-reflecting Lake.
And looking to the Heaven, that bends above you,
How oft! I bless the Lot that made me love you,"

Alessandro's voice moved through her hair and Bree sighed against his chest watching him flip the page in front of her.

"That one was really pretty," she whispered as he kissed her temple. She turned around and went up on her knees to kiss him. "Thank you." She snuggled against him, playing with the dark hair on his chest. "I remember when Colin would go out of town for some reason or another, he used to write Carrie these long rambling romantic letters and I remember being so jealous, wishing that I had someone to do that for me."

"Ah, then I shall make a note of that the next time I have to leave on business. I think I can spin some pretty words when I need to. Let's see: There once was a girl named Brianna, hmm…what rhymes with Brianna?" he asked.

Bree laughed and smacked his chest.

"No, no. I got it," he said smiling. "There once was a girl named Brianna, who's body so well filled my hands-a—"

"That doesn't rhyme!" Bree objected, giggling as Alessandro laid her back on the bed and hovered over her.

"Excuse me, I'm having a moment of literary genius here," he protested. "Now where was I?"

"You were butchering the English language," Bree said.

"Ah," Alessandro smacked her thigh. "Behave. Oh yes. There once was a girl named Brianna, whose body so well filled my hands-a. Her eyes were so pretty and she squealed when I'd bite her ti—"

"Alessandro! Stop!" She curled up as she dissolved in giggles.

Alessandro pulled her hands and up over her head. "There once was a girl named Brianna…Wait, how did it go again?" he asked.

"No, I beg you. No more. Leave it to the professionals."

"There once was a girl named Brianna—"

"Oh lord," She rolled her eyes.

"Whose body so well filled my hands-a. Her eyes were so pretty and she'd squeal when I'd bite her titties and every time I looked at her my cock did hard stands-a." He grinned at her, his dark hair falling over his eyes.

Bree stared up at him and tried to fight it but the laughter came sputtering out until she couldn't breathe.

"Oh, so I'm not appreciated in my own time, eh?" Alessandro lamented, which only made Bree laugh harder.

When she could control herself, she wiped her eyes and shook her head. "I meant to say that I liked this better because I don't have to sit at home reading your letters. I'm here with you."

"Well, yes. It'd be rather pathetic of me to be on my honeymoon alone, wouldn't it?" Alessandro cracked.

Bree smacked his arm. "Can you be serious?"

"Nope sorry. The blood flow hasn't spent too much time near my brain today so I think it's suffering for it." Alessandro lowered his head and nibbled on her neck making Bree sigh. "Mmm. I'm hungry. You hungry?" He slid off the bed and went to the dinner tray.

Bree sat up but he shook his head. "No, stay there. Lie back." He grabbed the fruit off the desert tray and climbed back onto the bed.

"What do you think you're doing?" She asked as he placed a row of grapes down her chest to her stomach.

"Eating," Alessandro explained, kissing his way down to her mound, grabbing the grapes with his tongue and feasting his way lower and lower.

Bree arched and offered herself up to him even more. He then looked up at her from between her legs and grinned devilishly.

"Oh, I have an idea…" he dug through one of the bags on the carpet and lifted the string of jade beads from the sex shop.

Bree shivered in anticipation and bit her lip.

He eased the beads in to her slowly, catching her small gasps in his mouth. "Good?" he asked, smiling smugly.

"Oh yes," Bree sighed, trembling.

Alessandro moved down between her legs and flicked her clitoris lightly with his tongue. He grabbed an orange segment and squeezed it against her pussy.

"Oh fuck!" Bree cried out, the small burst of pressure trickling down her folds.

He licked up the tart juices and Bree gripped his hair, rolling her hips against him.

"Oh so good…" She moaned.

He jerked the beads gently inside of her, tugging and releasing so they rubbed against her walls with deliciously sweet friction. He caught her clitoris between his teeth and sucked, sending her higher and higher towards what promised to be a very sharp orgasm. "Like that?"

"Oh yes, please…don't stop…" Bree begged. Her chest rising and falling with her quick panting breaths.

"You almost there, darling? You going to come for me, love?" Alessandro asked nuzzling her thighs with his cheeks.

"Ohhhhh! Oh don't stop…fuck…more…more…"

He sucked her clitoris harder, stopping only to rub a piece of mango along her folds.

Bree dug her head into the mattress and whimpered his name over and over as her nerves raced higher and higher. "Now…oh

God…"

And then he was pulling on the beads, the hard jade rubbing against her wet folds, the contrast making her body bow and then buck with a stunning, mindless orgasm. "Oh yes!" she cried out, falling back against the mattress. "Oh fuck me…" she moaned, staring up at the ceiling. Her nerves popped beneath her skin as he pulled at the last of the beads. "We're definitely…doing that…again," she sighed.

Alessandro laughed smugly. "Now, my darling, you will get on your knees and turn around because I need to get inside of you again."

"Mmmm," Bree moaned in agreement sitting up and turning away from him.

"Grab the bars so I can fuck your beautiful body good and hard," he groaned in her ear, behind her.

Bree's juices trickled down in anticipation, despite still trembling from her orgasm. "God Alessandro…you make me so…" she sighed, looking for the right word.

"Yes, darling?" Alessandro asked, rubbing her stomach with the palm of his hand as he positioned himself over her.

Bree arched against the delicious heat of his body. "Insatiable. I…never stop wanting you…wanting this…"

"This?" he asked, rubbing her folds with the head of his cock.

"Oh yes…" Bree moaned as he inched into her slowly so that she could feel every hot, hard inch of him. "Oh God yes…"

He pulled back just as slowly, making her whimper and then cry out blissfully when he slammed into her.

Her fingers tightened around the bars and she pushed back against him.

Alessandro groaned and she felt his head drop against the nape of her neck. "Fuckin' hell. You beautiful woman." He gripped her hips and thrust in quick deep bursts. He groaned her name as he rammed into her again and again, making her sensitive folds clutch him greedily. "Love you…Christ, I love you so much."

Bree moved with him, sliding beneath his warm, damp chest as they worked together towards an orgasm that promised to explode through her with the force of a freight train.

And when Alessandro's fingers moved down between her thighs, the lightest flicker of his finger was all it took.

Bree arched and her pussy tightened around his cock, feeling him swell and surge into her with his own release.

They fell against the bed together and for a minute Bree revelled in the feel of his strong body covering her. Then he moved off of her and pulled her onto his chest so that she could feel the racing beat of his heart against her face.

She felt him kiss the top of her head and fell asleep with his fingers stroking the damp skin of her back.

CHAPTER NINETEEN

"Dardano, I did not sign up for a honeymoon in Paris just to spend my time trimming hedges," Bree insisted as one vine nearly smacked her in the face once she clipped it after a stubborn struggle. Her back was beginning to get sore and she was starting to sweat. Sweat! In the middle of January! Not that her body knew it. Even buried inside one of the worker's thick coats and wearing working gloves over her pretty black leather ones, she was damn cold!

"I already told you, Brianna, then go inside," Alessandro pointed out motioning his head towards the estate.

Though the mansion was large and considerably warmer, it was also bustling with staff, aka: strangers.

"No thank you," Bree tossed back throwing the dead vines into what she had first mistakenly called the brochette, which made the field hand next to her, Gaston, dissolve into loud burly laughter.

"Darling, a brochette is the equivalent of a shish kabob," Alessandro explained, biting his lip not to laugh. "You mean brouette,"

"Bare-oo-ett," Bree repeated phonetically. She spent most of her time chasing the closest 'brouette' down because it was a large round cylinder, almost a tube-like barbecue used to burn the dead vines. It was bliss to be next to it. Every few minutes Alessandro appeared next to her and they warmed their hands together and he explained some of the workings and history of the land to her.

They had arrived that morning and Bree thought they were just going to spend the day traipsing around the mansion drinking wine and eating cheese. It was winter, she figured nobody would be working in the fields. Hadley quickly disabused her of that notion. The work never stopped on a vineyard. Ever.

Then she figured since Hadley was the acting boss for the Dardano vineyards, he merely sent the workers out and stayed in the mansion overseeing it all.

Wrong again. Kevin Hadley was the kind of boss who liked to get his hands dirty and he and Alessandro were in their element, working and joking and having a grand old time, making Bree wonder if Alessandro forgot he was supposed to dislike the man.

Apparently all was forgiven on that score. Alessandro saw Hadley as simply a man who Bernardo had used to try and get Alessandro moving on wooing Bree and since Hadley was obviously besotted with Meggie, he was no longer a threat.

Bree would have been insulted if she didn't love her husband so much. Not that she wanted him to be jealous of course. Certainly not, Bree thought dryly as she snapped another tough vine.

She silently admitted that she did kind of like digging around in the dirt. She liked the earthy smell. It reminded her of playing in the dirt with her brother back in Colorado. Her grandmother had nearly had a coronary when a five year old Bree and Brian had dug up her tulips and made an utter mess of themselves and the dearly departed garden.

She had spoken to Brian after breakfast. The boys were at her grandmother's and Brian was spending the morning with them. Her brother sounded a little off but when Bree pressed him about it, he told her he was just coming down with a cold.

Will wanted to know if they were bored yet.

When Bree relayed that question to Alessandro, her husband had choked on his coffee and fell off the bed in a fit of laughter.

"Was' so funny?" Will asked apparently able to hear Alessandro through the phone.

"Nothing, sweetie. Daddy just saw something funny on T.V," Bree lied. "Are you and Gianni being good?"

"I always a good boy," Will assured her. "But Gianni went number one in Gappy Dardano's eye."

Then it was Bree's turn to choke on her laughter after that beat of amusement, Bree felt a twitch of unease that Will was now referring to Bernardo as his grandfather. Strictly speaking, she supposed he was, by marriage anyway but that didn't make the idea sit any better with her. She was glad for the distraction of working in the vineyard, but was even more glad when Hadley suggested they leave the rest to the workers and go inside for lunch.

While the servants got their meal ready, Hadley served them warm spiced wine that made Bree shiver in utter bliss as it warmed her from the inside out.

"Pace yourself, darling," Alessandro warned in amusement as he watched her across the table.

"Mmmm, bite me, darling," Bree said with a smile, taking another long gulp.

"Here, have some cheese," Hadley said lifting the tray to her.

Bree took a wedge of cheese off the tray. The white cheese was creamy and tangy and almost melted on her tongue. She cradled the mug between her hands and took another gulp. "This wine is delicious," Bree said, pausing to hiccup. "Is it Dardano wine?"

"One of our most recent batches. Right before the first frost. Not our best," Hadley said. "I'll take you down to the cellars after lunch and you can try our best bottles. Over eighty years old."

"Well, I think this one's yummy," Bree insisted, the warmth spreading all through her body and making her feel a little languid.

"That's the difference between a professional and a novice," Alessandro said winking at her.

"Right. That and ego," Bree said throwing a piece of cheese at Alessandro's head.

Lunch was a delicious chicken and pasta dish followed by fruit in a creamy wine sauce.

The cellars were huge with hundreds of bottles of, according to Hadley, varying quality, lining the walls.

Bree couldn't really tell the difference between the different kinds of wine but she figured that may have been because she was admittedly a little woozy by now.

"You're supposed to be spitting it out after you taste it," Alessandro said after she tripped against him.

"Ew," Bree insisted. "That's gross."

He shook his head and laughed as he helped her back upstairs.

"Why don't you two spend the night here?" Kevin asked after dinner as Bree stuck her head out the window in the living room, trying to clear it a little.

Meggie was doing business in Italy and would be stopping to

spend a few weeks with Kevin on her way back to New York. The two of them would return to the states together.

Bree nodded eagerly, anxious to see her friend again. "Oooh. I like that idea. Yeah. Let's stay, Alessandro and then in the morning, we can have wine with our toast! Oh hey, that's funny, huh. Wine, toast, get it?" Bree giggled. *Oh wow. Her head was feeling really, really fuzzy.*

"Okay, let's go to bed," Alessandro said rising from the couch after he and Kevin finished discussing the plans for the vineyard in the coming year as well as the progress it had made thus far.

Bree gasped. "Alessandro! We can't have sex in someone else's house!"

Alessandro blushed and placed a hand on her back, leading her towards the stairs after wishing Hadley a good night. "It's my house, darling," he reminded her.

"Oh well, that's okay then, but you can't be loud though cause that would still be rude," Bree said, reaching down and squeezing Alessandro's ass. Gosh, her hubby had a really nice tight ass.

"Here we are," he said, leading her into one of the mansion's many bedrooms.

"Alessandro, I hass…have…a little confestion to make," Bree said leaning her head on his shoulder.

"You do?" he asked placing her on the bed and bending down to remove her shoes. Bree lay back and stared up at the spinning ceiling.

"Mmhm. I think…I'm ina...Little drunk bit."

"Really?" Alessandro asked with feigned surprise.

"Really," she assured him. She suddenly popped up in bed as something occurred to her. "Oh my gosh, Alessandro. Guess what?"

He jerked back in surprise. "Yes, darling?"

"I think I know why," she pressed a finger to her lips in a shushing motion.

"Pray tell, why?" he asked, laughing.

Bree threw her arms around Alessandro, toppling them both onto the carpet. "You have to warn your customeners…customers. The wine might make them a little tipsy. Oh my God. We should have sex now, don't you think?"

She curled up against him and sighed. Her husband made a really good pillow.

She fell on top of him and smiled as she found herself pressed against her favourite spot. She wriggled her hips a little and giggled when she heard him groan. "Bonjour, monsieur," Bree smiled, his arousal making itself more prominent.

He smacked her behind. "Behave." Alessandro pulled her off his lap and set her back on the mattress.

"But I don't want to behave."

"Darling, you're drunk."

"And horny. Like, a lot. Wanna do something about it?" Bree said, reaching down and rubbing him over his pants.

He took her hand and moved it off of him. "I will not take advantage of you in this state, love."

"'Take advantage'? What are you, a girl? It's only taking advantage if I don't want to and…mmmm. I so very much do," Bree sighed climbing back on top of him. She lowered her mouth to meet his and kissed him, sighing at the delicious feeling of him pressed hard between her legs and the yummy taste of him.

"Brianna…" Alessandro warned, sliding his fingers into her hair.

She rocked her hips and nibbled on his lips, trying to distract him. "God you're delicious, Alessandro. Has anyone ever told you that?" She ran her tongue down along the thick column of his neck, inhaling the strong manly scent. "You're delicious and hot and hard and I love how you feel inside of me."

"I've guessed that, darling, by the scratches you leave down my back," he said with a small laugh.

She slapped his chest. "Don't be vulgar."

Alessandro laughed. "Oh, I beg your pardon. Really, Brianna. We should get some sleep."

She bit his nipple lightly through his shirt as she made her way down. Stubborn man. "No we should get some orgasms." She grinned up at him and played with the waistband of his pants.

"What happened to we shouldn't have sex in someone else's house?"

She pressed her finger to her lips. "You'll just have to be very, very quiet. Shhh."

"I hate to remind you, darling but I'm not the screamer of the two of us, remember?" Alessandro asked hissing as her hand inched under his boxers.

"Oh well then I'm going to have to change that, won't I?" Bree asked lowering her head.

But her stomach seemed to have other ideas. She went still as it fluttered nervously.

"What is it?" Alessandro asked.

Bree took a deep breath and shook her head. "Nothing. Really." She groaned as her stomach rumbled uneasily. *Oh man…*

"Are you feeling all right?" Alessandro asked cautiously.

"Um…no," Bree replied and moved quickly off the bed, her hand clamped over her mouth. She barely made it to the bathroom, fearing for a blank moment because she had forgotten that she wasn't back home. But she managed to make it to the toilet bowl just in the nick of time.

"I hate to say I told you so but…well…you're sort of doing that for me," Alessandro said, leaning against the doorway with his arms crossed over his chest.

Bree groaned. "You're mean."

"So, no orgasms then?" Alessandro joked and she could hear the amusement in his voice.

She tried to think of a snappy retort, but her stomach lurched again and she decided to save that for later.

"Mmmmm coffeeeeee," Bree sighed after the warm liquid slid down her throat.

"Good morning, darling," Alessandro said brightly, sending needles of pain shooting through her head. He dropped a kiss on her throbbing head and sat across from her at the table. "Where's Hadley?"

"Not so loud. Please," Bree cringed, rubbing her temples.

He slammed the coffee pot down on the table with more force than she thought was necessary.

She glared at him and he gave her wide smile.

"Sorry, my love. Couldn't resist the opportunity for a little revenge, you know?"

Bree whimpered, holding her head up with the heel of her hand against her forehead. "If I had the energy, I'd take that croissant there and shove it so far up your ass the pointy end would come out your nose."

Alessandro chuckled and took a sip of his coffee, turning to the window as they heard a car coming up the driveway.

Bree followed him to the door as they watched the iron gates swing open once Kevin punched in the security code and Meggie give her a little wave through the windshield.

After parking the car, Hadley came around and opened the door for Meggie.

He held her close as they walked back to the house. Meggie laid her head on Kevin's shoulder as they walked together.

Bree rushed out to greet her friend. "I've missed you so much!"

"I need to make a couple of calls but I think I can get the priest here this evening," Kevin announced, kissing Meggie briefly before walking on ahead of them to Alessandro in the doorway.

"Priest?" Alessandro asked.

"Dardano, how'd you like to be my best man?" Kevin asked.

Bree stared at Meggie, who was beaming. Her friend lifted her hand to show off a square cut yellow diamond on her left hand.

"I promise, no purple taffeta."

The sun was setting, showering the inside of Kevin Hadley's study in gold and violet as the priest read from his bible.

Bree felt Alessandro's eyes on her as she listened to the familiar words.

Meggie's wedding wasn't any more conventional than Bree's had been but her friend didn't seem to mind at all as she looked up at Kevin with tears in her eyes. It was just her and Kevin, Bree and Alessandro, and the priest.

Bree was sure it may as well have just been Meggie and Kevin there for they only had eyes for each other. She blinked the moisture from her eyes as she listened to the priest tell Kevin that he could now kiss his bride. Bree felt Alessandro's eyes on her and when she lifted her gaze her eyes warmed at the love she saw in them.

I love you.

I love you too.

Later, after a quiet dinner, Bree sat on the edge of the bed, running her toes through the carpet as Alessandro undid his tie.

"How's your head?" he asked.

"Better," she assured him. The sharp throbbing had lessened to a slight tickle of pain on the fringes of her mind.

"You know what this wedding was missing?" Alessandro asked, leaning over the night table and switching on the radio in the digital clock. He changed the channels until he seemed to find a song he liked. A simple piano melody Bree didn't recognize. He lowered his hand to her. "May I have this dance?"

Bree smiled up at him and slipped her hand in his. "Why certainly, Sir." She closed her eyes and just swayed to the soft music as he led her. After a minute, she looked up at him and pressed her mouth to his jaw, slowly working her way upwards to his lips.

Her fingers went down to the buckle of his belt.

She looked up at him as their mouths met again…and again…

"What ever happened to we shouldn't have sex in someone else's house?" Alessandro asked and Bree could feel him smiling against her skin as he pulled her towards the bed.

"I guess you'll just have to be quiet," Bree whispered as she lowered him onto the bed.

"He loves me, the way I always dreamed someone would. He really does," Meggie said and Bree smiled at the soft hint of awe in her friends' voice.

"He wouldn't be worth anything if he didn't," Bree insisted as they sat inside the house, watching Alessandro and Kevin as they worked outside.

"What about you and the dark prince?" Meggie asked with a snort of amusement.

Bree's smile wavered slightly.

"What?" Meggie pressed.

"Nothing. It's…really, nothing."

"Uh uh. Don't you start that. The man is so over the moon for you, a moron could see that. So what's the problem?" She tucked a lock of black hair behind her ear and leaned forward.

"There's no problem at all, here. That's the problem," Bree sighed, leaning her head against the couch and staring up at the white ceiling. "There's never a problem when it's just the two of us."

"Ah, but Daddy-In-Law Lecter gets in the way, huh?" Meggie remarked.

"God, Meggie. I'm afraid to push Alessandro too hard because…"

"You're afraid he'll choose his father over you?"

"I'm terrified of what Bernardo could turn him into so everything in me screams to get Alessandro the hell away from

Bernardo. But how do I do that without losing him myself?"

"You don't. You bide your time. Seriously, Bree. You can't push this yet."

"God, everyone keeps telling me that but I don't know if I can wait."

Bree and Alessandro left Meggie and Kevin to enjoy some time alone and went back to their hotel to enjoy the rest of their honeymoon. The newlyweds would be joining Bree and Alessandro for dinner on their last day in Paris and would travel with them back to New York.

Bree felt as if she and Alessandro lived in a perfect bubble for the next few days. They enjoyed the city, they made love, they made plans for the future and Bree wished she could believe in Alessandro's words and promises but in the back of her mind, Bernardo's influence resided, like a huge looming dark cloud.

"How would you like to make a detour to London before we go back home?" Alessandro asked pocketing his cell phone.

"London? Why?" Bree asked rubbing a towel through her wet hair.

"We could try and find out who is in that tombstone Sister Brannigan told you about." Alessandro took a seat at the foot of the bed.

"You think they'll just let us in there and tell us after Mr. 'Naples' went to all this trouble to keep it a secret?" Bree asked.

"Oh of course not. We'll probably have to resort to scheming and all manner of chicanery," Alessandro replied with a smile. "You up for it, darling?"

Bree giggled. "Always."

Plot 777 was just that. A plot. No tombstone and it was virtually undetectable unless you knew where to look. Which they didn't.

But as Bree waited out in the hall and Alessandro sat in front of the man behind the desk at the cemetery they had a plan to find out.

"I'm sorry, Sir but we can't just move a body to accommodate someone else."

"I already told you. My mother did not want my father buried next to that woman. I don't care what her family says. I don't have to tell you what will happen if your mistake is not corrected very soon, do I?" Alessandro said, sitting with his arms over his chest, the picture of menacing authority.

The bald man's black beady eyes widened in his head. "Oh no. No, Sir. Not at all."

"Thank you. Now I'd like to show you exactly where I would like my father to be buried." Alessandro stood up. "He was very much into astrology you know?"

"Oh no! Oh this is a disaster!" Bree exclaimed tearfully bursting into the room.

"Can I help you?" the man asked as he and Alessandro got to their feet.

"I just realized my poor husband has bluebells growing near his grave," Bree wailed. She pulled out a few tissues from the box of the desk.

"And?"

"He was allergic to bluebells!" Bree said.

The man shook his head. "Allergic?"

"Yes. He hated them. I can't believe of all the rotten luck. I mean why didn't you tell m…m...me. Th...th…that…they…g…g…grew…"

"But he's dead," the man reminded her.

"So?" Bree asked, blowing her nose. She looked up to see Alessandro behind the man, barely able to suppress his laughter.

"Excuse me? We were in the middle of something," Alessandro reminded the man.

"Oh yes, yes, of course. Please. Miss, have a seat, right here." He took the box of Kleenex and handed it to her. "I will be right back."

"You're just gonna leave me here?" Bree asked sniffling.

"I promise. I'll be back in a few minutes. I just need to clear some things up with this gentleman. Please, help yourself to some coffee over there." He pointed to the coffee pot next to his desk and turned towards Alessandro, following him out the door.

Bree waited until she was certain Alessandro and the man had left the building and rushed quickly to the computer. She scanned the files of the different plots until she came to the one she was looking for. It was listed under Sister Brannigan's name as she expected it would be. Bree quickly printed out the information, not wasting time to read it. There wasn't enough time. It listed the location of the plot and who was inside. She had to stifle her curiosity now and tuck the pages into the pocket of her coat.

"There's no name," Bree said as they walked around the cemetery. "Dammit. Someone really does not want us to know who is buried in this damn grave. All it says is that the body is a female and she was buried in 1951. Alessandro, do you think…" Bree stopped as an idea came to her. "What if this is Francesca? I mean, what if she didn't jump off that cliff after all, but ran away to London?"

"Why?" Alessandro asked.

"Don't know. Wait, this is it," she said halting Alessandro when she found the plot by following the image on the map.

"This is it?" Alessandro asked kneeling down and reading. "Wait, there are words on it but it's in some language…I can't… 'a leanbh a chroí'." He looked back at Bree in question.

"What the hell does that mean?" she asked.

"I was hoping you could tell me. It sounds Gaelic, doesn't it?"

"Mmm. Maybe, but I'd be the wrong person to ask. The most I learned of Gaelic was the bad words," Bree admitted with a snort. "Write that down and we can ask my grandpa."

Alessandro stood up and Bree felt a beat of unease realizing he was standing on some poor girl's grave. The other graves were huddled close around it, as if hiding its existence from prying eyes.

CHAPTER TWENTY

"Mommy!" Will shrieked, jumping into Bree's arms and nearly sending her toppling backwards onto the sidewalk in front of the O'Reiley pub.

Brian smiled at her, holding Gianni who was squealing in delight and reaching for Bree as well. "Welcome home. Come on in. We were about to have lunch."

"Yeah. You can come say hi to Becky." Will scrambled down off of Bree and grabbed Alessandro's hand, pulling him into the pub.

"Becky?" Bree asked.

Brian's smile wavered and he passed Gianni over to Bree before following Alessandro and Will into the pub.

"Come see my mommy, Becky!" Will said and Bree stopped in her tracks.

"Oh hell no!" she exclaimed staring at 'Becky'. Rebecca, the bane of Bree's existence.

The blonde woman smiled mockingly at Bree. "How ya doing?"

"What?" Bree asked but the question was directed at her brother and not the skank in front of her.

"So how was Paris?" Rebecca asked moving right past Bree to practically press her body against Alessandro.

"Seriously, what?" Bree demanded, glaring at Brian.

"Hey, Alessandro. Great to see you again."

"Stop talking. Stop talking now before I ram your botoxed head through this table!" Bree hissed lunging at her. Brian grabbed her quickly and held her back.

"Sorry. Bree's a little bit touchy about that whole Vegas thing I guess. But hey, looks like it all worked for the best, huh?" Rebecca winked at Alessandro

"Brian, can I talk to you in private?" Bree demanded.

"Look, I know what you're going to say but I can tell you right now that I know what—" Brian insisted.

"Now," Bree snapped grabbing his hand and pulling him towards the corner.

Rebecca took a seat across from Alessandro at the table.

Bree scowled and grabbed Alessandro's hand too, pulling him out of his seat and away from the pariah slut that was Rebecca.

Bree smacked her brother's chest. "You remember that movie Fatal Attraction, Glenn Close and the bunny rabbit?"

"Oh for God sake, Bree, stop. I'm a big boy, okay? I don't need—"

"Wait, so is your brother Michael Douglas or is he the bunny rabbit?" Alessandro joked.

Brian rolled his eyes. "I'm perfectly aware of what Rebecca was like but I can tell you that she's changed."

"Into what exactly? From a cobra to a scorpion?" Bree snapped. "No way, Brian. You cannot be seriously considering getting involved with her again. Did you not learn your lesson the first time?"

"How many times have you heard that said about yourself, huh?" Brian pointed out. "I mean none of us is perfect, Bree. If you deserve a second chance, why doesn't she?"

"Because you're my brother. You're family. When it comes to family all bets are off."

"Look, Brianna, I know that the two of you don't like each other and I admit perhaps I shouldn't have exploited—" Alessandro began but Bree pointed a finger at him.

"Don't you start! This woman broke my brother's heart and has made it her mission in life to destroy me- Oh God," Bree groaned watching Gianni giggling at Rebecca as the skank made funny faces at him. "I'm going to have to wash him in bleach."

"Bree! Darling, you're home!" Alison said coming out from behind the counter.

"Hi, Grandma. I've missed you." She hugged the older woman, glad for the distraction.

"How was your trip?" Alison asked. "Is it true that Meggie and Kevin Hadley got married?"

"Yep. Is Grandpa around? We were hoping to ask him about this phrase we found on a grave on London. It's in Gaelic, we think."

"Oh, no. He's actually at your da's. They're going to go fishing this weekend."

"Okay, I guess I can swing by there on our way home."

"So tell me about your trip. But first, have a seat. What would you like to eat?"

"I've been dreaming of your chowder since we landed," Alessandro said reaching for Alison's hand.

She smiled at him and patted his shoulder before taking everyone else's order.

"How are you, sweetheart?" John asked coming out from behind his desk in his study, his eyes sad.

Bree swallowed hard, feeling like she was five years old again. Her Grandpa Joe's arm tightened around her in a gesture of comfort.

"Good, daddy," Bree said. "I'm happy." For the most part, that was true.

"I'm glad, honey. How was Paris?"

"Wonderful," Bree told him. They stood awkwardly.

"And the boys?"

"You know, daddy, you wouldn't have to ask if you would just bother to visit with them once in a while," Bree finally burst in frustration. Inwardly she grimaced at her short temper.

She half expected her grandfather to scold her for flying off the handle but was surprised by his silence.

"Drop by the Dardano mansion for tea? I don't think so Bree," John scowled.

"Why not? Grandma's done it a few times now. She doesn't even have to see Bernardo at all. She comes by, Rafe or Vanessa the nanny answers the door and Will and Gianni spend time with her upstairs. She cares enough about me and them to make the effort." Bree bit her lip, hard. She would not cry like a little girl, begging for her father's affection.

John sighed, grabbing his jacket. "Sweetheart, wait here for a minute. We're not finished with this discussion."

"Daddy, I actually just came by to talk to grandpa. I know you guys have to leave soon."

"Please. Just sit down and wait for me."

Bree sighed but took his seat at the desk.

"Give yer pa a chance, Bree," Joe said. He reached over and stroked her head after she'd rested it on her arms.

"He doesn't want a chance, Grandpa. He wants to change my mind. Alessandro is my husband. He's the father of my children."

"He also belongs to a family we've been at war with for more years than you've been alive. Yer Grandma and I, we love you and we've seen enough of this vendetta to know that the way to end it is not to dig our heels in until you see reason. We love you, no matter what. That is the most important thing. Yer an O'Reiley, no matter what your last name is now. "

"Alessandro and as much as I hate to say it, Bernardo, have stuck to their end of the bargain. My family doesn't even try to mend fences—" Bree rubbed her temples. "You know what? No. I'm not going to get into this again. I wanted to see you because we found something in London that we were hoping you could translate for us. There were these two words written on a plot. They're Gaelic, I think." She handed him the paper where she had jotted down the words.

Joe glanced down and then looked up at her. "Hmm. Well, that first part is 'my child'. That second bit there is along the lines of 'my darling' or 'my treasure'," he explained to her. "Where did ye see this again?"

My child. Bree looked at the words after Joe handed the paper back to her. Child. What the hell? What did this have to do with Francesca and who was this man who was paying the now deceased Sister Brannigan to maintain it for him.

Francesca had committed suicide in Gallway.

Adriano was dead.

Hadn't she?

Wasn't he?

Bree's mind was racing and then it stopped on a distracted dime when she spotted her mother's name on a file folder, sticking out from under her father's other papers. "What is this?" she asked pulling it out from under the other sheets. Opening it, she realized that it was police notes about Alessandro's shooting and Angela was among the main suspects.

"What ye got there?" Joe asked, coming up beside her.

"Bree, leave that alone!" John snapped coming into the office.

"Daddy, what is this? Is mom a suspect in the shooting?"

"Sweetie, I mean it."

"Don't do that. Alessandro is my husband, I have a right to know. Did mom shoot... Oh God…She did, didn't she? Mom shot Alessandro!"

"Bree, listen to me. You can't go off and just—"

"What? Tell Alessandro?" Bree snapped. "Do you think I would?" She clamped a hand over her mouth. What was the alternative? Keep it secret? Look at him every day for the rest of their lives and have this secret hanging over their heads.

Pass the sugar, darling.

My mother shot you.

How would you like to go out for dinner tonight?

My mother tried to kill you.

Gianni got an A in school today.

My mother shot you.

I'd like us to have another child, sweetheart.

My mother tried to kill you.

Bree felt as if she would be sick. "What are you going to do about it?" she asked him.

"I don't know yet. We're going to see if we could explain to the judge that she was afraid for your life."

"Is she being charged?" Bree asked, the words spilled out of her mouth but she felt as if she was looking down on herself, somewhere outside of her body. Oh God. What do I do? What is the right thing to do?

"Not yet. I'm trying to do what I can to keep this secret. You let me handle this and I promise you, we'll come to the best possible solution for your mother," John assured her.

Bree closed her eyes shaking her head. "I can't believe this. What the hell was she thinking?"

"Aye, well, she was thinking that she was protecting her little girl, is what she was thinking. Wrong though she was. I don't think ye can blame her and I know fer certain that ye'd be doing the same, now wouldn't ye?" Joe asked her, placing a hand on her shoulder.

He was right. She would have done worse in the name of protecting her family.

But now, protecting one side of her family meant betraying the other.

"Are you all right, darling?" Alessandro asked as he carried Gianni in on his shoulders. Will was already pulling off his gloves and kicking off his boots as soon as he stepped over the threshold.

All three of them were equally wet and flushed from playing in the snow.

Bree had begged a headache and stayed inside, working her nails to the skin, wondering how the hell she was going to live with this info over her head.

"Mommy, can we haf mashmmellies in da hod chocowate? And can we haf cookies?" Will asked.

"First, pick up that drippy mess you're scattering over the pretentiously expensive carpet before Grandpa Lecter has a coronary," Bree scowled, biting her lip guiltily when Alessandro stared at her in disapproval over Will's head.

"I sowwy," Will said trailing back and picking up his boots and gloves. He gathered the mess in his arms and grinned up at Bree. "Cookies now?"

"After we get you in your jammies, 'kay?"

"Okay," then he took off running towards the stairs, colliding with Rafe. "Sowwy Ralphie. You haf to go make hod chocowate and cookies, 'kay?"

Then he continued on his journey up the stairs.

"Yes, I'll get right on that, Master William," Rafe said dryly.

"How's your head?" Alessandro said, rubbing the back of her neck as he set Gianni down on the couch.

"Better. So how did the snowman building go?" Bree asked, gathering Gianni in her arms after she sat next to him. This has to be the most important thing. Gianni and Will and the family that Alessandro and I are making.

But she's my mother.

Who treats you like a pariah because you married Alessandro.

"Well, let's just say that I seriously doubt architecture will be one Will's future career options," Alessandro cracked. "Come on you," he picked a damp Gianni up. "I'll get these two in their…what did you call them 'jammies'?" He leaned down and dropped a kiss on her head. "Be back in a bit with some aspirin. Love you."

Bree leaned against the back of the couch and tried to blink away her tears.

"Can you say 'jammies', Gianni? Ja-mmies?" she heard Alessandro ask as they made their way upstairs.

"Your cookies and hot chocolate, Mrs. Dardano?" Rafe announced bringing the tray to her a few minutes later.

"Thanks, Rafe," Bree replied, distracted.

The butler stared at her curiously. "Is there something wrong, Mrs. Dardano?"

"What? No. Why?" Bree asked, lost in her thoughts.

"You called me Rafe. You never call me Rafe. It's always Ralphie," he reminded her.

"Oh. Right. Just feeling a bit under the weather, I guess. Sorry, Ralphie. Better?"

Rafe rolled his eyes. "Quite."

Once Alessandro and the boys returned, they sat around next to the fireplace and had their chocolate milk and cookies. "Okay, your turn, Will. 'B' The minister's cat is a…?"

"Big cat!" Will exclaimed clapping, knowing he'd got it right.

"Yay!" Bree clapped proudly.

"Aaaay!" Gianni echoed.

"Okay…um…the minister's cat is a…botoxed, cat," She joked. "Named Rebecca."

Alessandro choked on his hot chocolate.

"Ooooh, dat's a big word, mommy."

"Mommy's such a joker, isn't she, Will?" Alessandro threw a marshmallow at Bree.

Gianni stuck out his hand to Bree. "Mufdits?"

She held the marshmallow up to his lips and stuck her tongue out so that he would do it too. His tiny tongue darted out and his face screwed up at the chalky consistency. He shook his head. "Nugm mufdits, mumumy."

Bree blinked and looked at Alessandro who looked equally as surprised. "Did he just say 'mommy'?"

"Gianni, can you say it again? Can you say mummy?" Alessandro asked smiling.

He stuck his hand up towards his father and the cookie Alessandro was eating. "Mufdits?"

"Where's mummy, Gianni? Where's mummy?" Alessandro asked.

Gianni turned towards Bree and smiled. "Mama."

Bree clamped a hand over her mouth, tears of happiness filling her eyes.

"That's right, Gianni. Good boy!" Alessandro said, bouncing him as he smiled proudly at Bree. "Can you say it again? Can you say 'mama' again?"

Gianni shook his head and turned his attention back to the cookie. "Mumnngh Meep Deet?"

Alessandro scraped out a chocolate chip and placed it in Gianni's mouth. It got a much better approval than the marshmallow.

"Can you say Will, Gianni?" Will asked. "Can you say my name, dis time?"

"Heeee," Gianni remarked, giggling at his brother.

"Will," Will pressed. "Here. I give you cookie."

"Not the whole thing," Bree insisted holding his arm back. "Just a teeny tiny bite."

"Say 'Will', Gianni," he urged giving him the tiny piece.

Gianni's little mouth worked around the piece of cookie and he looked over at Bree. "Mama."

Bree leaned over and kissed Gianni's forehead.

Later that night, Alessandro was curled up around her, neither of them yet asleep as they talked over this major milestone.

This has to come first. This family, Bree thought in the back of her mind. "Alessandro…I…" she opened her mouth, trying to force the words out.

"I'd like us to have another baby, Brianna," Alessandro murmured, cupping her stomach.

"A baby?" Bree asked, the words coming out choked. Ohnononono.

"Yes. Maybe we could try for a girl, this time. A precious little thing as beautiful as her mother?" he asked, nuzzling her ear as he reached up to cup her breast.

"You don't think it's a little soon?" Bree asked, her mind racing trying to find any reason she could that didn't involve 'my mother shot you'. "I mean, Gianni isn't even walking yet."

"Well, no. I just can't get over how happy I feel doing something so simple as playing with our children, Brianna. Watching them tonight, I thought my heart would burst with it. I mean seriously, this morning, Gianni laughed for about ten minutes straight because Will was standing on his head and I found myself laughing with him."

Bree, you are going to burn in a very special hell if you don't tell him the truth right fucking now!

She looked up at him and smiled, moving on to her knees and straddling him. "But honey…I was just getting used to having our sex life back. I was kind of hoping to enjoy that for at least another year or two."

"Mmmm, you make a good point," Alessandro groaned as Bree sat down against his erection and rocked her hips ever so slowly.

"I mean, you remember not having sex, right?" Bree grinned, brushing her lips across his.

"Yes…not an enjoyable time," he admitted, reaching up and cupping her bottom.

Hell, Bree. The very special hell.

Bree swatted the annoying voice away and set about distracting both her husband and herself.

"Run, Daddy! Run!" Will exclaimed giggling, running back into the house through the backdoor, following Alessandro who was trying to dodge a snowball wielding Brianna.

"Oh. Oh, is that they way we're gonna play? Fine, you little boarding school, silver spoon-fed playboy. Let's play," Bree said, trying to shake the snow from her clothes after Alessandro shoved a snowball down the back of her coat.

"What the hell is going on here?" Bernardo barked, storming into the room. "What is this damned racket?"

They all jumped, startled and turned in unison.

And Gianni burst out crying in Vanessa's arms from their position on the floor where they were playing with his blocks. "Maaaammmmaaaa!" He stretched his arms out to Bree.

Bree picked him up and glared at Bernardo.

Alessandro scowled at his father. "Was that really necessary?"

"Aww, come here, sweetie. It's okay," Bree said gathering Gianni into her arms. The baby's cries lessened as he leaned his head on Bree's chest and grabbed her necklace with his fist. "Don't worry."

"You scare da baby," Will scowled at Bernardo. "You don' haf to yell. We playing, nod being bad. You always so mean."

Bernardo's eyes hardened and Bree was about to give him what for if he was even thinking about scolding Will too but Alessandro diffused the situation.

"Darling, why don't you take the children upstairs?" Alessandro said.

She hesitated, wanting to hear if Alessandro was gonna dare to get into it with his father.

"Go on with your mummy, Will," Alessandro said, cupping Will's head.

The little boy pursed his lips and stared up skeptically at Bernardo. "You no yell at my daddy, 'kay?" he warned and Bree had to bite her lip not to laugh.

Alessandro met her eyes and she could see the flicker of amusement in his eyes as well.

"Come on, Will. Let's get you washed up and ready for dinner," Bree said. "Vanessa, you want to help me get Gianni's bath going?"

She led the way out of the living room and halted at the bottom the staircase. "Tell you what," she whispered handing Gianni back to Vanessa. "Why don't you go on ahead and I'll meet you up there in a few minutes?"

"You're gonna listen in, aren't ya?" Vanessa asked with a small smile.

"I'll see you upstairs," Bree pressed, trying not to smile back.

"Tell me what happens," she urged and then turned and climbed up the stairs

CHAPTER TWENTY-ONE

Bree moved quietly and pressed herself against the thick oak doors that separated the foyer from the living room.

"What on earth was that?" Alessandro asked.

"Why don't you tell me? I feel like my home has been turned into a zoo, for God sake. There's no order at all. The children run around, undisciplined, screaming. I walk in and Brianna is attacking you."

Alessandro chuckled. "For goodness sake, Father. The children were just having fun. Now I understand that may be a foreign concept for you but I'm not about to keep my children from enjoying themselves."

"It seems to me that is all they do. I don't see you teaching them the things they need to know to survive in the positions they will grow into. I don't see you teaching them to be worthy of the Dardano name," Bernardo accused.

Bree clenched her fists at her sides but held herself still, wanting to hear what Alessandro would say to his father.

"Now the other one, I could understand as he will be free to do whatever he wants when he becomes of age, but Gianni is our blood. The Dardano legacy runs through his veins."

"Alright, stop this. Right now. You need to understand something, Father. Will is as much my son as Gianni is, of my heart if not by blood and from this moment, I would appreciate it if you never again refer to him as anything less. Do you understand?"

Bree smiled, her heart warmed by Alessandro's defense of Will.

"Alessandro, you're completely losing sight of what we are trying to do here. Need I remind you that the fate of this family rests on your shoulders? Do not forget where your loyalty is supposed to lie—"

"Oh don't do that. Don't you question my loyalty. An O'Reiley woman is my wife, she is the mother of my children," Alessandro snapped.

Bree's smile faltered at the reminder that her whole marriage was supposed to be nothing more than a coddling of an old man's curse. She believed it was so much more now, but it still irked her to remember how they had tried to manipulate her.

"Gianni is not even a year old yet. I'm not going to start indoctrinating him on life according to the Dardanos while he can still be an innocent little boy. He deserves better."

"There is no better life than that as a Dardano. We hold the world in the palm of our hands and you need to teach Gianni how to hold on to that power."

"I know full well what being a Dardano means and so will Gianni and Will, but I want more for him. I want him to know what it is to laugh and to play and to not feel like the whole world is out to get him, to find joy in simple things and not just how many zeroes are in his bank account. And more than that, I want them both to grow up and know that power is not everything. It is necessary, yes and I will teach them how to squash their enemies, how to hit first before they can destroy you but I will also teach them that without love, without a family, none of it means a good God damn. I want them to be worthy of that love when it comes, and to not be so wrapped up in this legacy and this power that they lose sight of love when it's right in front of their eyes."

Bree closed her eyes, blinking back tears. He was here, putting their family first, just as she had always wanted him too. How could she dare do anything less?

"Dear God, she has you completely turned around, doesn't she?" Bernardo asked in angry disbelief. "This woman is completely controlling you and you can't even see it."

"Oh for God's sake, Father. Brianna does not control me. This isn't a war!"

"That is certainly what it looked like to me when I walked in here," Bernardo said.

Alessandro laughed. "Oh that. It was nothing more than a silly snowball fight."“Alessandro, listen to me. You have to lay down the law with that woman. She can’t think that she can have any influence over you whether it’s in your business or as the head of your family. You have to show her who’s boss.”

“Oh that’s Will or Gianni, Father,” Alessandro joked. “Trust me.”

“This is not a joke, Alessandro. Would you wake up, dammit!” Bernardo yelled at him, making Bree jump on the other side of the door.

“You’re right, Father. It’s not a joke. It’s a private matter between myself and my wife.”

Bree blinked at the steel in Alessandro’s voice.

“You can advise me on matters that have to do with my position as your heir, you can advise me on matters of the Dardano business holdings, but when it comes to matters involving my marriage and how I raise my children, there you may not intrude. Now good night, Father.”

Sex as procrastination. That had to be a new one for Bree. She lay her head on Alessandro’s chest, still feeling the rapid beat of his heart against her ear. She shivered, the damp flush on her skin beginning to cool. Alessandro was panting as he drew the blanket up over her shoulder and hugged her. After dinner they had come upstairs and Bree had every intention of telling him about her mother’s involvement in his shooting but then he wanted to talk about his argument with his father and Bree put it to the back of her mind.

Alessandro brushed the curve of her bottom with his hand. “You know what I kept thinking when my father was going on and on about loyalty and how I had to step in line, blah, blah? I kept thinking, ‘I hope I don’t miss Gianni’s bath, maybe I can get him to say daddy’.”

Bree smiled at him as he kissed her forehead. She ran her leg up alongside his and kissed his mouth.

“I actually felt a little…relieved, I suppose. Is that terrible? I love my father but I admit it felt good to draw a bit of a line in the sand with him.” He trailed his fingers up and down her spine.

Bree took a deep breath. “Alessandro…I…um. I need to tell you something.” She ran her fingers along his chest, biting her lip as she looked down at him.

"Well that sounds ominous," Alessandro smiled.

"Yeah, well, that certainly fits," she admitted.

His smiled faded, but he cocked an eyebrow. "Ominous like 'I accidentally dented your car' or like 'I switched the sugar in your coffee with arsenic'?"

Bree thought a moment. "Kinda in between I guess."

Alessandro stared up at her and then moved to sit up. Bree pushed her hair behind her ears and followed him. "What is it?"

Bree stared down at the blanket, picking at it as she tried to find the words that would tell him what he needed to know but wouldn't make him want to throttle her or Angela. There weren't any such words, she guessed.

"Go on, Brianna. Whatever it is, we'll work through it. Is it about the boys?" he asked.

"No, they're fine. This isn't about them."

"Is it you?" Alessandro asked, his eyes suddenly flickering with panic. "Is something wrong with—"

"No, I'm fine too," she assured him quickly, taking his hands.

"Is it…well…are you pregnant again?" Alessandro asked and Bree felt a guilty pang at the beat of hopefulness in his voice.

"It's about my mother."

Alessandro's brows came together in confusion. "Angela? What would your mother have to do with us? Unless she's all of a sudden decided to accept that her daughter is an adult and not a O'Reiley pod child—"

"Alessandro, please," Bree hissed in frustration, her fingers squeezing his.

Something in her voice must have worried him because he pulled back a little and studied her face. "All right. Go on."

"I know who shot you," Bree said. There. Like a Band-Aid. Quick and…well, hardly painless. She took a deep shaky breath and blinked away the burning in her eyes that threatened to become tears. Her hands trembled in his and she felt him release her fingers but then clutch them more tightly.

"You do?" His voice cracked.

"Yeah," she exhaled. "Now you have to believe me, I didn't know at first, I swear I had no idea but—"

"Who?" Alessandro asked.

Bree's heart stopped a little as she recognized that cold steely tone in his voice.

Alessandro clenched his jaw. "Who, Brianna?"

The look in his eyes told her he'd put it together and wanted her to say the words.

Bree lowered her head, closing her eyes and blinking the moisture from her eyes, but the tears fell anyway. "My mother, Alessandro. My mother shot you."

He pulled his hands away from her and Bree felt a moment's panic that she should have never said a word; that she should have kept this secret and that now she would lose him. The weightless feeling terrified her and Bree scrambled forward and grabbed his hands again. "Alessandro, please. Please you have to bel—"

"Bloody fucking Christ, Brianna!" Alessandro hissed, shaking his head and getting to his feet, wrapping the sheet around himself. "How long have you know? How long?"

"Not long, I swear. I swear, Alessandro I had no idea until I went to see my grandfather and there it was on my dad's desk," Bree told him.

"That was…what…almost a week ago, Brianna. How the hell could you not tell me?"

"Oh gee, I wonder. I mean, you're taking it so well," Bree snapped then covered her face with her hands. "I'm sorry. I'm sorry, I have no right to get pissy with you."

"You're damned right you don't. All these days, these nights you've sat across from me, you've lain next to me knowing who nearly killed me and you said nothing."

"What was I supposed to do, Alessandro? Rat out my mother?" Bree asked.

"I'm your husband, your loyalty is to me," Alessandro insisted.

"Oh don't you start with that loyalty crap when up until recently Bernardo had to only snap his fingers and you went to him like some fucking lap dog."

"Say what you will about my father but when he makes a promise he honours it," Alessandro tossed back.

"Oh you don't need to tell me. My family has been suffering at his hands for years because of one very specific promise he made," Bree hissed trying to keep her voice down even as her anger was getting the better of her.

"He's not the one who's reneging on the terms of the vendetta, your mother seems to have done that by putting a bullet in my back like a vintage cowardly O'Reiley," Alessandro snapped.

"Oh it's really easy to take the high ground now that the tables are turned isn't it?" Bree shoved at his chest. "What about you, huh? What about when it was your father? What about when it was my brother in law Charlie? You remember Charlie, don't you, Alessandro? At least I didn't help my mother shoot you which is more than I can say for you!"

Alessandro shook his head and gave her a sad smile. "So much for the famous O'Reiley forgiveness.

Bree moaned and leaned down, burying her face in the mattress. "No…dammit, no, I didn't mean to throw that back—"

"Never mind, Brianna. It's obvious that I'm never going to be able to make that up to you." He turned away from her and bent to retrieve his clothes.

"What are you—stop, Alessandro, you're not going anywhere." She grabbed his pants out of his hands. "I told you the truth, knowing who you are and what you are capable of, I told you the truth because I trust you."

"Once you've deemed it convenient for you," Alessandro shot back.

Bree punched his arm. "Convenient? Are you…are you fucking kidding me? My mother tried to kill my husband. Now maybe in your Dardano universe that's pretty common but not in mine."

"Ah but you forget, darling, you're a Dardano now," Alessandro reminded her coldly.

"I am your wife, that doesn't mean I can just forget my other family."

"They've certainly forgotten you," Alessandro said, his dark eyes cruel.

Bree stared at him. "You son of a bitch."

"Quite. Well, if we're done here," Alessandro pulled his pants out of her grasp and proceeded to get dressed.

"Where are you going?" Bree asked.

"Maybe I'll go visit your mother, let her have another shot," Alessandro replied.

"Dammit Alessandro, I told you! Doesn't that count for anything? I could have kept this a secret but I told you." Bree got up onto her knees and pulled at his arm. "You think it's easy for me to turn on my mother? Regardless of what they all think of me, I can't just turn on my family," Bree said.

"And yet that is what you've been asking me to do since day

one!" Alessandro shouted at her. He glanced quickly at the door and lowered his voice as he buttoned his pants. "You seem to think it's so easy for me to just turn my back on my father but when the tables are turned your loyalty remains with the O'Reileys, not with me."

Bree cringed, afraid he'd wake the children. "If that was true, I would never have said a word."

"My father is all I have, Brianna. You give up Angela and you still have a whole brood of O'Reileys to pat you on the head for being a good girl. I turn on my father and that is it. I have no one."

"No one? So me, Will, Gianni, we're no one?" Bree spat.

Alessandro grabbed her arm. "Don't. Don't you use those boys to make yourself look like the innocent in this. Though, I shouldn't really be surprised at what you'll do, should I? I mean, you're not above whoring yourself to keep me quiet after all." He pushed her away from him and Bree fell back against the mattress.

"How dare you—"

"I mean, that was what tonight was about, wasn't it? You bring me up here to fuck so I won't be too upset when you have your little moment of confession?"

Bree blinked, and at her guilty flush his eyes seemed to grow colder. "What are you going to do?" she asked quietly, the tears streaming down her face.

"Sunshine, anyone tries to kill me, I destroy them. That is how I survive. That's how the Dardanos operate."

"You'd kill her? You'd kill my mother?" Bree asked wide-eyed. No, she couldn't believe that. She knew that wasn't the man she married, the man she loved.

Alessandro leaned over her. "Maybe round two will convince me not to."

Bree jerked away from him. "What?"

"Come on, darling. Let's have another go, and if you're good enough, maybe I won't throw your precious mother's sanctimonious ass in prison and if you're an especially good fuck, I promise not to kill her." He smiled coldly.

Bree slapped him. "You bastard. Get out! I hate you! I hate you!" she attacked him, scratching and slapping at him.

He grabbed at her arms and hauled her up against his bare chest. "You're killing me, you fucking bitch. You're fucking killing me. I don't know what to do. What is the right thing, Brianna?

What you tell me? What my father tells me?"

Through her haze of anger Bree could see the tears in his eyes and she softened. "Alessandro…"

"No, don't!" He threw her on the bed and stormed out of the bedroom.

"Alessandro, wait!" Bree pleaded, grabbing her robe and rushing out after him. She followed him out into the hall and down the stairs as he put his shirt on before opening the front door. "Please, I'm sorry I didn't tell you before. I swear I am but I'm just where you are in all this. I don't know what the right thing is to do."

Alessandro stopped and Bree rushed ahead, grabbing this momentary opportunity.

"I love you, Alessandro. You are everything to me. You and our sons, but please. Please, I am begging you with everything I have, to let this go with my mother."

"So you're putting her—"

"No!" Bree cupped his face, her heart breaking at the dampness on his cheeks. "No. This is not about her, this is about us, Alessandro. You and me. If you go after my mother, if you take your revenge on her, we can never come back from that. She's my mother. My mother. You will be the man who killed my mother."

He pulled her hands off his face slowly. "The thing about my father is that for all his supposed immorality, for all his selfishness and evil, I am his son. That is the most important thing to him. With him, I come first." Alessandro sniffled and cupped the side of Bree's face. "You changed my life. But it will never be enough, will it? Why can't I come first with you?"

"You do, oh you do, I swear," Bree promised, she reached up on her tip toes and pulled his face down to meet her mouth.

For a second he responded and she felt a tiny burst of hope in her heart but then she felt it, the door came down between them as solidly as if it had been a physical thing.

He pulled away from her and shook his head and reached past her to the doorway.

"Alessandro, please. Where are you going?" Bree begged, bereft.

He studied her and shook his head. "I don't know."

And then he was gone.

Bree awoke in the darkness after what had to be only a few minutes. She looked at the clock on the night table. Three a.m. Sleep eluded her without Alessandro next to her. After another ten minutes of staring at the ceiling, recriminating herself for telling him about her mother, fearing what he was doing, where he was, Bree threw aside the blankets with a grunt of frustration. Wrapping a robe around herself she left the bedroom, just to give herself something to do. Maybe she'd go down to Alessandro's study and get some of her own work done. Her father had mentioned wanting to buy a new property to convert into one of their hotels.

Bree paused at the bottom of the stairs when she heard something. It reminded her of wind chimes. They didn't have any. No. Not wind chimes, music. A piano. Was he home? Part of her was afraid to face him in case he was still furious with her. Part of her was afraid to face him because she'd have to ask him where he'd been and what he'd done.

She followed the sound to the ballroom and almost didn't go in but she stiffened her spine, knowing nothing would be solved by hiding in the bedroom like a scared little girl.

He was sitting at the piano, head bent as he played, fingers moved slowly, uncertain as if he was trying to remember the right notes.

She knew when he noticed her because his fingers stilled over the keys. Alessandro had told her he had lessons once, as a child and that the sound had always soothed him.

She knew well that her husband needed soothing. But would he welcome it from her and did she really want to soothe him? He had left her. She'd been honest with him after all, and he'd treated her like shit. He'd been ugly and vicious and downright mean.

Bree halted in the doorway. The room was dark, though the moonlight provided enough light through the windows that she had no trouble seeing him.

"Come on in, then. No point standing there like a damned shadow," he said softly. He didn't turn around.

Bree grit her teeth and walked in, stopping when she was right behind him.

"Do you want a divorce?" Alessandro asked, his fingers still against the edge of the piano keys.

Everything in her recoiled. "No," she hissed, horrified that he'd even brought up the hateful word.

"Come sit," he said, still not looking at her. He made room on the black leather bench.

She sat next to him, facing away from the piano. "Alessandro, where did you go tonight?" she forced herself to ask.

"Your mother is going to turn herself into the police tomorrow."

Bree jumped, startled. "You went to see my mother?"

"I went to kill her," Alessandro said. "I was going to kill her, Brianna. I loaded my gun and drove to her apartment. An eye for an eye, only like you say, someone slaps us, we run them over so I didn't go there intending to just shoot her, I meant to kill her. I didn't even feel guilty about it. It was all very clear and calm in my head."

Bree couldn't breathe, waiting for him to go on.

"But as I sat outside her building, I saw the diamond bracelet I gave you resting on the floor of my car. Remember? You'd been in a panic thinking you had lost it a few days ago when we took the boys to the park?"

Bree nodded.

"I sat in my car and it occurred to me, who I was."

Bree shook her head, not understanding.

"I'm a Dardano. My father killed your husband and yet you love me. I helped my father set up your brother-in-law and you love me. You gave me Gianni and you let me call Will my son. Knowing all that, how dare I ask you to prove your loyalty? How dare I call you terrible names and leave you alone?"

Bree lowered her head, tears filling her eyes.

"I'm a monster, Brianna. I have this beautiful woman who loves me unconditionally and all I could think of is my pride, that all-important Dardano pride." He hesitantly reached a hand over to hers on her lap, but pulled it back at the last minute. "I feel like I'm being torn in two different directions. I kept telling myself in that car that I was in the right. Angela deserved no mercy. She was my enemy because she had tried to kill me. If I begin to show mercy now, I won't survive. I am not worthy to be a Dardano if I am weak."

He took a deep shaky breath. "And for a split second I thought, I want you to love me more than I want to be a Dardano."

Bree lifted her head in surprise, afraid to hope he was finally able to make the break from his father.

"No, please. Let me finish. I don't think I ever felt more afraid or more alone than in that second. And weak, Brianna. I despise weakness in anyone, but most of all in myself. I didn't know what to hope for, to hope that you left me so that I could go back to being a strong Dardano worthy of my father, or to hope that you forgave me so that I could remain your husband and a father to our children. So I went up to see your mother, knowing that only when I looked at her, would I know who I was. She opened the door and I heard your words in my head. You didn't want me to go after her for our sake, not hers and I saw what you meant."

Bree closed her eyes, swamped with relief.

"I felt ill. Physically ill. You could forgive me for being the son of the man who killed your husband, but this, killing your mother, there'd be no coming back from that. No forgiveness and it mattered more than my next breath that I kept your love no matter the cost, to myself, to my pride. That's power to have over someone. Do you understand what I'm telling you?"

"Do you think it's any different for me?" Bree asked.

"I thought it was. You have that power over me and as much as I love you a part of me hates you for it. That's why I lashed out at you and I am so, so sorry for it," Alessandro said, his voice cracking.

"So where are we now?" Bree asked nervously. "I hate that the thought of losing you terrifies me, Alessandro. I'm not a weak woman. You make me weak. So if we resent these things about each other, how the hell is this ever going to work? Every time we get angry at each other we'll attack each other? I can't live like that and I don't want our children to live like that."

"Can you forgive me for how I behaved tonight?" Alessandro asked.

"Can you forgive me for not telling you sooner?" Bree countered.

Alessandro was silent for what seemed like an eternity. "Yes, because I understand what it is to be torn between your family and the person you love. I understand better than anyone and I should have understood that it was the same for you."

"We can't keep hurting each other because we're afraid, Alessandro. If I'm going to prove to you that you come first in my life, you have to do the same. That means with Bernardo." She held her breath, waiting.

"No one will come between us again. I swear to you on my life, Brianna. Not my father, no one," he cupped her face, his dark eyes glittering with the fierceness of his words.

She should have felt reassured, but deep inside, a seed of unease she couldn't explain still remained.

CHAPTER TWENTY-TWO

Bernardo was not with them at breakfast that morning. He'd passed by briefly and glared at Bree, who tried not to gloat but couldn't resist lifting her eyes to him and narrowing them in obvious disdain. He couldn't miss the message in them. You can try all you want, but you'll never take him from me.

He glared at Alessandro too, who was not as visibly defiant, and told them he had an early business call to make. Alessandro turned and focused on Gianni who hadn't quite yet managed 'daddy' but was getting closer. "Dodo," he cooed, mangling 'Daddy' and 'Alessandro' together.

Bree's shirt was still damp with coffee from when she'd nearly choked on it a few minutes ago, hearing that for the first time.

Alessandro flushed with what Bree could imagine was guilt as his father passed his seat. He lifted another spoon of oatmeal and mashed raspberries into Gianni's mouth. The baby smiled and tried to reach for Alessandro's tie.

Besides the baby and Will who was going on about how much fun he was gonna have with Vanessa today after the nanny promised to take him to see 'Kungfu Panda', breakfast was a pretty quiet affair.

After the emotionally draining discussion last night, Alessandro and Bree hadn't made love. He'd merely curled up around her and drawn her close to him as they drifted off.

Bree looked down at the display screen of her cellphone and groaned. Alessandro followed her gaze and kissed her cheek before grabbing a bagel and disappearing into his study.

She tried for a light greeting but was met with a barrage of fury from her father. "Yes, daddy. I know about Alessandro's visit to mom's…Well that's the right thing to do considering she did try to kill him…"

Vanessa blinked in surprise and mouthed 'Holy crap.'

"He could have but he didn't…he wanted to leave it up to the justice system, 'cause you know…it works so well." She rolled her eyes at Vanessa who snorted.

"Daddy…Come on…He did it for me…Because he loves me…Daddy…listen I…Daddy-Daddy-Daddy!" Bree was losing her patience, the man was not letting her get a word in edgewise as he ranted about how Alessandro had threatened Angela and how her mother had turned herself in that morning and…

Vanessa lifted the baby towards Bree and as if he knew what she needed, Gianni extended her arms and shrieked happily, "Maaaamaaaa!"

"Look, daddy, I really gotta go, Gianni needs me. I'll talk to you laterokaybyebye," Bree said quickly, hanging up the phone. "Good God!"

"Family. Gotta love them, huh?" Vanessa snickered.

"Uh, with my family trust me, that's a bigger chore than for most. Come here, you good little baby," Bree took Gianni from Vanessa. "You did such a good job for mommy."

"Bob," Gianni echoed with a giggle. He leaned his head against hers and blinked his beautiful brown eyes at her. "Meedee bob, mamma."

"Yes you did," Bree kissed his forehead. "Okay, I have to get ready for work." She passed Gianni back to Vanessa

She loved him for offering to come with her, but Bree told Alessandro that this was something she had to do on her own.

"It's just that I don't want her to upset you by going off on another vintage O'Reiley tirade." Alessandro said rubbing Gianni's stomach as the baby giggled up at him. "Daddy, Gianni. Daaaa-deeee."

"Deeeeee," Gianni smiled waving his fists enthusiastically.

Bree tossed him the baby's shirt and threw the old shirt, decorated thoroughly with the morning's raspberry mush, into the hamper.

"Alessandro, the woman shot you. I think she pretty much hit the max on upsetting actions."

"Mama!" Gianni burst reaching for a fistful of Bree's hair when she bent down to kiss him.

"Alright then, up it is," Bree said gathering her hair up and going back into the bathroom to look for a hair tie. "So what's the plan for today?"

"Daddy is gonna pay hookers!" Will exclaimed coming out from under the bed. "Look daddy, I find your udder shoe." He held up the black shoe Alessandro had been looking for the day before.

"Hmm, and who threw it under there to begin with?" Alessandro asked.

Will grinned and shrugged. "Maybe you should ask Gianni."

"Uh tell me again, what daddy is going to be doing today?" Bree asked pressing her fingers to her mouth to stifle her laughter.

Will bit his finger and looked from Bree to Alessandro, knowing he'd said something amusing but not sure what. "He gonna pay hookers," he giggled.

Bree bit her lip but couldn't keep back a giggle.

"Hooky. Now stop corrupting our child," Alessandro insisted with a laugh.

"Ugh," she groaned. "Okay. Let me give my pretty baby a kiss goodbye."

"Gianni's nod pittie. He a boy!" Will insisted as he bounced on the bed.

His cell phone rang for the umpteenth time that morning. "Bloody hell," Alessandro groaned. He turned the phone off, letting it go to voicemail.

"My handsome, handsome baby. That better?" Bree asked Will who nodded as he scrambled down to the carpet to scratch behind Luke's ear. "And my other handsome baby." Bree kissed the top of his head. "Okay, I gotta go. Maaan. I really don't want to do this."

"Ahem," Alessandro cleared his throat.

Bree smiled and went to kiss the top of his head but he moved his head back so that he caught her mouth with his own. He cupped the back of her head and held her still as he kissed her.

"Ewww, daddy! Give mommy back her mouth!" Will insisted.

"Daddy!" Gianni exclaimed.

Alessandro and Bree broke apart, startled. "Did he just-?" he asked, his face lighting up.

"He did," Bree agreed. "Can you say it again, sweetie?"

"Nopsie songiemybadbydoometimdodoay," Gianni babbled, blowing a raspberry.

Alessandro picked him up. "Please say it again, Gianni. Please say it for Daddy,"

Gianni giggled and grabbed Alessandro's nose.

"Okay. I gotta go visit my gun toting mother in prison," Bree leaned her head against the door. "Oh God, I must really be a Dardano now if I'm making jokes about my psychotic relatives."

"Darling, let me change and call Vanessa and I can come with you," Alessandro insisted.

"No, daddy. We gonna pay hookers today!" Will insisted.

"Ah, see? Now how can I compete with that?" Bree asked with a smile.

"I didn't expect to see you here," Angela said after the guard let Bree into the cell.

Brian was already visiting with their mother and was sitting with her when Bree arrived.

"Yeah, well, considering you shot my husband, I figured I should put in an appearance."

Angela shook her head. "I'm not proud of what I did, but I would do it again in a heartbeat."

"God, mom, what the hell were you thinking?"

"I was doing what I had to to protect my little girl," Angela insisted, her eyes filling with tears.

"Never mind that you could have hit me. Never mind that Will and Gianni were standing right there and they had to watch their father's blood spilling out on to the floor."

"Bree," Brian said, placing an arm on her shoulder.

"I did what I did to get you away from those monsters," Angela said.

"That wasn't the deal, mom!" Bree insisted. "I mean, what did you think would happen? You'd shoot Alessandro and Bernardo wouldn't retaliate? I mean for God's sake, that's what he does! We do something or he does something and then the other side takes revenge and on and on it goes for over fifty years now! Alessandro and I were putting an end to it all!" Bree insisted.

"And that's why Alessandro came and threatened me into

turning myself in," Angela hissed.

"You put a bullet in his back! I say forcing you to turn yourself in as opposed to the alternative is pretty generous on his part!" Bree reminded her.

"All right, that's enough," Brian insisted, pulling her back.

"What? Are you taking her side in this?" Bree snapped.

"I'm not taking anyone's side," Brian said.

"How stupid am I, huh?" She turned into Brian's arms. "I came here to see if my mom was okay. When am I gonna learn that as long as I'm with Alessandro, according to you, I might as well be dead."

"No, sweetie, that's not what I'm saying at all," Angela pleaded reaching for her.

"No, it's what you're showing. And it's what I see in your eyes every time you look at me. I'm going home to my family. To people that love me."

Bree came into the house and heard yelling. Very angry, distinctively ominous Dardano yelling.

She was about to burst into the living room to ask what the hell was going on when out of the corner of her eye she saw Will at the bottom of the stairs, his head covered by his arms, resting on his knees. Hearing her, he lifted his head and Bree felt an emotional punch in the stomach at the tears running down his face. "Sweetie, what happened?"

"I din' mean it, mommy. I promise! I…I…I…" Will choked on his sobs before his face crumpled and he threw his arms around her.

She gathered him close and picked him up, rubbing his back and trying to soothe him. She was torn between storming into the living room and punching both Alessandro and Bernardo for whatever the hell they were arguing about that had made her little boy so distraught and staying here to soothe her son. Bree ran her fingers through Will's brown hair and decided she'd try to get the story from him first. "It's okay, baby. Just tell mommy what happened. Where's Vanessa?"

When Will's sobs lessened he pulled and rubbed his damp eyes. "She up wif da baby. I got away 'cause I knew Gappy Lecter was gonna yell at daddy. He always yell at daddy now when daddy say he loves us. He's our daddy, Mommy. In't dat his job?"

"Yes, yes it is and don't you worry, your daddy loves you more than anything in the whole world. Now tell me what happened, huh?"

"It wasn't my fault. It was da baby. Vanessa dropped her coffee and it broke on da floor and Gianni was going really fast to the glass before Vanessa could get to him and I was closer so I runned to stop him and I banged in to da ugly vase on da table and it fallded down an broke. I din' mean to break it mommy. I swear I din'!" Will explained, his lower lip quivering.

"And that's why Bernardo's yelling? Because of a stupid vase?" Bree asked, furious.

"Well, now they're yelling about stuff I don' get but he came in and got mad at me and I was wewwy scared 'cause I know he don' like me too much then daddy wanned to know what da boody hell was going on," Will said, mimicking Alessandro's expression. "Dat's when they started yelling at each udder and daddy told Vanessa to take us upstairs."

"Will, you listen to me. Your daddy is right, you didn't do anything wrong, okay? You did a good thing trying to help your little brother so that he didn't get cut. That's more important than a stupid vase. And you're right, it is an ugly vase. Butt ugly," Bree said.

Will smiled through his tears. "Vewwy butt ugly."

Bree kissed his cheek. "I'm very proud of you for looking after your little brother."

"Dat's my job, right?" Will asked, sniffling.

"You betcha, kiddo. Now can you do me a favour and go upstairs for a little while?"

"You gonna yell at Gappy Lecter too?" Will asked.

"Nope, I promise. No yelling," Bree assured him. She was gonna lay down the law and if Bernardo had a problem with he could shove it where the sun didn't shine. But first, a little eavesdropping was in order.

"I love you, Mommy." Will said, hugging her.

"Oooh, I love you too, babe."

After Will disappeared from the top of the stairs Bree moved to the doorway to the living room.

"The whole point of marrying an O'Reiley was to prove my loyalty to you. All my life I have done nothing but prove my loyalty to you. And now, because I have the temerity to actually love my wife and put her needs first you seem to see this as some kind of a betrayal?" Alessandro hissed.

"Her mother nearly killed you. Your precious Brianna would be the final nail in the O'Reiley coffin if she would testify against Angela."

Brianna stepped back in shock. Testify against her mother? Could she do it? It was one thing to confess to Alessandro that her mother had shot him but…Oh God. To actually step up in front of everyone and testify to it? Bree squeezed her eyes shut in frustration and was surprised to hear Alessandro give voice to exactly what she was thinking at that second.

"You know, I am so sick of being pulled in two different directions all the time. I feel like I'm being ripped in half because for some reason, you only want me happy if it's under your thumb. You know what? Brianna is my wife, she is the woman I love and that means I don't want her hurt. I made my point to Angela and I'm letting the police handle the matter however they like because I do not want to put my wife through denouncing her own mother on the stand. She's been through enough with those people."

"You know as well as I do that John is going to fix her confession and the evidence to get her off," Bernardo sneered.

"Oh well it takes one to know one, doesn't it?" Alessandro pointed out. "Look, you are my father and I love you. I will always love you. But that love is not an all or nothing proposition. Brianna is my wife. Will and Gianni are my sons. You are all my family, but if you push me, Father, if you force me to choose between you and them you will not like the choice I make. You are never to treat William the way you did today, ever. Am I making myself clear?"

"Is that a threat, Alessandro?" Bernardo asked, his voice cold.

Bree felt her body stiffen with nervous tension. Her heart was racing, both with nervousness and joy that Alessandro was drawing a line in the sand with his father and that he was sticking up for them over Bernardo.

"Remember, Father, you raised me. You raised me to be a Dardano. That's who I am and I'm sure you know exactly what that means."

Along with her joy and nervousness, Bree felt an undeniable stirring of arousal at the power in his words.

She jumped, startled when Alessandro stormed past her. He turned in surprise to see her there.

"Were you listening at the door?" he asked, his dark eyes glittering, his face flushed from the heat of his argument.

Bree smiled up at him and grabbed his collar. "I love you so much." She brought him down to her level and captured his mouth.

Bree asked Vanessa if she could take the boys to the park for a few hours. The nanny, relieved that she was still employed, agreed and gave Bree a knowing wink before she left. Knowing how stressed Alessandro was over the fight with his father, Bree suggested he might like to relax in a nice bubble bath.

He initially resisted until Bree gave him a saucy grin that told him without words that he wouldn't be in the tub alone for long.

After Will assured Bree that they would of course be good boys, she closed the door and turned towards the stairs.

"You think you've won, don't you?" Bernardo said coming out of the living room into the foyer.

Bree's heart jumped in her chest and she reluctantly turned to face him. "I don't consider Alessandro a game."

"Let me assure you that my son will always remember who is he and where he came from. No insignificant little tart is going to change that."

"You know, I thought I would feel a lot more triumphant over the fact that Alessandro told you where to stick it, but right now, the most important thing on my mind is that my husband is hurting. He needs me. That is your big mistake, my dear father-in-law. I actually care about Alessandro as a person. I care about when he's sad or confused and needs someone to help him shoulder his troubles. You only see him as someone to be dictated to."

"Enjoy your victory while it lasts," Bernardo said. "Before I allow you to turn my son away from his legacy, from his destiny, I will rain down destruction on you and everyone you care for."

Bree fought the icy fear that slithered down her spine and forced herself to meet his gaze and not waver. "You can stuff your threats. Alessandro may always have the bad luck of being spawned by you, but he is my husband. He is the father of my children. It won't be long before you are totally irrelevant." And with that she turned and made her way upstairs to Alessandro.

CHAPTER TWENTY-THREE

She slipped out of her clothes and wrapped her peach satin robe around her. She peeked her head into the bathroom and watched for a second as Alessandro lay in the tub, his head back, his eyes staring up at the ceiling. She could practically hear the doubt and self-recriminations over his behaviour with his father going through his mind. "Somebody want some company?" she asked from the doorway.

He lifted his head and smiled at her. "I was thinking maybe you forgot about me."

"Never," she promised, grinning at him. As he watched, she slid the robe off her shoulders and let it pool at her feet.

His dark eyes flickered hungrily over her. "Water's still warm," he assured her.

"Goody," she said climbing into the wide tub. He was right, the water still held the slight sting of heat as she sank into it and turned away from him, letting her back come against his chest. "Mmmm," she sighed, leaning against the hard, damp wall of his chest. "This is heaven."

"Not quite, but we're on the right track, sweetheart," Alessandro murmured in her ear as his hand came up to cup her breast. "How long do we have?"

Bree reached down under the water to stroke his strong muscled thigh. "In real time, maybe three or so hours. In fantasy land, time has stopped."

"Oh, I think I like fantasy land. Can we stay here forever?"

Alessandro asked and she could hear the smile in his voice.

"We can do whatever you want," Bree told him turning around to capture his mouth.

"Oh that's a very loaded proposition, darling."

"I'm up for it if you are," Bree promised.

He groaned and squeezed her nipple, making her insides clutch with anticipation as he kissed her again. She could feel him growing thicker against her bottom and Bree wiggled back to press more firmly against him.

"Sit on me," he urged, bucking his hips slowly against her.

Bree reached around and closed her fingers around his cock, hearing his breath hitch behind her. She moved her fingers back and forth along the impressive length. God but he was beautiful. Her body was greedy, eager to be filled again. Bree positioned herself over him and sank down on the thick shaft, moaning at every hard inch.

"Fuuuuck," Alessandro growled behind her and Bree agreed.

His fingers sought out the folds of her pussy and stroked the bead in the center as he wrapped an arm around her stomach and guided her back and forth on his cock.

"Oh Jesus," Bree moaned as his fingers worked to draw her nerves tighter and tighter. Her pussy rubbed deliciously against the hard, swollen friction of his shaft.

He guided her and worked her body into a frenzy. "Come for me, darling. I want to feel you come all around me."

He pressed his hand against her stomach and Bree briefly wondered if she should go off the pill. Maybe it was time for another baby, another child to cement her connection with this man who owned her, body and soul. She jumped a little when she felt his teeth dig into her shoulder with slight but definite pressure. The walls of her core tightened around his cock in response and she felt him swell inside of her. His fingers worked her faster, determined to bring her over with him.

"Oh yes…Oh God…" Bree sighed. Her body moved, thrusting with him, sliding against the soapy muscled wall of his chest.

"Beautiful…so God damned beautiful," he groaned into her hair. "Love you…love you."

"Don't stop, Alessandro. Oh, don't stop," Bree begged, shivering as her orgasm began to tug at her belly before spreading outward and exploding through her blood. She arched back and the walls of her pussy convulsed around him, working her body to bring her man to his release.

And then he was there, swelling and stretching her and spilling into her with a cry of her name against her hair. He bucked hard behind her and Bree bore down against his hand as his fingers continued their sweet torture, ringing yet as second, sharper orgasm from her.

They fell back together and Alessandro sucked lovingly at her neck as he panted against her skin. "Shall we dry off and take further advantage of this stoppage of time?"

"Oh hell yes," Bree sighed with a happy shiver.

"You have that look on your face," Alessandro said, smiling as he tucked a damp lock of her blonde hair behind her ear.

"What look?" Bree asked, resting a hand on his flushed chest, propping herself up on one elbow. She could feel the racing heart beneath.

"The look of a woman who's been rather well fucked, darling," he grinned smugly.

She punched his chest lightly. "Ego much?"

"I see nothing wrong with taking pride in a job well done," he pointed out.

"Oh of course," Bree said, laughing and dropped her head on his chest.

"I love seeing you like this. It reminds me of the house."

The house always meant the abandoned house where they first met, where they'd not known who each other was.

"I still can't think of that place without feeling nostalgic and yet relieved we're not back there," Alessandro admitted, stroking her back with light fingers.

"Relieved?" Bree asked.

"I remember feeling that I'd never been happier or felt worse at the same time. I fell in love with you in an instant, and yet I knew that I had to fulfill my father's order. Marry an O'Reiley, provide an heir. At the time I didn't know you were one. I feared I'd never see you again, never touch you, kiss you, make love to you. It felt like I was cutting off a piece of myself I would never get back. Maybe if I had never known you, I could have gone ahead with my father's dictate and it wouldn't have bothered me. But I did know you. I hated that panicky feeling. I never want to experience anything like that again," he explained.

Bree dropped a kiss on his chest. She knew what he meant. "I'd rather have what we have now." She felt a surge of giddy joy. She had him. Here, in the real world, no hiding away, no living in a fantasy bubble. Here in the everyday life like she'd always hoped.

"Downstairs with my father, I hated hurting him, and I know I did but…" He took a shaky deep breath. "It occurred to me that I can't allow myself to be spilt in two the way I have been. I love my father, but you and the boys, you're my future. I can't live my life for him because someday, as much as I don't even want to contemplate it, he'll be gone. I have to put you first. I want to be a good husband to you, a good father to Will and Gianni."

"You are," Bree assured him rubbing his stomach.

"Thank you for saying so." He threaded his fingers through her hair, massaging her scalp gently. "You and the boys are my first priorities from now on. I promise you."

Bree blinked away the threat of tears. "I love you," she whispered, brushing her lips across his. "I love you so much."

He caressed her back, moving lower.

"Speaking of the house, do you remember what I told you when we were there about wanting to build up something that was mine, something no one could take away from me?"

"Mmm, I remember everything, my love," Alessandro said, burying her face in her neck, running his mouth up along her skin.

Bree shivered pleasurably. "I still want that."

"So…you want to start your own business?" Alessandro asked her.

"I do. I mean, I don't know what yet, but yeah…"

"I'd be proud to help you start—"

"Oh no," Bree cut him off quickly. "No. I don't want any kind of backing or anything."

"Oh, well, don't be ridiculous, darling. Why wouldn't you want to make it easier on yourself by getting a financial leg up by your disgustingly wealthy, handsome husband?"

"Oh and let's not forget modest as well," Bree joked, rubbing her leg against his.

"Sorry, I don't believe in false modesty. I am filthy rich," Alessandro smiled.

"And handsome. Can't forget handsome," Bree insisted, moving her body over his so that she was now straddling him.

"Well, I haven't broken any mirrors thus far," Alessandro shrugged.

"Some might even say sexy," Bree said, leaning down and kissing him. "Some might even say definite fantasy material."

"Oh?" Alessandro remarked, sliding his hands up along her sides. "Do tell, what kinds of fantasies?"

"Oh dirty, dirty, dirty fantasies. Things that would just make you blush to the tips of your itty bitty toes," she purred kissing his throat.

"I'm afraid I'm going to need a more comprehensive example," Alessandro said and she could feel the head of his cock nudging against her backside.

"Well, I imagine this hard, muscled body inspires many women's most primal urges."

"Oh urges?" He reached up to cup her breasts, running his thumbs over her tight, aroused pink nipples.

"Mmmm, urges to be taken by such a sexy man. Thrown down and just ravaged."

"On the floor? Oh my, that is dirty," Alessandro joked.

"Uh huh. And they must wonder seeing this tall, muscled body, if you are…proportioned well." Bree rocked her hips against the head of his cock.

"Oh, and what would you imagine they'd think?" Alessandro asked, taking his cock in his hands and moving her hips up so that he could rub the now swollen head of his shaft against the slick folds of her pussy.

"Oh yes, definitely…ah fuuuck," Bree moaned sinking down on him and arching back. "Definitely well proportioned. I'd imagine their mouths practically water, imaging this cock, imaging sucking it, fucking it, feeling every hard delicious inch ramming into them."

Alessandro lifted himself up so that he could sit up with her and catch one of her breasts in his mouth.

Bree grabbed his head and writhed against him.

"More, tell me more," Alessandro insisted, rocking his hips beneath her, driving up, deep.

"I imagine their pussies get very wet and their walls throb, imagining this beautiful hard cock fucking them. They imagine riding you, faster…faster. They imagine sinking their teeth into this beautiful skin as you ride them, like a beautiful animal, sweat shining on your skin as you fuck them harder…harder…Oh God,

Alessandro…Oh God…" Bree bucked her hips as her clitoris scraped wonderfully against the thick damp skin of his powerful cock.

"Don't stop," Alessandro ordered. "Tell me what you want. Tell me what you fantasize, darling."

"Oh, I don't have to fantasize, baby," Bree smiled possessively at him. She bit into his tight and now slick shoulder, damp with the sweat of exertion. "I have you to fuck me anytime I want, as hard as I want."

Alessandro flipped her onto her back so that her head was at the foot of the bed. "And how hard does my darling wife want it?" he asked plunging into her again.

"As hard as my darling husband can give it to me," Bree taunted arching as he filled her again.

Alessandro grabbed her wrists in one hand and pinned them over her head. "Oh he can give it to you hard, my love. He can fuck you…and fuck you…and fuck you until you can't walk," he growled possessively, punctuating his words with deep, penetrating thrusts of his cock.

"Oh yes! Yes!" Bree cried, feeling her orgasm churning and climbing through her blood.

"Your husband can fuck you so deep and so hard that you can still feel him in this beautiful tight, wet pussy, hours later. In fact…Fuuuck…ah Brianna…" The movements of his cock grew harder, more brutal and she could tell he was almost there too. "In fact…tonight at dinner. I'm going to keep my eyes on you and every time you look into my eyes…oh yes…fuck…fuck me back like that," he ordered as she snapped her hips up to meet his relentless movements. "Every time you look into my eyes, you'll remember my cock in you like this…deep and hard and I'll look at you and know how wet you are…and how hot your pussy is and how you're counting down the minutes until…mmmm fuck! Tonight, when I can fuck you again…and again…and ah yes, darling! Yes, Brianna!"

Bree screamed out his name as he ground his hips against hers, so that his cock rubbed against every inch of her pussy, driving, throbbing and then she felt the hot thick spilling of his seed into her and she fell over the edge with him.

She came into the house and heard giggling.

"Dat's a purple twee. Dat's too funny, daddy," Will said.

"Daddy!" Gianni squealed.

"Well, who says trees have to be green? How about a red doggie, Gianni?" Alessandro asked.

Curious as to what on earth they were doing, Bree walked into the living room. The coffee table was covered with paper, as was the floor beneath it where jars of water and paint rested. At the mention of a doggie, Gianni looked around for Luke who barked and rushed towards him. Gianni saw her standing next to the couch and his face split in a grin.

"Mama!" he pointed at her with a red finger.

Alessandro and Will turned and Bree burst out laughing. Her son had a bright splotch of yellow paint on his forehead and her husband had a purple smudge on the end of his nose and a streak of green in his hair.

"It looks like Debbie Travis made you her…um…" Remembering the kiddies, Bree caught herself and smiled. "Female dog."

"Mommy, we making pictures!" Will exclaimed.

"I can see that. Looks like you're having a good time." By comparison, the one who should be the most filthy, Gianni, was pretty spotless except for his hands. Bree imagined Alessandro was careful to keep the baby clean but neglected to extend the same diligence to himself.

"Ralphie screamed and ran away," Will laughed.

Bree snorted. "Uh, yeah. I can imagine."

"Mommy, tell Daddy twees are suppose' to be gween."

"Well, what about in the fall?" Bree countered.

That gave the little boy pause.

"When I was a little boy, we had art lessons and my teacher, Ms. Orgalthorpe was this old…" Alessandro smiled up at Bree. "female dog. Every single thing had to be perfectly proportioned with all the right colours and shapes etc… I always wanted to give my houses big bubbles blowing out of the chimney or give my dogs rabbit ears and once I drew this tree with chickens in it instead of leaves. The old bat was not amused."

"But now you a growed up and can do whatever you want right?" Will asked.

"And so purple trees it is," Alessandro insisted.

"Oh and look, mommy. We make hands. Dis one is mine." He

held up the paper with the image of blue hands. "And I writed my name all by myself." William, like Alessandro called him. Not just Will.

"Wow. I'm impressed."

"Well, Daddy told me da letters but I writed dem on da paper," he amended.

"Good job, kiddo." Bree took a seat on the edge of the couch and Gianni extended his arms to her. She gingerly picked up the baby, careful to keep his hands away from her skin.

"And dis one Gianni," he handed her the other paper with small baby hands in red. "Dat one daddy had to write da name."

Bree looked back and tried to imagine taping these up on the refrigerator, but that was in the kitchen, where they would hardly see them.

After they cleaned up for dinner, Alessandro taped them to the wall of their bedroom on either side of the mirror. "Better than any Picasso if you ask me," he insisted.

"Damn right," Bree agreed meeting his gaze in the mirror. Her baby's hands, her little boy's hands, put up with pride by her husband. My family, Bree thought. Mine.

Sister Brannigan's belongings were strewn between them on the couch. "I can't ask him that," Bree insisted. "Hey Grandpa, before your sister threw herself off a cliff, did you ever happen to notice if she was knocked up under her dress?"

Alessandro rolled his eyes. "Well no, not if you put it so colourfully."

She picked up the locket and opened it, looking at Adriano's face and then looked over at her husband. "Geez. The poor girl never really had a chance." She snorted.

Alessandro smiled at her. He picked up the paper with the address on it.

"Come on," Bree looked at Adriano's face. "Gimme something, dead grandpa-in-law."

"There's no way in a town the size of Galway that Francesca could have hidden a pregnancy. No bloody way. I mean, do you remember that time we went to Gordie's house and Will said that thing about how your grandmother didn't put corn in her clam chowder? The next day, I walked into the pub and at least three different people came up to me and were telling me different ways they prepared their corn for their clam chowders. That was corn,

Brianna."

"Okay, so this can't be Francesca's baby." Bree twirled the locket around her fingers. "But then how do you explain this?"

"What? The locket?"

"It's Francesca's obviously. Look at it. The cover is dented." Bree held it out to him.

Alessandro picked it up and ran his finger over the silver dented cover. "I don't see the connection."

"Only one thing makes a dent like that." Bree pointed out.

Alessandro shrugged "A tiny hammer? Like one of those blasted IKEA Alex keys."

Bree smacked his arm. "Allen keys and no. Those are teeth marks, Alessandro."

Alessandro studied the piece of jewellery with renewed interest. "How can you tell?"

Bree snorted. "You've obviously never been in labour."

"No, I'm afraid I haven't been so blessed." Alessandro smiled and picked up his tea from the coffee table, taking another sip.

"Well, biting into something sometimes helps take the edge off the fact that you're trying to push something the size of a pot roast out of an opening the size of your nostril."

"Mmm, charming," Alessandro grimaced. "I'll make a note to Cook to take pot roast off the menu for a while."

"So if this is obviously Francesca's locket and that grave isn't supposed to be Francesca's baby then why is the damn thing dented? Maybe she took a trip and then came back?" Bree asked.

"I seriously doubt a young girl could leave a village like Galway for that many months, come back and everyone not know why," Alessandro pointed out with a smirk.

"Gah!" Bree burst in frustration.

"Stop dat, Gianni. Gimme da gween." Will reached over and grabbed the crayon out of the baby's hand.

Gianni's little brow furrowed and he tried to reach for Will's hand and get the crayon back but Will held his hand away, far out of the baby's reach.

"Meeeeeeeeeeeeeeee!" Gianni shrieked.

"No. Is' my crayon," Will insisted.

"Caaaaa. Bah deemmeee!" Gianni demanded.

"No. I need dem. You nod colouring."

The baby's lips quivered but instead of crying, he took his little hand and smacked it down on Will's leg. "Bah! I wat. Geee caaaa!"

Will shoved at the baby and Gianni fell over sideways. "Don' hit me. I bigger den you."

"Will! He's a baby!" Bree insisted coming around to Gianni's side.

"So? He a baby, nod a dummy," Will said. "I don' touch tings dat ain' mine."

Seeing his mother, Gianni gave full reign to a wail and reached up for her. "Mamaaaaaa!"

"Oh sure. You cry only fo' mommy to see," Will rolled his eyes.

"I don't want to see you hit your brother again, got me?" Bree said.

"I din' hit him. I pushded him. He hit me!" Will said.

"You know better," she countered.

"Yeah, I know he hit me," Will said stubbornly sticking out his lower lip.

Vanessa snorted. "Will, he wanted to color with you."

Gianni squirmed in his mother's arms, wanting to go back down. He laughed and made his way back to Will and his pictures.

Will sighed. "Oh brother. Okay, fine. Here." He pulled an extra page from his stack and put it beside him for Gianni.

"Will he's not going to be able to re—" Bree's words were cut off by the fact that Gianni had grabbed the leg of the coffee table and was currently pulling himself to his feet. "Oh my God!" Both she and Vanessa shrieked at the same time.

Startled, Gianni fell back onto the carpet and turned to his mother with a 'what the hell?' expression on his face.

"You wanna try again, baby?" Bree asked standing up behind him.

"Heee!" Gianni smiled reaching for the table leg again.

"Guess why you love me?" Alessandro asked, smiling, coming into the living room.

"He's gonna stand up!" Bree hissed, trying not to shout and scare the baby again.

"You can do it, Gianni!" Will said.

"He's what?" Alessandro asked, wide eyed. He rushed towards them, excitement and pride in his eyes as he watched Gianni struggle to get to his feet.

Gianni stuck out his tongue and with a look of sheer Dardano determination struggled unsteadily to his feet. He looked around and bounced his chubby legs, a look of surprise at seeing the world from a new height on his face. He giggled at Will and turned to Alessandro. "Daddy!"

"Yay!" Will exclaimed softly, following Bree's lead and clapping very gently.

Then Gianni looked down and his face clouded. "Uh…oh…" he murmured, his lower lip quivering as it must have occurred to him that he didn't know how to get back on the floor.

"Ah, no problem, my little handsome boy. Here we go, see?" Alessandro took his hands and pulled them away from the table. He eased Gianni back down on to the carpet.

"Yeeeey!" Gianni squealed. "Gen dooo, daddy." He reached for the coffee table again.

"Now, don't you want to know why you love me?" Alessandro asked, grinning.

"Do tell," Bree said.

"Vanessa, can you watch the boys for a little while?"

"Sure," Vanessa said.

"Wonderful. We'll be back in about an hour. Darling, come with me." With that he wrapped his arm around Bree and steered her towards the door.

He took her to an abandoned building. A bar she suddenly recognized. She turned to Alessandro and gave a gasp of surprise.

"How the…what...how?" Bree asked.

He laughed behind her. "Go on in then, darling." He smacked her bottom lightly and she kicked him before she entered the bar.

"It's yours. If you want it that is," Alessandro said crossing his arms over his chest.

Bree looked at him, and her smile wavered. "Tell me you didn't buy it for me. Alessandro I told you I didn't want you to—"

Alessandro held up his hands. "I promise. I promise I didn't buy it for you. I simply asked your aunt's father if he'd be interested in selling it. His exact words were 'To you? Not on your life.' Then I explained it would be for you and that made him change his tune. You can meet with him tomorrow if you like."

Bree clamped her hands over her mouth to contain her squeal of excitement and then jumped into his arms. "Oh I love you! I love you, love you, love you!"

"You should. Jack O'Reiley is an arse."

"Oh wow," Bree said looking around. "This would be perfect,

Alessandro. There's the bar where we could have hunky bartenders serving drinks with dirty names, tables where we could serve some simple dishes, like wings and stuff." She walked to the opposite side of the bar. "And here, here would be the stage. Blues, jazz, maybe some rock to shake things up every once in a while. None of that pretentious piano lounge music stuff. We could make some room in front for dancing." She ran to the opposite wall. "And here the pool table. Maybe darts too. Have you ever played pool?"

"Snooker?" Alessandro asked.

Bree blew a raspberry at him. "No not Snooker. Pool. American pool."

"I suppose you'll have to teach me. Now, let's go back to the part about the hunky bartenders," he asked cocking an eyebrow.

"Oh…um…you?" Bree lied wrapping her arms around him.

"Is that right?" Alessandro asked with frank disbelief.

"Sure, you know how to put together 'oral sex' and 'multiple orgasms', right?" Bree asked grinning.

"I've been told I'm quite well versed on those subjects," Alessandro said leaning down to nuzzle her neck.

Bree poked him in the chest. "I can't wait to get started. I'm gonna talk to Uncle Jack and then start looking at paint samples. You want to help me pick out swatches?"

"Oh God, not swatches," Alessandro groaned. "Brianna, just hire someone to do it. I can have the top painters in the city come and-Ow!" he exclaimed when she punched his arm.

"Bite your tongue. I'm gonna do this myself…well…you're gonna help me and so is Brian."

"Am I?" Alessandro asked.

"Yes, because you love me and I shall repay you with mind numbingly hot sex," Bree promised, leaning in and biting his ear lobe gently.

"Done," Alessandro agreed with a groan. "Oh and there's something else I wanted to tell you. It's about your mother."

Bree pulled back nervously. "Okay."

"I gave my statement to the court today. I refused to press charges against Angela and I asked that if they do indict her, that's she's given just some time under psychiatric care," he told her.

Bree blinked in surprise and then again because tears were filling her eyes. "You…did that…for me?"

Alessandro kissed her forehead. "I'd do anything for you, my love."

Bree cupped his face and kissed him, her heart nearly exploding in her chest with the intensity of her love for this man.

As they got ready for bed that night, Bree handed him a small box.

He draped his shirt over the edge of the bed and took the box. "What? It's not my birthday."

"I know," Bree said smiling.

He opened the box and then looked up at her with a beat of confusion before realization dawned and he quickly looked back down at the box.

Of her birth control pills.

CHAPTER TWENTY-FOUR

"Meee 'atch, daddy. Meee," Bree heard Gianni say as she came into the living room.

"It's a little big for you, don't you think?" Alessandro said and he smiled up at her as he held Gianni on his lap, zipping up his coat. The weather was warming up and all the snow had completely melted, but the ride would still be a little chilly for the baby.

"Noooo, 'atch," Gianni insisted reaching for Alessandro's wrist.

"Where are you guys going off to?" Bree asked pouring herself some coffee from the pot still on the table. "You shouldn't have let me sleep in."

"You were rather tired, I imagine," he replied winking at her.

Bree grabbed a grape off the table and threw it at his head.

Gianni picked it up as it fell in his lap and brought it to his mouth.

"Oh, hang on there, little one," Alessandro grabbed it and broke off half, giving one piece to Gianni.

"Mmmm," the baby murmured in approval.

"We gonna wide da horsies," Will explained popping up from the front of the couch.

"Gianni too?" Bree asked nervously. "I don't know, Alessandro."

"Oooooo!" Gianni insisted.

"He won't be by himself. I'll carry him in front of me, darling."

"Ah there you are, Alessandro. There are some business matters we need to discuss. Come with me to my study," Bernardo said, coming into the room.

Alessandro's face fell and he shifted his disappointed gaze to Bree who grit her teeth.

"Father, I was planning to take the boys riding today."

"Well, the horses aren't going anywhere are they? This is important," Bernardo insisted.

"Seesees," Gianni smiled, tugging on Alessandro's sweater.

"No horsies, Gianni. Gappy don' wan' daddy to haf no fun," Will grumbled under his breath.

Bree's heart broke for Will but Gianni, not understanding continued to smile at his father.

"Seesee's, daddy?"

"We can discuss things later, Father," Alessandro insisted.

"Oh for God sake, Alessandro. Why does everything have to be such a battle with you lately? Bah! Never mind. I know exactly why," Bernardo glared at Bree who crossed her arms over her chest and glared right back.

Alessandro rubbed the back of his neck and propped Gianni on the couch. With a sigh he got to his feet. "Very well. Will, can you wait an hour for us to go outside?"

Will shrugged, obviously disappointed. Bree stiffened in irritation.

"Here, Gianni, you wanna play with daddy's watch for a little while?" He took the expensive watch off his wrist and handed it to the baby.

Gianni giggled happily and lifted the shiny thing on his palm. "Ooook, mamma. 'atch. Daddy 'atch."

"I promise, I won't be long," Alessandro said, touching Bree's arm. She echoed Will's shrug. "Fine, Father. Let's get this over with. I can spare an hour but that's all."

"Of course," Bernardo said and Bree glared at him when the corner of his mouth lifted in a smirk before he turned away.

Son of a bitch.

"Bu'ness takes long time. We nod gonna get to go on da horsies today," Will said.

Bree sighed and walked over to Will. "Tell you what kiddo, why don't we go ahead and start without daddy. He can join us when he's done."

Will beamed at her. "Really?"

"Sure thing. Come on, Gianni. Let's go riding, huh?" Bree said, picking him up.

"Daddy 'atch," Gianni said showing it to her.

"Yeah, lucky boy. You have daddy's watch. If you want, you can throw it in the horse poop."

Vanessa joined them and rode with Will as Bree rode with Gianni, holding him close as she moved the horse at a gentle trot. "You like the horsies, Gianni?" Bree asked, tickling Gianni's tummy.

The baby giggled and tried to turn his head to face her. "Seesee's, mommy. Mo' da seesee's."

"Faster?" Bree asked, laughing. The baby showed no fear when it came to the horses at all which surprised her a little. Will was much more gung ho, jumping into things. Gianni was quieter and she was worried the big beasts would scare him. But no, she had raised his tiny hand to pat the horses and he'd laughed when the horse nudged his baby fingers. "Peee, seesee's. Seesee's," he urged, bouncing against her.

She trotted a little faster and he squealed in delight. She followed Vanessa to a small group of trees where they stopped to rest. "You wanna feed the horsies some sugar, Gianni?" Bree asked sliding off with him and pulling out the small bag from her pocket.

"Eeed, seesee's," Gianni nodded.

"Look, Gianni. Watch me," Will said, showing him how to do it. His face was flushed from the ride and a few locks of his dark hair were damp and sticking to his forehead.

Bree put the sugar cube in Gianni's hand and lifted it to the horse's mouth.

Gianni shrieked in anticipation and laughed sweetly as the horse took the sugar.

"Mommy, daddy's coming!" Will exclaimed happily and true enough when Bree turned, there was Alessandro on his own horse, riding towards them. "You came to play, daddy?"

"Of course," he assured him giving Bree and apologetic glance.

"Daddy, oook! Eeed seesee's," Gianni said tugging on the bag wanting another sugar cube.

"Are you feeding the horsies?" Alessandro asked, kissing Gianni's head.

Gianni nodded.

"Dare I ask if he lost my watch?"

Bree pulled it out of her pocket and handed it to him.

"I love you," Alessandro said.

Bree grunted but gave him a kiss.

"You understand that I have to give in sometimes to keep the peace, darling, don't you?" Alessandro urged.

"Mmm," Bree said. "Fine, fine. At least you're here."

"That I am. And ready to play," he grinned.

They rode for another hour and Alessandro explained to Will that all the land spread out before him would be his and Gianni's someday.

"How come not now? We live here," Will pointed out.

"That's true, but you're still little. When you get big, then you can own all of this."

"Wow. I can't wait to get growed up. Growed up's get to do whatever dey want and dey get lots of grass and trees too. I wanna name this tree, Jack, when I growed up." He pointed to a tree ahead of them.

"After your uncle?" Alessandro asked, lifting his eyebrow.

"No!" Will laughed. "From da Jack and the Beanstalk, Daddy."

Bree laughed and fed Gianni some water, noticing his flushed face. It was getting warmer now. "Why don't we go back. It's getting a bit warm for the baby."

"Is nod hot," Will countered.

"Well, maybe not for you but Gianni's smaller," Bree explained.

"Vanessa, you wanna take the boys back and we'll join you later? There's somewhere I want to show Brianna." Alessandro said, his eyes warm as they met Bree's with unmistakable intent.

"I bet there is," Vanessa snickered. "Come on kiddies."

"I gotta say, the last time you said you wanted to show me something, I ended up with a bar. I can't wait to see how you top that this time," Bree joked as she followed Alessandro on her own horse.

He slowed the mount and pulled up next to her. "Well, it's not quite the same," he explained with a grin. "I've been dying for the weather to warm up again because there's this gorgeous little clearing at the end of the grounds and I thought it would be the perfect private place to take my wife for a deliciously debauched picnic."

"Really?" Bree asked with a grin as a thrilling little shiver darted through her blood. "You said 'private'. How private are we talking here?" She hadn't noticed it before but he had a pack tied to his horse.

"I promise. No one will see."

"It is still technically morning, Alessandro," Bree pointed out.

"Since when is my wife a strictly night time woman?" Alessandro asked, cocking an eyebrow.

"Very funny. I'm just saying how do you know nobody is going to be walking around?"

"Would you trust me, darling?" Alessandro insisted.

"Well. I am hungry," she admitted with a sassy grin that told him food wasn't what she was hungry for.

The last time they had made love outside had been in Ireland. It had been black as pitch outside. Now it was very much daylight.

Alessandro led her over a small bridge that covered the pond. He led her along the bank and then stopped when they came to the high stone wall, the opening of which led to the orchard with apple, peach, orange and cherry trees. She followed him through until they reached the end of the orchard and he stopped the horse when they reached the bank of the river again. The apple blossoms from the trees reached over them like a canopy.

"Oh wow. This place is gorgeous."

"I thought so," Alessandro agreed. He got off his horse and moved over as she dismounted. He caught her by the waist and helped her down, smiling at her. "When I first saw this place, I knew that I wanted to lay you down on the soft grass and make love to you right here. The workers won't arrive for another few weeks so it's perfectly private." He lifted his fingers up along her ribcage over her blouse.

"Oh, I married a genius," Bree said burrowing closer to him and wrapping her arms around his neck.

"Quite," he nodded.

The branches cast shadows on the grass as Alessandro spread the blanket down and placed the basket in the center. "We have fruit and pasta, chicken salad."

"Yum," Bree said kneeling down and lifting her hands to his chest. "We should eat first."

"I suppose," Alessandro said, sitting next to her.

"Yeah, I mean, we don't want it to spoil," Bree said handing him a paper plate and a plastic fork. She giggled when he grunted and reached in the basket for a bottle of wine.

After they ate, they lay on the blanket and stared up at the blue sky. "Did you ever play the cloud game?" Bree asked him, as she felt his fingers in her hair.

"The what?" Alessandro asked.

"My siblings and I, back in Colorado, when we were little we used to lay on our backs in my grandparents' backyard and play the cloud game for hours."

Alessandro shook his head blankly.

"Like, okay, look up at that cloud and tell me what you see," Bree said, pointing up at the closest cloud above them.

"What do you mean, what do I see? It's a cloud. I see a cloud," Alessandro insisted.

"No, what do you see? Like when you go to a shrink and they make you look at ink blots," Bree explained.

Alessandro looked over at her. "How much wine did you drink?"

She smacked his arm. "I'll go first. I see a rabbit."

"A rabbit?" Alessandro asked, laughing.

"Yeah, the top of that one is shaped like ears, long rabbit ears."

"Ah, I see what you're doing now. All right then. That one there…looks like…" Alessandro squinted his eyes as if hard in concentration. "An airplane."

"Oh, yeah. I see that," Bree agreed. "Okay, what about that one?" She pointed to a cloud to Alessandro's right.

"That one looks rather like my wife's sweet pert little ass," Alessandro joked.

"After two kids? You're delusional," she said laughing. "My turn. I think that one looks like…" Bree tilted her head.

"My wife's beautiful round breasts," Alessandro injected.

"Stop that!" Bree said, giggling.

"Excuse me, I'm just playing the game."

"No, you're not. You're being a horny guy."

Alessandro pressed a hand to his chest as if she had wounded him. "To prove it to you, I say we compare." He undid the buttons of her blouse and Bree was laughing too hard to stop him.

She shivered when the breeze hit her skin. Alessandro's eyes flared hotly but he tore his gaze away and then looked up at the sky. He looked back at her and nodded.

"I was right, see?" He said with a mischievous grin that reminded her of Gianni.

"Oh I see all right," Bree snickered.

Alessandro lowered his mouth to hers and he grabbed her by the waist, moving on to his back and bringing her with him. "Ah now, let's see. That cloud—"

"Hey, it's my turn now," Bree objected.

"I'm new at this game. You should let me have more turns. Now where was I?" Alessandro looked up at her. "Ah yes. I think that cloud right there looks like…" his hand moved down between her legs and cupped her core through her jeans, making Bree jump. "My wife's beautiful warm pussy," he said huskily, pressing his fingers against the material so that it rubbed against her folds that were getting slicker with each second. "But I think we're going to have to see it to compare."

He flipped her onto her back again and pulled off her clothes until she was completely naked.

"Oh yes. I'd say I'm very good at this game, darling." Alessandro ran his mouth up her thigh and Bree held her breath as the heat of his mouth danced over her slick skin.

When his lips closed over her clitoris, Bree stared up at the clouds she could no longer see because her vision blurred with the haze of pleasure and she had to agree that her husband was very, very good at the game.

His tongue was slow and lazy, as if they had all the time in the world. Bree arched and behind her she could see the canopy of pretty apple blossoms. Some of them fell with the breeze, landing near her head. When she tilted her head forward again, she could see the sun and the beautiful blue sky, dotted with clouds. She closed her eyes and saw red, the warmth of the sun bathing her face. She moaned as Alessandro's tongue moved deliciously between her thighs, the blanket soft against her back. She took a quick nervous scan of the area, even though he had assured her no one would see them. They had the high stone wall ahead of them, the orchard blocking the view of the house and the bridge hiding them even further. The soft movement of the pond filled her ears and Bree felt as if she herself were swimming, floating.

Coming.

"Oh God…" she sighed, biting her lip, trying to be quiet, just in case. Her body trembled with anticipation of the heated explosion just moments away.

Alessandro's fingers were determined, yet gentle as they kept her thighs spread. His skin was warm against hers and he dotted sweet kisses along her slick folds before thrusting his tongue deep into her pussy and making her come apart with a cry of ecstasy.

Bree gripped his hair as her body bowed, suspended in delicious pleasure before coming down with a sated sigh of release. "Holy…fuck," she sighed. "You're too good at that."

He smiled smugly at her as he climbed up her body. "My pleasure." He dropped a kiss on her stomach, making her giggle. "You're like gold all over, especially out here in the sun." His hands came up to her breasts and he kneaded them gently, rubbing his thumbs over the rosy nipples. "Beautiful," he sighed. "You stop my heart with how beautiful you are, Brianna."

Bree shivered at the soft passion in his words. "Ditto," she said, sliding her fingers through his hair. She cupped his face and brought him closer so she could kiss him.

He groaned into her mouth and Bree slid her hands into the back of his shirt, feeling the warmth of his skin as the sun hit his back. She began undoing the buttons of his shirt but decided she wanted to see every inch of him become exposed with her full gaze so she pulled back and smiled at him before motioning him onto his back.

Alessandro gave a small chuckle as Bree laid him flat against the blanket and climbed over him. She finished unbuttoning his shirt and lowered her mouth to the crisp dusting of hair on his chest. She flicked her tongue over one nipple, then the other, loving the sound of his needy growl. The sun beat down against her back now, mixing with the light breeze and making her shiver. "You're all hard and beautiful," she remarked.

"Well, hard, certainly," he joked.

Bree looked down and smiled at the bulge in Alessandro's pants. She shimmied down and pressed herself against his erection. She bit her lip as she ground her hips against him, sending a fresh burst of pleasure through her blood.

Alessandro arched his head and clenched his teeth in obvious bliss. Bree did it again, watching the sun and branches make beautiful shadows on his face as he tilted his head back and along the column of his neck. Bree leaned down and ran her mouth along the thick column of his neck.

"I love you," Bree whispered in his ear.

His erection got thicker between her legs.

She sighed and kissed him, feeling him slide his fingers in her hair before she moved lower still. When her face was level with his groin, she smiled at him. "Yeah?"

"God, yes," he pleaded.

She undid his zipper and helped him push his pants down past his hips, freeing his cock. He was already long and nearly fully erect when Bree took him in her hands. He felt like warm steel and beads of his arousal peeked through the head, beckoning her tongue. She heard him hiss when she licked the drops, the taste of him unbelievably arousing to her because of its familiarity. The taste of his cock in her mouth, the feel of the warm skin was like another part of herself, separate from her and yet connected to her very soul. Bree sucked the head slowly, feeling a deep tug of primal pleasure as Alessandro made his familiar sounds of greedy, needy ecstasy. She cupped his sac lightly as he sucked him. She loved that she knew exactly how to touch him, suck him, love him. Bree smiled as she thought about how marriage was supposed to be boring, the sex was supposed to get mundane, normal, run of the mill. Certainly not her marriage, she thought with a little thrill. She could never imagine sex with this man becoming run of the mill. She felt such joy in touching him, in knowing this body as well as she knew her own. When he touched her, it was as if he made love to her very soul, and Bree felt it was the same for him.

"Fucking Christ," he moaned, bucking his hips, wanting her to take more.

Bree obliged, burying her nose in his male scent. She looked up and Alessandro's teeth were clenched and his head was arched back. His body was flushed and his stomach tightened and released as he panted.

"Wait…wait…" he pleaded, pulling her away and up. "I need to get inside of you now. God I need to feel you tight around me…" He pulled her up over him. "Oh sweet fuck…" he moaned as Bree felt him guide her down onto his shaft.

"Ah yes…" Bree cried as he filled her, hard and deep. She arched back and he moved her hips back and forth, angling her so that her clitoris rubbed against the warm damp skin of his shaft.

Outside, in the middle of the day, buck naked, Bree thought with a small giggle. No. Definitely not mundane. She felt a shiver shoot through her and knew she was almost there again. Bree fell forward and Alessandro grabbed the back of her head and brought her mouth down over his as he pushed into her again and again.

"What is my gorgeous wife smiling about?" he asked, his eyes shining with desire.

"Happy," she explained, kissing him, tasting him. "Just happy."

He groaned and wrapped an arm around her waist, flipping her onto her back without pulling out of her. "Ah, then I consider it my duty to always make my gorgeous wife smile," Alessandro said, his breath hot against her face as he drove into her again and again.

She dug her nails into his bare back and moaned. "Oh yes…yes…" She brought her knees up and tightened her thighs around him.

His tongue slid into her mouth, mimicking the movements of his body. "God…" he groaned, snapping his hips, fucking her closer and closer to the edge.

Bree could feel him swell and throb inside of her and knew he was close. Now, she thought for a second. Let it happen now, out here in this beautiful place.

"Love you," he growled, meeting her gaze as he pumped with increasing speed.

"Oh, I love you," Bree shivered, feeling her belly tighten with impending release. "Alessandro…Alessandro…" She tilted her hips when she felt him release into her with deep, hot spurts. The feel of his release and the image of his essence bathing her womb, possibly creating another baby triggered her own orgasm.

"Brianna…Brianna…" he panted against her face, his eyes tight as he was overcome with pleasure. She held him close until they both stopped trembling. He fell on top of her and Bree could feel his breath, quick against her breasts.

"Perfect," Alessandro sighed. "Always so bloody perfect."

Bree ran her fingers through his hair and stared up at the sky. "It really is," she agreed.

He ran his fingers along her belly. "Is it normal?" He asked.

She'd been married before. He hadn't. She would certainly know. "If you're lucky," Bree replied.

"I expected to tolerate marriage," he confessed, running a finger along the curve of her breast. "I never expected this. This all-consuming thing. Nobody I know wants their wife like I want you, Brianna. They're married but they have women on the side. I don't want anyone else."

"Good, 'cause I'd kill you," Bree laughed, though she knew what he meant.

He smiled and propped himself up on his elbow. "That's why I love you." He lowered his head to her breast and groaned.

So did she, feeling the flickers of desire grow again.

"Fuck…I want you again." He moved his hand between her legs and Bree trembled at his touch. "I just fucked you and I want you again." When he was ready, he pushed into her pussy again. "Bloody hell, this can't be normal."

"Mmmm," Bree agreed, wrapping her legs around his waist. "It's better."

CHAPTER TWENTY-FIVE

"A bottle of your best sparkling cider, Louise," Alessandro said smiling up at the red headed woman.

"Spar-," her eyes moved over to Brianna and her mouth fell open. "Oh my, are you-," she began excitedly but Brianna cut her off

"Oh no," she shook her head quickly. "Or, well, we're trying but we don't know yet."

"Oh how wonderful!" Louise exclaimed. "One bottle of sparkling cider on the house."

Alessandro saw Brianna's gaze move over his shoulder and her beautiful blue eyes hardened.

Alessandro turned around and saw Rebecca walking in with an older man.

"That is Rebecca being a two timing skank. She's supposed to be all in love with my brother and here she is walking in with a guy old enough to be her father," Brianna snapped, leaping up from her chair.

Alessandro was barely able to get across the table to grab her hand in time. "Oh no you don't."

She pulled her hand away. "I'm not letting her get away with this."

"No, Brianna. Brianna!" Alessandro hissed helplessly as she stormed towards Rebecca's table.

"Well, isn't this nice? Does my brother know you're

screwing around behind his back?" Brianna asked, a hand on her hip.

"I beg your pardon?" the man asked.

"You shut your mouth, Bree!" Rebecca hissed. "You don't know what you're talking about. This is simply a business dinner."

"Perhaps it's better if we do this some other time?" the man got to his feet.

"No, please. It's all right. She's just unbalanced-" Rebecca insisted sending Bree a murderous glare.

"It's perfectly all right." With a stiff nod the man stalked away.

Rebecca glared at her. "Congratulations. You just cost me a million dollar account."

Brianna crossed her arms over her chest. "Oh don't worry. I'm sure with your talents you could earn another mil in no time. I'll tell them to clear a street corner for you."

Rebecca lunged for her and Alessandro stepped between the two women.

"Brianna, come on," he said guiding his wife away from the table.

"What? I'm not a child. I can handle her."

"I'm sure you can." He informed the waiter they would be taking their bottle of sparkling cider home. "But you're letting your emotions get away with you. Your brother is a grown man and can handle himself."

Brianna blew a raspberry at him.

"Oh yes, quite mature. Let's go home." He guided her towards the entrance.

"Damn, I forgot my purse," Brianna said turning back.

"All right. Don't dawdle," Alessandro demanded.

Rebecca stormed past them, making sure to push against Brianna on her way to the door.

Alessandro watched Brianna's eyes widen and she took a step toward the woman.

He gripped her arm. "Your purse, darling."

Brianna rolled her eyes and walked back towards the

tables.

Alessandro held the door open for Rebecca as they walked out.

Bree lifted her purse from the chair and was making her way toward the door when a popping sound made her halt mid step. It almost sounded like... Her fingers tightened around her purse and she hesitated a moment before pushing the door open to leave. She expected to see Alessandro and Rebecca through the glass but didn't. A knot tightened in her belly and she rested her hand on the steel bar of the door tilting her head to look for Alessandro's car. She pushed her nervousness away. He was probably waiting for her inside the car. She opened the door and jumped when she heard Alessandro's voice coming from the direction of the car.

"Brianna! No! Stay inside!" Oh God, she'd been right. It had been a gunshot that had made that noise.

She heard him but didn't see him. An icy dagger of fear sliced through her and she was torn between running towards him and staying put as he ordered her.

"What's going on?" Louise asked.

Then there was more popping and Bree screamed and ducked, bringing Louise down with her. "Alessandro!" she cried.

She could see him now, or more accurately, she could see his car door open and then close. Bree felt a small beat of relief. Alessandro had bulletproof glass installed in every car they used so for the moment he was safe.

Assuming he hadn't already been shot.

"The police are already on their way." Louise explained.

"Thank God," Bree said. Her phone rang in her purse and she scrambled to answer it, recognizing Alessandro's cell-phone number. "Are you all right?"

"I am. It's Rebecca. She's been shot. I'm going to drive her to the hospital."

"Rebecca's been shot?" Bree asked. She despised the woman but…God. Her next thought was of Brian. She'd give anything to not to have to make her next call. "Louise's called the police. They're on their way."

"Good. You stay there and then ride with the police. Meet me at the hospital."

"Alessandro who shot"

But he'd already hung up.

Her heart was racing the entire time she rode to the hospital and she felt like she couldn't breathe until she set eyes on Alessandro again.

When Bree got there the nurse told her that Alessandro had dropped Rebecca off and then left. "Left? Where?" she asked desperately.

"He didn't say but he told me to tell you that he'd meet you back here when he was done and that you were to wait for him," the nurse explained.

"Bree?" Colin asked coming out of the elevator.

Bree groaned, not in the mood for any kind of confrontation but he surprised her by not looking at her like he wanted to shove her head through a meat grinder. "What's going on? Is it Will?"

"No. No, he's fine. There was a shooting outside Callini's. Rebecca," she explained.

"Somebody shot Rebecca?" Colin asked. "Who?"

"I don't…Oh God…no," she moaned, her knees buckling. She covered her mouth and held onto the counter of the nursing station to keep herself upright. "What if they weren't aiming at Rebecca? What if it was Alessandro? They wanted to shoot Alessandro."

"Bree. Bree, calm down, okay?" Colin said, holding her arms.

"He went after whoever it was, Colin! Don't tell me to calm down! It's Arturo, right? It has to be Arturo." She jerked out of his grasp.

They both got to their feet when Alex came out of Rebecca's room. He met Bree's gaze and shook his head. "They used a hollow point bullet and it hit her in the chest. There's nothing we can do."

Bree looked at Rebecca's door and then back at Alex. "Then…what? That's it? You're not even gonna try?"

"We're getting the OR ready but…it doesn't look good."

"Jesus Christ," Bree burst, pushing past her and storming into Rebecca's room. "All right you listen to me, you bitch. You are not doing this to my brother."

Rebecca's face twisted in obvious pain and she opened her eyes then looked at Bree and groaned. "Oh geez."

"You make this big stink about how much you love Brian, well you prove it. You fight."

Bree tried not to notice how her arch-enemy was as white as the sheet. All she saw was her brother and how, misguided though he was, he loved this woman. How destroyed he would be if she died.

Rebecca gave a pained weak laugh. "Right. Like you…give a damn."

"I have hated you for years…but I never…not this," Bree admitted uncomfortably. She'd just been in the wrong place at the wrong time.

Rebecca snorted. "Well hell, looks like your problems are gonna be over soon, huh? With me out of…the way, your brother can move on. I always thought it…kind of funny," Rebecca groaned, her eyes staring up at the ceiling. "You and me. How alike we are."

"That's the pain medication talking," Bree sneered.

"I think that's the only reason why Michael paid me any attention when we were kids. I reminded him of you." Rebecca said.

"Yeah, let's not do the whole trip down memory lane or you're going to remind me that I hate you and would like nothing more than to pull the plug."

"Do me a favour?" Rebecca asked.

"I'm not doing anything for you. You're getting better and you're getting out of here, preferably out of New York and out of my life."

"I know you don't believe this but…loved your brother. Only man…tell him for me…please."

"Dammit Rebecca, stop this. Stop with the deathbed crap."

Her eyes met Bree's desperately and then seemed to glaze over and Bree could feel her enemy's life slipping away with each beep of the monitor. She nodded slowly. "I'll tell him," Bree said, her eyes burning.

"Thank—"

And then there was nothing but the long final note of the monitor.

The doctors rushed in and Bree wiped her damp cheeks, horrified at her tears over a woman she despised. She stopped when she met Brian's panicked gaze.

"No," he pleaded. "Oh no! Rebecca!" He pushed past Bree and tried to get past the doctors but they wouldn't let him enter the room.

Not that it mattered at that point. Rebecca was dead.

Bree wrapped her arms around her brother, holding him as they sat in the waiting room. His head was on her shoulder and he looked utterly lost. She knew what he was feeling. Exactly. For all her hatred of Rebecca, Brian had loved her, as she had loved Michael. Now Rebecca was gone.

Bree took a deep shaky breath. Alessandro, where are you? She was afraid that she knew exactly where he was. She knew him too well. He'd gone after the shooter.

Oh God. Bring him back safe. Please.

But what if whatever Alessandro was doing went against God? Would God turn away and leave Alessandro to whatever danger he was facing?

She saw Andy coming out of the elevator and shot to her feet. "Tell me he's all right. Where is he? Why isn't Alessandro with you?"

"He asked me to stay with you. He's fine," the bodyguard assured her.

"Why isn't he with you?" Bree pressed, her heart racing.

"He's got everything under control and told me to tell you not to worry. He'll be here as soon as he can."

"Does he know who did this?" Colin asked, getting up from his seat.

Andy looked over at Colin and Bree saw the blank look settle over his face. He certainly wasn't going to tell this man anything.

Bree turned to her brother, torn between wanting to stay and comfort him and wanting to go track down her husband.

"You know who did this, right?" Brian asked coldly.

Andy gave Brian the same expressionless look.

"You take me to them. You take me to whoever did this. Now," Brian ordered.

Andy didn't move.

Brian grabbed his collar and Bree tried to pull him away.

"Brian, don't!" she pleaded but if she was worried that Andy would fight back, she hadn't needed to. The bodyguard simply pulled Brian's fists off of him.

"Step back."

"You're going to take me to wherever Alessandro is."

"You're going to sit down and wait for Mr. Dardano," Andy countered.

Luckily, they didn't have to wait long. Shortly after the hospital staff took Rebecca to the morgue, Alessandro came out of the elevator.

The tension in his body seemed to drain when he saw Bree and she threw her arms around him.

"Oh thank God!" she cried. She noticed with a start that he smelled like soap and that his hair was slightly damp.

As if he'd showered.

She shivered but realized that he was shaking too and it eased her nerves a little to know that whatever he had been doing, it wasn't something that he took lightly.

"How is she?" Alessandro asked.

"She's dead," Brian snapped. "You tell me who did this. You take me to them, right fucking now."

"Christ," Alessandro said, covering his mouth. He moved his gaze to Brian next. "You don't need to worry about the shooter. He's been taken care of."

"Did he tell you why he did it? Is he working for Arturo? Is Arturo back?" Bree asked, her heart in her throat.

Alessandro gave Colin a look of irritation and pulled Bree off to the side. Brian stubbornly followed them. "I'd rather discuss this with my wife in private," Alessandro insisted.

"Yeah well, I don't give a flying fuck what you'd rather. You tell me why the woman I love is dead."

Alessandro took a deep trembling breath. "He shot the wrong woman." His eyes moved to Bree and they were filled with both rage and panic. He ran a shaking hand over her hair.

Bree took a step back and raised both her hands to her mouth as horror washed over her. "Oh God."

Brian closed his eyes and fell against the back of one of the chairs.

"He was informed by Arturo that I would be with my wife at the restaurant, a woman with blonde hair and he was to take both of us out."

"Oh, and I went to get my purse and…oh! Oh Brian!" Bree turned to her brother.

He shook his head. "Don't. This wasn't your fault." His gaze shifted to Alessandro. "So Arturo is back. I'm helping you take him down."

"No!" Bree exclaimed. "Brian, please. You don't know what he's capable of."

"I just saw what he's capable of Bree. I'm not letting him get another shot at you. I'm not letting him take out one more person I love," Brian vowed.

"Alessandro, tell him how dangerous Arturo is, please! Tell him that—"

"Brianna, Brian has every right to go after Arturo. I would do the same thing. I am going to do the same thing."

"Oh that's great. So you're going to turn Brian into a killer like you?" Colin asked coming up behind Bree.

"The sniper was instructed to shoot a hollow point bullet into my wife, the mother of my children. Don't you stand there with your sanctimonious airs simply because you've lost the balls your ex-wife stole from you."

"You son of a bitch!" Colin lunged at Alessandro but Bree rushed quickly to hold him off.

"Colin don't!"

"Why not, huh, Bree? You worried your husband will take me out?"

"Don't tempt me, Neally," Alessandro snapped.

"That's enough!" Bree cried. "Alessandro, please. Can we just go home? I need to set my eyes on our babies. I need to hold them," she pleaded pressing her face against his chest.

Alessandro wanted Gianni and Will to sleep in the bed with them tonight and Bree didn't mind in the least. He absently played with Will's curls as the little boy slept pressed against him. Gianni slept peacefully against Bree and she and Alessandro whispered as they dozed.

"It's so easy for me to forget that other part of our lives when I see you like this, with Will and Gianni. Tonight, that was kind of jolt," Bree admitted. "You're so good with them."

"That's because I love them. That makes that other part necessary," Alessandro said. "I know getting married wasn't really your choice—"

"Of course it was my choice. I love you," Bree rushed to assure him.

He gave her a small smile. "That's not what I mean. I have no doubt that you and I would be married. We were meant to happen, darling, because we are the other half of each other. I only mean that you agreed to marry me because of the vendetta. I don't think it really occurred to you the things that you would have to allow for. What being a Dardano truly entailed. Who I would have to be sometimes."

"I knew you weren't exactly squeaky clean," Bree tossed back with a snort. "That you had people trying to kill you, that you used violence to protect yourself. I accept that. I've lived in the same world." She tucked her hands under the blanket so he wouldn't see them shaking.

"Do you?" Alessandro asked, raising his eyebrow. "I don't think you do."

"I just can't have Brian... Alessandro. I can't worry about him too. Please. I'm begging you, turn him away."

Alessandro sighed and shook his head. "How can I do that and not be a hypocrite? How can I when I think he's right to want his vengeance. The fact that you'd ask me to go against who I am, tells me that it's easy for you to say you accept that part of my life but you really don't. That man that accidentally shot Rebecca, I killed him, Brianna. I pictured his bullet finding its intended target and I had no conscience, no guilt over ending his life. I don't usually enjoy that part of myself but it's necessary to keep me alive. But when it's personal, when it's a personal attack against my family, oh, that I enjoy. I enjoy taking my revenge against an enemy who dares to touch the people I love."

Bree shuddered. She understood…in theory. But to have him spell it out like that, so frankly, terrified her. "I would do anything to protect you and the boys too," she said, though the words sounded weak to her own ears.

"Yes, but you wouldn't enjoy it."

"You can't make me believe that killing is so easy for you," Bree pressed. "I saw you when you were holding Gianni. You were practically shaking."

"Yes, because it was your fucking purse that saved your life tonight. Not me," he sneered and Bree was shocked at his self-loathing. "That man could so easily have taken you from me because my guard was down. Even though I should have known to make certain there is never a threat to you or the boys no matter where we go. But I was lulled. Soft."

"That's not true. Alessandro, you can't keep thinking that everyone is out to get you and stay sane," Bree reached over to stroke his cheek.

He placed his hand over hers and closed his eyes. "I should be. I need to keep that wall up. But I need you and the boys at the same time. My father is right," he snorted. "You make me weak, but I'm afraid of what my life would be if I lost you or our children. I'd know nothing but hate and darkness. That's why I held Gianni so close. I look at him and you and Will, you're my light."

CHAPTER TWENTY-SIX

"Tada!" Bree said saucily after blowing a paint chip off her bangs and hopping up onto the bar.

Alessandro looked up from his sweeping.

Three weeks later and the bar was ready for its grand opening the following week. They had hired people to do some of the reconstruction but for the most part, Bree was happy with the bar as it was.

She'd gotten a local up and coming blues band to perform for the opening night. Bree had joked it would assure Bernardo didn't attend, being obsessed with opera and disdaining any other type of music as he did. No such luck. He'd smiled and told her he was looking forward to it.

To hurry the process along, she, Alessandro, Vanessa, Hadley, Meggie and Brian had taken up some of the painting and cleaning. She thought it would help keep Brian busy, though he still held his grief in his eyes.

Alessandro's eyes flared with hungry understanding as he stalked towards Bree on the bar.

"For good luck, you know? You're supposed to christen any new place." She said, wrapping her legs around his waist and drawing him close to her.

"Ah, a good luck fuck, as it were?" he joked, sliding his hands along her thighs, lifting her skirt as he went along.

"I love how eloquent you limeys are," Bree teased, tugging lightly on his earlobe with her teeth.

"Limey?" Alessandro asked, smacking her bottom.

The bar had only the small row of lights over the bottles of liquor. The rest of it was bathed in darkness as they were preparing to go home.

"Well, I do confess, we English do like to get straight to the heart of things," he moved his hand under her skirt to find her damp heat.

Bree moaned and found his mouth as his fingers slipped past her panties to touch hot wet heat. She slid her tongue in his mouth to stroke invitingly along his and her hands went to the belt of his jeans. He'd worn jeans so he wouldn't dirty any of his more formal trousers and Bree had spent half her time enjoying how delicious his ass looked in the casual wear. "You should wear them more often," she insisted. "Positively mouth-watering." She pushed the zipper down and eased her hand inside to find hard heat.

"Mmm, ditto," he joked, pressing a finger against her clitoris and rubbing slowly. "In your pretty spring frocks, all I can imagine is pushing them up around your waist and doing all manner of naughty, debauched things to you," Alessandro purred, pushing her panties down to her ankles.

Bree kicked them off her sandals. "Really? Naughty, hmm?"

"Oh indeed," he nodded, sliding a long finger into her, making her head arch back at the exquisite pleasure. "Highly improper. Things that will make your pretty cheeks blush." He added a second finger and began pumping slowly.

"Well…mmm. God…I gotta say, since meeting you…Ah…ah…it takes a lot to make me…blush. Oh!" Bree cried out when his other thumb came between her legs to rub her clitoris while his fingers pumped faster…harder.

He removed his hand just as she was about to go over, making her cry out in desperation.

"Hey!" she protested. But her emptiness was short lived as Alessandro pushed her skirt up and replaced his fingers with his tongue. "Oh fuck me…" Bree moaned arching back. She propped herself up on her elbow as she watched him spread her open and lick her damp folds with diligent purpose.

He was finely attuned to her body enough by now so that as soon as Bree was teetering on the edge of her orgasm, he stopped again.

She smacked his shoulder. "You're mean!"

He smiled at her, his mouth damp. "Mmm, I want to feel you when you come, darling. I want to feel you squeezing me when you lose control. Will you forgive me when I let you come with my cock in this delicious body?" He asked, nuzzling her neck and sliding his hands beneath her dress to knead her breasts in his warm hands.

Bree moaned when he kissed her and pulled her off the bar to set her on the leather stool in front of it. "Well," she said, pulling his jeans down to free his straining erection. She took him in her hands and stroked slowly, feeling him swell and feeling his grunts of pleasure against her hair. "That all depends on how hard you work for my forgiveness. Will you work hard, my love?" she asked, licking at his lips in a beckoning motion.

"Very…" he assured her bucking his hips to thrust through her fingers.

She stroked the tight sac at the base of his cock and heard him whimper as she rubbed the head of his cock against her soaked pussy. "Very hard?"

"Oh yes." His fingers dug into her thighs as he spread even more open for him and with on fierce, hard thrust, impaled his cock deep inside of her.

"Oh God!" they both cried out at the same time as the explosive sensation seized them both.

"Do you know yet?" he asked her, his voice tight.

She shook her head. Her cycle had never been regular. Maybe they'd know next week. Maybe she'd just be late. But maybe…just maybe…

It wouldn't take long, they both knew it and their gazes locked with united purpose.

"Fuck me…" Bree sighed, dropping a kiss on the end of his nose. "Fuck me, Alessandro."

He held her thighs open and began thrusting fast, too caught up in the electricity they generated between them for long leisurely lovemaking. They would go home and take their time

Bree gripped his shoulders and worked with him as he drove into her again and again. "Oh God…yes…don't stop…" she moaned, burying her face in his neck, sucking at the racing pulse.

"Fuck…" he groaned. "Brianna…Brianna…Beautiful…Love you…"

Then she clamped tight around him as her nerves burst beneath her skin. He came at the same time, his eyes closing tight at the same time hers did as their mutual climax rocked through them at the exact same time.

As their movements slowed, Bree shivered. It didn't happen often, but when they did come at the same time, it always shocked her and made her feel just that little bit more certain that their souls really were connected.

"Fucking Christ, I love you," he groaned into her hair, rocking slowly, softening inside her but still apparently unwilling to pull out.

"Mmm, love you too," she kissed his neck and rocked with him hoping that if it hadn't happened yet, this would be a perfect time, when they'd come together.

United in both body and soul.

Bree felt something against her stomach. A poking…no…tapping. As the haze of sleep began to lift she heard Alessandro's voice.

"Anybody home in there?"

She giggled and opened her eyes. "What are you doing?" She looked down at him, his head level with her stomach.

"Just checking," he confessed.

"And were you expecting an answer 'cause that would be hell-a impressive," Bree laughed, propping herself up on her elbows.

"Well, she is a Dardano after all," Alessandro winked.

Bree sighed. "Alessandro, I don't want you to be disappointed—"

"Oh, I'm not, darling. I'm not. If it doesn't happen this month then we'll just keep trying. Won't that be fun?" he grinned at her.

"Well, even if this week goes by. I could just be late what with the stress of the opening tomorrow and all. You said 'she'. You want this one to be a girl?"

She sat up in bed and Alessandro dropped a kiss on her stomach before joining her upright.

"I won't be disappointed with another son. But I would like to have a little girl. A little wee girl with blonde pigtails and pretty lacy frocks and bows in her hair—"

"Ah, so you want a child from the 1950's?" Bree joked.

He poked her side. "What do you think of Gabriella Francesca Dardano?"

Bree smiled a little surprised. "I like it, but why Gabriella?"

"First painting I ever bought was Madonna and Child by Signorelli. He painted it in the 16th century and gave it to his daughter Gabriella as a gift. I always liked that name."

"I've never seen this painting of yours. Is it in London?"

Alessandro pressed his lips together and gave her a sheepish smile. "You could say that. I gave it to a friend."

"A friend?" Bree asked, cocking an eyebrow as she picked up on his tone.

"First girl I ever slept with. Lovely girl with long black hair down to her waist."

"Ah I see and it was worthy of a masterpiece, huh?" Bree pressed, enjoying the blushing in his cheeks. "I'm suddenly very aware of the fact that you've never offered me any priceless art. Maybe I should up my technique."

"Well, I confess I had no frame of reference as it was my first time, hers as well."

"How old were you?" Bree asked, her curiosity peaked.

"An untried, fumbling lad of fourteen," he admitted.

"Fourteen!" Bree exclaimed in shock.

"A late bloomer, I'm afraid," he said with a shrug.

She smacked his arm. "What are you talking about? You were practically a baby! What were you doing having sex?"

"You Americans certainly are prudish, aren't you?' Alessandro asked. He stroked her thigh. "Well, some of you, anyway."

"So you want to name our daughter after the first girl you had sex with?"

"No no," Alessandro laughed holding up his hands. "Gabriella was the artist's daughter."

"Mmmhmm," Bree said, her lips pressed together.

He followed her to the nursery to wake up Gianni to find that he was already awake and so was Will.

"But is okay 'cause my mommy is yo' mommy too," Will explained, both boys on their stomachs on the floor.

Bree blinked, wondering how Will had gotten Gianni out of his crib, but then she saw the fluffy Elmo chair propped against it and her heart fell into her stomach thinking how they both could have fallen. She was about to burst and scold Will but Alessandro held her back, wanting to continue to watch.

"Oooo," Gianni echoed.

"And den when you see my udder daddy in hev'n and he gonna

like you like Alessandro like me eben though he nod my borned daddy."

"Daddy," Gianni said. "Ada good mideed. Eee?" He held up his blanky and put it on Will's head.

"No. I don' haf one anymo. I a big boy now."

"Oy now?" Gianni asked.

"Yep and you gon' be big too. Den we can go to da park and pay ball."

Gianni crawled to the ball in the corner and pushed it back to Will with a giggle. "Baaa." He pushed himself up in a sitting position.

Will laughed and rolled it back to him.

Gianni clapped.

Will leaned over and patted his head. "Good boy."

Gianni patted Will's shoulder. "Boy." He leaned down and kissed Will's knee.

Bree couldn't breathe, her tears were rolling down her face.

"I love you," Alessandro whispered against her hair, his voice thick with emotion.

"Mama!" Gianni burst happily, throwing his arms up as he spotted her.

Bree stepped into the room.

"Hi mommy. Hi daddy. We was jus' talking bout tings," Will explained.

"Really?' Alessandro asked, sweeping Will up into his arms.

"Next time you want to have a heart to heart with your little brother, let me know," Bree insisted, rubbing Gianni's back.

"But you was sleeping," Will explained.

"Yes, but you could have dropped him,"

"Oh dat's silly, mommy. I never drop Gianni. He my brother."

Bree turned to Alessandro and shook her head, smiling. "How can you argue with that?"

"All right, you little troublemakers. Let's have breakfast and then head over to mummy's club, shall we? We have a lot of work to do before her party tomorrow."

"Pa-ee!" Gianni said clapping. He pointed to Will. "Ma boy."

"Dat's right, Gianni," Will nodded.

Then Gianni turned to Alessandro. "Ma boy?"

"Course daddy's a boy. Dat's why he's a daddy," Will insisted.

Gianni turned his head to Bree and poked her. "Ma mamma

boy?"

"Oh brother," Will shook his head and covered his eyes. "He needs work still," he explained to Alessandro with a shrug.

Wrong! Bree kicked the shoe off and it went flying across the room. Alessandro opened the bedroom door and caught the black open toed shoe as it came soaring towards him, narrowly missing his head.

"Nice catch, daddy," Will giggled. "Oooh, mommy, you look shiny."

Bree patted her red satin dress. "Thanks, sweetie. Has Vanessa dressed Gianni, yet?"

"Yep, he looks like he belongs on the top of a wedding cake," he snorted. "As do I." He slid a hand down his chest, covered by black linen shirt and black sport jacket.

"Where's your tie?" Bree asked.

"I hid it," he grinned.

She moved towards him quickly, her stomach a bundle of nerves and she fixed his collar. "Well, that's okay. You look better like this, more casual. This isn't one of your father's grand balls." She took a quick sniff of his spicy cologne. "Mmm, I like it."

"Do dat mean I can wear my runny shoes?" Will asked.

"No, it 'do' not," Bree insisted.

"JesusmarriedJoseph," he grumbled turning away back out into the hallway.

"Wait, wait. Let me look at your hair. You need a haircut. You're going to look like a dark haired Orphan Annie soon. Alessandro, can you run a tiny bit of moose through his curls, please?"

"Mommy, dat's a girl!" Will protested, patting his hair.

"Brianna, darling, calm down." Alessandro held her shoulders.

"I can't, Alessandro. Tonight has to go off without a hitch."

Alessandro rubbed the back of his neck. "I don't know, sweetheart. Perhaps we should postpone tonight's opening."

Bree stared at him. "Are you trying to give me a stroke?" She reached into the closet and pulled out more shoes.

"I'm only unsure about our security tonight. Will, do me a favour and go see if Gianni and Vanessa are ready," Alessandro said.

"Okie. And I nod wearing no mooses on my head, mommy."

Will scowled and left.

"What are you talking about, Alessandro? I think you and my father have every bodyguard in New York watching the club tonight. Arturo and his men aren't getting anywhere near us."

"I'd feel better if we were staying home. You could send someone in your place, like a representative," Alessandro said.

"Oh, so it's okay if someone else dies?" Bree asked shaking her head.

"As opposed to my wife and children? I hope that was a rhetorical question," Alessandro scowled.

"Alessandro, come on. We can't spend the rest of our lives hiding from Arturo. That's no way to live. I know that you'll keep us safe from him. I know it," Bree took a moment to wrap her arms around his waist.

"Well, I'm glad you have faith in me but I'm still not comfortable about this," he grumbled. "Knowing that son of a bitch is out there."

"We can't live our entire lives in hiding. You know what could help ease your stress?" Bree asked, smiling up at him.

"Mmm?" he asked cocking an eyebrow.

"Help me pick out shoes," she pleaded and rushed to the bed where she had dumped her wide array of heels.

"Hi. I'd like to welcome you all to the opening of Adresca. I really couldn't have done this without the help of my family and friends. I only hope I can keep that family tradition alive by dedicating this place to the head of both branches of the Dardano and O'Reiley family trees, Adriano and Francesca. Thank you to Don and his band for agreeing to play for us tonight. I hope everyone has an awesome time!" Bree said stepping off the stage to applause, less than enthusiastic from the O'Reileys specifically, but really, Bree didn't care. She'd only invited them to show people that she was the one making the effort. Brian and Beth were there and the rest of the O'Reiley brood followed out of curiosity.

The music started up and Bree looked around for Alessandro. She saw Vanessa over by the bar feeding Gianni juice from a straw.

"Have you seen my husband?" Bree asked.

Vanessa nodded. "He's outside talking to the security guys."

Bree sighed. "I wish he would just let them do their job and relax." She walked up to her brother, who was holding Will now.

"How are you doing, huh?" Bree asked him.

"I'm all right. I wanted to be here for you," he leaned in and kissed her cheek. "I see mom's here. Have you talked to her?"

Bree turned to look at Angela. "Yeah, she was telling me about her therapy sessions and how she only has a few more to go to fulfill the terms of her probation."

"That was a good thing Alessandro did for her," Brian said.

"Yeah well, Alessandro's a good guy. I just wish everyone else could see that."

"They will soon. Give them time," Brian said, hugging her. "This place looks awesome. I'm gonna go say hi to Colin. I'll see you later, buddy," he said, kissing Will's cheeks and setting him on the floor.

Alessandro who wrapped an arm around her waist and nuzzled her neck.

"Hey, there you are. I was beginning to forget what my husband looked like," Bree said.

"My wife, the comedienne," Alessandro said.

"Mommy. I gonna go get some juice," Will said.

"Is it all clear outside?" Bree asked.

Alessandro grumbled. "Two of the guards never showed up. I don't like it."

"Oh so we're down to ninety-eight guards instead of a hundred?" Bree exaggerated.

"Brianna, you can think I'm going overboard but until Arturo is dead, I'll gladly go overboard, all right?" He kissed her forehead and smoothed a hand over her shoulder, brushing it with his fingers.

"Fine, but just don't keep skulking around in dark corners or I'll be forced to find some other hunky guy to enter…" her voice trailed off as her attention moved from Will taking his juice from the bartender to the glass behind the bartender.

There were red dots on the glass.

Alessandro brushed her shoulder again and Bree followed a row of red dots from the glass mirror to the wall.

Some of the red dots danced over the guests and as an icy cloak of understanding fell over Bree, it seemed to grip Alessandro as well.

Then she turned to face him and there were red dots on his chest, as well as her shoulder, which he had been brushing, thinking it was a speck of dust.

"GET DOWN!" he screamed to everyone grabbing Bree by the waist and throwing her down while and trying to be heard over the music.

Chaos erupted as gunfire drowned out the sound of music and people fell screaming on top of each other as pieces of the wall and glass from the doors and the mirrors rained down on them.

The gunfire raged on and on for what seemed like an eternity.

Then there was silence.

CHAPTER TWENTY-SEVEN

She heard crying. Loud, frightened, screaming crying. Will or Gianni? Both. Bree tried to get up but Alessandro's weight pinned her down. "Alessandro?" she struggled to turn and see him but he was too heavy. Her leg caught against a piece of broken glass and she grimaced at the sting as it pierced her skin while she tried to move out from under him. He groaned over her, but said nothing.

"Mammmmaaaaaa!" Gianni cried grabbing on to a bar stool and pulling himself to his feet, trying to struggle towards her.

Bree lifted her head and managed to push Alessandro off of her but when she looked over at Gianni again she saw a tiny red dot against his stomach. "NOOOOO!" she screamed, diving for him. She threw him to the floor as more bullets exploded through the room.

"Everybody stay down!" Jack yelled after the gunfire stopped in case anyone was tempted to get up.

There were screams and whimpers of fear and Bree could hear her aunt Keira begging Jack not to go outside. She heard the peeling sound of wheels and only then did she risk lifting her head again. Gianni was squirming and crying beneath her and she saw Will hiding behind another bar stool, holding his arm and crying.

Bleeding.

"Mommmmyyyyy. I…I…owwwww. I…owww!" Will screamed.

She crawled over to him, dragging Gianni with her, terrified of letting her baby go. "Stay down, sweetie. Show mommy where it…oh God…" She'd prayed it was glass but couldn't tell.

"Noooooo. It hurts mommy! It h...h…h…h...urts!" Will shrieked holding on to his arm and not wanting to show her. Blood was gushing from his arm and a stream hit Bree in the cheek when she pulled his fingers off the arm. An artery.

Terror gave her an odd sort of calm as she tried to get him to take off his jacket so she could wrap it around his arm.

Gianni had his baby fists tight in the bodice of her dress and he was still screaming and crying.

Will refused to move his arm so she could take off his jacket. "Noooo! I can't, mommy! Nooo! It hurt!"

"Here. Here," Brian said crawling over to them and pulling off his own suit jacket. "Here, Big Guy. I just need to slide this around your arm okay so it can stop bleeding."

Will shook his head, his face white even in the darkness. "It g…g…gonna hurt, Unco Bwian."

"I know, buddy. But we have to try, okay? Why don't you squeeze mommy's hand if it gets too bad," Brian suggested, sliding the sleeves of his jacket through Will's arm and side.

Will grabbed Bree's hand with his own damp cold fingers and squeezed hard, crying as Brian tied the jacket around his tiny arm. The blood continued to flow but it wasn't gushing. She smacked his face when Will's eyes rolled back in his head and he went limp, falling forward against her and Gianni.

"WILL!" Bree cried, shaking him.

Brian lifted his fingers to Will's neck and nodded at Bree. "He's okay. He just fainted. He turned to Vanessa, who was lying on the floor, blood flowing from her chest. "Oh Jesus." He did the same for her and dropped his head on her chest. "There's still a pulse, thank God."

Bree crawled back to Alessandro praying with all her heart that he was all right. "Alessandro. Alessandro!" She had a flashback to their wedding. He'd survived that. Would he be as lucky a second time? "Oh please, God. Alessandro, open your eyes." There was a large puddle of blood underneath him.

"Daddy. Up! Daddy! Up!" Gianni screamed pointing his arms towards Alessandro.

"Kevin!" Meggie screamed and Bree looked over at her friend who was hunched over her husband, crying, bleeding from a cut on her forehead.

People were slowly starting to sit up and take inventory of the damage.

Alessandro's face grimaced as he regained consciousness. "Brnna?"

"Alessandro? Are you all right, Alessandro?" Bernardo asked, blood running down the side of his face.

"Can'…legs…Can' feel…legs," he groaned. His dark eyes were glazed with pain and confusion and the settled on Bree with a flicker of relief and desperation. "All right…?"

"Yeah. Yeah, I'm okay. Gianni's okay too," she assured him.

"Will?" he groaned.

Bree took his hand. "He'll be okay." He would, she told herself. There was no other fucking alternative.

"Be?" Alessandro asked, his eyebrows drawing together with worry.

"Please, don't worry. Just save your strength. Look at me. Alessandro!" Bree screamed as his eyes fluttered closed. Her knees were now soaked with blood. "Sweetie, please open your eyes. Don't leave me. Oh God. Oh God. Alessandro! Dammit! Don't you leave me. Listen to me," Bree pleaded, caressing his face, her tears mingling with the blood as it dropped onto his face. "Stay with me, baby. Stay with me."

"Alessandro!" Bernardo grabbed his jacket.

"Don't move him. We don't know how badly hurt he is," Bree insisted. Can't feel my legs…She pushed down a flare of panic at those words and forced herself to concentrate on getting Alessandro to regain consciousness. She tried to set Gianni down next to Alessandro but he refused to let go of her. Bree kept an arm around him and the baby leaned over and patted Alessandro's chest.

"Up, daddy!" Gianni whimpered, his cries lessening.

"Noooooo! Kevin!" Meggie screamed again and Bree looked over at her friend.

She could hear the sirens wailing in the background and Bree felt a tightening in her chest as she watched Meggie trying to wake her husband. There was blood along Meggie's collarbone, probably from broken glass, or maybe from clutching Kevin's body against her. He wouldn't be waking up, Bree thought, feeling nauseous, judging by the way his eyes were staring up sightlessly, lifeless.

"John!" Angela screamed, slapping his face as he lay on the

floor.

"Daddy!" Bree screamed. Oh please no.

She felt pulled out of her body as she scanned the room. She could tell who had died so far by the empty, terrified looks of the people who loved them. Her mother and Meggie had the same broken looks on their faces.

Bree's mind was spinning. She didn't know where to turn. Will was curled next to the bar, his small face pale and his curls, that just that morning had been in stubborn fluffy disarray, were limp and damp against his scalp. She hoped he stayed unconscious for just a little while longer so that he wouldn't feel any more pain.

People were crying out, some in pain, and some in grief.

Meggie was curled up on Kevin's chest…as if willing the sound of his heart to fill her ears again.

Max was tying what looked like a towel around his girlfriend Lily's bleeding leg.

Her mother was stroking her father's forehead, her tears falling on his face. Bree couldn't breathe. She didn't know where to turn first. Daddy…Please, daddy. Daddy…

"Daddy, do 'eep?" Gianni asked, putting his hands together against his cheek, motioning sleep.

"Yeah, sweetie. Daddy's just sleeping," she said looking down at Alessandro. She leaned down and kissed Alessandro's damp face.

"Up ime ow, daddy. Up!" Gianni insisted.

Alessandro groaned, his eyes fluttering open.

"Alessandro, son. Save your strength," Bernardo ordered.

"Father…m'afraid," Alessandro whispered.

"Don't you worry about a thing. You're going to be just fine, I swear to you," Bernardo vowed and Bree couldn't help admiring his strength in that instant.

She felt like if someone so much as blew on her, she'd fall apart. She jumped nearly a foot in the air when the paramedics and police burst into the bar.

Gianni burrowed closer to her and began to cry again in the confusion.

"My son. My son's been shot," Bernardo said grabbing one of the paramedic's and dragging them towards Alessandro.

Bree pointed towards Will and rushed over with another medic to show them Will's injury. "Alessandro's my husband. My son is injured too. I think something pierced his arm because the blood was gushing before we tied my brother's jacket around him.

"How old is he?" the medic asked holding Will's head.

"Five. He's going to be okay, right? Please, God tell me he's going to be all right,"

The medic pulled back, looked at the puddle of blood around the little boy, and avoided Bree's gaze. "He's probably in shock right now. Let's just get him to the hospital and we'll do what we can for him."

"What you can? What does that mean? You'll fix him, dammit!" Bree shrieked. She could feel her control slipping.

After one of the other men strapped Vanessa to a gurney and pulled her away Brian stood up and came to wrap his arms around Bree and Gianni as the medic took Will next. She assured them that Gianni hadn't been hurt but they still wanted to look at him just in case.

Gianni however, refused to be parted from his mother and shrieked bloody murder as the man tried to pull him away. "Nooooooooooooooo! My mammmmaaaa! Don meeee noooooo!" He then proceeded to bite the man's wrist.

"Christ!"

"Please, I'll bring him in later." She didn't know who to ride with in the ambulances. There was Alessandro being lifted on to the gurney and Will was being rolled away.

There was no reason to ride with her father. Bree closed her eyes and bit down the overwhelming urge to scream.

Brian insisted that she ride with him in his car and they'd meet the ambulances at the hospital. Bree nodded absently and let him guide her out.

"He's dead."

Bree jerked in her seat and looked up at her mother as Angela came out of the hospital room.

"Oh God," Brian buried his face in his hands and his shoulders shook with sobs. "I want to see him. I need to see him."

He rushed into the room and Angela took his seat next to Bree.

"How is Will?" she asked her.

"They gave him something for the pain. He's sleeping now," Bree explained. "Daddy's gone. I can't…Oh God…" Bree hugged Gianni closer to her and buried her face in his sweet smelling neck.

Angela leaned over and hugged her. "I'm so sorry, baby girl."

"Mom, I want to fall apart. I want to scream but I can't. I just…I feel like if I fall apart now I'll never stop."

"You're probably in shock, sweetie," Angela explained stroking her hair.

"This is all my fault…all my fault…" Bree moaned.

"Oh no, honey. Don't you think that," Alison said placing a hand on her shoulder.

"Grandma!" Bree wailed turning and wrapping her free arm around the old woman. "I killed him. I killed Daddy. I killed your son."

Alison cupped her face. "You stop that right now, young lady. You did not do this." Her eyes were hard with determination and Bree got the feeling she was trying to keep it together as well.

"No, a Dardano did it," Carrie snapped storming into the lounge, Alex rushing in behind her. "Are you happy now, you selfish bitch? Your husband killed my father."

Bree set Gianni down on one of the seats and shot to her feet. "He was my father too and Alessandro had nothing to do with this. It was Arturo. Alessandro is in there fighting for his life, so don't you fucking dare accuse him of anything."

"Oh right, no one should dare say anything against your prince."

"Carrie, Alessandro can't be held responsible—"Alison began but Carrie cut her off.

"Oh come on, Grandma. Bree chose her side a long time ago. She doesn't give a damn about Dad."

"You bitch!" Bree lunged at her, grief fuelling her desire to attack, to maim, to kill.

Colin caught her around the waist and restrained her. "Don't, Bree that's not gonna help anything.

"I loved Daddy!" She stopped when she saw Carlo come out with Bernardo. She pushed Colin's arms off and rushed towards them.

"How is he? How is Alessandro?" Bree asked, her heart racing so loud she could hear it in her ears.

"We've got him stabilized but right now we're having some trouble with his spine. There are fragments pushing down on some nerve endings and we're reluctant to operator in case we do more damage."

"What does that mean?" Bree asked looking from him to

Bernardo, who looked pale and so much older in the space of a few hours. "What? He was saying he couldn't feel his legs. Is he…Is he paralyzed?"

"It could just be temporary," Carlo assured her but Bree's legs were already buckling.

Bernardo caught her before she hit the ground as everything went black.

Bree opened her eyes to see Will staring down at her, his face and eyes were damp, but he gave her a smile that pierced her heart and lifted the cloud of the nightmare that had been this night. His arm was bound and strapped against his chest.

"Hi mommy," He dropped a kiss on her face and hugged her with his free arm. She could feel his small body still trembling. She felt a surge of anger at…everyone. Arturo, Alessandro, Bernardo, herself. How selfish they all were to drag this boy into their dangerous lives again and again, to fight their battles without thought to the tiny lives that were caught in the middle. Will deserved better than to grow up amongst all this violence. She sighed. What was the alternative though? Live without her soul's other half? Bree didn't think she could.

That made her the most selfish of them all.

"How are you feeling, sweetie?" Bree asked, running her fingers through his now dry curls.

"I okay. Dey gimme med'sin candy and it made me a wittle wooooo at first," he explained tilting from side to side and raising his free hand in the air. "But it no hurt no more so I okay wif da wooooo. Gianni crying lots. He wants you and nobody else. Nod eben me."

"We just wanted to make sure he wasn't injured. We'll bring him to you in a little while," Carlo explained.

"Thank you," Bree said, struggling to sit up in the bed. She still felt a little light headed and now nauseous as well. "How's Alessandro?"

"I heard Gappy Lecter say he was pawadised. Dat's good right?" Will asked. "Pawadise like hev'n but here."

Bree swallowed hard, not sure how to explain when she could barely digest the news herself. She had to be strong and stay positive. It was temporary. It had to be temporary. Please, God. "Baby, uh…Paralyzed mean daddy's legs aren't working right now."

Will blinked and she could see the effort to understand on his face. "Dey broken?"

"Yeah, but the doctors are gonna fix his legs right up very soon."

"Like my arm?" he asked pointing to it.

"Yep, just like that," Bree said, praying with all her heart that her words came true.

Carlo gave her a sympathetic but wary glance cautioning her with his eyes not to get her hopes up.

Bree felt Will poke her. "Mommy…Gappy go to hev'n, huh? Him and Meggie's husband? They wif daddy now?"

Bree didn't trust herself to speak. She nodded slowly.

"Dat's sad. The bad man did dat, huh?" he asked softly.

Keeping the truth from him certainly didn't stop her son from being terrorized. What was the use of lying to him now?

"Yeah, sweetie."

Her heart broke as she watched the fear in his eyes as the tears threatened. He blinked rapidly and his lower lip quivered. She saw him tuck his free hand behind his back, so she wouldn't see it tremble.

He shouldn't have to try to be so brave.

"Will, I promise. We'll get Arturo. We'll stop him and he won't come near you."

"But how, if daddy's legs don' work? He can't go get him," Will reminded her.

"We'll just wait for daddy to get better. You just watch, he'll be chasing you around in no time."

"How he gonna come home, mommy? He no can walk."

"Well, Will, we're gonna give your daddy a wheelchair to get around. You want to come help me pick one out for him?" Carlo asked.

That brightened Will a little bit but he looked at Bree with hesitation. She nodded. "Go ahead."

"I come back fast, mommy. Pomish," Will patted her leg and followed Carlo out just as his wife Tina brought in a screaming Gianni.

His little face was red and his dark hair was sticking up in disarray. When he saw her, his arms stretched out and his shrieks grew louder. "Maaaammmaaaaaaaa!"

"Here we go, Gianni. Here's your mama. Yeah, there we go," Tina leaned down and lowered the baby into Bree's arms.

"Oh, it's okay, sweetie. Mommy's here," Bree clutched him tight against her, feeling as if another part of her slid properly back into place.

"Just to make a note of it, you might want to take care of his fingernails," Tina joked with a small smile.

"Did you scratch Tina, Gianni, hmm?"

Gianni burrowed closer to Bree and stuck her necklace in his mouth.

"How's my uncle Jack?" Bree rubbed Gianni's back as the baby's cries slowed to whimpers and the occasional hiccup.

"He's all right. Arturo and his men made a quick get away."

Her OBGYN, Dr Caroline Murdoch, popped in and asked if she could speak to Bree alone. Bree nodded and Tina left them. "I wanted to talk to you about why you fainted."

Something in her voice made Bree's body go rigid with expectation. "I…thought maybe it was the shock of…everything," Bree whispered. Oh God. Oh God. She didn't know what she was bracing herself for.

"I know you and Alessandro were trying to conceive again. I want to tell you that you were successful. You're going to have a baby, Bree," she said.

Bree squeezed Gianni tighter and buried her face in his neck as the tears filled her eyes and streamed from her face. Oh God…Now? She was torn between joy and utter terror. They had done it, but how would Alessandro react when he found out, considering the condition he was in now. They had created another life.

Another target for Arturo.

CHATPER TWENTY-EIGHT

Bree kissed her father's cold forehead. They gave her some time alone with him before they wheeled him down to the morgue. "I'm going to have a baby, daddy," she whispered. "I'm so sorry you're not going to get to meet her. I'm so sorry," Bree moaned as her tears fell. Before Michael and Alessandro, her father had been her whole world. The only man whose acceptance ever really mattered to her.

And she'd killed him, just as surely as if she'd fired Arturo's gun herself.

What was it about her that made God want to torture her so damned much? Was it completely impossible for her to be happy without God taking something else away from her? She and Alessandro actually had a future, a real one and now God had to take something away just so she couldn't be completely happy.

She gave her father a final kiss and left the room to allow the men to take him.

She looked over at Brian, he looked exhausted. Vanessa's recovery wasn't looking good. The bullet had done some serious damage to her internal organs and she was being prepped for a second surgery because she'd begun haemorrhaging in the middle of the night.

Was it her destiny in life to destroy everyone she cared for?

She saw Bernardo sitting in one of the waiting room chairs, facing Alessandro's room.

Well, she wasn't completely to blame for tonight, now was she?

Bree grit her teeth and wiped her damp cheeks as she stormed towards him. She halted when she saw him cover his face with his hands. Bree's steps slowed as she moved towards him and took a seat next to him. His shoulders were hunched over with sadness and try as she wanted, Bree couldn't remain unmoved. He was a cold-blooded, heartless, murdering son of a bitch.

But he was a father whose child was in pain.

She thought back to Will and how close she'd come to losing him and her hand lifted to Bernardo's shoulder. She touched him for less than a second before Carlo came out of Alessandro's room and Bernardo leapt to his feet, Bree as well.

"There's been no change," he said somberly.

"Can I see him?" Bree asked, nervously.

"What can you do for him? I mean, you can't just leave him paralyzed for God sake!" Bernardo growled.

"For right now, we're just going to monitor his progress and see if the fragments ease their pressure from his spine on their own. Then we can go in and operate to remove them."

"And if they don't?" Bree asked, her mouth dry.

Carlo met her gaze. "I'd rather not speculate until he's had a chance to recover."

"If you don't fix my son, so help me—"

"You'll what?" he snapped, as he glared at Bernardo.

Bree had to admire him for that.

"You'll send Arturo on a rampage in the hospital?" he sneered.

Bree quickly rushed ahead before Bernardo put a hit out on the young doctor who had never been comfortable with the world his wife had been raised in. "Can I see him?"

"One visitor at a time and please, keep it short. I should warn you though, Bree. As you can imagine a lot of patients have a hard time dealing with the news that they're paralyzed, temporary…or not," Carlo gave a wary glance at Bernardo and then placed a hand on Bree's shoulder. "Just…don't take it personally, okay? He's still trying to process the news."

Bree shivered but nodded, hesitating now at the door. What would be greeting her on the other side? Alessandro, the man who loved her, the father of her children or the Dardano, the man who would feel he had lost his power and was now broken? Her hand trembled as she pushed the door open.

It was dark. Too dark and the only sound was the beeping of

his monitor. He lay on the bed, and for a moment Bree thought he was asleep.

She hated herself for the beat of relief as she turned to leave the room.

"Not worth the bother, eh?" It sounded like his voice, but there was no warmth in.

Bree turned back and walked towards the bed.

His dark eyes were staring up at the ceiling.

"How are you feeling?" Bree asked and felt a moment's disgust for the stupid question. She knew exactly how he was feeling because she knew him.

"How are Will and Gianni?" Alessandro asked, ignoring her question.

"Will's okay, enjoying the side effects of the pain killers they gave him after they pulled the fragments out of his arm," she said with an attempt to make him smile.

Nothing.

"And Gianni, well, you'd be very proud of our son. He beat them up until the doctors brought him back to me. He's sleeping now with Will and they're with my grandma."

"So, what's the body count?" he drawled coldly.

Bree blinked at his callous attitude. "Um…some people are still critical but so far…um…five people, a few from the other families. Kevin and…my dad," her voice broke at the end and Alessandro's gaze moved to hers, before he went back to staring at the ceiling. She watched his Adam's apple work to tamp down any obvious emotion.

"Well, one must say this for Arturo, he's certainly thorough. I'm surprised you're still here. Why haven't you skitted off back to the O'Reileys by now? Surely you've heard."

"Yes, I heard, but why on earth would you think I'd leave you? Especially—"

"What? Especially now that I'm a cripple?" he snapped, his dark eyes darting to hers, enraged.

Not at me, she forced herself to remember. He's suffering. He's lashing out, but still those angry eyes aimed at her made her wince.

"It's too soon to tell, Alessandro—" Bree offered but he cut her off quickly.

"Oh don't. Don't. Don't you start with that. The motivational garbage."

Bree swallowed and moved closer to him, tentatively. "I can understand you being angry. But please don't do this, Alessandro. Please don't shut me out," she pleaded sitting down and reaching for his hand.

It felt like he slapped her when he jerked his fingers out of her hand. She blinked back tears of rejection and forced herself to remember Carlo's words. "Tell me what you need. Tell me what you need me to do. How can I help you?" Bree urged.

"Leave."

"You know me better than that," Bree countered, taking a deep breath.

"Fine. Stay," he said as if he couldn't care less. That hurt. "What do you want?"

Bree looked helplessly at him. "I want to help you. I want…I want to tell you how sorry I am—"

"Why? Arturo's the one that shot me. Not you," he reminded her.

"Yes, but…but…" Bree lowered her head and took a deep breath, hoping that she didn't break down. Alessandro needed her strength now. He needed her despite his angry denials to the contrary. "You asked me to postpone tonight and…I didn't want to. I swear, Alessandro. I never imagined that—"

"Ah yes. I did ask you to postpone the opening tonight, didn't I?" Alessandro asked, his voice tight. "But you didn't listen to me, did you? DID YOU?" Alessandro yelled when she didn't answer quickly enough for his liking.

"No. No. No," Bree repeated, shaking her head as the tears fell. "And I am so, so sorry Alessandro."

"Yes, well, not as sorry as I am. Or Meggie or the sainted O'Reileys. I know if one of them had asked you to postpone the opening, you would have done it without question. But me, your husband?" he snorted and shook his head. "Well, I guess that's the crux of the matter isn't it? I'm your husband, but not by your choice, isn't that right?"

Bree lifted her head sharply and stared at him in disbelief. "Granted, I married you not because I wanted to but to end all the goddamned animosity between our families, losing my own family in the process, but it was not against my choice. I loved you. I love you and it is killing me, killing me to see you like this."

"Oh well then no one is stopping you from leaving, darling.

There is the door," Alessandro snapped.

"Oh I wish I could," she moaned, rubbing her damp eyes.

"Why don't you?" he pressed.

"I already told you, I love you and I know that you are just angry right now and you're feeling like your life is over but Alessandro—"

"My life is over," he snapped.

"Alessandro, I am sorry for what happened to you but—"

"I don't want your pity," Alessandro said, looking away from her.

"Good, because I do not pity you," Bree shot back, wishing she could shake him and make him see that they could work through this together!

"What do you want, Brianna? I have nothing for you now."

She took his hand and fingered the wedding band he wore. "I want for better or worse, in sickness and in health, as long as we both shall live. Those are the promises we made. Have you forgotten our vows?"

"No," he whispered thickly. "No I haven't forgotten and I'm…sorry for what I said earlier. You're right. I'm taking this out on you and you are not to blame," He looked up at her, his eyes red and he gave her a sad smile. "Kind of funny when you think about it. I certainly didn't expect to spend the rest of our marriage dead from the waist down."

"Alessandro, don't. It's too soon. There's no way of knowing how—"

"I know, Brianna," he insisted.

"Oh, so you're a doctor now?" Bree countered.

"I know," he repeated. "Don't worry. You won't have to look after a cripple the rest of your life."

Bree held her breath, afraid of where he was taking their conversation.

"You have enough work with our babies to chase after. You don't need me as an added burden so…" he swallowed hard. "I'll have my attorney draft up the divorce papers as soon as possible."

"What?" Bree asked, her voice cracking as her heart fell into her stomach. "You…w...want a divorce?"

He looked at her, his eyes roaming over her face as if it was the last time. "Yes," he lied.

She knew he was lying and he knew that she knew he was lying.

"And you don't need to worry about the vendetta anymore. I'll let my father know that it's what I want—"

"Oh for God's sake, Alessandro!" Bree burst in frustration. "I don't give a damn about the vendetta! I love you and I know you love me and I refuse to let you give up like this! But fine, if you won't fight for me, then fight for your children, dammit! Fight for Will and for Gianni and for the baby that I'm carrying now," she spat and then jerked back, stunned with her self.

Alessandro stared at her, his eyes moving to her belly and then back up to her face. He gave a burst of laughter that chilled her with its lack of warmth. "Oh we really do have the worst timing known to man, don't we?"

He doesn't want it, Bree thought.

"Oh that poor child. She's really going to have a rough go of it, won't she? Having a cripple for a father, although, it may be easier for her after all. Will and Gianni know what it's like to have me play with them, run around with them. Our daughter can't miss what she's never going to have," he said, shaking his head, his eyes full of pain.

"Stop it," Bree hissed.

"Brianna, go home. Take our babies and go home. I have nothing to offer you anymore."

"Don't do this," she pleaded, stroking his cheek. "Don't talk like your life is over."

"My life is over. Yours does not have to be. I love you too much to saddle you with a man who's as good as dead. Now go home. Go and be happy."

Bree shook her head and slid her hand to cup his chin. "You make me happy. Even if I want to clobber you over the head with a frying pan most of the time there is still no one else I will ever love as much as I love you, so you take that into account before you toss us away like we're nothing."

"That's not what I'm doing," he said, wrapping his fingers around her wrist. "I'm doing this for you."

"Bullshit. You're doing this because you're scared and I can't tell you how disappointing that is because the man I love, the Alessandro Dardano I know is not a coward," Bree reminded him, hoping she could make him angry enough to fight for them but he just shook his head listlessly.

"That man doesn't exist anymore."

"You're not thinking clearly, Alessandro. You just need some time to process this. You need to rest. We'll go home, and we'll curl up in bed and just shut everyone else out like we do sometimes and we'll fight this together," Bree insisted stubbornly as she softly kissed his cheek.

He lifted his shoulder, to push her away.

She swallowed down her bitter hurt and forced herself to plod on. "You can't just give up without trying. I won't let you,"

His eyes softened as he looked at her and he raised his fingers to gently stroke her face. Her tears fell to meet his fingers. "I'll never be able to make love to you again. I want you to be happy, Brianna. You won't have any happiness with a man who can never love you the way you deserve anymore."

"So that's all we have between us? Sex?" Bree asked, though she felt a little sick inside, thinking there was a chance they'd never have that physical connection again. No, as long as there was a chance he could recover, she would fight to help him get better, and even if he never walked again, the love she had for this man transcended the physical. She'd mourn the loss of that part of their lives but to hold on to him was so much more important. She could live without making love with him. She didn't think she could live without him. "When I found out who you were, I couldn't break free from this thing between us. We've gone through so much, Alessandro, and survived. Doesn't that prove that our love is strong enough to survive this?" Bree pleaded.

Alessandro said nothing, but she could see the tears gathering in his eyes.

"Look at me," Bree urged.

Nothing.

"Look at me!" she pressed. She reached over and grabbed his chin, turning his face back towards her. "Don't you dare give up. Not now. Not after everything we've been through to be together. Please," she moaned, leaning down and pressing her face next to his. "Please, Alessandro." She kissed his cheek and moved to his lips. She kissed him and felt him respond with a low growl as he opened his mouth under hers, meeting her tongue with his own for the briefest instant and sliding his fingers into her hair, gripping her tight. Bree felt hope burst through her and then just like that, the wall was back up again and she felt worse than she had before as he pulled away.

"You should go now," he said listlessly.

"What?" Bree asked.

"I love you too much to watch you waste your life away on me. Go and be happy."

"Stop it, Alessandro. You don't care what I want—"

"Get out," Alessandro pressed.

"You never cared about what I want—"

"Get out," he snapped.

"It was always about you and fulfilling what your father wanted. Do you think Bernardo is going to want a son who won't even fight—"

"GET OUT!" he shouted at her.

Bree leapt to her feet. She had to leave now before she grabbed the bed pan and brained him with it. "Fine. I'll go."

"And don't come back," he ordered.

"Oh, I'll be back, husband. You can count on that 'cause, you know what? You may be a Dardano but now so am I," she snapped.

She stormed out of the room, feeling with each step that she was losing her grip on her whole world. She slammed the door hard behind her, ignoring the chastising looks from the nurses. Bree covered her mouth but the sobs burst through as she slid to the floor. Bernardo came rushing towards her.

"What is it?" he asked. "Is he all right? What happened?"

Bree shook her head and forced herself to stand up. "No. No he's not all right. He's completely given up. I…I don't know what to do. He's trying to push me away."

"What? You can't let him do that. You're his wife, dammit. Act like it. You go back in there and you give him a reason to fight."

"I've tried—"

"Well, you're obviously not doing a good enough job if you're standing out here—"

"Oh God!" Bree burst pushing past him, afraid she'd kill him with her bare hands if she didn't get away from Bernardo. She didn't know where she was going until she found herself in the hospital chapel. She fell into one of the pews and covered her face, sobbing. She took a deep breath and stared up at the crucifix that hung behind the altar. "I don't know what to do. Please, help me. I don't know how to help him."

Don't come back.

Come back! Please don't leave me. Please don't listen to my angry words!

I'm nothing now. Half a man. Better she leaves now than to see that look in her eyes, that pity, that disappointment when she realizes I will never be the man I was, ever again.

Please love me even though I'm broken.

Alessandro wanted to scream. He wanted to rail at the world. His wife, his darling Brianna, she'd leave him soon. He knew it.

She'd go looking for a whole man.

He hated that man, who ever he would be. He would probably kill him, which would rather defeat the purpose of sending Brianna into another man's arms in the first place, wouldn't it?

He should have tried harder to find Arturo. He should have stopped at nothing, not let love distract him, his family, his peace, all distractions.

And now he'd paid.

Will. Good God, what if he'd been hurt more seriously? And Gianni.

There was a new baby. They'd made a new baby. Alessandro had never felt better or worse at the same time as when she'd told him that.

A little girl. Alessandro didn't know how he knew but he was certain. Because he wanted a little girl. And Dardanos always got what they wanted.

Except he wasn't really a Dardano now was he? Alessandro stared up at the ceiling, nausea churning in his belly. A Dardano was powerful, strong, lethal.

He was useless.

He was nothing.

Be a man!

Never again. He knew he'd never be worthy of the Dardano name again, because he would never walk again. This was his punishment for his many many crimes, for the lives he'd taken. He'd be helpless. A cripple.

Brianna could never stay with a helpless nothing like him. And if he wasn't a Dardano, wasn't that what he was? Nothing?

"Alessandro, what is going on?" Bernardo rushed into the room.

Leave me alone! Alessandro wanted to scream. Leave me alone

so I don't have to see that you hate me now.

Father, please don't stop loving me.

"I just spoke to Brianna and she says that you're pushing her away. Why?"

"It's for the best. I love her too much to have her shackled to a cripple for the rest of her life."

"Bah, Alessandro! That is the self-pity talking. Snap out of it. Brianna's place is by your side as your wife. It is her duty—"

"I don't want her with me out of duty, Father. I never did. I told her that I wanted a divorce. I'm setting her free and—"

"What are you think—"

"This is what I want. I want her free of me, without fear of repercussion from you. You will not stop her from leaving—"

"And what has Brianna said about your wishes?" Bernardo asked, taking a seat next to his bed.

"She thinks she can talk me out of it."

"Good. You're frightened now, my son. We'll get you the best doctors in the country, in the world, and you'll be up and about in no time at all."

"You don't know that, Father. You can't throw money at my legs and make them move. The Dardano will is not going to bring the feeling back where there is none."

"This is just temporary, my son. I'm sure of it."

"You can't possibly be," Alessandro insisted.

"You just have to believe—"

"YOU'RE NOT LISTENING TO ME!" Alessandro exploded.

Nobody is listening to me because I'm already nothing. In their eyes, I'm already insignificant. I might as well be dead.

Dead.

Dead.

Bernardo reached over and placed a hand on his arm. "Calm yourself."

Alessandro closed his eyes and wished for death. Goodbye, my Father.

Goodbye, Will. Gianni. My baby. I'm sorry. I'm sorry.

Brianna.

My love. My heart. I was happy for a little while. Thank you.

And then everything went black.

CHAPTER TWENTY-NINE

Bree prayed the entire way back to the hospital. An infection. Oh God, please. I can't…Please. Bernardo had sounded worried on the phone. For him to show weakness like that, it had to be bad.

She'd left Gianni and Will with Andy again, promising to bring them to visit Alessandro soon. As soon as he was out of the ICU.

Please.

"How is he?" Bree asked rushing out of the elevator and spotting Bernardo immediately.

Bernardo lifted his hands helplessly.

"What the hell happened?" Bree demanded.

"Well if you had been here, you would have known that wouldn't you?" Bernardo chastised. "If you'd stayed with him as you should, he wouldn't have given up and be willing himself to die."

Bree narrowed her eyes at him but didn't dare answer, fear and anger was churning inside of her. Damn him. Damn every last Dardano and their stubborn pride.

She pushed the door to Alessandro's room open. "What the hell do you think you're doing?" Bree demanded.

"Oh, so Father went and told 'mummy' on me, did he?" Alessandro asked, his face was flushed, fevered. He was sitting up now, propped against the pillows.

When she placed her hand on his forehead she wasn't surprised to feel that the skin was warm. "Damn it, Alessandro."

"Yes, we've established that already," he joked bitterly. "Really, darling. I know we Dardanos are usually a pretty powerful lot but even we can't manufacture infections of the blood…though my father did help me give this brat at Oxford the chicken pox once."

"Stop it. I know what you're doing. You're just giving up. You can fight this infection but you won't because you want to die, because for some ridiculous reason you think that you're half a man if your legs don't work." She dropped into the chair beside him so she wouldn't give in to the temptation to punch him. "Like your legs are what make you a man, a husband, a father. Well, I have legs too, I must be a man then."

"Now you're being ridiculous," Alessandro sighed.

"Well, I'm glad you recognize that. You can't give up, Alessandro. All right. Fine. You can't move your legs now but it's so early, Alessandro. You might still recover and let's say you don't, worst case scenario, you can still lead a full—"

"Stop it! I do not want to live like this. I refuse, do you hear me? Is it penetrating that stubborn skull?"

"Great so that's it? Never mind that I love you, never mind that you'd be abandoning your sons and this unborn baby."

"Gianni barely knows me and that baby inside of you won't miss me either."

"Of course Gianni knows you! You're his daddy. You don't think he'd notice if you all of a sudden just dropped off the face of the earth?"

"He's young. He'd get over it," he replied coldly.

"And what about Will? He's already lost one father. How dare you take another one away from him?" Bree hissed.

"I'm sure you could find another replacement soon enough. You're a beautiful woman."

Bree clenched her fists. "Are you trying to make me angry? I am asking you, Alessandro, please. I am begging you to fight. Just…try."

"Why?" Alessandro asked hopelessly.

"For us. You've claimed up and down for months that you loved me, you've put yourself in the path of bullets for me and now I'm asking you for this one thing, something so small, just not to give up and you can't give me that?"

"I'm doing this for you, Brianna. I'm doing this for our children. I will not saddle them with an invalid for a father. I will not burden you with having to play nurse maid to me for the rest of your life. I love you too much."

"Oh stop it. Stop hiding behind that when what you're really doing is wallowing in self-pity. I love you, you stupid jack-ass. And your sons do need you. Alessandro, you are the only man I will ever love. Ever. Whether your legs are working or not that is never going to change. I mean, give me a break, if I was able to love you through everything you've deliberately done so far, do you think I'd stop loving you over something you had absolutely no control over? Then you don't know me half as well as you think you do."

"Brianna, listen to me. This discussion is over. I won't allow our children to waste their years growing up with a burden like me and I won't allow you to either. I won't allow it," he insisted.

"So that's it. You'd leave your children without a father rather than have them help you with your wheelchair. You selfish, arrogant, son of a bitch," Bree hissed through her teeth as the tears burned in her eyes. "How can you tell me you love me, love our kids and do something so sick and cruel?"

"I'm doing this for the best. For all you."

"No! No you shut up, and you listen to me. You are still the same man. You are still the man I love, the stubborn Dardano ass who always gets what he wants."

"Brianna, no matter how much I might want to, I can't fix this."

Bree sat back down. "You don't know that. Let me help you. Let's do it together because damn you, I will not bury another husband. I can't…I can't…Alessandro, please," Bree begged.

He said nothing.

She closed her mouth over his. He softened and cupped the back of her head with a groan.

He smelled of medicine, antibiotics and IVs now. She missed his smell.

When they broke the kiss she felt encouraged that he didn't pull away. "This guy told me once that I was stubborn."

"A guy, huh?" Alessandro whispered.

"Mmm, ended up marrying him but, you know how that goes. So see? I'm stubborn, and that means I'm not going anywhere and you can't make me."

"You sound like Will," Alessandro said with a snort.

Bree smiled, her heart lightened by the less angry tone of his voice. Hopeful tears sprung to her eyes.

"Hey…" Alessandro asked, lifting his finger to catch her tears.

Bree shook her head. "I'm just…our babies and I…we all need you, Alessandro."

"I know," he said. He pulled back and looked up at her with sad brown eyes. "I love you."

"I know," Bree said, leaning down and kissing him again. She felt a fresh burst of happy tears when she felt him kiss her back.

Alessandro gave her a small smile and Bree took a deep shaky breath.

"Alessandro, I want you to promise me that you're going to fight,"

The smile wavered and he lowered his gaze. Bree took his chin in her fingers and gently lifted his gaze back to her. "Alessandro, come on. You have to fight. Don't you want to see our new baby when she or he comes? Don't you want to see Will on his first day of school? You know that's coming up this year. He's going to want you to hold his hand while he waits for the bus. What about Gianni? And I'm gonna need you. I'm gonna need you to watch me get bigger and bigger with this kid and still convince me that I'm beautiful. I'm gonna need you to grow old with me and tell me that you don't see my wrinkles or the grey in my hair."

"I want that," he said, his voice low, uncertain. "But…I've had more in my life than I've ever imagined I would. And I'm not talking about the Dardano power and privilege. I'm talking about a family of my own. You, our children. Having you love me despite my name. That's more of a miracle than I could have ever hoped for. I don't think I deserve to ask for another one."

Bree kissed his forehead. "You are the strongest man I know. I know that you can beat this."

"If I give you this promise, I have one of my own, Brianna," he reached down and took her hand. "If I fight this. If I fight to walk and if I don't give up, and if we find out that the paralysis is permanent…"

"No, Alessandro," Bree butt in, knowing where he was headed.

"If we find it out it is indeed permanent, I want you to promise me that you'll leave me."

Bree tugged her hand away but he gripped her fingers tighter. "How could you ask me to promise you that?"

"That's the deal, darling. I will try on that condition."

Bree closed her eyes. "How about you promise to fight and if we find out you really will never walk again, then we can cross that bridge when we come to it. We'll figure out what's best for our family then and only then."

Alessandro looked at her with obvious skepticism but nodded.

Bree gave a sigh of relief over the small but significant victory and moved off the bed.

"Wait, where are you going?" Alessandro asked.

"Remember those kids I mentioned?" Bree asked with a little grin.

Alessandro was out of the I.C.U two days later so Bree brought Gianni and Will to visit with him for a little while. There'd been no change in his paralysis but Bree was determined to look on the bright side. His fever was down, and his spirits were…if not necessarily 'up' then at least he wasn't suicidal anymore.

Vanessa had regained consciousness briefly. The doctors assured Bree that her body was recovering and that it was an exhausting battle so she shouldn't be worried if the nanny stayed under for a while yet.

Bree had briefly visited with Meggie that morning and she'd assured Bree that she didn't hold either Bree or Alessandro responsible for Kevin's death. She still loved them both and wanted to talk with Alessandro as soon as he was back home.

She could see Meggie struggle to be strong even with her heart broken and she'd thanked God yet again that Alessandro had survived.

"Knock, knock," Bree said popping her head in Alessandro's room. "I come bearing baby." She pointed Gianni at him, who wiggled so excitedly at the sight of his father that Bree almost dropped him.

"Daddy!"

Will burst ahead of her into the room. "Hi daddy!" He jumped up onto the bed and threw his arms around Alessandro.

"Careful Will," Bree warned.

"Uh oh," he moved off of Alessandro carefully and patted his legs. "I sorry. Mommy said yo' legs are brokded. Dey don' fix dem yet?"

Alessandro's face fell and Bree grimaced but she watched Alessandro close his eyes and gather his strength to smile at his son and she loved him so much in that second. "No, not yet, Will."

"But dey will soon, right?" Will asked.

Bree questioned whether it had been a good idea to bring Will and Gianni after all.

"I hope so," Alessandro said, his voice cracking.

"Me too, daddy."

"Come, Gianni. Come to daddy," Alessandro said raising his arms for the squirming baby.

"Are you sure?" Bree asked, hesitantly.

"Really, Brianna," Alessandro urged.

"Daddy! My daddy, gimme meedee daddy!"

"The king has spoken," Bree joked placing him in Alessandro's arms. She watched as Alessandro wrapped his arms around Gianni and kissed his head.

"Mommy say dat bad man shooted ebbybody." Will asked softly.

Alessandro gave Bree a chastising look and she glared back at him silently. What did he expect her to do, lie about it? Apparently so, she thought with a beat of annoyance.

"Don't worry, Will. Arturo is not going to hurt you anymore. We're going to make extra sure of that."

"But how, daddy? 'Cause yo' legs are brokded. What if he comes 'a fore you can fix dem?"

Alessandro wrapped a free arm around Will. "That's just another reason for me to make sure I get better, isn't it?"

Will nodded. "I help. I go down wif da doctor and pick out a chair for you. Can I ride in it wif you?"

Alessandro's eye flickered angrily and Bree held her breath. He didn't like the idea of a wheelchair but she hoped he wouldn't show his irritation over that in front of Will.

"Daddy, 'atch," Gianni said tugging on Alessandro's hospital bracelet.

Alessandro smiled at Gianni, the need to address using a wheelchair pushed aside for the moment. "Not exactly a Rolex is it, my boy?"

"Mee dis. My wan dis. Daddy 'atch," Gianni tugged on the plastic.

"Dat's nod a watch, Gianni. Dat's a sickie bracelet," Will explained. "Dat so dey know daddy's name."

"Up, daddy," Gianni said, tugging on Alessandro's hospital gown and motioning towards the other side of the room.

"Daddy can't get up. His legs bwokded," Will explained.

"Awww," Gianni leaned in and kissed Alessandro's cheek. He pointed to Alessandro's legs. "Owwie, daddy?"

"Yes, daddy's got an owwie. But you and your brother make it all better," Alessandro said kissing Gianni's cheek.

"We gonna help, daddy. Promise. Den you be up again. No time at all. Just watch," Will nodded stubbornly.

"Daddy 'atch?" Gianni asked, his attention back on Alessandro's wrist.

"Noooo," Will replied impatiently.

"Sorry, see? Daddy can't take it off." Alessandro tugged on it, trying to show him.

"Off. Me dis, daddy. Gibbit me wanned." Gianni pulled on the little silver snap, annoyed that he couldn't undo it. "Meeeeee! Dis!" he burst in frustration.

"Hey, you gonna be a good boy for daddy?" Alessandro asked.

"Awww," Gianni leaned his head on Alessandro's shoulder. "Gooo 'oy, daddy. Mee gooo." He stuck his thumb in his mouth.

"That's my boy." Alessandro rubbed his back and looked over at Bree. "Maybe you could get the doctor to give you an extra one?"

Bree nodded and left to go get a toy bracelet for Gianni to play with.

When she came back, plastic blank bracelet in hand Will had his head on Alessandro's chest and was rubbing tears from his eyes.

"I go be bwave now. I promise. But I was so a-scared dat you were going in hev'n like my other daddy. I don' care if you legs bwokeded. I just wan you here," Will said.

Alessandro's eyes were red and Bree watched him blinking back tears. "I'm not going

anywhere. I promise, son."

"Good," Will said with a shuddering sigh.

Bree almost left again to give them a few more minutes alone but Alessandro saw her and smiled.

"Look what mommy found, Gianni?" Bree said lifting the plastic bracelet for Gianni to see.

Gianni lifted his head and gasped, smacking his hands together. "Daddy 'atch!" he squealed in delight. "Gibbit me!" He extended his hand.

"Say please," Bree insisted.

"Mammaaaaa! Gibbit!" Gianni insisted.

"Say please," Bree pressed.

"Peeeesh?" Gianni asked.

"Good boy," Bree handed him the bracelet.

Gianni grabbed it happily. "Oook, daddy. My 'atch." In his enthusiasm, he poked Alessandro in the eye with it.

Alessandro groaned and covered his eye as Bree rushed towards him.

"Gianni! Daddy's legs aweady bwokded! Don' bweak his eye!" Will scolded.

Alessandro thought that was hilarious and burst out laughing, Bree couldn't help join him.

He looked over Gianni's head and mouthed the words 'thank you' to Bree and through her shimmering eyes, Bree mouthed back, 'I love you.'

"It's out of the question," Bernardo said turning away from her.

Bree grit her teeth and resisted the urge to smack her father-in-law over the head with the morning paper. "How can you say that? You have to be practical. I mean, how is Alessandro going to go to bed at night if he can't go upstairs to our bedroom."

"You'll occupy one of the rooms on this floor until he can walk again. Why are we even having this discussion?" Bernardo asked.

"Because what if he can't?" Bree whispered so that Gianni and Will, who were playing a few feet away in the living, room wouldn't hear them. "We have to think long term about this just in case things don't happen the way we want them to."

"If you fulfill your duties as a wife and help him fight, then my son will walk again. I refuse to entertain any other outcome," Bernardo growled at her.

"I cannot will Alessandro's legs to move," Bree hissed. "If I could give Alessandro my legs I would, but since I can't my duty as his wife is to support him regardless of what happens in the future. We could install one of those electric chairs that move up along the wall or a small elevator or—"

"I already gave my decision on this matter," Bernardo said and walked away from her.

"Yes, Sir, Mein Furher." Bree threw the newspaper at his departing head but he didn't acknowledge her again.

The sound of Gianni giggling brought her attention back into the living room and she saw Will building towers of blocks with his brother. Once finished he'd place his hand over the top, letting it hover as Gianni squealed with anticipation of the inevitable demolition. When it came, Gianni fell over on the blanket dissolving in laughter. Then they'd start again with Gianni helping him build a new tower. Bree watched them for a few seconds.

A loud clang of what sounded like a tray hitting the marble kitchen floor made Bree jump and Gianni go wide eyed with apparent terror. He covered his ears and shook his head. "Bang! Bang! Bang!" He fell over and covered his head.

Bree rushed over to him as he began shrieking fearfully. "Maaammaaaaaa!"

"Is okay, Gianni. Just a ting falled down," Will said patting Gianni's back but Bree noticed her little boy's hand was shaking.

"It's okay, sweetie. Mommy's here. That's okay," she crouched down and gathered Gianni into her arms.

"Bang! Mama. It bang!" he wailed into her shoulder, trembling in her arms.

"It was just a loud noise. Cook just dropped something, probably a whole big plate of yucky beets. Isn't that funny?" she said, forcing a laugh. Jesus Christ, how much more violence would her children be forced to endure? Again, Bree felt selfish for bringing her innocent babies into the Dardano world.

Gianni looked up at her, picking up on her tone he gave a small watery smile. "Ucky ee

"Yucky yucky beets," Bree repeated bouncing him lightly as her heart returned to its normal rhythm in her chest.

Gianni giggled and shuddered against her as the last remnants of his fear dissipated.

Bree looked over at Will. "You okay, sweetie?"

Will blinked and looked over at her, wide eyed and his lower lip quivered, but he set his chin like she knew he'd watched Alessandro do and nodded. "I bwave. I nod scared."

Bree smiled at him and kissed his cheek as she ran her fingers through his hair. "Wow. That is pretty brave. I know I was scared when I first heard the noise."

"Really?" Will asked hesitantly.

"Definitely," Bree nodded. Gianni echoed the gesture.

"Well, dat's diffen. You's a girl."

"Oh, is that so?" Bree asked setting Gianni on the blanket next to her. "So you think 'cause mommy's a girl she's a fraidy cat. Huh? Huh?" she asked poking him.

Will curled in on himself and giggled as he tried to avoid her fingers.

"But he's right," Alessandro said as Bree wheeled him into the house. Bernardo helped her get him up the stairs to the house.

"I dow, mamma," Gianni said pointing down and wriggling in her arms.

"You see? Alessandro understands that Dardano men do not give up. Making any additions to the house is admitting defeat," Bernardo gloated.

Bree patted Gianni's back. "He's not right. We can take the lifts out once you get better."

"I don't understand, Brianna. You keep insisting I fight to get better. How is knowing I can rely on technical conveniences to get around the house going to motivate me?"

"That is exactly the point I was trying to make," Bernardo said.

"You know what? He's in the house now, I don't need your help anymore," she snapped.

"As a matter of fact yes, I do have some business I need to attend to. Alessandro, you let me know if you need me." Bernardo said placing a hand on Alessandro's shoulder before leaving.

"Mamma, dow. Gibbits dow!," Gianni repeated.

Bree went to the couch and set him down on. Gianni shook his head. "No, up!"

Bree looked down at him in exasperation. "Now you want up?"

"Up voom, mamma. Gibbits voom!" He said pointing to Alessandro's chair.

"Ah, gotcha," she said moving back towards Alessandro.

Alessandro raised his arms to take Gianni. Gianni bounced happily as he sat on Alessandro's lap.

Bree almost warned him to take it easy but with a pang she remembered that he couldn't feel Gianni anyway.

"Voom, daddy! Voomie!" Gianni insisted wanting Alessandro to move.

"Daddy I gots a question?" Will said kneeling on the couch and shifting over to the edge so he was facing Alessandro.

"And what would that be, young William?" Alessandro asked raising an eyebrow.

"How you gonna get up da stairs wif da chair?" Will asked.

Bree crossed her arms and sent her husband a very pointed 'I told you so' look.

Alessandro ignored her and focused on Will. "We're going to be using one of the bedrooms down on this floor for a while."

"Excuse me?" Bree asked.

He rolled past her with Gianni who giggled happily as Alessandro wheeled around the couch and back to Bree. "Any chance your little tantrum is over?"

Bree scowled.

"No? Okay, Gianni, another round it is," Alessandro placed his hands on the wheels to move away but she gripped the handles to stop him.

"I'm serious, Alessandro. I don't want us to move into one of these bedrooms."

"What difference does it make?" he asked.

"The difference is that our bedroom is upstairs, it's not here," Bree insisted.

"Really, Brianna, be reasonable," Alessandro said insisted. "It much easier if we simply move down here for a little while and once I can walk again we'll move back up again."

"The nursery is upstairs! I can't be on a whole other floor from Gianni. What if he needs me?"

"Oh for goodness sake, you can use those baby monitor things we have," Alessandro reminded her, scowling.

"But Alessandro, what made living in this house bearable was that I could avoid Bernardo anytime I wanted by staying on the second floor for the most part. Now you're asking me to live on the same floor as Grandpa Lecter. No, forget it."

"Well, that's certainly your choice," Alessandro said, eyes darkening angrily.

Bree glared down at him, an odd sensation after getting used to staring up at him. "What the fuck does that mean?"

Will gasped. "Mommy! Dat's a bad word!"

Bree cringed, forgetting that Will and Gianni were in the room. "Could we continue this argument somewhere else?"

"There's no argument, darling. You are welcome to stay upstairs to be the near the children. I will sleep down here."

Bree clenched her fists at her side and tried to remind herself it was wrong to hit an invalid. "What is this, the eighteen hundreds? I'm not sleeping separated from you, that's just stupid!"

"What's stupid is that you've been touting the virtues of being practical and here you are insisting we install contraptions in the house when we have perfectly good bedrooms to occupy here on this floor."

"But none of them are our bedroom. I like our bedroom. It's like our little sanctuary from this nuthouse."

"It's not like it would be of any use to us for anything besides sleep anyway," Alessandro snapped at her. "I'm paralyzed from the waist down in case you've forgotten.

Bree blushed and glanced at the boys who were watching them with identical uneasy looks on their faces. "Can we not do this now?" she hissed.

"I'm perfectly fine concluding this argument right now, Sunshine."

Bree narrowed her eyes at him. "You are not moving down here,"

"I beg to differ, darling. I already told you, I'm not going to make you move into one of the bedrooms on this floor if you're not comfortable with that. I think I'm being quite generous here. In fact, I think I'd prefer it if you and I didn't sleep in the same bed until I'm back on my feet."

"That's insane, Alessandro! What if you—" she pressed her lips together to stop the negative words from escaping. She had to think positive.

"What if I never walk again? That's what you were going to say, isn't it?" Alessandro asked through clenched teeth.

Bree grimaced.

"Isn't it!" he yelled at her.

Gianni jumped in Alessandro's lap and placed his hands over his ears. "Nooooo! Noooooo dis! Nooooo dis! Me nooo wanned!"

"Mommy, daddy! You haf to stop yelling and be nice, right now!" Will demanded.

Bree grabbed Gianni off Alessandro's lap.

"Where do you think you're going?" Alessandro snapped.

"What the hell do you care?" Bree tossed back. "You want to be alone down here. Fine, come on, Will." She stormed out of the room and climbed the stairs up to the next floor.

CHAPTER THIRTY

She couldn't sleep. You stupid dingbat, Bree thought with burning self-loathing. Go downstairs and sleep next to your husband. She stubbornly stayed put and stared at the ceiling. Oh right. This is better. Stand your ground, make your point.

Sleep alone.

Dingbat! Dingbat! Dingbat!

Bree kicked the covers off with a burst of irritation. She grabbed her baby monitor and went downstairs. She went down the long hallway to the group of guestrooms on the first floor.

She had grudgingly helped Alessandro into bed, refusing to let Bernardo help her. The less she had him help with her husband, the farther away she could keep the bastard from poisoning Alessandro against her.

That was another reason she was giving in now. Better she stick with Alessandro wherever he went, even if he was being an ass.

She stopped, feeling a twinge of sympathy. Wasn't he certainly due? The man was paralyzed. He was going through this terrible time and they all had to make adjustments until things got back to normal…whatever that meant in the Dardano house.

"Oh God, please let things get back to normal soon," she pleaded, before she knocked on the door to Alessandro's room.

"Hello?" he called out.

He sounded alert, not sleepy, not like he'd been sleeping soundly and she'd pulled him from the bliss of oblivion.

Bree felt more than a little smug knowing that he couldn't sleep either. She turned the doorknob and poked her head in. "Can't sleep?"

"Mmm," he grumbled. "Missing my wife. Lovely woman. You wouldn't happen to know where she went, do you?"

Bree rolled her eyes. "I decided that it's more important that we aren't at odds than the fact that my husband is being a stubborn jackass."

"Pots…kettles and all that," he said, narrowing his eyes at her. "Is this your idea of an apology 'cause it's sorely lacking, darling."

"No, I'm not here to apologize because I didn't do anything wrong."

Alessandro sighed. "Then what, Brianna? What do you want?"

Bree pursed her lips and stormed towards the bed, pulling back the blankets and climbing into bed. "Go to sleep, Alessandro."

He snorted. "Apology accepted."

"Shut up."

She woke up to the sound of crying and opened her eyes and looked at the baby monitor. She groaned and rubbed her eyes.

"Mmngh?" Alessandro asked next to her.

"Yeah, guess who's awake?" She got up and promptly stubbed her toe on the unfamiliar foot of the bed. "Fuck!"

"Ahh, sweeter than the sound of birds chirping," he mumbled, rolling over and opening his eyes.

"Don't start with me," Bree snapped.

"Bring him down and we can just lie here for a while?" Alessandro offered, dark eyes raised in an attempt at meekness.

Bree laughed at the image of her powerful husband trying to look meek. "Mmph." She leaned over and kissed him. "Good morning."

She picked up Gianni out of his crib and Will came stumbling out of his room. "Daddy waked up yet?" he asked, curls out in comic disarray.

"Yep. Let's go hang out with him before breakfast. What do you think?" Bree asked.

Will nodded. "But you no yell no more 'kay?"

"No mo'" Gianni echoed leaning his head on her chest.

Meggie came to visit later that morning. Bree hugged her tightly. "How are you doing?"

Meggie shrugged. "One day at a time, right? How about you?

Everything okay with the baby?"

Bree touched her stomach instinctively. "Hardly any morning sickness. Thank God."

"How's Alessandro?"

"In complete denial, of course," Bree groaned. "I'm trying make the house easier for him to navigate but Bernardo refuses to make any improvements because of course his son is a Dardano and will not give in to this paralysis and gaaaah!" Bree groaned, leaning her head against the couch. "I'm sorry. Here I am going on about my problems when at least I have Alessandro around. I hope you can forgive me."

Meggie took her hand. "Don't worry about it. You should be grateful that Alessandro survived but trust me, don't ride him too hard about this. You have to do things his way right now 'cause he's the injured one. Whatever makes him more comfortable. I actually came by 'cause I wanted to tell you that I'm going back to Paris for a while."

Bree sighed. "Oh, no, Meggie. You need to stay in New York and be around family. You're one of the only friends I have now that I've gone to the dark side."

Meggie smiled ruefully. "That's not gonna change kiddo. You and me will always be buds. But I just need to…get away. I need to be close to him and I don't feel him here, you know? The vineyard was his life. It was a part of him and it was something he loved. I feel like if I go back, I won't feel so empty inside."

Bree's eyes burned. "I can't ever make up that loss to you but I want you to know how terribly sorry I am for what happened."

"Hey, no. No, okay? I don't hold you responsible for what happened at all so just put that from your head. Nothing that happened that night was your fault." Meggie gathered her in her arms and hugged Bree tightly.

Bree swallowed back her tears and forced herself to smile when Meggie pulled back. "But you'll be back, right?"

She shrugged. "To visit, but without Kevin…I don't know if I can ever see this place as home anymore."

"We miss you lots, Nessa. You come home today?" Will asked leaning his elbows on her bed.

"Not yet," Vanessa said, giving him a small grin.

"How come? Yo' eyes open now. Are yo' legs bwokded too?"

Bree grimaced. Crap.

"What?" Vanessa asked looking up at Bree.

She sighed. "Alessandro's paralyzed," she explained. It still made her a little nauseous and heartsick to think about his injury.

Helping him bathe had turned into a disaster. He'd snapped at her as she tried to help him and was in a foul mood for the better part of the past few days. He told her that he abhorred that she had to help him in and out of the tub, even though she tried to assure him she didn't mind. She was his wife and it was her duty to help him do these things. She even tried to make it fun and enticing by trying to make it sexual but that only made Alessandro more furious with her and he'd finally kicked her out, accusing her of trying to rub it in that he couldn't respond to her physically.

Humiliated, she had sat in the bedroom, tears running down her face until he called her back into the bathroom because he needed to get out of the tub.

He hadn't spoken a word to her until the next morning when he tried to apologize but Bree was too hurt to accept it.

Alessandro thought he was the only one suffering. Well what about her? Did that give him the right to use her as an emotional punching bag? Bree grabbed the kids and left, needing to be away from Alessandro and his foul mood, and Bernardo's disapproving glares for at least a few hours.

"Oh God," Vanessa gasped, bringing her hand to her mouth. "Permanently?"

"No," Bree assured her. "Or, well, we don't know for sure. We hope not," she amended. "What about you? Any news on when you get to blow this joint?"

"Been trying to talk the doc into it," Vanessa took a deep breath before going on. "Too tired to argue well enough."

"I'm sure Doctor Homewrecker appreciates it," Bree said.

"Mamma, dow," Gianni said, shifting in her arms and pointing to the floor. "Depfeedie. Oook. Dis. Depfeedie me dow."

Bree shook her head. "No, you can't touch that."

He pointed to the foot pedals at the bottom of the bed again. "Tat. Dow. Tat."

"No,"

"Noooo," Gianni insisted while contradicting himself by nodding.

Will went over to the empty bed on the other side of the curtain and pulled the curtain aside so they could see him. "He could play wif dis one, mommy."

"Heeeee," Gianni giggled, dancing in her arms and clapping. "Dow, mamma. Dow!"

"Smarty pants," Bree grumbled. "Don't let him hurt himself," she warned setting Gianni on the floor next to Will.

"Duh, mommy. I nod stupid," Will reminded her.

"Depfeedie. Oookie," Gianni said touching the foot pedal.

Will showed him how to press down and Gianni jumped as the buzzing noise started and the bed rose up and down.

"Eeeeeeee!" Gianni squealed clapping.

"Watch, Gianni. Up…and down."

"Uhhhd. Dow," he repeated. He pushed on the foot pedal but didn't have enough strength to push it down. "No dow?" He grabbed Will's hand and put it back on the pedal to do it.

"Here, I show you," Will wrapped his fingers around Gianni's hand and used his pressure to push the baby's hand down.

When the bed rose and fell, Gianni giggled in delight.

"So how they doing?" Vanessa asked, yawning.

"Will's arm is healing okay. He should have the bandages off sometime next week."

"Yeah, dey itchy!" Will called out, pointing to his injured arm. "But no hurt no mo'."

"Oh, well. That's important," Vanessa said with a small smile. She turned back to Bree "Any nightmares?"

"I think Gianni's been having them 'cause sometimes he'll wake up shrieking bloody murder in the middle of the night. Not like he's hungry but scared, you know?" Bree said concerned. She dropped her voice down to a whisper. "And Will peed in his bed last night. I'm so worried about what this is doing to them. God, why did Arturo have to come back into our lives?" she hissed. "I knew we couldn't possibly stay happy. Ugh!" Bree shook her head before she lost control of her emotions again. "I'm thinking we might visit Dr. Sheri today if she's free. She's helped Will a lot in the past. I don't know if she'll be able to do anything for Gianni though. Are there baby shrinks?" she asked ruefully.

"Hey, how about you, huh? You've had a hell of a month and you've been handling it all on your own."

"Oh, don't worry about it. You just concentrate on getting back on your feet again. I'm gonna need your help again soon."

"Heard about the new baby. Happy for you," Vanessa said.

"Thanks. See? I'm fine. I just need to concentrate on the good things. There's a new baby coming. The boys are safe and even though right now I want to ram his head through a wall, at least Alessandro's alive," Bree said, as if trying to convince herself that she had no reason to complain.

"Colin?" Bree asked, spotting him helping an old man into his wheelchair.

He lifted his head and smiled. "Bree. Hey." He straightened as the elderly man wheeled away.

"Hi Unco Colin!" Will said running up to him.

Colin swooped him up in his arms. "How you doing, buddy?"

Will shrugged. "Only a little bit okay. Daddy still brokded and he cranky and sad."

"Oh." Colin looked at Bree sympathetically.

"Yeah, well, he's having a hard time dealing, you know?" Bree asked uneasily.

"That's understandable. How are you coping?" he asked, reaching out and touching her arm.

Gianni shifted in her arms and looked down at Colin's hand.

"It's taking some getting used to. Let's just say it's a bit of a relief to take a break for a little while. I'm more worried about the kids though and this is affecting them so I'm hoping to get in to see Dr. Graham. She was a big help to Will a while back."

"Oh, yeah. I hear great things about her. You know she doesn't just work with kids, right?"

Bree narrowed her eyes but smiled in amusement. "Is that a hint?"

"Not a very subtle one, I know. Hey Gianni, how you doing, huh? Wow, you're sure getting big," Colin remarked.

"He sure is. He's almost standing all by himself now, aren't you, Gianni? You wanna show Colin?" Bree asked.

"Nooo," Gianni insisted, burying his face in Bree's neck.

"Oh, speaking of Mr. Cranky Pants, huh? He didn't get a lot of sleep last night."

Gianni lifted his head and then looked down, and it was then that Bree noticed Colin still had his hand on her arm.

"Dat," Gianni said.

Bree cleared her throat and took a step back, not wanting to make the movement seem like she was uncomfortable with Colin touching her. That was just silly. She may have had a bit of a crush on him when she was younger, jealous of Carrie's ability to make all the boys flock to her, but they were only ever just friends. It was normal that he'd touch her affectionately. He always was a touchy feel sort. Bree had always liked that about Colin.

"How about we go down and get something to eat in the cafeteria. I'm on my lunch now."

"So you're working here?" Bree asked.

"Volunteering a few hours a week. Gets me out of the stuffy office so I don't become some stuffed shirt mogul."

"Right, God forbid," Bree said with a snort.

"How about it, Will? You want some Jello?" Colin asked, bouncing Will in his arms.

"My dis," Gianni insisted reaching for Will.

"Only if is nod da gween Jello. I no like gween Jello no mo'," Will explained.

"He had a lot of green Jello when he was in the hospital," Bree explained with a smile.

"Oh then green Jello is off the table. How about some ice cream?"

"Deal," Will nodded.

"How about you, Gianni? Would you like some ice cream?" Colin asked, carrying Will over to the elevator.

"No," Gianni said, his dark eyebrows furrowed.

"Um, how about some Jello?"

"No," Gianni repeated.

"Someone a picky eater?" Colin joked as they made their way to the cafeteria.

"Only if you put a vegetable anywhere near him, but you like Jello and ice cream, remember, Gianni?" Bree asked.

Gianni shook his head and wrapped a tight fist in the collar of her blue silk blouse. "My dis mamma. No you," he insisted, looking at Colin.

Her mood was much improved as she waited outside Dr. Sheri Graham's office. The shrink had a half hour block open and was on her way to meet with them.

"So how are things going?" Sheri asked sitting across from them in the brown leather arm chair.

"We're hitting a bit of a rough spot again. Alessandro's paralysis is taking a bit more adjusting to than I imagined," Bree admitted, feeling her old miserable emotions returning.

"Do you think he'd be up to coming to a few sessions with you?" Sheri asked.

Bree snorted. "Hardly. Dardano men are strong. They don't go to strangers and air their dirty laundry," she said, mimicking Bernardo that morning.

"Will, how do you feel about your daddy not being able to walk?" Sheri asked.

Will swung his legs back and forth on the edge of the couch and rubbed his knee. "It...ummmmmmmmm. It make me sad."

"I bet. Are you sleeping okay?"

Will lowered his head. "Nod really. I haf da bad deems sumtines. And…um…I pee in da bed like long tine ago again. But ony one time. I 'member to be brave now."

"And how's Gianni?" Sheri asked reaching over and stroking Gianni's cheeks.

The little baby smiled at her and blew a spit bubble.

"He wakes up screaming at night and he jumps at any loud noises thinking they're gun shots," Bree admitted. "I don't know what to do. I mean, what kind of mother am I, right? Bringing my kids into this warzone. Being stupid enough to bring another one into it."

"We don't pick who we love. From what you've told me before, your husband is a good man. Only you can decide if you'd be willing to give him up for the sake of some sense of security that is never guaranteed in life."

No, she wasn't willing to make that sacrifice.

CHAPTER THIRTY-ONE

Bree stopped in the doorway to the bedroom, surprised at the sight that greeted her. A particularly hefty woman stood next to Alessandro who was laid out on a medical cushioned examining table. The woman, who had a wild cap of thick red hair had one of Alessandro's legs in her hand and was instructing him to try and push against it.

"Is she fixing yo' legs, daddy?" Will piped up, excited.

The lady and Alessandro both turned. The lady smiled at them. Alessandro didn't.

"We'll see if it does any good. Okay, that's enough for today, Bernice. This is my wife, Brianna. Our sons Will and Gianni."

"Daddy!" Gianni squealed happily, extending his arms to Alessandro.

Bernice turned and shook Bree's hand. "Pleasure ma'am."

"Uh hi," Bree said, caught off guard. Why would Alessandro hire a nurse when he insisted he didn't want anyone helping him?

No, he said he didn't want 'you' helping him.

Bernice turned and helped Alessandro back into his chair. Bree leaned over and passed a squirming Gianni over to him.

"Oook, mama. My dis," Gianni said, leaning his head on Alessandro's shoulder.

Bree gave Gianni a weak smile, the sting of rejection still burning in her stomach.

"Same time tomorrow, Mr. D?" Bernice asked.

"Yes, thank you," Alessandro said, not looking at Bree.

"We saw Unco Colin today. He buyed me a ice cream," Will said. "I don tink Gianni like him too much though. He throwed his Jello at him."

Alessandro snorted and tapped Gianni's nose. "That's my boy."

Bree's scowl deepened when she caught Will's smile fall from his face. Will had always considered Colin one of his favourite people.

"So Bernice? Where did she come from?" Bree asked, wrapping and arm around Will and pulling him against her.

"I hired her this morning. She's one of the best physical therapists in the field."

"I told you I was willing to help you between your doctor's appointments. Carlo was going to help me learn some exercises for you to do and you told me not to bother, that you'd get your physical therapy at the hospital."

"Ah well. I decided you were right, darling. Why go to all the trouble of going to the hospital when I can get my therapy at home?" Alessandro explained. "Mummy was right, wasn't she Gianni? Yes she was." Alessandro smiled at the baby who giggled.

"Waaa," Gianni agreed.

"So you hired Bernice, even though I told you I was willing to help you?" Bree countered.

"So your little visit with Colin, was that before or after your appointment with Dr. Graham? Or did you get so caught up with chatting up your old friend you had to reschedule?"

Bree narrowed her eyes, not liking the insinuating tone of his voice. "Before."

"Can you walk now, daddy?" Will asked.

Alessandro smiled at him. "Soon, young Will. How did your visit with Dr. Graham go, hmm?"

"I like her. She nice. She told me is okay if I'm 'fraid sumtines 'cause wha happen' was really scawy," Will explained moving from Bree to Alessandro.

"Mmm, that's good," Alessandro said. "But you know, it's important to be brave too so that we can be strong when scary things happen. That way we'll be able to fight."

Will nodded, slowly. "Yeah. I know."

Bree swore inwardly. She knew that wasn't what Will wanted to hear and she wanted to punch Alessandro. "Will, you want to do mommy a favour and go play with Gianni in the living room?" She picked Gianni up and placed him back in the stroller.

"Okay, but daddy, Dr. Sheri say next time she want you to come too," he said as he pushed Gianni out of the room.

Alessandro snorted. "Right, that's all I need now," he said when Will was out of earshot.

"So you'd rather have a stranger helping you? How reassuring."

"Oh please, Brianna. Don't take it personally. Bernice is trained professional."

"Where as I'm just your wife. I'm just the person who is supposed to help you through your hardest times. But no, you'd rather have a stranger do it. Got it, loud and clear, Alessandro, thanks." She turned to storm out of the room.

"Wait, wait." Alessandro reached out and grabbed the edge of her sweater, pulling her back. "Brianna, come on, please understand. I hate having you see me like this. I want to be the man that I was. Strong and capable."

"Alessandro, none of that matters to me," Bree tried to assure him. She kneeled down next to his chair.

"I know you want to believe that, and you want me to believe that but it kills me to be this broken shell of a man. If it wasn't for you and the boys, I would have put a gun in my mouth long ago."

Bree started, terrified. "Don't even say something like that!"

"My point is I love you, but I can't bear for you to see me fighting so hard to do the simplest things. It's emasculating and humiliating, Brianna. I can't bear for you to watch that. Please, do this for me, darling. Please, can you understand?" he begged, cupping her face.

Bree sighed. It hurt that he didn't want her to help him but she could understand his embarrassment. She knew she'd have a hard time with it too but …wasn't that what marriage was about? Sharing the good times and the bad was a part of it. "Yeah. Okay. But you have to understand, Alessandro, that I love you. That means I love you no matter what. I mean, if it was me, would you stop loving me because I couldn't walk?"

"Of course not. But it's different when I'm the one that's injured."

Bree left Alessandro alone and went to check in on Will and Gianni. Gianni was on the floor in front of Will playing with their toys.

"How's it going?" Bree asked sitting down on the floor next to them.

Gianni handed her a Lego block. "Do, mama. Dis." He pointed to the tower he was building.

"Mommy, am I nod aposed to like Unco Colin no mo'?" Will asked.

Bree blinked in surprise. "Of course you can like him."

"But daddy no like him and he likes Gianni better now 'cause Gianni no like him too," Will explained, his face utterly dejected.

Bree grit her teeth, forcing herself not to go back and tear Alessandro a new one for his thoughtlessness. "I promise, daddy doesn't like Gianni more than you. He loves you just as much. Daddy's just sad because he knows Colin can walk around and maybe play with you like daddy can't right now. We just have to work very very hard to remind daddy that we still love him the best, okay?"

"Of course, mommy! Colin nod my daddy. Daddy shouldn't tink dumb tings like dat."

"I agree kiddo," Bree said though she couldn't help the seed of resentment that Alessandro seemed determined to make loving him so damned hard.

Bree lay next to him, the man she loved, lust churning in her belly. Christ. Of all the worst damn times to get horny. She was still furious with him for his thoughtless comments earlier in the day but one thing Bree had learned about her relationship was she didn't have to like Alessandro in that particular instant to want him.

But there was nothing to be done about it. Or was there? Bree bit her lip and turned to face Alessandro's tightly muscled back and ran her fingers along the warm skin, lit by the moonlight filtering in through the window. Okay, so they couldn't completely make love but Carlo had assured her that there were plenty of things Bree and Alessandro could do together to retain that sexual intimacy between them. Bree licked her lips and pressed her mouth to his back in a soft, tentative kiss.

One good thing they'd always had between them was the sex. No doubt about that, Bree thought, her body already responding just from the memory. "Alessandro, are you awake?" He's not going to want to, her doubt warned. He's in a dark place and just might bite her head off for trying.

But she had to know for sure if there was any hope they could have at least that physical connection.

He'd already shot her down once while she was helping him bathe. Was she simply being a glutton for punishment or was it worth trying again?

Bree told herself she wasn't ready to give up on that part of their lives. Okay, so they couldn't have intercourse yet. They both had working fingers and tongues, she thought with another surge of lust. God, he was an amazing lover. Incomparable, completely attuned to her every need. Bree missed that.

"Mmm?" he asked sleepily.

She moved her lips up to his shoulder and bit ever so gently. "I can't sleep," she murmured in his ear. She moved one hand over his arm to dance her fingers through the dusting of dark hair on his chest. The edge of her fingernail grazed his nipple and Bree felt his body grow rigid and heard him groan. She smiled, imagining putting her mouth there.

His hand closed over hers. "Don't, Brianna."

Bree's mouth went dry and she felt a twinge of unease. "Come on, Alessandro. You know you want to," she teased, running the tip of her tongue along his shoulder.

"There's no point, darling," he replied, but she could heart the crack in his voice.

He wasn't unaffected. He liked what she was doing.

"The point is I love you. I love touching you and having your hands on me. We could do that, Alessandro," Bree reminded him.

Alessandro took her hand and turned to face her, putting her hand down on the mattress between them.

Bree fought the flare of rejection that made her eyes burn. "Come on, Alessandro. We can still—"

"No. We can't. Now can we stop this, please? I'm tired."

"Why?" Bree asked. "I mean, I know we can't make love completely but there are other things we can do."

"No," Alessandro snapped, his eyes cold.

"I repeat, why?" Bree insisted stubbornly.

"Why? Here," he grabbed her hand again and put it between his legs.

Bree glared at him and tried to pull her hand away but Alessandro wouldn't let her.

"Do you feel that? Or should I say, do you feel what's not happening?"

"Alessandro, I'm not an idiot. I know how your paralysis works. But just because we can't have intercou—"

"I want you, Brianna. Still, despite how worthless I feel and disgusted I am with myself, I still want you, still love you."

Bree sat up and looked down at him. "But then I don't understand. Why wouldn't you want us to at least make love that way if we can't another way. There's so much we can do still, Alessandro."

"Because. It would kill me. Part of what inflames my desire for you is your response to me. The sounds you make, the way your body moves, the way you look at me. I hate that inside I'm so full of my desire for you and then I look at my body and nothing happens. Inside, I want to bury myself deep in you and never stop, never let go and I know that physically I never can again. Please, Brianna, just…let it go."

Bree stared at him, blinking back tears. She sniffled and forced herself to speak. "Right. Because that's just what's best, huh? Don't push, don't press, don't upset the careful order of your wallowing in self-pity because God fucking knows this is only about you!"

Alessandro sighed and turned his face away from her.

"No, dammit. Listen to me."

Alessandro turned back to her and rolled his eyes. "Brianna, you asked me to fight. I'm trying. I'm doing what you asked. That has to take all my energy right now. I can't give you what you want."

"Because you refuse to. What exactly are you fighting for, Alessandro? You're fighting to walk again. Well, what happens if you've pushed all of us away and no one is around to celebrate you getting back on your feet?"

"And what is that? A threat?" Alessandro asked.

"Noooo," Bree moaned in frustration, burying her head in the pillow. "You think I just love you because you're good in bed, Alessandro? For God sakes Alessandro if that was all I wanted then—"

"What? Has Colin offered to step in on stud service?" Alessandro snapped.

Bree stared at him and wound her fingers tight in her lap to keep from slapping him. "Sex is not what our marriage is about. Sex is not why I love you and why I thought you loved me."

"I do love you. That hasn't changed and never will. But you just have to accept that we won't be intimate that way ever again. Maybe it would be best for you to take a lover, to fulfill needs that your eunuch of a husband can't."

Even as he said the words, Bree could see the hatred blazing in his eyes and knew the words were bitter to him. "Just not Colin. Promise me it won't be Colin. I'd appreciate it if it was someone I didn't know."

"Promise…promise you…" Bree couldn't speak she was so furious. "You're giving me permission to cheat on you? To go out and find some other guy? To let him put his hands on me? To put his mouth on me? You won't care if maybe I slum it a little and go down to a bar and pick up some boy toy for the night and have him fuck me? You won't care that another man will take what belongs to you, Alessandro?" Bree taunted.

Alessandro gripped the back of her head and pulled her down, capturing her mouth in a kiss that sent Bree's senses spinning. He thrust his tongue in her mouth, and Bree nearly came just from the potency of his taste, missing him so much. Bree pulled back and smiled at him triumphantly. "You fucking liar," she drawled.

"Shut up," Alessandro growled, and once again captured the lips that would belong to him and no other.

He thrust his tongue into her mouth, branding her as he always did. He didn't have to, Bree thought. She would never belong to anyone but him. His fingers twined in her hair, holding her head still, as if he was afraid she'd pull back. Her fingers slid along his chest, up along the tight muscles of his shoulders to the warm column of his neck.

She could feel the strong, racing pulse there. As long as that could still be felt, Bree could deal with anything else. She moved her mouth against his, tasting him, drowning in the taste that was a combination of coffee and the cherry lollipops he had shared with Gianni and Will earlier that day. His lips still held the faintest trace of sweetness and Bree ran the tip of her tongue along the skin.

"Help me up," he urged against her mouth and she eased back to help him sit up. "Sit on me," he ordered.

Bree blinked, disoriented for a second thinking he meant on his shaft. No.

She saw the flicker of disappointment in his eyes at her confusion and she quickly kissed him again, straddling his hips with her legs. His mouth ran along the curves her face, her eyes, her cheeks.

His hands went to her breasts, stroking the nipples and sending bursts of electric sensation through her body. Bree cried out and arched, bringing his head to them, urging him silently to take them into his mouth.

"They're already growing," he murmured, kneading her breasts with his fingers, the heat from the palms of his hands driving her insane. He nuzzled them with his mouth, looking up at her, his eyes full of wistfulness and need. "Christ, you're so beautiful." He lifted a hand up to push a lock of her hair behind her ear.

The gentle gesture brought tears to her eyes.

"I don't deserve you. I know I don't. I've been moody and cruel and thoughtless," Alessandro sighed, sliding his hands down her waist.

"Stop it," Bree insisted, digging her fingers into his shoulders. "Don't think about anything but us, but right now."

"Why?" Alessandro shook his head. "Why are you doing this? You don't have to pretend you want me. You can't possibly want me like this."

Bree cupped his face. "I'm doing this to show you what we're fighting for. To show you how much I love you, how much I do want you. Love me. That's all I want Alessandro. Just love me," she urged, linking her fingers with his.

She lowered her mouth to his neck, sucking at the pulse at his neck before moving down to his chest. The dark hairs tickled her tongue before she found the erect pebbles of his nipples and flicked them.

A soft thud made her look and Alessandro had his head pressed against the headboard, his eyes closed and his teeth pressed together.

"Good?" she asked with a soft smile before sucking at the sensitive skin.

He gasped. "Brianna…"

"That's right. Let me make it good for you."

Alessandro shook his head and grabbed her. "You can't," he growled stubbornly. "No matter how much you want to, or I want to. I can't come. I can't get hard and I can't fuck you and spill myself inside of you. That connection. My body into yours, leaving that part of me in you. That always felt like coming home for me, Brianna. Now I feel lost. How can you fix that?" He set her down on his thigh, after pulling off her panties. The coarse hair of his body rubbed against her clitoris, making her moan. "Come for me." He guided her hips back and forth.

Bree wanted to assure him they'd have that connection again. They'd fight as hard as they could to make it happen. But she couldn't make that promise and she wished he would believe that while she'd miss that connection, he was a part of her soul, so far beyond the physical connection.

But he didn't believe her. That hurt. Hurt more than she thought it could. How could they have any kind of future if he didn't trust in her love for him? Hadn't they moved past that?

"I can't feel it," Alessandro groaned, torment evident in his voice. "I can't feel you on my skin, can't feel how wet you are." Pain-filled eyes lifted to hers and Bree felt so guilty.

Was she being completely selfish, pushing him to try and accommodate her desire for him when he wasn't ready? No, she thought stubbornly. They needed this intimacy for their marriage, not just to get her off. She took his hand and lifted her hips, placing his fingers between her legs. "Feel me. Feel how much I want you. Feel how much I love you, will…Oh God…" she moaned when he thrust his fingers into her, "always love you."

Alessandro let out a primal possessive sound as he curled his fingers inside of her and Bree clamped down around them. "So warm and wet," he ground as he moved his head to her breasts and took a nipple into his mouth.

Bree cried out as he stroked her walls, pumping his fingers back and forth inside of her. "Can you feel me now?" she asked, cupping the back of his head, burying her face in his hair. "Can you feel how wet I am for you?"

Alessandro moaned in agreement and fucked her with his fingers as his tongue flicked over her breast, trying to give each nipple equal attention. "Come for me. Let me feel it."

He rubbed her clitoris with his thumb as he thrust his fingers at a quick determined pace.

Bree hissed, feeling the tension begin to tighten in her belly. She felt a beat of disappointment war with the urge to let go and give in to the explosion waiting just there over the edge. She didn't want it to be over too soon. She'd missed Alessandro's hands on her for so long. She wanted more. She wanted it to never stop. "Please…" she whimpered, wanting him to slow down, wanting him to keep going.

He cupped the back of her head and kissed her again, thrusting hard one final time before Bree cried out into his mouth. Her orgasm thundered through her and she gripped his shoulders to anchor her to the earth. As she fell against him her eyes locked with his. "I love you," she sighed, kissing him as she felt him pull his fingers out, leaving her empty again.

"I think you should go back to our old bedroom now," he said, his voice tight.

Bree went still, the icy shock of surprise paralyzing her. "W...what?"

"You were right," Alessandro choked. "It's easier if you're closer to—"

"Why?" Bree asked, a wealth of pain in that one word. "Didn't I just prove to you that no matter what I still want you? Still need you? I mean, didn't what we just shared mean anything—"

"That's my point, Brianna. I didn't share it. I never can again."

"STOP IT!" Bree exploded sliding off the bed and wrapping the sheet around her. "Stop pushing me away. You're not even trying. I know you liked touching me. I know that meant something to you and things could be so amazing between us still if you just—"

"Buck up and deal with what I've got instead of what we had?" he sneered.

"Yes!" Bree spat. "Damn you, yes! Why are you so determined to ruin this when I know you love me? I know what we do to each other, how we make each other feel. You can deny it all you want but I see how you want me every time you look at me. Why won't you let us be happy?"

"Because there's no point. I want you, but I can never do anything about it and you unman me by making me try to fulfill needs that I never will be able to again."

Bree stared at him, tears pouring down her face. It hadn't worked. "I 'unmanned' you. Stupid me. I thought I was showing you how much I loved you. Thanks for setting me straight." She picked up her robe and slipped it on, turning and hiding her naked body from him.

"Brianna…" his voice was almost apologetic and she whirled around, anger churning through her.

"What?" Bree snapped.

His dark eyes glistened with tears that he'd refused to let her wipe away. "Nothing."

She walked upstairs in a trance of soul wrenching pain. She went into Will's room and nudged him awake. "You wanna come sleep with mommy?" she asked, her voice trembling with the effort not to break down.

Will turned and blinked sleepily at his mother before raising his arms to her. She gathered him in her arms, taking a small bit of comfort from him. Bree carried him into her old bedroom and set him down on the bed.

When she lay next to him, his hand went to her face but he kept his eyes closed. "Daddy make you cry again?" Will asked.

Bree bit her fist to keep her sobs and screams inside.

CHAPTER THIRTY-TWO

They hadn't spoken in almost a week except for the most cursory sentences. If it wasn't for the boys, Alessandro doubted Bree would have said a word to him at all. It was what he wanted of course. He wanted her to leave him the bloody fucking hell alone. He didn't want her to look at him and see how lacking he was. He was trying. Nothing was happening. Nothing would happen because this was his punishment. God was turning him, who had revelled in his strength, in his power to dominate others and bend them to his will, with violence, with no compunction at all, into a weak, pathetic useless waste of space in this world. Someone worthy only of pitying glances. Ah the great Alessandro Dardano. Not so great now, are you, ol' boy?

And now this.

"I thought it might interest you to know what your dear Brianna has been doing with her days instead of being here by her injured husband's side." Bernardo said.

Will, who had been playing with Gianni, helping him stand up again and again, stopped and turned to Bernardo, irritation furrowing his small dark brows. The temporary nanny, Darcy, Dara, Debbie or something, gathered Gianni up in her arms and prepared to leave the room.

"Nooooooooo!" Gianni insisted, wanting to continue to play where he was.

Alessandro gave the nanny a nod, indicating the boys could stay.

"Unco Colin her fend," Will injected quickly before Bernardo could spill the news.

Colin. Just the name made Alessandro's gut burn. He knew the man wanted his wife, even if Brianna was too blind to see it. The moron had been cuckolded by the paragon of supposed virtue, his wife Carrie and now he had finally opened his eyes and seen what Alessandro had known all along. Brianna put every other woman in New York to shame. No woman could come near her beauty, her passion, her fire.

Colin had tossed her aside for the angelic Carrie and now he was changing his mind.

Oh no you don't, you miserable fucker.

"Her friend indeed," Bernardo drawled, his Italian accent thick with unmistakable implication.

"Dat's da truth. He no make her cry all da time." That was directed at Alessandro, with small dark accusatory eyes. "He nice."

Alessandro couldn't look at those eyes without feeling a sickening pang of guilt. She's mine! He wanted to scream. Mine! Mine! Mine!

"Oh yes. Very nice. He was very nice when he held her at the cemetery and very nice when he was dancing with her at Adresca."

That made Alessandro's head lift in surprise.

"Oh yes, my boy. She's been there, cleaning up the rubble and word is that she's working on re-opening it. Her friend Colin has been quite helpful in that endeavour."

"I don' like how you say dat," Will said scowling.

"Really young William, I only speak the truth," Bernardo taunted.

Alessandro's mind was racing. NO! Not Colin. He could not let that imbecile take Brianna away from him. He'd have to be eliminated somehow. Alessandro began to plot all the different ways he could ensure that Colin Neally stayed away from his wife, permanently. They all involved grisly, violent methods. He could not be allowed to win Brianna.

But hadn't you ensured his victory by pushing her away, a small voice taunted. He had no one to blame for this but himself. It was what he wanted really, Alessandro told himself, for Brianna to move on. Leave him so that she wouldn't see him grow into an old invalid. Weak and disgusting.

Oh and he'd disgusted her, Alessandro had no doubt about

that. She hadn't tried to touch him since that last pathetic attempt at lovemaking. Sex. Hardly lovemaking, he thought, forcing down the bile that rose at the memory.

"Leave me alone, father." Alessandro said, wheeling away. He didn't even have the dignity of storming out. No dignity, ever again. He couldn't even go to the fucking bathroom by himself and had to have implements attached to him because he couldn't even feel when he had to relieve himself. I can't. I can't do this anymore.

He was effectively pushing away his family, the only thing that had ever truly mattered to him. Even Will, who had looked at him with such hero worship once, now looked at him with accusation and incomprehension.

Nothing was changing. He would live like this limp, useless creature forever. No matter how much physical therapy he did, his legs would never work again. He'd tried to fight. He couldn't anymore.

Gianni was too young to understand now but soon he'd look at him in the same way. Even now, he was constantly asking for Alessandro to 'up' with him, to play with him as he used to. Gianni would grow up and feel the burden of taking care of his 'poor crippled old man'. He wouldn't want to bring his friends around to see his disgusting father. Bernardo would instil in Gianni the need for strength, power and domination. Gianni would see that Alessandro was lacking in all those things and feel sorry for him, come to be ashamed that he had been sired by such a pitiful creature.

After searching for the tiny key, Alessandro unlocked the bottom drawer of the night table where he kept the spare gun.

The new baby would never know him as strong, powerful. She would see only her poor daddy who needed special care. She would grow up never knowing what it was like for daddy to play with her because he couldn't get out of his wheelchair.

They'd all love Brianna's future husband more, Alessandro thought bitterly, hating himself for the tears that rolled down his face. She would find someone else. No man would be able to resist her and she would find someone else who didn't push her away, didn't disgust her. He gave a bitter snort, remembering the gypsy Ruthie's prediction of a third marriage. Looks like that would come to pass after all.

But not Colin, Alessandro hissed inside. His father would know what to do afterwards.

His father would know what to do when he found Alessandro's body. Colin would never get his hands on Brianna. Bernardo would make sure of that, because Alessandro was too much of weakling to do it himself.

He wouldn't leave a note. He wouldn't weaken himself further by trying to explain the unforgivable. And oh, he knew Brianna would never forgive him for this final act of cowardice. Ironically, he thought that anger, that rage would help her move on.

Alessandro started at the taste of the cold metal in his mouth. He took a deep breath and willed himself to pull the trigger. He closed his eyes and saw Brianna's face, smiling at him, her arms wrapped around him and he willed himself to feel her strength to use it for what must be done.

He gripped the barrel and forced himself to move his finger towards the trigger.

My beloved.

"DADDY!" Will screamed in the doorway.

Will covered his eyes and shook his head and screamed. "Noooooo! No! No! No!"

Alessandro stared at him, wide eyed, frozen with disbelief over what he'd been about to do, what he'd been about to do to Will. Alessandro dropped the gun. "It's all right, Will. It's all right, look. See? I don't have the gun anymore. See?" He tried to reach out for Will but he couldn't manage it in the chair.

"Gaaaaaapppppyyyyy!" Will shrieked and turned, running out of the room to get Bernardo.

"No, Will, don't!" Alessandro pushed himself too far in his bid to stop Will and fell out of the wheelchair, hitting the hardwood floor with a dull thud. "Bloody hell," he groaned, rubbing his head after it hit the floor.

"Alessandro, Alessandro! What on earth?" Bernardo asked, rushing in, Will close behind him.

"I'm all right, just help me back into the chair," Alessandro said.

"The child came running at me screaming about a..." he stopped after helping Alessandro into the chair and started at the floor, spotting the gun. "What in the world...Alessandro! Madonna mia, what were you thinking?"

"He put it in his mouf. Like dis! Like dis!" Will explained, motioning with his finger in his mouth.

"I was thinking that I can't leave like this anymore, Father," Alessandro snapped. Then he shook his head. "But I understand now that I can't possibly do that to the people I love."

He moved to look at Will who looked white as a sheet.

"You're damned right you can't! We are Dardanos and we do not give up! We do not take the coward's way out, my son."

"Father, just let me talk to Will alone, all right? Just leave us for a little while."

Bernardo shook his head but Alessandro insisted and Bernardo raised his hands in defeat. "Bah! The boy stopped you from your stupidity. Maybe he can make you see sense."

Will turned to leave but Alessandro called out to stop him. "I want to explain what happened. I want—"

"No! I don't wanna talk to you no mo!" Will shouted and moved to the door.

"William, you stay right there. I want to talk to you," Alessandro ordered.

The little boy turned and scowled, but didn't leave. He crossed his arms over his chest and glared at Alessandro, silent.

"I'm sorry for what you saw. I understand that it was the wrong thing to do and I want to explain—"

"I don' wanna no explains!" Will yelled. "You wanna go away up in hev'n like my daddy. But you was gonna do it on purpose! Nod an asiden' like my daddy!"

"You're right to be angry with me—"

"Good. 'Cause I is."

"Okay. But I realize it was a mistake. I was feeling very very sad and I didn't feel like…" Alessandro struggled to explain such complex feelings to a five year old. "I will never do anything like that again. I swear to you, Will. I promise."

"You pomish you be my daddy, and you was gonna break dat pomish. But I don' care 'cause I don wan you fo my daddy no mo! You mean, and you make mommy cry. You don play wif us like afore. You like Gappy Lecter, nod my daddy." Will's lower lip quivered and he looked away.

"You know why I can't play with you like before but it doesn't mean I don't still love you. That's part of the reason I was so sad. I felt like I wasn't good enough to be your daddy anymore."

"I nod talking 'bout yo' legs. I little but I nod a dummy. I know yo legs are brokded. But is yo' brain brokded too? You can still laugh and play wif me and Gianni. We don haf to play running. But you no want to no more." Will sniffled and his face crumpled. Shamefaced, he whirled around and faced the wall.

God help him, Alessandro thought. What the bloody hell was he doing to Will, to his family? There had to be a way to live with this weakness and make some sort of peace with it because he could never bear to leave Will the way he had planned. He could never bear to destroy his son like that.

"My son..." Alessandro whispered, his eyes burning. "I hate you seeing me like this. I hate that I used to be able to run with you and play ball with you and now I can't, I hate it. But I love you. You and your mother and Gianni, I love you all so much. That's why it hurts so much."

"But is nod yo' fault. Is Arturo's. But if you gonna shoot da gun in yo' mouf, dat would be yo' fault," Will insisted. "Wha' happen if you get better but den you can' come back 'cause you dead? Den what?" He turned his head, eyes blazing and tears trailing down his cheeks.

"We don't know if I'll ever walk again, Will."

"So? But you be here. I lie afore." He turned back to face Alessandro. "I say I no wan you to be my daddy no mo. But I mean da daddy you is now. Da mean one. I wan my nice daddy back. If you no do dat. I no talk to you no mo."

"Fair enough," Alessandro nodded sniffling.

Will looked at him skeptically. "Sooo?"

"If you can forgive me, I will try and be better. Nicer," Alessandro explained, feeling a rush of strength come over him. He'd try even when he feared he couldn't try any more, for this little boy, for his family. Alessandro tentatively extended his arms to Will, praying that the little boy didn't reject him, praying that even though he was weak and crippled, this boy would still love him.

Will stepped forward into his arms and hugged him tightly. "Deal," he said, sniffling. Alessandro picked him up and set him down on his lap, feeling a pang of sadness that he couldn't feel Will's small frame.

Will lay his head on Alessandro's shoulder. "So you no do dat ever again? Promise?"

"With all my heart," Alessandro agreed. He still didn't feel worthy enough to be in their lives, but they didn't deserve for him to take the coward's way out. He loved them too much for that.

"Good."

"So…uh, how about you and I keep this little episode from mummy, eh?" Alessandro asked.

Will lifted his head. "If she ask, I no lie 'cause dat's bad."

"Fair enough," Alessandro said with a grimace though he tried to be secure in the knowledge that Brianna wouldn't very well walk in out of the blue and ask her son if Alessandro had put a gun in his mouth. He gave a wry snort and eased Will's weight from one thigh and suddenly stopped, realizing what he had just done.

What he had just felt. Alessandro's heart stopped in his chest as he realized with a rush of exhilaration that he had felt, for a moment, the pressure of Will on his legs. He set Will on his feet and was crushed under the weight of disappointment that he no longer felt anything when he rubbed his hand along his thigh. No sensation at all. But he'd felt it. He knew he had.

Hadn't he?

Bree felt guilty as she walked through the door. She hadn't wanted to come home. Home. This Dardano tomb had never felt like home to her but because of Alessandro and her boys, it had been bearable. But lately, with Alessandro's angry behaviour and her children's lack of joy, not even they could make her stay longer than she absolutely had to. Bree found herself looking forward to throwing herself into her work, getting Adresca back on its feet.

She couldn't even have Alessandro help her with that because she just knew he'd snap at her if she asked. She missed doing things alongside him, watching him transform from polished suits to grimy jeans and still look so devastatingly handsome he stole her breath. She would have never have imagined the silver spoonfed Dardano golden boy would be so at ease working with his hands. They would work, laugh and be so comfortable with each other that the absence of it all made her heart ache.

Even with Colin, as comfortable as she was with her ex-brother-in-law, there wasn't that same indefinable thing that she had with Alessandro. Like a joined magic. Two souls that fit together like pieces of a puzzle and moved together through the world, linked. But lately, when Bree thought of Alessandro, she felt a dread in the pit of her stomach. An uncomfortable knot that told her nothing she did would be right. He'd snap, he'd yell, he'd push her away.

For a few moments, in the ease of Colin's company, Bree could forget. It was getting to the point where she was looking forward more and more to seeing Colin and less and less to facing the husband who she feared would never let her in again.

There was a man she didn't recognize taking measurements along the wall over the staircase. He turned to her and nodded. "You must be Mrs D?"

"Uh…yeah and you are?" Bree asked walking to the bottom of the stairs.

"Name's Bob. I'm installing the lift here for your husband."

Bree blinked. "Wait, what?" She felt a trickle of hopefulness shiver under her skin but she tamped it down quickly. She didn't want to get her hopes up in case she was misunderstanding.

Rafe passed by then. "It seems Master Dardano has finally gotten his head out of his rear end."

Bree stared at the dour butler, her eyes wide.

He shrugged. "It had to be said." He continued on towards the living room.

Bree stared after him in disbelief.

"That one's a hoot, inn't he?" Bob, the handy man asked before getting back to work.

"A hoot. Ralphie. Sure," Bree snorted in disbelief. She shook her head, fearing this house was finally driving her insane. When she went into the living room, she was surprised to hear laughing.

Alessandro had Gianni in his arms and was holding the baby over his head, pretending to be flying with him. The scene stopped her heart. Her baby was giggling and squealing, but it was Alessandro who had her attention.

He was smiling.

Alessandro's smile wavered when he saw her and his eyes flickered with something she'd come to recognize in her husband's eyes as guilt.

"Mommy!" Will came running towards them and threw his arms around her legs.

"Hey little man," Bree leaned down and picked him up and that's when she noticed he was trembling.

"Please don't go away 'gain. Please stay home now," he whispered fervently. "Please stay here wif daddy all da time now."

"What's going on?" Bree asked, her brief beat of lightness

replaced by worry. She looked over at Alessandro who sighed and set Gianni down on his lap.

Will covered his mouth and shook his head. Then leaned his head against Bree's and whispered in her ear. "Ask daddy. Please ask daddy 'cause I promise I no say."

"Okay someone explain to me what is going on here," Bree said, her worry growing. She rubbed Will's back until he stopped trembling.

"It's all right Will. I'll tell her. It was wrong of me to ask you to keep it from her."

"Keep what?" Bree demanded, panicked.

"Will could you stay with Gianni while I talk with mummy in the bedroom?"

"Okay. But please mommy, don' be mad at daddy. He was really, really sad and I stopped him," Will pleaded as Bree set him on the floor.

"I'll hold off on making any promises until I hear exactly what it is daddy did," Bree said turning and following Alessandro as he moved past her into the hallway.

Alessandro grabbed a key out of his pocket and unlocked the bottom drawer of the night table. When he turned with the gun in his lap, Bree stared at him uncomprehending.

"What the…" Her legs gave way beneath her and she fell against the bed. "Oh my God! Will said…and he said…"

Alessandro raised his hands. "I know that it was a stupid thing to do and I'm so so sorry that I even thought of it but you have to understand—"

"I have to understand? I have to?" Bree yelled. "I am sick to death of trying to understand. How could you even contemplate such a thing? How could you think of doing something so cowardly and selfish?"

"I know. I know. But I felt like I was losing you, losing everything. That you couldn't possibly want me like this—"

"You're the one who keeps pushing me away, pushing everyone away!" Bree shouted at him.

"Well, from what I hear Colin has been doing quite a good job of picking up my slack now hasn't he?" Alessandro scowled.

Bree narrowed her eyes. "Andy, right? What? Has he been coming back every day and giving you and Hannibal Lecter little reports? But never mind. Stop trying to change the subject. Explain to me what the hell you were thinking?" She suddenly got to her feet. "Wait. Will said he stopped you. What did he mean by that?"

Alessandro's cheeks reddened with shame and Bree's rage, born of terror at how close she'd came to losing this man, the image of him lying dead by his own hand, exploded. "Did he see you? Did he see you with the gun? Did our five year old son see you almost commit suicide?"

"Yes," he said softly. "Brianna, you have no idea how sorry—"

Bree slapped him across the face. "You selfish son of a bitch."

CHAPTER THIRTY-THREE

"Oh. Ow! Bloody hell," Alessandro groaned, his eyes tight as his hand went to his face.

Bree felt a surge of satisfaction when she saw the red imprint of her hand on his skin.

"Fair enough…Damn," he worked his jaw and grimaced. "I know I deserved that."

"Oh good. I'm glad you approve," Bree hissed.

"Brianna—" Alessandro sighed.

"Don't!" she snapped. "I don't want to hear a damned thing you have to say. How could you…How could—"

"I thought you said you didn't want to hear—"

"Shut up!" she screamed. She took a step back and covered her mouth. "And that you would let Will watch? I mean, how sick is that?"

Here Alessandro glared at her indignantly. "I did not let Will watch. That's unconscionable. I merely forgot to shut the door."

Bree forced herself not to lunge for him again and tear his eyes out. "Oh, you forgot?"

"Brianna, I wasn't thinking clearly. I have never felt so low in my life."

"Yeah well you have no one to blame for that but yourself," Bree shot back. "For over a month now we have been bending over backwards, walking on eggshells around you. Poor Alessandro, you've had it so rough. One bump in the road and you put a gun in your mouth."

"I would hardly call this a bump in the road, darling," Alessandro scowled.

"You want to talk about bumps in the road? How about growing up knowing that you are never anybody's first choice? How about finally meeting a man and thinking you were going to spend the rest of your lives creating the family you always wanted, only to have him die? Murdered by the family whose sole existence is to destroy yours. How about meeting a stranger and connecting with him on such a deep level only to learn that he's a Dardano, a part of that family that wants to destroy you and has been brainwashed by his monster of a father to get you pregnant and carry on the god forsaken Dardano legacy—"

"Brianna—" Alessandro objected but Bree leaned over his chair and glared at him.

"I'm not finished! How about feeling that you have finally found the other half of your soul that you have been missing your whole life, trying to get over the fact that not only is he supposed to be your mortal enemy but his father killed the man you were supposed to spend the rest of your life with? How about thinking that you have finally found the one person who when he looked at you, always made you believe that you were the most precious thing in the world to him? Then coming home to discover that had it not been for your five year old son, you would have come home to that man's brain splattered against the wall because he couldn't bear his one 'bump in the road'. That this man who you thought loved you beyond anything, did not deem you worthy enough to live for just because his legs didn't work!" Bree concluded, tears streaming down her face.

Alessandro was silent and awestruck as he stared up at her. He lifted his hand to wipe her tears but she smacked it away.

"Don't! You don't get to comfort me after almost making me come home to your corpse. What the fuck do you know about hardship you silver spoon fed, had everything handed to you on a platter, selfish bastard? You've never had to fight for anything. You've been raised to think the world revolves around you, while I was raised having to scrape for the slightest crumb of love and approval from my family. How dare you? How fucking dare you?"

Alessandro nodded, his eyes red. "I know, Brianna. Please, I know. But this time, I was the one who didn't feel worthy of you. I was the one who didn't feel like you could love me like this—"

Bree gripped his face and got to her knees in front of him. "Don't you get that I would have followed you?" she hissed, licking the saltiness of her tears from her lips. "Don't you get that it if it wasn't for Will and Gianni that if I came home and found you dead, I would have picked up the gun and put it in my own mouth?"

Alessandro shook his head. "Don't even think about—"

"What? And you can? You don't get it, do you? You don't understand that what I feel for you is completely irrational, completely insane and all consuming and true. Even if you never walk again, it will not change one iota of this bond between us…or this bond I thought was between us," she said, her voice cracking.

Alessandro leaned forward and pressed his forehead to hers. "I'm sorry. I'm so sorry. I'll be different now. I swear to you, I'll change. I think I've hit the lowest point today."

"I want to believe you," Bree sniffled. "But you have to believe me, Alessandro. You have to believe that I would never abandon you like this. I would never leave you while you were suffering like this. I want to take care of you, to help you get back on your feet and help you even if you never do, but you have to let me fight with you."

"What on earth is all this yelling? Can't you possibly do anything other than shriek at my son like a damned fishwife, for God's sake?" Bernardo barked coming into the bedroom.

Bree stiffened and got to her feet, glaring at him. "You. This all your fault, you bastard! You pushed him to this point" She lunged at him.

"Brianna, don't!" Alessandro insisted.

Bernardo grabbed for her flailing arms as she unleashed her fury on Bernardo, slapping, shoving. "All right that's enough!" he said, holding her arms at her sides as Bree tried to break free. "You will calm yourself down and comport yourself with the dignity deserving of the Dardano name. Do you understand me?"

"What I understand is that you have got that man so turned around that he feels like he's nothing if he's not perfect. That he's not worthy of living if he's not the perfect Dardano specimen. You did this,"

"Oh and where were you, my dear? While my son was suffering you were off rekindling your passions with your old flame weren't you?" Bernardo hissed.

"All right that's enough," Alessandro snapped behind them.

"If you think I will allow you to disrespect my son by taking Colin Neally as your lover then you sorely underestimate me, Brianna. You will stay here in this house where you belong and fulfill your duties as befitting the wife of a Dardano or so help me I will—"

"I said that's enough!" Alessandro barked.

Bernardo released Bree and she rubbed her wrists where his fingers had gripped her painfully, her blood chilled by the vehemence of his words.

She turned to Alessandro. "We are leaving this house. You can choose to stay if you want but I'm not staying in this house for one more second, and neither are my sons. Do you understand me, Alessandro?"

Alessandro raised his hands. "Okay, Father, can you leave us alone?"

"Alessandro, you shouldn't over exert your—"

"Oh stop it!" Bree snapped. "Stop babying him he's a grown man for God's sake."

"Really, Father. Let me handle this. Leave us, please," Alessandro said.

Bernardo stepped back towards the doorway and then turned back and glared threateningly at Bree. "If you make him suffer any—"

Bree slammed the door in his face and turned to Alessandro who was fighting a smile.

"You're really not intimidated by him at all, are you?" Alessandro asked.

"Please, he gives me the heebie jeebies. Can we focus please?" Bree insisted. "I want us to leave, today. We can stay at a hotel for a while. The ones in town are all wheelchair accessible."

"But did you see when you walked in? I'm having a lift installed like you wanted and I thought we could move back upstairs. I thought we could maybe try and get things back to normal."

Bree leaned against the wall and crossed her arms over her chest. "I don't know, Alessandro. I…appreciate the effort but I can't help thinking that things would not have gotten this bad if it wasn't for your father. His influence on you is just toxic. I mean, can't you see that?"

"I know my father is not…" Alessandro shook his head. "He's

my father." He shrugged. "Lord knows he's a lot to take and sometimes I wish I could tell him to go to hell but he's family, Brianna. But I do understand what you're saying. I can't live with his stifling and domineering if we have any chance of surviving in this marriage. And more than anything else, I want to make this up to you, to make up for my shameful behaviour. You are everything to me, Brianna and I'm so ashamed of myself that I made you doubt that for even a second. I want to make that up to you and if that means we get out of this house and make a go of it on our own then…yes. That's what we'll do," he nodded resolutely.

Bree stepped away from the wall, afraid to hope that he meant what he said. "Are you sure? I mean…we'll leave this house and live in our own place? Raise our boys without Bernardo skulking in every corner?"

"Well, he is my father and I don't want to abandon him but…I know that you and the boys have to be my priority."

Bree looked at him cautiously, not sure she could trust him. "Okay. Okay."

"So who's going to tell my father?" he asked with a small smile.

"Oh that's all you," Bree insisted raising her hands and stepping back.

"I thought you weren't afraid of my father?" Alessandro countered.

"See but this can be part of your recovery, you know? Standing strong, metaphorically speaking."

"Uh huh, chicken," Alessandro teased.

Bree smiled and got on her knees in front of him. "Thank you." She leaned forward and kissed him. "Thank you." She stood up. "I'm going to go tell Bob his services are no longer required and you can tell Bernardo to go to hell…er…tell him that we're moving, I mean." Bree rushed out of the room, renewed joy making her feel like she could float down the stairs.

After speaking to Bob, Bree spotted Will's head peeking around the corner of the living room doorway. "Daddy okay?"

"Daddy is fine."

"I did a good ting, right? Even though you yell lots?" Will asked uncertainly. "You say sumtines when you yell it don' mean you no love me. So you still love daddy, right?"

Bree picked Will up and carried him into the living room. "I will always love daddy. That's never gonna change. But guess what?

We're going to be moving out of the house."

Will's face fell. "But I don' wanna move! I wanna stay wif daddy! Mommy we haf to stay! What if daddy gets sad again and gets da gun again?" he asked, his eyes panicked.

"No no, sweetie. Daddy's coming with us." Though Bree felt another beat of anger towards Alessandro and what he'd done to their son.

Will's face split with a beaming grin. "Really?"

"Really," Bree mimicked.

"Oh yay!" Will exclaimed.

"Yay!" Gianni echoed.

"Is Gappy Lecter moving wif us too?" Will asked, his smile wavering.

"Not a chance," Bree whispered.

Will leaned in close. "Good, 'cause I no like him," he whispered.

Colin was already hard at work at Adresca when Bree arrived, dreading the discussion they were about to have. He smiled when he saw her. "Guess what I just did?"

She smiled guiltily at him. She wanted to tell herself that she hadn't sensed the feelings between them turning to more than friendship on his end, and that she hadn't used them to keep him around to ease her loneliness, to keep her company, but the truth prickled at her conscience.

Colin picked her up and twirled her around the room. "I got a band lined up to play for the re-opening."

Bree cried out in excitement and hugged him. "Really? Oh my God, Colin, that's incredible!"

"They had heard about what happened of course and took a bit of convincing but I managed to assure them that security would be even tighter than before and after a loooot of arm twisting, they said yes."

"Thank you so much." She went to kiss his cheek but he turned at the last minute and caught her mouth.

She was so stunned that for a moment, Bree couldn't move. He took that for acceptance and deepened the kiss. Funny that as a teenager she would have given everything to have him kiss her the way he was now, yet now she felt…nothing. It was a pleasant kiss. A good kiss filled with obvious passion on his part but Bree's world didn't tilt on its axis, her mind didn't go senseless and her heart didn't race in her chest. He wasn't Alessandro. It was that simple and clear. Bree pulled away gently, guilt settling like a stone in her belly.

He looked at her expectantly, waiting.

"Colin, we have to talk."

"Bree, look, I know that was a stupid thing to do," Colin began as Bree pressed her fingers to her mouth.

"Oh good," she whispered, her nerves churning uneasily. "I'm glad you get that."

"But I'm not going to apologize for it," Colin insisted and Bree stared at him.

"Come on, Colin—"

"No, you come on. You have to know how I feel about you now."

"Now…" Bree said, squeezing her eyes shut. "That's the funniest part of this whole thing. That this is happening now."

"I don't know what changed but—"

"Everything, Colin," Bree reminded him, moving towards the bar and easing herself onto the stool. She had a brief memory of Alessandro taking her right on this stool and she slid off, uncomfortable with the memory while trying to let Colin down. "Everything changed. You…you were with Carrie."

"Right," he snorted bitterly. "And look where that got me. Divorced from the woman I thought I would spend the rest of my life with and in love with her sister."

Bree gasped and quickly shook her head. "No…no you're not. You're just…lonely," she finished lamely.

Colin rolled his eyes. "Bree—"

"I love Alessandro," Bree injected quickly before he could continue. "I moved on, Colin. You will always be the first guy I had a crush on but…" she shrugged. "Alessandro is my future."

"Bree, the man has treated you like garbage from the second he met you. He only sees you as a means to give his father those all important Dardano heirs."

"That's not true!" Bree insisted, hotly. "Okay, fine, Alessandro's been having a hard time lately but who wouldn't, Colin? The man is paralyzed for God's sake. And he's promised things would be different now. We're moving out of that house of horrors and we're going to be a family, away from Bernardo."

"And you really believe that? You really think that if you just move that it'll change anything, that Alessandro will suddenly become an upstanding citizen out from under Bernardo's influence—"

Bree shook her head. "Don't you start with me too, Colin. I've heard that song and I know how it goes no matter who's singing it. If you want to stay my friend then you have to hear me, okay? I love Alessandro. He is my husband. He is the father of my children. He is the man I want to spend my life with. I'm sorry if that hurts you but you are just going to have to accept that, okay?"

"I just hate that you're hurting yourself over a man that is so bad for you."

"I'm a big girl, Colin," Bree snapped insulted. She hated when he did this, treated her like a two year old. "I can take care of myself."

"Right, well what about Will and Gianni?" Colin pressed.

Bree grit her teeth and grabbed her purse. "That's it."

Colin grabbed her arm as she went to the door. "No, Bree. I'm sorry. I'm sorry."

A blinding pain suddenly shot across her abdomen and Bree's legs buckled from underneath her. She would have fallen if Colin hadn't caught her.

"I…Oh God…" The twinge eased but came back with the force of a punch and as Andy burst in, demanding to know what had happened, Colin scooped Bree into his arms and ordered the bodyguard to call the hospital. "Something's…wrong, Colin. Oh no…the baby! Something's wrong with the baby!"

"Colin was with her?" Alessandro asked, his voice cold as Andy explained that Brianna was at the hospital. His heart had stopped when he heard the news. My fault. Oh God. My fault. And then rage was warring with his panic. He would have to have a little chat with Neally. He tried to push down his fury, afraid God wouldn't allow Brianna and the baby to be all right if he was having murderous thoughts about the man who wanted to be her lover.

"If she's not sleeping with him yet, rest assured, my boy, she will be soon," Bernardo had insisted.

He tried to explain to his father that he and Brianna needed their own place. Bernardo countered that Alessandro was allowing her to have too much free reign in their marriage. He had to put his foot down, beginning with Colin. Alessandro was well aware that the imbecile lusted after his wife but he'd hadn't seen any sign that Colin's feelings were being reciprocated. He tried to stay secure in the knowledge that Brianna's loyalty was to him and to their children.

But he'd been pushing her away. Was she seeking comfort in Colin's arms? No, Alessandro told himself. Not Brianna. Not with the bond they shared. He would surely know. Wouldn't he?

"You have given your heart to a woman well versed in the art of deception, my son. Believe me. There is no woman on this earth who is above treachery. I have tried to teach you to keep your heart hidden, strong. To let no woman weaken you, but you would not listen," Bernardo said sadly. "I suppose I shouldn't be surprised at your stubborn will. You are a Dardano after all."

"Father, stop this. I trust Brianna," Alessandro insisted, but inside he felt sick with doubt. He wasn't a whole man. He knew that. And a passionate woman like his wife…and especially the way he'd been treating her lately, was it really so far fetched that she would turn to someone who could fulfill her needs.

"My boy, when are you going to stop causing yourself such pain and understand that I am the only person you can trust? I, your father, am the only person who will ever be completely loyal to you."

Alessandro had demanded that he drop the subject. "Brianna will never leave me."

Bernardo snorted at that. "Why? Because you're paralyzed? Out of some sense of wifely duty? What happens when you can walk again? No, my son, no. You must put your wife in her place, subservient to you and you must never allow her to control your emotions, never allow her to weaken you."

"I said that's enough, Father!" But the seed of doubt had been planted and Alessandro felt a niggle of fear. What would happen when he walked again? He had pushed her away, been so cruel to her in his pain, what if she had turned to Colin and what if her feelings for her first love had been rekindled? Would he lose her?

Had he lost her already?

Alessandro prayed all the way to the hospital, for his wife, for his unborn baby, for their future together.

He wheeled up to the nursing station demanding to know how his wife and child were doing. The nurse looked over his shoulder in confusion.

"Oh. I'm sorry. I thought he was the father."

Alessandro turned and felt a murderous rage thunder through him when he saw Colin sitting next to Brian.

"She is my wife," Alessandro hissed.

The nurse paled and gave him a weak smile. "My apologies, Mr. Dardano. Your wife and baby are doing just fine. She's resting now."

"What the hell happened?" Alessandro demanded.

The nurse jumped and she looked around for help. "I…It was …high blood pressure, th…that's all. Really, she'll be just f…fine."

Stress. My fault. He turned and glared at Colin. Colin stood and glared right back.

"High blood pressure. I wonder what could have 'caused that?" Colin sneered.

"Dude, ease off," Brian warned.

"No, no. Please. I'd very much like to hear about Colin's opinion on my wife's health. In fact, I'd very much like to have a chat with Mr. Neally in private. Shall we?" Alessandro asked, pointing to the lounge.

"Oh, I don't think that's a good idea," Brian pointed out, shaking his head.

"Come now, we're both civilized men, aren't we, Colin?" Alessandro asked, keeping his rage from his voice.

Colin narrowed his eyes, obviously skeptical but he turned and led the way into the lounge.

Brian grabbed the handles on Alessandro's wheelchair, making as if to follow him inside but Alessandro turned his head.

"You should stay out here in case there's any news on Brianna," Alessandro reminded him.

"Just don't do anything stupid, okay? Bree doesn't need the added stress of bailing your ass out of jail."

Alessandro snorted and wheeled himself into the lounge after Colin.

"Let's just cut the crap, shall we? Go ahead with your cave man spiel about asking me to stay away from your wife because my first priority is Bree and making sure she's all right. I'd like to get back out there in case the doctor comes back with anymore news," Colin insisted.

"Let's just say it's in your best interest to keep your fucking hands off of my wife."

"Or what, hmm?" Colin countered, leaning against the table with the coffeemaker and paper cups. "You'll have daddy put a bomb in my car?"

"Really, what do you take me for, Neally? Nothing so impersonal. If you were to ignore my wishes, I would personally wrap my hands around your throat and pop that sanctimonious head right off your shoulders," Alessandro explained smiling.

Colin sneered. "You know, ever since you walked into New York you acted like you owned Bree."

"Oh, you know very well Brianna was mine before I even set foot in New York City. We met in the middle of that snow storm, remember? We took shelter in that abandoned house. I made her mine then, Colin. Quite thoroughly and repeatedly," Alessandro said, relishing the jealousy on Colin's face.

"And once she found out who you really were she wanted nothing to do with you. I remember that," Colin spat back. "But you couldn't leave her alone, could you? You had to keep pushing at her and breaking her down, using her children to trap her into some farce of a marriage just to satisfy Bernardo's wishes."

"Brianna loves me," Alessandro reminded him. "We have a bond, a connection that you could never hope to understand in your narrow little world."

"And what did you do with that love, hmm? You hurt her. You pushed her away. So Bree turned to me. I was the one whose shoulders she cried on. I was the one who was there for her. Now you're scared aren't you? Bree is realizing that she deserves to be happy. She deserves to be with a man who doesn't tear her down. Who doesn't simply want her to be a Dardano brood mare," Colin shot back.

"As opposed to a man who ignored her for her sister?" Alessandro drawled with disgust. "You could have had her. A diamond among shards of glass and you tossed her aside for a milksop of a girl who cuckolded you at the first opportunity," Alessandro taunted.

Colin jerked away from the table, violence in his eyes as he stood over Alessandro, fists clenched at his sides.

"Go ahead," Alessandro goaded. "You think this chair is any kind of handicap against a lily livered shit like you?"

Colin snorted. "I have more respect for myself than to beat up on a cripple. It must be very painful for you. I'm trying to understand,"

Alessandro's heart raced, images of crushing Colin against the wall with his chair running through his mind.

"You know, all the time Bree was crying in my arms, I tried to tell her that it must be very difficult for you dealing with your new physical limitations. I pity you really and believe me so does Bree."

Alessandro clenched his jaw so tight his teeth hurt.

If she's not sleeping with him yet, she will be soon.

Not if I kill him first.

"I know you have deluded yourself into thinking that you and Bree have some fated kind of destiny because that's what daddy led you to believe."

"So…what, you think that you're the better man? In what universe could you ever compete with me? Brianna is mine, in every way. She is the mother of my children. She is carrying my child inside of her. She will never, never love you the way she loves me. The kind of passion and love Brianna and I have…you can't even conceive of. Makes one wonder doesn't it? I mean, Carrie obviously found you lacking in the passion department otherwise she wouldn't have fucked around with Dr. Winters now would she? Are you sure you were doing it right?" Alessandro laughed.

Colin lunged for him and Alessandro grabbed his throat and with his other hand he grabbed Colin's wrist, pressing his fingers into the space between the wrist and the forearm to 'cause the maximum amount of pain. He brought Colin's arm down so that his fingers were pressed between the steel spokes of the wheels in Alessandro's chair. He had only to press his elbow into the button that would move the chair forward and slice Colin's fingers off. "Now that I have your undivided attention," Alessandro pressed his other thumb forcefully against Colin's windpipe so that he couldn't cry out in obvious pain. "You will keep away from my wife. You will not so much as breathe on her. The only way you will put your limp little fingers on my wife is in your dreams."

Colin gurgled, enraged.

Alessandro pressed his fingers in harder and Colin's eyes widened as he tried frantically to dislodge Alessandro's grip on him. "A simple blink for yes will do, ol' boy."

"Dammit, Alessandro! Let him go!" Brian ordered, bursting into the lounge.

Alessandro ignored him, pressing his fingers against Colin's throat with more and more pressure, wanting to kill him, practically salivating with the urge to snap this man's neck for lusting after his woman.

"Alessandro!" Brian repeated, pulling against his shoulders.

Just a little more pressure and he wouldn't have to worry about this son of a bitch touching Brianna, kissing her, making love to her because Alessandro couldn't. Hate burned through Alessandro, the likes of which he didn't think he'd ever experienced.

"Stop!" Brian yelled pulling Alessandro's arms away from Colin.

"I'll kill him! I'll fucking rip the flesh from his bones with my bear hands!" Alessandro shouted as he struggled against Brian's grip.

"You fucking lunatic! I won't rest until Bree is safe from you, I swear to God!" Colin cried between coughing fits. "I won't let you destroy her with your psychotic Dardano influence, and don't think I'm letting you turn my nephew Will into a carbon copy of you either."

"You stay the hell away from my family! Brianna will never be—"

"That's enough!" Brian shouted stepping between Alessandro and Colin. He glared down at Alessandro. "You need to calm the fuck down and forget about Colin, you got me? You go out there and you focus on my sister. She should be your first priority. Do you hear me?"

The red, violent haze began to lift from Alessandro's mind. Brianna. Yes. He needed to focus on her. She was everything. She and the boys. Colin was irrelevant. He would never violate what Alessandro and Brianna had built.

Alessandro would kill him first.

CHAPTER THIRTY-FOUR

Bree's eyes felt heavy as she struggled to open them. The familiar sound of the hospital monitor confused her. What the…oh. Her cheeks flamed in embarrassment remembering how she had let Colin kiss her and how she had tried to let him down easy because he wasn't Alessandro. She sighed her husband's name and opened her eyes.

Alessandro smiled at her, his fingers stroking her hair. "Welcome back, sweetheart."

The reason she was in the hospital came back suddenly as well and her hand went to her stomach as panic froze her. "Oh God, the baby! Is it—"

"Fine. I swear, darling. The baby is fine. Just became a little excited that's all."

"Are you sure?" Bree asked, wide eyed. "I don't know, Alessandro. It hurt so bad. I was sure that something was wrong. I would never forgive—"

"Darling, darling, look at me, eh? Breathe, darling. Calm yourself." He cupped her cheek and guided her breath back to normal.

Bree focused on his eyes and the peace she had always found there. Peace and passion. What a bizarre combination was her connection to this man.

"There we go, eh? Better?" Alessandro asked, his fingers stroking her skin.

Bree nodded slowly.

"That's my good girl. Now. The doctors said it was stress that 'caused your body to react as it did. I'm so sorry for that, sweetheart." Alessandro leaned his forehead against hers. "I'm so sorry I contributed to that. But I promise, from now on, things will be different. I will help ease your stress, not make it worse. I wanted to tell you, I spoke to my father and we'll be moving out at the end of this month. We need some time to make the house a bit more accessible until I get out of this thing, eh?" he said.

"The house? What house? And oh my God what did you tell the boys? They must be out of their minds, especially Will. He so doesn't need to go—"

"Brianna. Brianna, breathe, breathe." He inhaled and exhaled dramatically, guiding her. "Think of happy places and babbling brooks and that...what do you call it? That plinky plunky music with the rainforests that always makes me feeling like going to the loo."

Bree laughed and shook her head. "I'm okay now. Really. But what did you tell them?"

"I just told the nanny to tell Will that you were just going to spend the night in the hospital for some tests for the baby and that it was all perfectly normal and there was no reason at all for him to worry."

"So you lied to our son?" Bree scowled.

He brought his fingers together, about an inch apart. "Only a little lie. Forgive me?"

Bree rolled her eyes but smiled, loving his teasing manner, a welcome change from the past few months. "But wait. I don't want to spend the night. I feel perfectly fine now. Why can't we go home?"

"The doctors want to keep you overnight to make sure your blood pressure doesn't spike again."

"Maaan, I'll be bored out of my skull if I have to spend—"

"No you won't. Because I'll be here with you," Alessandro assured her.

"What do you mean?"

"Well I paid the nanny handsomely to agree to stay the night with the boys so I could keep my beautiful wife company."

Bree cocked an eyebrow.

"All right, yes so I'm laying it on rather thick but I have much I have to make up for, Brianna," Alessandro said seriously.

"Yes, you do," Bree nodded. "And what kind of wife would I be if I didn't let you, I guess."

Alessandro took her hand and smiled.

"Oh, but I was with Colin when I collapsed. Is he still here?" Bree asked. She watched Alessandro clench his jaw.

"Colin. You want to know about Colin?"

"Don't say it like that. Colin is my friend, okay? That's all. Maybe I admit I was leaning on him a bit more than I should have because my husband was being a grade A jackass and maybe I gave him the wrong idea but that ends now, Alessandro. I told him that we can't ever be more than friends because…well…idiot that I am, I'm in love with my husband." Bree leaned over and stroked Alessandro's cheek.

He grinned at her. "Well, then I have a bit of a confession to make. Colin said some things to me and the sound of his voice irritated me so I had one of those clowns with the big red noses in the paediatric wing turn him into a balloon animal. A giraffe I'm afraid. Sad fate it was," Alessandro joked with no sign of remorse at all.

"Stop that!" Bree said laughing.

He kissed her hand. "I was so afraid I'd never see you smile again. Brianna, I will spend the rest of my life trying to make you happy, trying to make up for what I put you through. You believe me, don't you?" Alessandro asked, turning her palm and kissing it.

"I believe that you love me. That's all the happiness I need. I also believe that you did say something to Colin that you're not telling me, right? What, something along the lines off, 'keep your mitts of my wife'?"

"I did not," Alessandro insisted. "Well…I didn't say 'mitts' anyway."

"Alessandro…" Bree groaned resting her forehead on the heel of her hand.

"Brianna, you said so yourself, the idiot is in love with you. Mind you, I don't blame him but the line has to be clearly drawn."

"Right, but I'm the one that needs to draw it. Not my caveman of a husband. I'm perfectly capable of taking care of myself, you know? You're just like Adriano!"

Alessandro blinked. "Wait, we're talking about my grandfather now?"

Bree shrugged. "I don't know. I just…had this bizarre dream

about your grandfather only it wasn't him it was you. And I wasn't me, I was Francesca."

"And you were mad at me because…?" he pressed.

"I don't remember. Something about a dress that you didn't want me to wear because the guy that delivered the bread kept looking at my legs…er Francesca's legs."

"Okay, darling, you don't think maybe it's just the medicine the doctor's prescribed to lower your blood pressure?" Alessandro asked cautiously.

"No…er…maybe but, anyway. I ended up throwing the sewing machine at your head."

"What sewing machine?" Alessandro asked.

"Francesca's sewing machine. Keep up, would you?" The full memory of her dream suddenly hit her full force and Bree suddenly shot up in bed. "Oh my God that's it!"

"What? Is it the baby? Are you in pain?" Alessandro asked, panicked.

"No, no. Adresca. Back at the studio in Paris! When that guy was looking at my legs. I remembered the back label of one of the dresses. It didn't occur to me until just now. I had completely forgotten about it. I thought I was just doing a tribute to Francesca and Adriano by naming the bar after them but I must have subconsciously remembered the name from the clothing label. That's what it said. 'Adresca'." Bree exclaimed.

"Well, maybe the designer was Italian?" Alessandro offered. "I can already see your fanciful gears turning and running away with you. I give you that there may have been a child between Francesca and my grandfather and that the child died but you're assuming that Francesca…what, had a clothing line on the side?"

Bree scowled. "Well, no, but…Adresca? Come on, Alessandro. That name is not that common. Francesca was dirt poor, she'd be handy with a needle and thread just out of necessity. There's no harm in following the lead and seeing where it goes."

"Ah well, that remains to be seen, doesn't it?" Alessandro warned.

"What do you mean?" Bree asked.

"Well, explain to me your thought process here. I know what your thinking but I want to hear you say it out loud."

Bree held her breath afraid to say it out loud. Afraid of what it meant. "What if she didn't die on that cliff, Alessandro? What if

Francesca never commited suicide at all?"

"You think she's alive?" Alessandro asked.

Bree hesitated. "Well…I don't know about that. She'd be…how old now?"

"Oh, in her seventies at least. But Brianna, just think about this for a second. My father holds your great aunt personally responsible along with Old Man O'Reiley for the destruction of his parent's marriage. If Francesca was still alive, I hate to say this to you but my father would most certainly go after her."

Bree bit her thumbnail. He had a point there. Knowing that Adriano had gone to his grave loving another woman, that Bernardo had to grown up without his father's affection because of Francesca's rejection and supposed death…there was no way Bernardo could know Francesca was alive and not rain his vengeance down on her.

"I'll make some inquiries but darling, I know how romantic you are. I don't want you to be disappointed," Alessandro said.

"Mmm, I guess you're right. I just…" she shrugged. "Something tells me that there are too many unanswered questions here. But, anyway. Tell me about this house."

"Oh no, darling." Alessandro smiled. "That is a surprise."

"What? Why is it a surprise? This is our house we're talking about."

"Just…shh!" Alessandro insisted, pressing his finger to his lips. "Let me do this for you, Brianna."

"Well, you know I'm not going to stop asking," Bree insisted. "But anyway, maybe you should go see the doctors about getting a cot in here if you're spending the night."

"Or you could just scoot over and I could sleep wrapped around you like I really hope you'll allow me to," Alessandro said.

Bree smiled at the pleading in his eyes. "I would like that. Do you need—"

But she didn't need to continue 'cause as she moved over to make room for him he was pulling off his shoes and then his shirt. Bree took a moment to appreciate his naked chest before he turned the wheel chair around so he could lift himself onto the bed. His powerful arms displayed taut muscles as he moved onto the mattress. Bree helped him brings his legs under the blanket. She slid down so she could lie next to him, her face against his chest. She shivered against, missing the feel of his arms around her after so long.

"Comfy?" Bree asked.

Alessandro made a groan of approval. His fingers moved through her hair. "I can't believe I've been so stupid. I can't believe I almost gave this up, touching you, looking into your eyes. You do forgive me, don't you, Brianna?"

Bree blinked back tears and nodded, running her fingers along his lips. "Do you believe that I love you? No matter what? That I would never leave you because you can't walk?"

"But you turned to Colin. I hate it but considering how I treated you I can understand if you went looking for comfort from a…friend."

She looked up and saw him push the word out through his teeth. "Alessandro, there is nothing between Colin and me. Yes, I may have felt something for him once but I'm your wife, Alessandro. Yours. I'm completely devoted to you and our family. I promise. Now I know you must have given Colin an earful when you got here. Will you tell me what you told him?"

"No. Leave it alone, Brianna because I don't want to add to your stress. Happy thoughts remember? Think of the baby," Alessandro reminded her, running his hand over her belly. "Can you feel her yet?"

"Not yet, but why are you so convinced it's a girl? I mean if this kid comes out with a penis you are going to be very sorry."

"I was right about Gianni, wasn't I?" Alessandro said continuing to stroke the small rise of her stomach.

"Oh please, that was pure Dardano ego talking because you wanted your all important Dardano heir to carry on the precious legacy." Bree poked his chest. "Now you're just thinking this one is a girl 'cause you already have your heir so you don't care which one comes out."

"That's not true," Alessandro insisted. He tapped her nose. "I happen to very much want this one to be a girl. Honestly I won't care. I'll adore it if it's another son but…I don't know, just the image of a little girl to dress in pretty frocks with blonde hair like her mummy. That picture warms my heart."

"Ha. Careful what you wish for. My daughter will certainly know how to wrap daddy around her little finger."

Alessandro's grin widened. "I look forward to it."

"Hmm, and do you look forward to the boys coming around

when she's a teenager?"

The smile wavered. "My daughter is not dating until she's thirty. At least."

"Oh, is that how it's gonna work?" Bree asked laughing. "I'm afraid you forget that I'm a girl too and we all know how well I deal with being told to stay away from the bad boys. I expect it'll be even worse if she has both the Dardano and O'Reiley stubborn genes. I predict you going grey very early Mr. Dardano."

Alessandro leaned down and cupped her behind. "Well, I'm very lucky that you didn't listen to all the nay-sayers and I promise to do my best from now on to never give you 'cause to regret it."

Bree ran her fingers along his chest. "Just love me, and never forget that I love you. That's all I want." She reached up and kissed him, her body responding instantly. She pulled away guiltily. "I'm sorry. I didn't mean to start anything and make you—"

Alessandro brushed his lips across hers. "I'm sorry for that night. More sorry than you'll ever know. I was so selfish that night, Brianna."

"No, I should have understood how hard that would be for you."

"There was no excuse for my behaviour, darling. None. You were right. There are many ways we can make love and I'd like us to try again. I don't want us to lose that passion between us and wait until I can walk again."

Bree pulled back nervously, not relishing the thought of another rejection if Alessandro got frustrated again. "I don't know Alessandro. I don't want to push you if you're not—"

"I hurt you. I know. But I swear, I want to fight for our marriage just as much as you do, and that means keeping every part of it alive. I'm paralyzed, not dead. Loving you makes me feel more alive than I've ever been before. I want that intimacy back. When we can make love properly, I don't want us to be strangers to each other. I know there are other things we can do."

Bree jumped a little when she felt his finger between her legs.

"Will you let me, darling? Let me make it up to you?"

"What? Here? Alessandro, what if someone comes in? A doctor or—"

Alessandro smiled and kissed her lips as he parted her legs. "Then I suppose you'll just have to be quiet, sweetheart."

Bree left him sleeping. There'd been no recriminations this time, no rejection from him, but she could see in Alessandro's eyes the flicker of sadness that he couldn't go further. He wanted more and couldn't have it. It made her feel guilty and Bree wasn't sure she could make the effort next time if she knew that inside, Alessandro wasn't happy.

But it was so important. Bree felt it deep inside of her. They had to keep this part of their marriage alive. But even if it meant a constant reminder if what they couldn't have? May never have again? Yes, Bree thought. Oh yes, they had to power through those negative feelings if they had a hope in hell of surviving. She thought again about Dr. Sheri and thought maybe a session on her own was in order.

Bree O'Reiley seeing a shrink, she thought with a snicker. Some would say that was long overdue.

But first thing's first. She rubbed her rumbling stomach. She was craving something salty. She just knew if she rang for the nurse she'd be told that they weren't going to give her any middle of the night snacks 'cause it wasn't good for the baby.

Or worse, they'd come at her with the Jello. The green Jello that she doubted was really Jello. She'd made Jello at home. It was nothing like the fibrous, stiff, gummy thing they served in those stupid round plastic cups.

Salt and vinegar chips. Oh God, her mouth was salivating at just the idea. "I hear ya, babe," she said, rubbing her stomach. She'd just have to get past the night nurse. She slid out of bed and eased the door open slowly, looking back to make sure Alessandro didn't wake up. When she turned back towards the outside she jumped and almost screamed at Andy's wide imposing body blocking the doorway.

"What are you doing here?" Bree hissed.

"My job," Andy replied.

"Well, Alessandro is in here with me so you can go now."

"Nope. Sorry."

Bree narrowed her eyes at him. "I don't think you're sorry at all. I think you enjoy your power a little too much."

The corner of his mouth lifted slightly in an almost smile.

"Yeah that's what I thought. Look I'm just going to the vending machine down the hall okay?"

"No."

"Is that like your favourite word or something? Geez. I'm having cravings here."

"Then I'll call the nurse and maybe she can—"

"No, no!" Bree whispered fiercely. "Hey, I got an idea. Why don't you go get it for me? So help me if you say no again I'm going to slam this door against your nose."

"Sorry. Can't," Andy said, his eyes blue eyes twinkling.

"Cute. Come on, Andy. I'll stay in my room, promise. Remember, I told you Alessandro's in here with me. I'm perfectly safe. The vending machine is just down the hall—"

"No."

Bree growled in frustration and then smiled. "You can come with me."

Andy looked skeptically down at her but seemed to be considering it so Bree pressed her luck. "Yeah, and you can totally see my room from there."

"No."

Bree poked him in the chest. "You know, I think maybe you are a Dardano and you just don't know it. Oooh, Vanessa! Hey Vanessa!" Bree called out from under Andy's arm as she saw the nanny walking towards the elevators. The young woman gave her a tired smile and adjusted her purse strap

"Hey, just finished my weekly poking and prodding before I head over to your place. How is the baby? Brian told me you'd been brought in. You're not having any more pains are you 'cause I can go call the nurse—"

"No, I'm good. I was just wondering if you could go grab me something from the vending machine."

"I told you I don't think that's a very good idea," Andy warned.

"You shush!" Bree insisted.

"Cravings, huh? I hear they're a real bitch. My aunt Cassie, when she was pregnant with my cousin Dwight, she used to have cravings for sausages, not the breakfast kind but the kind they make in Europe that have that yummy spicy, hammy taste. You know, it's been a long time since I had that kind—"

Oh God. She really was recovered, Bree thought wryly.

"Yeah, could you go over to the vending machine and grab me a bag of chips? Salt and vinegar. Please," Bree pleaded, licking her lips.

"Sure thing. Sorry Andykins. Girls gotta stick together,"

Vanessa said and Bree smiled smugly at her bodyguard.

She hopped back on the bed and opened her bag of chips. She took a deep breath, inhaling the tart scent and sighed. Her stomach rumbled again in response. "Yeah, I know," Bree agreed. She looked down at Alessandro's still sleeping form.

"Want one?" she asked pointing a chip at him. "Oh, sorry. Can't. You're sleeping. Guess I'll have to eat them all myself then." She popped the chip in her mouth and moaned, letting it soften and dissolve in her mouth.

Alessandro shifted in the bed, taking a deep inhale and his brows came together as he could obviously smell her chips.

Bree whimpered in protest, and hid the bag behind her.

"Wha's smell?" he asked slowly opening his eyes.

"Hmm, what? I don't smell anything," Bree replied, putting on her most innocent face.

Of course, the man could see right through her and he cocked an eyebrow as he reached behind her and pulled her arm forward bringing the bag of chips with it.

"Brianna, really," he scolded.

"What? I got it for the baby. She was craving them."

Alessandro snorted. "The baby, huh? That can't be healthy for the baby."

"Sure it is. It's potato. The baby needs carbs too."

"Nice try. Give me the bag. I'll get the nurse to bring you some carrots or Jello or something," Alessandro insisted.

Bree jerked the bag away from him. "Noooo!"

"Come on, sweetheart. Just give me the bag," Alessandro reached for her arm.

"No! It's mine."

"Oh for goodness sake. You're worse than Will. Give me the—"

In normal circumstances, Alessandro was stronger then her. With his disability, his upper body had to compensate and was made even more powerful and he had to barely tug on her and she was sprawled on top of him, the bag of chips crushed between them.

She smiled down at him. "Ha. See, now I got you right where I want you. What if for every chip you let me have, I'll give you a kiss?"

"Mmm, with a mouth full of salt and vinegar. Tempting," he

said sarcastically. "Methinks…no."

"Really?" Bree asked, rubbing her body against him and stopping when she felt his shaft suddenly twitch between them.

They both looked down at the same time. "Did you feel that?" Bree asked, a flare of hope bursting through her body.

"I…I felt something," Alessandro admitted, dark eyes wide with uncertainty, as if he was afraid to hope.

Bree didn't mind, she'd keep enough hope for both of them.

CHAPTER THIRTY-FIVE

"Do you feel that?" Carlo asked pushing the back of his hand against Alessandro's foot.

"No."

Bree stood on the other side of the room. Every question and answer breaking her heart a little more. She could see Alessandro retreat further and further into himself with every 'no' he gave. Had the brief sensation just been a fluke?

"It's not uncommon for paralyzed people to feel tiny bursts of sensation here and there over time. The brain is continually firing off stimulating neurons and sometimes a cluster of nerve endings in under the skin will receive the message."

"So this was nothing?" Alessandro asked, his face dark, eyes cold.

Guarded. He's afraid to hope.

"No, I didn't say that. This could be the first hint that you're beginning to recover. If the sensations begin to return with more frequency, then I would say that you'll be up and about again in no time. I just want to be completely honest so that you understand what this may or may not mean."

"But in your professional opinion, is this a good sign?" Bree urged.

"Bree, I'd rather not guess and raise your hopes. Now I'm gonna go set up some x-rays for you, Alessandro so we can have another look at your spine and see if there are any changes that could allow me to give you a more positive prognosis," Carlo informed them before leaving them alone.

"Figures, doesn't it? Don't raise your hopes but stay optimistic. Spoken like a true doctor looking to avoid a malpractice suit," Alessandro grumbled as he moved back into his chair.

"Well, take my word for it then. I think this is a very good sign," Bree reached down and kissed his cheek.

"Spoken like a true wife," he said with a smirk. He sighed. "I'm going to go wheel myself into oncoming traffic."

"Alessandro, come on."

"Sorry, bad joke. I know. I just need to have some time to myself for a while, sweetheart. I'll be back in plenty of time before we leave for home."

Bree grimaced, wishing she knew what to say to him. "Alessandro, you can't just—"

He raised his hand to stop her. "Please, darling. I don't want to argue with you. I just need a minute to myself. I'll be roaming the halls." He wheeled out of the room after she helped open the door for him.

She groaned when she saw Bernardo at the nursing station. Visiting hours had started up again and there he was circling them like a vulture.

"Alessandro, how is the baby?"

The baby. Not, how is Brianna? Nice. Bree rolled her eyes. She was just the carrier of the latest Dardano heir after all.

He nodded at his father but continued to wheel away.

"What is wrong?" Bernardo asked finally turning and acknowledging Bree's presence.

"Nothing. He just…we thought he might be getting some feeling back in his legs but Carlo told us not to get our hopes up," Bree explained.

"What so you're just letting him go off alone? Why aren't you following him and comforting him like a good wife should?" Bernardo demanded.

"Oh geez. Here we go. You know, do you know another song 'cause that one's getting real old." Bree suddenly smiled. "But you know what? It's okay because I won't have to put up with you much longer."

"Ah yes, you think you're going to be moving, don't you?" Bernardo sneered. "Let me assure you, Brianna that my son will be staying in the mansion, with me where he belongs. He is nowhere near ready to move out of his home."

"Boy are you ever scared of me," Bree gloated. "That's why you want to keep Alessandro in that looney bin with you, right? You're afraid that I'll finally be able to turn Alessandro away from you and show him how to actually be happy. Oh by the way, we'll be needing the key to the storage rooms so we can get an early start on packing." Okay, so the morning had started off in the toilet but it felt good stick it to Bernardo and tell him they were going to be free of him.

He gave her a small patronizing smile. "My son chose well in you. You have gumption and certainly have the strength and fire to help lead the Dardano legacy. I'll give you that, but believe me my dear you won't be going anywhere. My son and my grandson will be staying in their home to claim their birthright. And you will stay by his side as is your d—"

"Duty as a wife, gotcha." Bree rolled her eyes. "We'll just have to see about that, won't we?" She turned away from him and asked the nurse when Dr. Graham would have an opening so she could book a session with her.

She was glad to be home and even more glad that Will had no idea of the real reason that she had spent the night at the hospital. He was cheerfully playing with Luke on the carpet.

"Mamaaaa!" Gianni squealed, bouncing in her lap, pointing to the book she had opened in front of them.

He was pointing to the picture of a blond lady who was pregnant.

"And see, she's gonna have a baby, just like mommy."

Gianni turned and pointed to Bree's stomach. "Eebee?"

"Yep. The baby is in here."

"Me, eebee." He patted his stomach.

Alessandro snorted from his place at the desk doing some paper work. "That would be an impressive feat. Even for a Dardano."

"Mommy, was I smart baby?" Will asked, playing with Luke's paws. The puppy barked and licked his face.

"What do you mean?" Bree asked.

"Da baby passed da tests right? Dat's why you get to come home? Dat means da baby really smart. Did I do good on my tests 'cause I no 'member taking dem inside yo' tummy."

"Ahhh," Bree looked over at Alessandro, not sure how to explain without divulging that she'd been in danger of losing the baby.

"I'm sure you were absolutely brilliant, young William," Alessandro replied with a soft smile, though Bree could see his sadness was still there even if he tried to hide it.

"I tink so too. I mean. I brilliant now, right?" Will reasoned.

"I can feel him beginning to shut down again and it terrifies me," Bree said, leaning her elbow on the arm rest of the couch. "He's trying so hard to stay positive. I can see it in his face, in his eyes. Alessandro is fighting with all his might not to fall back into that black hole but every let down is just chipping away at his resolve and I don't know what to do anymore."

"What do you think you should be doing?" Dr Sheri Graham asked, tapping her chin with the end of her pen.

"I don't know, encouraging him, I guess. Not making things harder for him. Not fighting with him when he blows up at me, understanding that he needs to deal with things in his own way. Not feeling hurt that he still wants Bernice to help him with his therapy and not me."

"Did you hear what you just said?" Sheri asked, coming forward in her seat. "Not feeling hurt. Like it's something you can control. If someone hurts us, we feel hurt, Bree. We don't instinctively rationalize that they didn't mean it. That rationale comes later, with time and reflection but in that moment, you feel what you feel because that's the way our minds work. We can't control how things affect us, only how we respond to them."

"Okay I guess then I should respond when he hurts me by understanding. Better?" Bree asked with a snort.

"Should? Says who?" Sheri asked, leaning back. "I mean, why can't you chew him out when he snaps at you?"

"Because…" Bree insisted. "Because I'm afraid that I might push him too far and that he might…" she lowered her head and shook it as she picked at her jeans.

"He might try to kill himself again?"

"Yeah."

"Do you think that's why he contemplated suicide the first time? Because he was feeling pressure from you?"

"Well…no. I…I don't know. That's the problem. I have no idea how I'm supposed to act around him anymore."

"And that makes you feel…"

Bree threw her hands up and got out off the couch. "How am I supposed to feel? Yeah, it's frustrating. How do I get past that?"

"Why do you feel you have to get past it? You certainly have the right to feel frustrated. I mean, Bree, the man you love, the man you promised to spend of your life with is pushing you away. He's been dealt a terrible blow. We don't know if he'll be able to walk again, that is a devastating thing to try and deal with not only for him, but for you. You need to give yourself permission to acknowledge those things. You say you don't know how to act around him anymore. How did you act around him before the shooting?"

Bree leaned against the wall and snorted. "Alessandro and I have a very…uh special relationship."

"Right, because his father was allegedly responsible for the death of your previous husband."

Bree snorted. "Ironic isn't it? I mean, I can get past that and get past this stupid vendetta between our families and marry him. We've been through so much to be together. So much. And this is what's tearing us apart now? The fact that he can't walk?"

"That must make you very angry," Sheri remarked.

"It makes me beyond angry I just…sometimes I just want to stand in the middle of the room and scream."

"Angry at whom? Who would you scream at?" Sheri pressed.

"At Alessandro!" Bree burst and then clamped her hand over her mouth and shook her head. "God, no. I didn't mean—"

"Yes, you did. Because that's how you feel."

"But how can I be furious at him for something that is not his fault?"

"Is there a part of you that thinks maybe it is his fault?"

"What? That he can't walk? That's insane."

"No, the shooting," Sheri corrected. "Your husband is part of a very violent family if what the newspapers claim is true. Is there a part of you that thinks if he wasn't who he was, he wouldn't have gotten shot?"

"I live in that same world, even if the O'Reilieys aren't exactly as bloodthirsty as the Dardanos. He's the one that wanted to postpone the opening of the club. I was the one who didn't listen."

"So you feel guilty about that?"

"Of course I do," Bree said, her voice breaking.

"And so you think you have to make up for that by bowing

down to him at the risk of your own feelings?"

"Yes," Bree sniffled, blinking back tears. "But I'm tired of it. I don't know if I can do this anymore. I mean, I had hope that things were getting better between us. He says we're going to move out of Bernardo's house but I'm afraid he won't follow through with it because Bernardo will manipulate him somehow. Now instead of just shutting down on me completely, I can feel it a gesture at a time so I'm not quite sure if it's really happening or if I'm just overreacting."

"That must make you feel very resentful of him."

"How can I resent him? I love him so much. He's the father of my sons and this unborn baby—"

"One of your sons was wounded in the shooting, right?"

Bree swallowed hard. "Will." She looked up at the ceiling. "He adores Alessandro. He has from day one. He's part of the reason I gave Alessandro a chance and forced myself to get past the Dardano name."

"And then it was because of Alessandro's family that your son was wounded. Your father was killed that night as well, wasn't he?"

Bree placed her hands on her hips. "Right, so what kind of mother am I to keep my children in that family, right? I must be the most selfish woman in the world to put my children in harm's way just because I can't stop loving their father!" Bree covered her face with her hands as her guilt and anger swamped her and her tears slipped through her fingers.

"No, that's not what I'm saying at all. I'm trying to make you see what is really at the root of your feelings here."

Bree looked up from her hands. "I don't know that, that's why I'm here. Isn't that your job?" she scowled.

"I think you do know," Sheri countered, studying her carefully. Waiting.

Bree slid down the wall to the floor. "I hate him. As much as I love him, I hate him."

"Why do you think you hate him?"

"He doesn't love me as much as I love him."

"Do you believe that?"

"Not…" Bree struggled for the right words. "All my life, I've just wanted someone to put me first. I thought Alessandro was that man. But even after everything Bernardo has done, I mean, Arturo wouldn't have ever shot Alessandro if Bernardo hadn't raised him to be a monster, even knowing that, Alessandro refuses to cut his ties with his father. So…yeah, I guess I do blame Alessandro for getting shot. God, that sounds so horrible." Bree covered her face with her hands again.

"No. It sounds human. Your husband is choosing his father over his wife and his children, putting them all in harm's way in the name of loyalty to a man who you feel is destroying him. It'd be human for you to feel resentment for that and maybe…seek comfort in the arms of an old friend?"

Bree sighed. "A part of me will always love Colin but…it's just not the same anymore. For everything Alessandro has put me through, I can't stop loving him. I can't. It might not be healthy or sane but it's like…he's a part of my soul. I think that's why it feels like such a betrayal when he pushes me away."

"So could you maybe be getting back at Alessandro in some small way by spending time with Colin?"

"I told Colin it wasn't going to happen," Bree said. "Figures, huh? Once he finally wants me back I'm in love with some one else."

"So you acknowledge that you turned to Colin because Alessandro was pushing you away, and now you feel like it might happen again. Do you want Colin to be there for you in case Alessandro does push you away or do you want to fight for your marriage?"

"I want Alessandro. Nobody else. But I feel like if I can't get him away from Bernardo that it's just going to get worse and worse and his father's influence is going to pull him away from me forever. If it wasn't for that godforsaken vendetta, Alessandro and I could be happy."

"Bree, listen to me very carefully. You can't control your father-in-law. You can't control Alessandro and you can't even control Colin. The only person you can control in this situation is you. The only way to do that is by being completely honest with yourself. And if you want your marriage to have a hope in hell of surviving you have to be honest with Alessandro."

"How can I possibly do that?" Bree groaned. "I'm afraid if I push him, he'll retreat further away from me."

"Honey, you just told me you think that's what he's doing now. You're walking on eggshells around Alessandro, waiting for the other shoe to drop. You say he's changed. Do you think he might be pulling away from you because you've changed as well? Maybe he's afraid that because he's paralyzed, you don't see him as the same man anymore and that you altering your behaviour is seen as proof of that in his eyes."

"So what do you suggest I do? Go home and yell at my husband?" Bree asked with a snort.

"Exactly," Sheri suggested, smiling.

CHAPTER THIRTY-SIX

"I no dis," Gianni insisted, pushing aside his bottle and reaching for Will's cup.

Will moved the cup out of his reach and took a long drink from it then blew a raspberry at Gianni. "You hafta drink from da baby bottle 'cause you still a baby. I's a big boy."

"Will, it's not nice to tease your brother like that," Vanessa insisted.

"I 'oy. Gibbits, 'oy." Gianni reached for Will arm and tugged on Will's black t-shirt. Gianni blew a raspberry back at Will.

"See, he do it back. Dat's nod nice either. No, you can' haf it. Nyah, nyah."

Gianni grabbed his baby bottle and threw it at Will's head. "Gibbits me!"

"Ow!" Will exclaimed after the plastic bottle konked him on the head. "Daddy, he hit me!"

Alessandro looked up from his paper and cocked an eyebrow. "Seems to me the bottle is what hit you, and I'd say you deserved it."

"I din' nod!" Will exclaimed.

"Oh really, did you not just taunt him with, and I quote 'Nyah, nyah'?"

"So?"

"So, Nyah, nyah gets you bashed over the head with a

baby bottle," Alessandro explained. "But Gianni,"

Gianni's dark head turned and Alessandro almost laughed as he watched the guilty flicker in Gianni's brown eyes school themselves into mock innocence. A Dardano to the core, aren't you, my boy?

"Daddy," Gianni said with a smile.

"No hitting. Understand?"

Gianni shook his head. "No 'it." He turned back to Will and grumbled with irritation when he noticed that Will had slid out of his chair and was now on the other side of the room. "Daddy. Up!" Gianni demanded, wanting to be taken over to where Will was.

"Oh no, my boy. You're going to have to figure that out yourself."

"No 'eff. Up!" Gianni said. Seeing that Alessandro wasn't going to help him, he stubbornly scrambled off the chair. He held on to the seat and looked around for the next thing he could grab on to. He wrapped his hands around the table leg and then fell against the couch. He grabbed the back and pulled on the fabric to anchor himself until he got around to the arm of the couch and then the cushion.

Will was too entertained by Gianni's trek to move from his place at the wall and by the time he realized how close Gianni was, his little brother was nearing the end of the couch.

"Uh oh, whatcha gonna do now? No where to go," Will taunted.

Gianni looked around with a scowl and Alessandro and the nanny were both watching the unfolding scene with interest. Alessandro wheeled around to the other side of the couch so he could get a better look. He suddenly realized that the only way Gianni was going to reach Will was if he walked over to him. Would he do it? Would Gianni take his first steps now? Alessandro wanted to call out to Brianna, who was up in the bathroom looking for scissors to cut Gianni's hair, but he didn't want to startle Gianni.

Gianni bounced on his legs uncertainly and stretched out

one arm to Will while his other hand stayed firmly gripped in the seat cushion. "Wanned! Gibbits."

"Come get it," Will teased, excited now as it occurred to him that Gianni would have to walk towards him. "Look daddy. I tink he gonna walk now! Come get it Gianni. You can do it," he teased him with the cup and Gianni looked about ready to wail at him.

He let go of the couch and fell promptly on his diaper cushioned butt. But he grabbed the cushion again and pulled himself up. "Mee dood it gibbits me dat," he grumbled as he moved closer to Will and look skeptically at the distance between Will and the couch. He let go of the couch but didn't move, apparently trying to find his balance.

"Good boy, Gianni," Alessandro exclaimed, feeling a rush of pride. "You can do it. Walk for daddy, eh?"

"Ah, I finally found it, stuck under that whole pile of cotton—" Brianna stopped as she took in what was happening. "Oh my God, is he walking?"

"Mama, dat!" Gianni insisted pointing at Will. The gesture made him lose his balance and he almost fell again but he quickly grasped the couch cushion again.

"Are you gonna walk for mommy?" Brianna asked excited.

"No 'ak! Gibbits dat, mamma," Gianni insisted.

"Nope. You haf to come get it," Will teased holding the now empty cup out towards Gianni and then jerking it back.

Gianni let go of the couch and took one…two…three steps, reaching Will and falling against him while Brianna shrieked happily.

"Hey! You did it!" Will exclaimed, falling with Gianni to the floor.

"Well done, Gianni!" Alessandro cried clapping and laughing.

Brianna grabbed Gianni and picked him up in her arms. Smiling down at Alessandro in delight. Alessandro reached up and took Brianna's hand to indulge in a brief moment of shared pride. He tried to push away the negative knowledge that now Gianni would be walking and he still wouldn't. He tried to stay happy but the dark cloud was there. Brianna must have seen it in his eyes because she reached down and kissed him.

Gianni, however couldn't care less about the milestone he'd just achieved. With a single-mindedness befitting a Dardano he pointed down at Will and his cup. "Gibbits!"

Alessandro looked at Will. "I'd say he deserves it now, don't you?"

Will sighed dramatically. "Ooookaaay. Here," he lifted the cup up and handed it to Gianni who clutched it to his chest triumphantly.

Gianni then looked inside the cup. "Awww!" he remarked, turning the now empty cup over. He looked down at Will and threw the cup at his brother's head.

"Alessandro, I'd like to see you for a moment," Bernardo said coming into the living room. "Would you come into my study? It's very important."

"Father, Gianni just took his first steps," Alessandro said proudly.

Bernardo beamed. "Ahhh, brava, my boy, brava!" He reached over and kissed Gianni's cheek.

The little boy grabbed a handful of Bernardo's salt and pepper hair and pulled hard. "Me dis!"

"Oh, what a grip, uh?" Bernardo said, laughing as he pulled Gianni's fingers out of his hair. "That's some strong Dardano muscle."

"What's so important?" Brianna asked scowling.

Alessandro sighed inwardly. Really, this animosity between them was becoming tiresome. Maybe when they moved and there was some distance they could be more civil to each other.

"It's just some private business I need to discuss with my son," Bernardo explained, piquing Alessandro's curiosity.

"Daddy will be back, Gianni," he tugged on Gianni's foot. "That's my good boy."

He followed Bernardo into the study and waited as Bernardo turned and locked the door. "So what was so important?"

Bernardo sighed and Alessandro felt a prickle of unease at the pained look on his face. "Ah my boy. I want you to understand that what I'm about to do, I am only doing this because I love you. You know that, don't you, Alessandro?"

Alessandro nodded nervously. "Of course, Father."

Bernardo pulled out a disk and popped it in the computer. "I know this will be painful for you to hear, but I think you must understand just where you stand in Brianna's heart."

Alessandro looked at the disk. "I…I don't understand." He swallowed hard.

"I know you don't. I hope this will make things clear for you. You have such a good heart, my boy. Such an open heart and I have long felt that your Brianna was taking advantage of your feelings for her. Well…now…now I have proof."

Alessandro blinked and had the most absurd urge to cover his ears with his hands like Gianni did. "What are you talking about?"

"I think this will explain it all." He pressed a key and Brianna's voice came through the small speakers on the desk.

"I hate him. If it wasn't for Will, I would have never given him a chance. It makes me beyond angry. I don't know if I can do this anymore. This stupid vendetta between our families was why I married him. I can't stop loving Colin! I don't love Alessandro as much as he loves me. Bernardo raised him to be a monster. I blame Alessandro for getting shot. After everything Alessandro has put me through, it's just not the same anymore. Colin is a part of my soul. Figures, huh? Colin wants me back and if it wasn't for this stupid vendetta and that Alessandro can't walk, I could finally be happy. I'm tired of it."

Alessandro felt nauseous. He couldn't even see his father anymore. No. No. There had to be some mistake. Brianna loved him…he KNEW she loved him.

"I'm so sorry my son," Bernardo said sitting in his chair.

But it was Brianna's voice. COLIN. She loved Colin. Not him. She'd always loved Colin. The vendetta…the fact that he couldn't walk…that was the only reason she stayed married to him.

Colin was a part of her soul.

Alessandro felt a rage so strong that if Brianna had been standing in front of him, he would have easily killed her.

Lies. All lies.

No. No, all this time, she couldn't have lied all this time. Every time she touched him, kissed him, smiled at him.

She stayed married to him because of the vendetta…and out of pity because he couldn't walk. Alessandro would have very easily wrapped his hands around her beautiful lying neck.

"Alessandro, can you hear me?" Bernardo asked and Alessandro realized with a jolt that his father had been talking and he hadn't heard a word.

"I didn't want you to be blinded by your own feelings. Brianna is your wife but you must never forget that it is you who must hold the power over her. You must never weaken yourself under her."

Weak. Yes. How pathetic he had been. Loving her, opening his heart and soul to her, thinking he had someone who would love him without conditions, someone with whom he could create the family he always wanted.

The vendetta. The fact that he was crippled. That was all that tied her to him. It was right there in her own words. Her own sweet voice that had whispered in his ears that she loved him while he'd made love to her.

"Oh God…yes…I love you…I love you…Don't stop…"

Had she been yearning for Colin the whole time?

The pain of it was crippling him. He couldn't breathe. Be a man! Be a Dardano. Alessandro felt the protective wall shoot up around his heart in one quick instant. Dardanos weren't weak and stupid like he had been. Dardanos didn't let their emotions blind them. Love was for fools. Love made men stupid. But oh, she would never make him stupid again.

Oh, how Alessandro would make his darling wife pay.

"No, no, no, no, no!" Gianni cried pulling his head out from under Bree's grip.

"Gianni. It don' hurt. Promise. Look see?" Will said, pulling up a brown curl. "It's okay cause hair no haf feelings. Watch." He took one strand and pulled. "Ow!"

"No wanned. No!" Gianni insisted, pushing Bree's hand away.

"Dat did hurt, mommy," Will said. "How come?"

"One of life's greatest mysteries," Bree replied wryly.

"I tink so too. Maybe daddy know."

Bree looked back towards the hall that led to Bernardo's study. They'd been in there a long time. Whatever they were discussing, Bree bet it wasn't anything good. Bernardo was probably trying to convince Alessandro not to move out. Bree gritted her teeth. Well, dream on, Grandpa Lecter. As soon as the house was ready, they were so out of here. "Come on kiddo, hold still for mommy," Bree pleaded grabbing Gianni's head again. She'd focus on this for now and trust that Alessandro knew how to handle his father.

"No 'till! No 'till, mamma," Gianni protested.

"Look, Gianni. Watch," Bree made a quick snip of a piece from his bangs. Then she held it up to show him. "See? That didn't hurt at all, did it?" She let the wisp of hair fall from her fingers to the towel on the floor.

Gianni looked at his hair falling from Bree's fingers and his brown eyes widened. He screamed in horror.

"Uh oh," Will said plugging his ears.

"No, honey. It's okay. Look, look, huh?" Bree reached under her hair and snipped a small lock of her own.

Gianni stopped screaming and stared at the hair and Bree's apparent calm.

"What's going on?" Alessandro asked, wheeling back into the room. Bree turned and smiled at him.

He looked at her, expressionless at first and then smiled back.

She looked at him curiously and felt a twinge of nervousness in her belly. Whatever Alessandro had talked about with his father, it hadn't been good.

"Daddy ook!" Gianni pointed down at all the hair strewn

over the spread towels. "Oook, no! No, no!"

"I'm trying to cut his hair," Bree explained. "But someone is not took keen on the idea."

"What don't you just let a barber do it?" Alessandro asked.

"Because. I can do it. I did Will's hair and he didn't give me this much grief."

"See Gianni? I no give mommy geef. You shouldn't either."

Gianni blew a raspberry at his brother.

"Now granted, Will was asleep when I did it, but still. Hey, maybe that's it? Maybe I should wait until his nap," Bree said putting the scissors down. "Your hair gets a last minute stay of execution, sweetie." She kissed the tip of Gianni's nose.

"Heee," Gianni grinned and followed the scissors with his eyes as Bree put them back in their plastic sleeve. "Mmm," he said with a curt nod.

Shortly after the sound of the doorbell, Rafe came in and announced that Bernice had arrived for Alessandro's physical therapy session.

"Oh good," Bree said. She picked up the towels and cleaned up any stray hairs that may have fallen. "Debbie, can you watch the boys for a little while? I'm going to help Bernice and Alessandro today."

Alessandro stopped his chair on his way to the door to greet Bernice and turned in question back to Bree. "You're what?"

Bree placed Gianni in his baby swing and went to Alessandro. "I said, I'm helping you out today." She greeted Bernice and pushed Alessandro towards the bedroom.

"I thought I made my feelings on that matter quite clear," Alessandro said.

"Oh, you did. But that didn't work so well for me seeing as I am your wife and my place is to help you in your recovery."

"Ah yes, you are my wife, aren't you, darling?" Alessandro said.

The tone of his voice perturbed Bree and she looked

down at him in confusion.

"I think that's a very good idea, Mrs. Dardano. It can only help Alessandro to have his wife there encouraging him," Bernice said, laying the blue mat on the floor at the foot of the bed.

"Excuse me. I am sitting right here," Alessandro sneered.

"And now you'll be on the mat. Let's go," Bernice said. She locked the wheelchair and slid her hand under his arm to help him out of it.

Bree moved to Alessandro's opposite side and helped move him to the floor.

He glared up at Bree furiously and she glared right back. Dr. Sheri was right. She couldn't walk around being Miss Mary Sunshine hoping not to make Alessandro upset. That was NOT the woman he married.

He continued to glare at her as she took instruction from Bernice and helped massage Alessandro's legs. She took careful mental notes of different exercises she could do with him.

"Bernice knows what she's doing. She doesn't need you here," Alessandro growled at her.

She helped Bernice hold Alessandro up after the woman set up the steel guides for Alessandro to balance himself with as he made his way upright from one end of the bars to the other. Bree tried to stay strong as she watched Alessandro drag his feet helplessly, unable to place any weight on them at all.

He must have seen the sadness in her eyes because he snapped at her. "I want you to get out, Brianna."

Bree jumped at the vehemence in his voice and tried to remind herself it was his pride talking. She had to stand her ground and not allow herself to be bullied by him. The woman he married gave as good as she got.

"No you don't," Bree insisted. "You're just being stubborn."

That made him laugh, but it had a bitter edge to it. "Me? Me?"

After helping Alessandro back into the chair Bree assured Bernice that she would be helping Alessandro with his bath from now on. "It's my job as his wife after all," Bree insisted after bidding the nurse goodbye.

"All right, Brianna, that's enough. You can drop the act," Alessandro scowled.

"Oh, it's no act. Now that, before, with me trying to go out of my way to accommodate you, that was an act and you know what Alessandro, I'm done." Bree placed her hands on the arm rests of his wheelchair on either side of him and leaned over him. "I'm your wife and that means when you're in pain, when you're hurting, my place is by your side, helping you get better and I'm not letting you push me away again. You push me; I'm just going to push back because I love you. If you don't believe me, well I'm just going to have to prove it to you." She grabbed the sides of his face and kissed him, trying to show him that her passion for him was still very much alive and that she wasn't going anywhere.

She could feel him pulling away even before his lips left her. He wasn't there, inside. Alessandro's lips were on hers and for a second, she could feel his tongue reach out to meet hers and then he groaned and it was like she felt something switch off in him and he pulled away from her.

"What?" Bree asked.

"Why do you even bother?" Alessandro asked, wheeling away from her. "It's not like we can ever do anything about it so why start something I can't finish?"

Bree took a deep breath. "We're not having that conversation again. You are my husband and I'm not going to stop showing you affection."

"You're wasting your time, Brianna." He wheeled towards the bedroom door to leave but Bree stepped in front of him.

"Wanting to show you that I love you, I don't consider that a waste of time. Now you promised me that you were going to try, are you telling me you're backing out of that now cause if that's the case, you'd better let me know right now."

"Really, so that you can save your energy for Colin?" Alessandro countered with a lift of his eyebrow.

Bree stiffened. "Is that what this is about? Colin? Are you kidding me?"

"Well, he is your true love, isn't he?" Alessandro sneered. "I know how you felt about him when you were younger."

Bree dropped into the off white satin lounge chair that was propped up against the wall next to the door. "You've…rendered me speechless."

"Well, I'd say your lack of a denial speaks volumes," Alessandro said with a look of disgust.

"Does it?" Bree asked leaping out of the chair, frustration and indignation churning through her blood. "Oh, then please, just so there are no misunderstandings, let me be more clear." She took the crystal vase off the dresser and threw it at his head.

He ducked and it narrowly missed his head before smashing into the wall.

"How's that?" Bree spat and turned and stormed out of the room.

She was shaking with rage when she burst into Bernardo's study, finding him looking out the window. "I don't know what you said to Alessandro to make him so surly, but let me make it very clear that I am not going to allow you to drag him down. He needs encouragement and he needs to know that we love him no matter what."

"I don't need you to tell me what is best for my son, Brianna. As for what I said to him, let's just say that I took the blinders off of him."

"You know what? I don't even know what that means, and what's more I couldn't give a damn. Pretty soon we'll be moving out and you'll be nothing more than an annoying relative we have to put up with at Christmas and Thanksgiving."

Bernardo smiled at her. A patronizing grin that sent a flare of unease through her but Bree stood her ground. He put his hands on the back of his black leather chair. "I can see why my father fell for your great aunt Francesca and why he allowed her to destroy our family. That you possess the same fire cannot be denied. It's part of the reason I deemed you as the only O'Reiley worthy of the Dardano legacy. But you also possess the same selfish spirit as Francesca. You want everything your way. My dear, you married a Dardano. You are the mother of a Dardano. Your wishes are absolutely irrelevant. My son will never turn his back on his father, on his heritage. He is the heir set to take over the mantle when I am gone. Do you really think you can take him to go live some ridiculous apple pie existence behind some O'Reiley white picket fence? The very idea is laughable."

Bree grit her teeth, trying not to be swayed by Bernardo's words. Alessandro loved her. She trusted in that and that meant that he would put her and their children and the happiness of their family first. She trusted that.

So why was there this voice of doubt that made her body tense as if preparing for an attack she didn't know she was supposed to be expecting?

CHAPTER THIRTY-SEVEN

She asked Vanessa if the nanny could stay for dinner and watch the boys that evening as she and Alessandro would be taking dinner in their bedroom.

Bernardo scowled at them. "We have dinner in the dining room. We do not eat in our bedrooms like uncivilized people."

"Oh don't worry, you're not invited," Bree said with a smile.

Will giggled and tried to stifle it when Bernardo glared at him.

"Alessandro and I will be spending a quiet romantic evening together, alone," Bree announced.

"I beg your pardon?" Alessandro asked, wheeling into the dining room.

"Mommy wants to be womantic wif you, daddy," Will explained.

Alessandro looked warily at Bree and she took his nervousness for uncertainty over what exactly she was expecting from him.

She walked towards him and took his hand. "I thought it would be nice if you and I spent sometime alone."

He took his hand back and wheeled past her. "I don't know, Brianna, I've got a lot of work to do for Dardano Enterprises. I was just thinking of grabbing a quick bite at the table and then staying at my desk for most of the night."

"You can put it off, can't you?" Bree urged, disappointed. "I mean, you're the boss, right?"

"Yes, I am. That means I have more responsibilities than everybody else. I have more on my plate. Sorry, darling but this paper work has to be ready by tomorrow morning. I'll take a rain check, eh?"

She caught Bernardo watching them from his place in the doorway.

He was smiling.

"Bree, we need to talk."

Damn. Bree turned and forced a smile at Colin. She really wasn't in the mood to deal with him today. Not after the night she'd had. Alessandro hadn't come to bed. She'd fallen asleep waiting for him and when she'd woken up and realized it was the middle of the night and he wasn't beside her, she felt a moment of panic. Maybe he had hurt himself, fallen and wasn't able to get back in his wheelchair.

But no, he'd been sitting at his desk where she had left him. And he was fast asleep, chin on his chest.

"Can't leave me…," he'd murmured when she kneeled down and tried to wake him up. His small voice broke her heart.

She'd stroked his face and he leaned his forehead against hers. "You lied. You don' love me,"

Bree kissed his face and tried to rouse him from the grip of whatever awful dream he was having. "As if I could help it, silly man. You're my soul, remember?"

He woke then. Brown eyes filled with such pain that they shocked Bree. Granted, he'd been a bit off with her lately but where was this pain coming from? She'd thought things would be getting better between them. In an instant the pain was gone, replaced by…nothing. A cold wall Bree couldn't penetrate.

She'd asked him what he'd been dreaming about. He'd said nothing and she fell asleep feeling more alone than when he hadn't been next to her.

And now Colin. She didn't know if she had the energy to push him away or just let him lift her out of her morose mood.

"Colin, I'm actually here with Vanessa. She's getting her last check up today. I'm also making sure everything's okay with the baby."

"Yeah, I just wanted to check up on you and see how things were at home."

"Um, good," she lied.

Of course, he'd known her long enough when she was lying and he gave her a look of obvious disbelief. "Really?"

"Colin," Bree warned.

Gianni who had been silent thus far, blew a raspberry and clutched his fist in her blouse. "No," he exclaimed simply and leaned his head on Bree's shoulder.

"Will, honey. You wanna take your little brother and go to the waiting room. You can wait with Vanessa for me there." Bree leaned down and put Gianni back in the stroller.

"Noooooo! Mamma! Up!" he protested loudly.

"Is okay Unco Colin. I still like you if Gianni don'," Will assured Colin before pushing Gianni away.

"Can we talk in the lounge?" Colin asked.

Bree looked behind her at Andy who stood only a few feet away. "I don't know, Colin. The walls have ears, you know?" she tilted her head towards Andy with a wry grin.

"Well that's nice. Now they're monitoring who you can and can't talk to?" Colin asked.

"It's not like that. Come on, Colin."

"Isn't it? Bree, don't you see what they're doing? They've already pulled you away from your family. Now they're cutting you off from your friends. Have you forgotten how dangerous these people are?"

"Colin, stop!" Bree snapped. "Considering the things we talked about the last time, I don't think it's unreasonable for Alessandro to not want me to talk to you. I mean, you all but asked me to leave him," she hissed, dropping her voice.

"Because I want what's best for you. Alessandro is exactly like his father, no matter how much you want to believe otherwise. He practically threatened to fit me for cement shoes and chop off my hands off if I so much as looked at you again."

Bree sighed and pulled him off to the side. "I am a big girl, Colin. I don't need you to look out for me. I know you're my friend—"

"Bree, I love you," Colin whispered. "I know you know that."

. She shook her head. "We've been through this, Colin. I love Alessandro. I'm committed to him. I know he can be a little…uh…intense but if he imagines a threat…or in this case I guess…sees one pretty clearly, he fights to eliminate it and does whatever he has to. So do I, remember? Now Colin, hear me, okay. You have to stop this. I'm serious. I…uh appreciate that you're concerned about me."

"Concerned? Bree—"

"Don't!" Bree pleaded, lifting her fingers to his mouth. "Please don't say it again."

Colin sighed. "Look, just promise me that if you need me, you won't hesitate to call, okay?"

Bree wanted to say no, that she wouldn't need him but a selfish part of her refused to turn him away. Alessandro certainly wasn't making an effort to be her friend as well as her husband. If he didn't step up, what right did Alessandro have to tell her who she could be friends with? She had a history with Colin. He was one of her oldest friends.

Who was now claiming to be in love with her. Bree groaned. No, this was a bad idea no matter how she wanted to justify it. She opened her mouth to tell him that she really didn't think they should talk for a little while.

"Darling, there you are. Colin, this is becoming a habit, eh? Whenever I want to find my wife, I should just look for you now, shouldn't I?" Alessandro asked, wheeling up to them.

"Alessandro," Bree stepped closer to his chair and leaned down and kissed his cheek, not sure who she was trying to put the show on for, Colin or Alessandro.

He smiled up at her as if he saw right through her. When didn't he? Bree thought with a snort.

"What are you doing here?" Bree asked.

"Well, you mentioned you had an appointment with the OBGYN, I thought I should be here with you as your husband," he spoke to her and yet his eyes were locked on Colin and Bree felt a shiver of unease at the violence that emanated between the two men. "Colin, I hope all is well with you,"

He might as well have been saying that he was going to run Colin down with his car, judging by his tone.

"Perfectly fine," Colin said.

"That's good. I hope you continue to be well. I hope nothing happens to change that."

"Hmm, if I didn't know better I'd almost think that sounded like a threat," Colin said stepping forward.

"Okay, we'd better get going," Bree grabbed the handles of Alessandro's wheelchair and pulled him back. "Colin… Please think about what I said."

"You have a good day now, Colin," Alessandro called back as Bree wheeled him away.

"Alessandro, really," Bree scolded.

"What?" Alessandro asked, his voice thick with feigned innocence.

"What, he asks," Bree said. "You have to stop this. I mean it. Nothing is going on between me and Colin."

"Not for lack of trying on his part, I'm sure."

Bree stopped the wheelchair outside of her doctor's office. "Can you try and hear me? What Colin does or doesn't want doesn't matter to me. I am your wife. Yours, and that is who I want to be. I love you, even when you make it damned hard, I love you. I get the feeling that you're doubting that lately and I don't get where this is coming from."

"Fine," he pushed the word out through his teeth.

"Fine? Just…fine?"

"I can only trust your word. Isn't that right, Brianna? I can only believe the words that come out of your mouth," Alessandro said. He reached up and took her hand. "Of course I believe you, darling."

He didn't. She knew it. She could see it in the flicker of his eyes.

"Look, we'll talk about this more at home, okay?" Bree said.

Alessandro shook his head and brought her hand to his mouth. "Nothing to talk about, sweetheart. Everything is quite clear." He pressed his lips to the back of her hand and Bree shivered at the coldness in his voice.

She was overwhelmed by a sense of frustrated helplessness.

Dr Murdoch came out and ushered them into her office. "Bree, Alessandro. How are you?"

Bree forced a smile. "Anxious to make sure that everything's okay." She got up on the examining table.

"I'm sure everything's all right. Let's have a look, shall we? Have you been feeling any pain?"

Just in my heart. The thought came and Bree pushed it away stubbornly. Wallowing was not going to fix anything. Bree needed to act to fix what was happening between her and Alessandro. She could not give up. "No. No more pain since I got home."

"That is good to hear." She ran various tests on her before bringing the ultrasound machine forward so they could see the screen. "Okay, here we are."

The sound of the heartbeat filled the room and Bree's vision with blurred with tears and she looked at the tiny body on the screen. "Do you hear that?" she asked, turning her head to look at Alessandro whose eyes were red. "Do you see that?"

"I see her," Alessandro said, awe in his voice.

"Her?" Caroline asked. "Did someone tell you it was a girl?"

"You mean it's not?" Bree asked, lifting her head in surprise.

"Well, I don't know. Do you want to find out?"

"Alessandro's just convinced it's a girl so I got used to thinking of her—it like that," Bree admitted.

"You'll see, I'm right," Alessandro said and he gave her a small smile.

Bree's heart tightened in her chest at the first genuine smile she had seen on his face in days.

"It might be a little early but if the baby co-operates we might be able to get a look one way or the other. Would you like to know?" Caroline asked.

Bree looked at Alessandro and he nodded quickly, excitement evident on his face.

"Okay. Let's see what we have…or don't, as the case may be," the doctor joked. After about a minute, she spoke again. "Well, looks like you were right, Alessandro."

Bree gasped and leaned up on her elbows to get a better look. "It's a girl? You're sure?"

"Mind you, when you come for your next ultrasound we'll know for sure but judging by the screen right now. I'd say we've got Baby Girl Dardano."

She heard Alessandro gasp and let out a chuckle of delight as he pressed his hands together. "I was right. You see? We're going to have a little girl."

This time, when he took her hand and kissed it, Bree shivered at the true emotion behind it.

"Can we get a picture of it?" she asked, sitting up.

"Sure thing," Caroline said. Handing them the photo, she left the two of them alone and told Bree to make sure to make her next appointment before she left.

"Look at her," Alessandro said, awestruck as he stared at the grey photo. "I thought Gianni was the most beautiful perfect thing I'd ever seen but look at her, Brianna."

Bree smiled and came up behind him and lay her chin on his

shoulder. "I felt that way when I first saw Will and then Gianni and now her too. It's always the same with a new baby. Looks like this one is already going to have daddy wrapped around her little finger, huh?"

Alessandro looked back at her. "I'm going to be a good father to her, I promise, Brianna."

"I know you are," Bree said, kissing his cheek.

"I know I haven't been easy to live with lately. I…I'm sorry about that. I'll try to change my behaviour." He reached back and cupped her cheek, bringing her face closer to his so he could kiss her.

Bree whimpered, wanting so much to hope he meant it, but afraid to get her hopes up just to have him fall back into his awful mood. She pulled away shakily. "I just want you to believe in me. Believe in us and our family. If something is bothering you, I want you to tell me so that I can help you. Promise me you won't shut me out again, Alessandro. That's all I want."

"Dardano men are not really known for their sensitivity and ability to articulate emotional weakness," Alessandro explained.

"Well then it's a good thing I love you despite that pesky Dardano-ness of yours," Bree said with a grin, buoyed with delight by the promise of better days ahead.

Will, was not as taken with the photo of the new baby as the grown ups around him. "It look like Mr. Potato Head."

"I'm sure your baby sister will appreciate that," Alessandro said with a wry grin.

"A girl? It's a girl?" Will asked with a grimace.

"That's right," Bree announced as Vanessa and Brian congratulated them.

"I can play wif Gianni but what we gonna do wif a girl?" he asked, handing the picture back to them. "Nope, send it back and get another boy dis time."

He could feel his legs. Alessandro stared down at his thighs and held his breath. He wheeled back closer to the wall of the warehouse as Andy and Morgan dragged an unconscious Colin into the room.

Then, no he couldn't. Bloody fuckin' hell. He couldn't take this much longer. There'd been twinges here and there. Hopes rising and then dashed. No amount of Dardano will could control the sensation or lack thereof in his legs.

He'd woken up twice now in the middle of the night to painful spasms in his leg muscles. Sharp enough to make him groan. Once, Brianna had roused slightly and turned to him, wrapping an arm around his waist.

"'kay?" she had murmured before drifting off again.

He had almost pulled her close, missing the sweet warmth of her body but then he remembered her words. She loved Colin. Not him. Never him. Alessandro took her hand and pulled it off of him and back on the mattress.

He almost told her about the pain but then he remembered: "I'm your wife. It's my job to help you. I would never leave you, especially not because you can't walk."

Never going to leave him.

As long as he couldn't walk.

Because she was his wife.

She loved Colin.

"What the…?" Colin asked, coming to as Andy pulled him onto the chair and tying his arms behind the back.

"I think you and I need to come to a new understanding," Alessandro said wheeling towards him.

She loved this pathetic creature.

Alessandro had given her everything, loved her with his entire being and Brianna loved this sorry excuse for a man.

Well, could he really blame her? What kind of man was Alessandro now, he asked himself. Trapped in a chair. Useless.

Ah, but even before then, she had loved Colin. Her first love. Even before the ending of the vendetta, when Alessandro could walk. When he had power, stature, Brianna had loved this imbecile.

She'd only married him to end the vendetta, to keep her family safe. Every smile, every touch, every time she let him fuck her, it was to keep her family safe.

Oh she may very well have enjoyed it, Alessandro thought, burning. She was well schooled in the art of betrayal and deception but Alessandro knew well enough when a woman was enjoying herself in his bed.

But it had meant nothing to her. He'd given her his heart. His soul.

And it had meant nothing.

Alessandro fought back the red haze of rage and lifted his gaze to Andy. He needed to concentrate. He wanted to enjoy this.

But even that was dimmed for him because he couldn't get up out of the chair and beat the shit out of Neally like he wanted.

He nodded at Andy and the bodyguard punched Colin across the face.

"I do believe I was quite clear in that I wanted you to keep your fucking hands off my wife," Alessandro insisted.

Colin groaned, blood streaming from his split lip. "You don't deserve her. You have her locked up in that mausoleum like some—"

Alessandro lifted his gaze to Morgan, who drove his fist into Colin's stomach. "You talk too much, ol' boy. I think it impairs your ability to listen. I thought I was quite cordial in my request but unfortunately you've pushed me to use more…definitive tactics."

"Right," Colin said. He leaned forward and spat in Alessandro's face.

Alessandro clenched his fists to keep from reaching forward and snapping Colin's neck. He wiped his face and smiled coldly at Colin.

How could Brianna even compare the two of them? After everything he'd done for her.

Alessandro couldn't understand it. Brianna had been practically disowned by her family for marrying him. She'd cried in his arms because her family couldn't accept that she loved him. She'd didn't have to be as sweet to him, as passionate with him, as loving to him as she had been. If it was all a lie, all an act, why had she fought so hard for their love? Was it just to sell it all the more? Was she playing the part so well so that Alessandro would never have 'cause to doubt her feelings? And why did it matter? Why not just marry him with the clear understanding that it was to end the vendetta and nothing more?

His mind raced as Andy and Morgan beat Colin to a bloody pulp. Alessandro didn't know what to believe. The proof was there in her words on that disc. So why was he punishing himself? Why didn't he just throw her out and leave her to her lover? What was to be gained by shackling himself to a woman who didn't want him?

Was his pride worth his own suffering?

He wanted to punish her, but at his own expense?

God he loved her. How pathetic he was, even knowing she wanted someone else, every part of him ached for her.

"Brianna is my wife. She promised to love, honor and obey me. To stand by my side. To sleep in my bed. I will not allow her to steal my balls the way Carrie did to you. I do hope you understand."

Colin glared hatefully at him through a mess of bloody bruised flesh. "You're crazy. I'll get her away from you if it's the last damn thing I do."

"I'm afraid you won't get the chance," Alessandro explained, clucking his tongue.

"Why? You'll have your goons kill me 'cause you're not man enough to do it yourself? Ain't that just like a Dardano? Get others to do your dirty work for you."

"Oh, no. See, I don't want to get myself all scruffed up and bruised beating the life out of you like I wish I could. Brianna wouldn't like that very much, and well, I have a date with my wife and I rather we not spend it unpleasantly." He looked at his watch and smiled. "I really must be going now."

Andy tipped the chair over and Colin hit the floor with a painful thud.

Alessandro pulled out a lighter from his pocket. "I do hope you understand. I wish this was avoidable but you brought this on yourself." He lit the end of a piece of paper while Morgan poured kerosene all throughout the room. "Brianna is mine and I certainly won't lose her to a pathetic loser like you."

"Bree loves me and you can manipulate her all you like but she is never going to truly love you, no matter what she says. She only thinks she loves you because she doesn't know the monster you are."

Alessandro waved his hand, tossing the lit paper in the air. It fell to the floor and the room went up in flames behind him. "I'm a Dardano, I always win." He wheeled out of the room with Andy and Morgan, leaving his enemy to die.

CHAPTER THIRTY-EIGHT

Bree came into the bedroom after picking Gianni up from his nap and found a pink summer dress hanging over the foot of the bed. There was a note in Alessandro's handwriting placed on top. 'Put this on.'

"What?" she asked picking up the dress and looking behind her.

Gianni reached for the soft material.

She wasn't sure what to think but she set Gianni down on the bed and put the dress on. "'kay. Now what?"

Gianni lifted his hands to express that he had no idea either. She came down the stairs and Will was at the foot of the stairs smiling and practically giddy, his hands over his mouth.

Her suspicion was immediately raised but she felt an excited shiver go through her. Whatever Alessandro was up to, it was something good.

"So, you wanna tell me what's going on?" Bree asked.

"It's a supise," Will explained. "You look pittie, mommy."

Gianni was playing with the straps of her dress and tried to bring a strap to his mouth.

"A surprise. Okay. So I put the dress on. Do you know where your daddy is?"

"Daddy say fo you to go to him. He say you know where."

Bree shook her head. "Well, daddy's wrong. I haven't a clue."

"He say if you don' know den fo' you to member da baby."

Vanessa, newly re-installed in her position as the nanny came out into the foyer. "Oh don't you look gorgeous? I saw this commercial one time where this woman was out in a field of flowers and she was dancing around and waving her arms, I think it was a commercial for tampons or something. You totally look like that woman."

Bree smiled at her. "I'm so glad you're back."

"Aw, ain't you just a peach? Now don't you worry about a thing. You just go find that hot husband of yours and I'll keep the kiddies busy." Vanessa reached over and took Gianni from her arms.

Her hand went to her stomach, knowing suddenly where Alessandro was. She looked at the glass doors that led to the backyard. "You boys take it easy on Vanessa, okay? Remember, she just got out of the hospital." Her heart was racing in her chest. She was so afraid to get her hopes up that Alessandro had planned some romantic time for them, that he was pulling himself out of his melancholy.

"Mommy, we know thaaaat," Will said rolling his eyes

"Oh and for God's sake, if you see Bernardo looking for Alessandro, sit on him if you have to but don't let him interrupt us," Bree added to Vanessa.

"Will do," she promised.

It took Bree a while to get to the spot without a horse but she found the canopy of apple blossoms and she couldn't keep the shiver of pleasure from her body as she recalled the last time they were here. She could see Alessandro's chair and then his dark head bent as he looked in what looked like a basket on a blanket from his position on the ground. He looked up at her when she reached him.

"Hey," Bree said. "What's going on?"

He smiled up at her and extended his hand for her to take it and sit down beside him. "You look lovely."

"Thanks."

"I'm calling in that rain check from before. Dinner. Just the two of us. Sparkling apple cider," he held up the bottle and then something mouthwateringly familiar in two white Styrofoam trays.

"Is this—" she opened the tray and squealed.

"Bangers and mash, flown in from one of the very best pubs in London," Alessandro announced.

"From London? Wow, I'm impressed," Bree smiled.

He poured the cider in a glass and handed it to her and then filled his own. "To a new start." He held up his glass for a toast.

Bree looked at him hesitantly, afraid to hope that he meant it. "What do you mean?"

"I mean that you and our children mean everything to me. There is nothing I wouldn't do for you, Brianna."

"I…I know," she said slowly.

"I know that we didn't get off to the best start. I know that you married me to end the vendetta—"

"Alessandro—" Bree objected but he lifted his hand to stop her.

"But I hope this can be a new start for us. Let's put everything in the past aside and just concentrate on us, our family and continuing the Dardano legacy. Nothing is more important to me than family, Brianna. Nothing."

Bree blinked. There was something in his voice, in his tone that gave her a flicker of unease. Maybe it was the way he lumped in the Dardano legacy with their family. Maybe it was the look in his eyes when he mentioned putting things in the past. Bree forced a smile. Dammit, he was trying. The least she could do was do the same. After so long, Alessandro was making an effort.

"That's all I want, Alessandro. Us, our family. That's all I've ever wanted," Bree urged. "I love you so much."

Alessandro smiled and cupped the side of her face. "You do don't you?"

She thought she might have imagined it, but did his fingers tremble when they touched her? "Of course."

"And nothing matters more than our family. Does it, Brianna?"

"You know that, Alessandro."

"Yes, of course I do. You wouldn't lie to me about that. Would you, darling?"

Bree stared at him and shivered. Something was wrong. Something was…off in his eyes when he looked at her. "What's going on, Alessandro? Where is this coming from?"

He smiled, but the look didn't reach his eyes. "I'm sorry I ever doubted your loyalty, or your love, darling. I promise. It will never happen again."

He looked like a predator, toying with his prey, ready to squash it. Bree had seen that look before, but never directed at her.

But then, in the next instant it was gone and Bree wondered if she'd imagined it because his eyes softened and filled with love as he moved closer and pressed his lips to hers.

Bree cupped his face and deepened the kiss. She'd imagined it. She was just letting the past few months get to her. He was trying, she had to fight too. She had to have faith in their love like he was trying to do. "You're everything to me, Alessandro," she whispered against his face. "You believe me, don't you?"

He shivered against her and then smiled at her. "I have a gift for you." He reached to the basket and pulled out an envelope. She noticed it was one of two envelopes in the basket.

"What's that one?" Bree asked, looking in at the one he'd left inside.

"Oh, that? Nothing. That's work I packed in here by mistake. This is the one for you."

Bree raised an eyebrow but decided to concentrate on the envelope she held.

"Open it, darling."

She pulled out a picture of a house. There was something familiar about it…Bree gasped and brought the picture closer. "Is this…the house?"

The house. The abandoned house where they first met and took shelter and claimed each other's souls.

"It is. I bought it."

"This is the house you were talking about? This is going to be our home?" Bree asked, her eyes filling with tears of happiness, everything else was forgotten as she leapt onto him after he nodded. How could she doubt him after he was so obviously trying to change? They really were going to leave this place. They were going to get away from Bernardo. Bree rained kisses on his face.

They were going to be happy.

"Shhh, Gianni. You can haf dis one, but you haf to shhh!"

"No. Mouf dis. 'oy mouf dis."

Alessandro pressed his fingers to his lips as he and Bree slowly peeked into the nursery together.

"No. Stop dat. I don' wan dat one. Dat one is minty." Will pushed Gianni's hand away. "Dat's fo you."

Gianni picked up another candy from the bowl and smiled at the shiny blue wrapper. "Peeee."

Will popped another chocolate in his mouth and helped Gianni undo the wrapper to his. He bit Gianni's chocolate in half and gave him the smaller piece.

He dropped the small bit in his hand and Gianni giggled. “Keddy!”

“Shhhh!”

Gianni squeezed his fist around the chocolate and put his whole fist in his mouth. “Mmmmkeddymouf.”

Will popped another chocolate in his mouth. “We haf to save some fo tomowo,” he explained through cheeks filled with chocolate.

“Oh I wouldn’t worry. Mummy and daddy could always buy more,” Alessandro explained from the doorway.

Will and Gianni both jumped and turned identical chocolate smeared guilty faces towards them.

Gianni reached into the bowl and grabbed a handful of chocolate and lifted it towards them. “Keddy, daddy?”

Alessandro tried to bite back his laughter as Brianna stormed into the nursery. “All right, hand it over.”

“What?” Will asked, sliding the bowl under Gianni’s crib.

“Nice try. Now, Will,” Brianna insisted extending her hand.

“Awwww. No keddy?” Gianni asked as Will grudgingly handed up the bowl.

“Good lord. Are you trying to put yourselves in a diabetic coma?” Brianna asked, handing Alessandro the bowl and picking up Gianni.

“Looks like mummy isn’t the only one with a sweet tooth, huh?” Alessandro teased.

“Really, mommy. Is’ jus candy. Is nod like I go rob a bank,” Will grumbled as Brianna handed Gianni over to Alessandro and grabbed Will’s hand to drag him to the bathroom to clean him up.

Brianna stared down at Will for a stunned moment and then shook her head, fighting laughter. “No, but you know very well that you’re not allowed to sneak in candy…” She went on scolding him as they disappeared down the hall.

“And what do you have to say for yourself, Gianni?” Alessandro asked, propping Gianni up on his feet.

Gianni smacked chocolate smeared, damp hands on both sides of Alessandro’s face and planted a wet kiss on him.

“Trying to butter up daddy so you won’t get in trouble, eh?” Alessandro asked. “That’s my boy,” he chuckled.

Gianni bounced excitedly on Alessandro’s thighs and

Alessandro froze. He could feel him. Alessandro's arms tightened against Gianni's waist and he picked the baby up, and then set him back down on his thighs, in case it was just a temporary spasm.

No. It was still there. The feeling. The sensation. A rush of pain accompanied it but Alessandro tried to push past it because there was the overwhelming feeling to…move.

Alessandro moved Gianni to one arm and looked down at his feet. Gianni looked down with him and then back up at Alessandro, seeing nothing on the floor of any interest. Alessandro couldn't break his gaze away from his feet. He took a deep breath and moved his right foot.

It moved. Straight off the foot rest. "Oh bloody hell. Oh God," Alessandro whispered, his heart racing. He swallowed hard and tried to lift his leg to put his foot back on the foot rest.

He was able to do it. It took all his will power not to scream for Brianna. He clutched Gianni tight to him and buried his face in his son's neck and he shook with triumph.

"Daddy?" Gianni asked looking at him curiously.

He kissed Gianni's face. "Daddy's okay. Daddy is absolutely brilliant." He could feel his legs. He could fucking feel his legs again!

Alessandro didn't dare say a word to Brianna. Part of him was still afraid it was a fluke. He needed time to know for sure. Five minutes became half an hour, then another hour and then another and then the whole day.

And the feeling in his legs didn't disappear.

He feared that if he said anything to Brianna he'd see relief in her eyes instead of joy. Relief that her obligation to him would soon be over.

That son of a bitch Colin hadn't died in the warehouse. He had been pulled out of the burning building by Charlie Donovan who had been down on the docks doing business.

But Colin was still unconscious and as long as he stayed that way, Alessandro couldn't be fingered as the one who tried to kill him.

"Look me in the eyes and tell me you didn't do this to him," Brianna had asked him when Brian had arrived with the news.

Alessandro had looked at her and lied. "Of course not, darling. I was here with you, remember our picnic?"

Brianna had been skeptical so he'd done what he had to divert her off her suspicious track. "Has it occurred to you that this could be another attack from Arturo?" He felt a beat of guilt but pushed it down. There was no place for guilt if he wanted to keep his family together. "I mean, if he's got men watching us then he knows how much Colin means to you. Perhaps he hoped that by attacking Colin he could scare you, send a message."

"Well, I guess we'll know what happened for sure when Colin wakes up." She'd cupped his face and Alessandro had had to use every ounce of Dardano willpower to look into her eyes. "I know you, Alessandro. I know how you felt about Colin. Tell me if you did something to him."

"Brianna, look at me. How could I have done anything to him? Yes, I hate him and I'm not wringing my hands over his injuries but it's simply a matter of logistics, sweetheart. I couldn't be there and here at the same time. I understand your skepticism. But I was in my father's office taking care of some business for him."

"And you didn't send anyone to do anything to Colin, either?"

She either had to believe him, trust him, or admit that she didn't believe him and that would 'cause a rift in their marriage that he knew she wanted desperately to heal.

He could see the indecision in her gaze and it made him nauseous with self-hatred.

But he had to stick to his story. His whole life depended on it.

Brianna may have married him because of the vendetta, she may have lied and stayed with him out of some fear for her family and obligation because of his injuries but he could manipulate the situation to his own ends.

She did harbour some feelings for him, if her reaction over the house was to be trusted and if that had been a lie as well, what better victory than to kill her lover? She'd turned to Colin because of him, of his coldness to her. If Colin was out of the picture, then Brianna would be his forever, she could genuinely come to love him.

If not, well, he could still hold her to him through their children. And there were the terms of the vendetta to keep as well. As long as they were together, there would be peace between their families.

It would be easier if she genuinely did love him.

But the words on the disc taunted him.

Could he have been wrong? Brianna was so loving towards him, even when she was angry at him, there was love there in her eyes mingled with passion. It just didn't fit with the words he'd heard her say. So many times, he wanted to ask, to throw the disc at her and tell her to explain herself. But he didn't dare because what if she had meant what she'd said on the disc?

And if she didn't, if there was something wrong with the disc, what other option did that leave him?

That Bernardo had tampered with it?

No, that was inconceivable. His father was a master manipulator, and schemer with a questionable moral compass, but Alessandro knew his father loved him. It was that surety that comforted Alessandro through every phase of his life. Alessandro's whole life was a testament to his father's love for him. Bernardo was cruel, but he would never do something so sick and cruel to his own son.

So that left Brianna. Brianna and her beautiful lies.

And Brianna could be controlled and made to love him. Alessandro would keep her at any cost.

And that meant keeping Colin out the picture. Permanently.

He met with Rafe after dinner and his father's doctor examined him in the basement. Alessandro tested himself by trying to get out of the wheelchair for the first time. With Rafe's help, Alessandro tried to get to his feet.

Holding on to Rafe's arms, for the first time in months, Alessandro stood up.

Alessandro pocketed the now empty vial and after dumping the doctor's scrubs he'd used as a disguise, wheeled towards the elevators just as Carrie was coming out.

"You…" she sneered. "I know you think you've gotten away with what you did to Colin, but I swear to God I am going to make you pay."

Alessandro clucked his tongue and shook his head. "I understand you're under a lot of stress so I'm not going to take that little tirade personally. How is your ex-husband, by the way? I certainly hope his recovery is going well."

"Your sincerity is overwhelming," Carrie sneered. "I see your hand all over this because Colin was getting close to my sister."

Alessandro lifted his hand to stop her. "What happened to

Colin is unfortunate and while I'm certainly not weeping over it, I had nothing to do with what happened to your precious Colin."

"Bull," Carrie said. "And as soon as Colin wakes up he is going to rat you out for the psychopathic bastard that you are."

"Yes well, you will ring me up when that happens. I'll be at home on the edge of my seat," Alessandro said with a snort. He fingered the vial in his pocket. If he had his way, Colin would never wake up.

"Father, I have something I want to show you," Alessandro said after Bernardo let him into his study. "Please, lock the door."

"What is it, Alessandro? Nothing's wrong I hope."

Alessandro struggled to his feet and Bernardo instinctively moved to help him but Alessandro raised his hand to keep him back. "It's all right. Just..." He took a deep breath and while his muscles were still very weak and it caused him some pain, he slowly stood up.

Bernardo's eyes widened and he cupped his hands over his mouth in shock. His eyes filled with tears as he looked at Alessandro and he reached over to take Alessandro's shoulders and pull him in for a hug. "Ah, Brava, my son. Brava!"

Alessandro buried himself in his father's embrace, feeling Bernardo's love and pride wash over him.

"Have you told Brianna the good news?" Bernardo asked helping Alessandro ease back onto his chair.

Alessandro's stomach tightened with guilt. He shook his head. "Not yet. I...don't know if I should."

Bernardo sighed and sat back behind his desk. "Because of Colin. Have you been taking care of that situation?"

"Yes. I just came from the hospital. He shouldn't be waking up for a long time. I know that if Brianna finds out I can walk, she'll leave me. I need more time."

"Time to what?" Bernardo said. "My boy, you are much too emotionally involved with this woman. It was your grandfather's weakness as well."

"Why is it a weakness, Father? I mean...all of the pretense, all of the lies. Why is it always so necessary to be so damned invincible, indestructible all the time?" Alessandro asked.

Bernardo stiffened. "My boy, listen to me very carefully. We are Dardanos and just by that very name will always be a target. We must never, ever let our guards down. Our enemies will always try to destroy us. I may push you to be strong, be hard for your own protection."

"I understand that in regards to our enemies but…when I'm with the boys and Brianna…it's as if…I feel like I can breathe, Father. Do I have keep my guard up around them as well?"

"Ai, Madonna, Alessandro where you get these fanciful notions I don't know, are you forgetting the disc you listened to. Your precious Brianna lied to you, has been lying to you this whole—"

"I haven't forgotten," Alessandro snapped. "What I'm saying is maybe with time…"

"What? If you stay in that chair and continue to lie to Brianna then perhaps she will come to love you? Alessandro, where is your backbone? She is your wife. A Dardano, her feelings about you are irrelevant. You have to take control of this situation. You cannot spend the rest of your life in that chair out of fear that your precious Brianna will leave you. You make it impossible for her to leave. You simply do not allow it."

"What? Have a woman who hates me bound to me forever? I can't live like that, Father. Maybe you can but I am not you. I am my own man."

"You are wrapped around Brianna O'Reiley's finger is what you are," Bernardo said with a snort of disgust.

Alessandro shook his head. "I was hoping for some advice from my father. I should have known better. You don't give advice, father. You dictate. I suppose I'll have to figure this out on my own." Frustrated, he turned away and almost asked his father to open the door for him, but he managed to turn the knob and hold it open by himself.

He was in a very different kind of hell now. First, it had been the horror of being broken, of his body betraying him, of being less than a man.

Now his body was working as it should, fully as it should. As he lay in bed next to Brianna, her arm wrapped around him while she slept, he had to move the lower half of his body away from her so that she wouldn't feel how much he wanted her.

Wanted a woman who loved someone else.

Fuck, but his father was right, he was completely enraptured by this woman. He couldn't seem to help himself. The lies he had to tell were eating on his conscience, another development that loving Brianna had brought him. Alessandro usually had no problem lying to get what he wanted, but looking in her eyes and seeing her look back at him while he lied to her face was getting more and more difficult. Did Brianna feel the same unease lying to him about her feelings, or was that look in her eyes genuine? He didn't know what to believe anymore.

CHAPTER THIRTY-NINE

Alessandro was happy to be alone the next day, with the exception of Gianni. Bernardo was out doing business and Brianna, after an argument in the morning, insisted on going to visit Colin in the hospital and took Will with her. Gianni was suffering from a cold and so Alessandro was on babysitter duty until Vanessa, who had an early morning doctor's appointment, was scheduled to take over in the afternoon.

Maybe he was a glutton for punishment, but he wanted to hear the disc again, needed to hear for his own sanity that his loyalty should rightly belong to his father; that he didn't need to feel any guilt over his lies; that Brianna had really been lying to him all this time. As he unlocked his desk which held the disc, he heard giggling coming from the foyer.

Alessandro looked up and Gianni was no longer in the living room. "Well, bloody hell, that was quick."

He wheeled out to the foyer and saw Gianni climbing up the stairs. "And where do you thing you're going, eh?"

Gianni turned his head and squealed, caught, but continued on his journey.

Alessandro had no choice but to follow him before the baby fell. Where the heck was the baby gate? Will must have forgotten to put it back after he came down the stairs. He took a quick glance around to make sure that he was indeed alone and stood up out of his chair.

With practice, he was getting more used to putting his weight on his legs again so he could climb the stairs with minimal trembling or pain.

"Alessandro? Alessandro, you son of a bitch, where are you?" Carrie demanded from the living room.

Bloody hell, had he left the back door open after he came back in from playing with Will outside that morning?

Alessandro looked around frantically, hearing Carrie's feet coming closer. He was trapped in the center of the staircase. He'd never get up to the top or down back in the chair in time.

Gianni let out another giddy shriek as Alessandro scooped him up into his arms and Carrie came out into the foyer, having followed the sound.

She looked up at Alessandro standing on the stairs and the angry tight line of her mouth suddenly curved in a wide triumphant smile. "Gotcha."

Alessandro walked slowly down the stairs. Stay calm. He forced himself to stare straight at her, and not waver. Do not show one ounce of weakness.

But his arms were so tight around Gianni that the little boy began to squirm in protest.

"Ow, daddy."

Alessandro eased his grip. You are in control of this situation. You are a Dardano. You do not cower.

"I should have known," Carrie sneered. "Though I'm not surprised even I'd say this is pretty cold. To play on people's sympathies when all along it was a ruse."

"Are you done?" Alessandro asked, his legs were shaking and he wasn't sure if it was because of his weak muscles or fear.

Dardanos are never afraid.

"Oh not by a long shot. You know, if this had happened to anyone but my witch of a sister, I'd be pitying the poor bimbo but the fact that it's her whose eyes you're pulling the wool over makes me want to laugh my ass off. Now, here's what's going to happen, Alessandro. You're going to the police and you're confessing what you did to Colin."

"Am I?" Alessandro asked wheeling back into the living room, Gianni on his lap.

"You are, unless you want your precious Brianna to learn the truth."

When he stopped and turned to her, Gianni giggled and blew a raspberry at Carrie before pointing down on the floor. "Dow, daddy." Alessandro placed Gianni on the floor and grabbed his baby bottle from the coffee table and handed it over.

"See, that puts me in a quite a difficult position, darling Carrie. I can't very well confess to something I didn't do."

"I know you were responsible for what happened to Colin, just like I know you were in his hospital room the other day and you did something to put him into a coma!"

"Hmm, you certainly paint me as quite the nefarious criminal. I'm impressed with your courage."

Carrie shook her head and lifted the corner of her mouth in a smirk of disgust.

"No really, I mean, here you are accusing me of all manner of atrocities and yet you've come here to face big bad Alessandro all alone," Alessandro smirked.

Gianni pointed behind Carrie and said, " 'afie," Before she could turn and see Rafe behind her, the butler plunged a needle into her neck and the woman collapsed in his arms.

"Awww, dow." Gianni said looking back at Alessandro.

"No worries, my boy. Carrie's just going to take a little nap for a while," Alessandro said. He ordered Rafe to tie her up and lock her in the basement for now.

He needed time to figure out a way to ensure Carrie kept her mouth shut when he released her because he knew he couldn't keep her there forever.

"Seepy?" Gianni asked, placing his hands together on his cheek as Rafe carried Carrie away.

Before Alessandro could answer him, the doorbell rang signalling Vanessa's arrival.

"Perfect timing," he snorted as he wheeled to the door and answering.

"Ugh. Remind me to never, ever, ever, let myself get shot by one of your relatives again. I mean the traffic getting back here was ridiculous. Turns out there was this accident involving a truck carrying these blue footed chickens but then it took even longer 'cause you're not allowed to have blue footed chickens in the U.S so the guy got arrested then we had to wait until all the chickens were rounded up. But one guy got pissed and didn't want to wait so he ended up running over one of the chickens and then he got arrested. Hey how come Ralphie didn't answer the door?" Vanessa asked.

"'afie seepy," Gianni explained crawling towards the foyer.

"Hmm, I didn't know robots slept," Vanessa said reaching down and picking Gianni up. "Missed me, kiddo?"

Gianni pressed his hand to his mouth and blew her a kiss.

"You are just a precious little heartbreaker aren't you?" Vanessa cooed.

"Yaaaa," Gianni nodded.

"So Bree still at the hospital?"

"Yes, weeping over Colin's dead corpse if there's any justice in the world," Alessandro grumbled under his breath but Vanessa heard him.

"Careful, someone might think you don't like him too much," Vanessa warned wryly.

Brianna arrived later in the day and Alessandro tried to be understanding as Will went on about how sad it was to see his 'Unco Colin' with his eyes closed.

"But da doctor say he no seeping. He jus no can open his eyes. In't dat sad? I mean, I can open my eyes all da time. See? Watch." Will slowly blinked at him. "I hope I don' neber get what Unco Colin haf. Maybe dey can put some chicken soup in his needle? Make him all betto 'gain?"

"Honey, why don't you take Gianni and go play? Mommy wants to talk to daddy for a little while."

Alessandro felt his stomach tighten with apprehension and he wanted to call Will back, knowing that Brianna was less likely to tear him limb from limb if Will was there.

"I need you to do me a favour," Brianna said sitting on the couch and reaching to take his hand.

Alessandro blinked in surprise. "What do you mean? What's happened?"

"It's Beth, and well, Max actually," she said, her eyes bright with nervousness.

"Beth your sister?"

"Yeah, it turns out like a couple of months ago some guy was going around attacking the sorority girls at the university. I guess a few weeks ago he attacked Max's girlfriend Lily or something and Beth ended up stabbing him, thankfully before he could hurt her. But um…it looks like Max helped them hide the body…except…"

"What? He's not really dead?" Alessandro asked waiting to hear how she wanted him to help.

"Oh no, he's dead. That's not the problem. There's this tape. A… um, security camera that shows Max leaving the house with the body."

"How do you know all this?" Alessandro asked, fishing through her words for the kernel of an idea of an opportunity he could use against Carrie.

"Max made Beth admit all this to me. Colin is usually our tech guy but, well...I know my husband has some…er…talent in fooling the police too," Brianna said wryly.

"Oh, well. I'm quite flattered. So, what exactly do they want me to do?"

"If there was some way that you could doctor the footage?" Brianna asked.

Alessandro smiled. "Darling, I will do what I can."

Brianna threw her arms around him. "Thank you, Alessandro." She kissed him firmly on the mouth and Alessandro felt that tightening in his belly again, but this time it was guilt.

He went down into the basement, where Carrie was locked up. She screamed expletives at him at and when her tirade was over, Alessandro smiled at her.

"What the hell is that look for?"

"Gotcha, yourself, darling," he taunted.

It was while he was fixing the footage Max had given him that the doubts about the disc Bernardo had played for him began to plague him with ever growing strength.

Alessandro couldn't contemplate his father doing something so cruel but…Bernardo would certainly know how. Hell, Bernardo had taught him how to fiddle with electronics when he was still a teenager.

And he wanted Alessandro under his control, under his roof.

Knowing that Alessandro was trying to keep his family together and that entailed moving into their own house, out from the Dardano mansion, would Bernardo try to turn him with false information?

Brianna had been so sweet and loving to him lately, but she hadn't allowed him anymore wallowing. She pushed him to get better and didn't take any of his crap anymore. She was back to the Brianna he adored, who fired his blood as opposed to the doting 'yes woman' she'd been when he'd first been injured.

She was so excited when she was bathing him last night and he'd been completely unable to hide his arousal at her touch. "Do you think that means you're getting better?" she'd whispered huskily in his ear as she reached into the water and took him into her hand.

It didn't sound like relief that she would be able to leave him for Colin soon, who though he was now awake, had no memory of what had happened to him, leaving Alessandro further in the clear for now. It had sounded like anticipation for when they would renew their lovemaking. Lord knew he was dying to get back inside of her. It had been so long since he'd felt her so warm and eager around him. But shouldn't she be dreading that he would want to make love to her if she intended to leave him for that imbecile?

The doubts were there and he hated them. He was used to feeling sure about everything, in control always.

He snorted at that as he went about his work. He hadn't been in control for a second since Brianna O'Reiley Donovan Dardano had crashed into his life.

Video doctoring completed he looked at the disc on the table. Part of him wanted to smash it to pieces because no matter the outcome, someone he loved had betrayed him.

But he couldn't go on like this, looking into Brianna's eyes wondering if she was lying to him, wondering if every precious memory he held close to his heart was a lie.

Wondering if every precious memory he had of his father was a lie. If his surety in his father's love for him was nothing more than the manipulations of Bernardo Dardano, master puppeteer, if all these years, Alessandro was simply being controlled at the heir to the Dardano Empire, not loved.

Because no father who loved his son would rip his heart out the way Bernardo had done by insinuating that the love of Alessandro's life had lied to him.

"Well, Father, you're always going on about how Dardano men need to be strong. How we need to never back down in the face of fear." With those words in his head, Alessandro popped the disc into the editing program.

It would tell him if the disc had been doctored in anyway by showing him where the audio had been split or filled in. Alessandro's heart was beating so fast he could feel it throbbing in his ears as he watched the readings onscreen and waited. Brianna's beautiful voice filled the room. With truth or lies?

His fingers itched to stop the audio. He didn't want to know. It would be too painful either way.

And then the line on the screen spiked to show a split in the audio.

And then another.

And then another.

There were at least a dozen splits in the audio but Alessandro couldn't see them all because his vision had blurred with tears.

Oh Brianna. My darling. My heart. My beloved wife…

Oh Father.

Alessandro bent double as the sorrow in his heart threatened to steal his breath. Alessandro bit his fist to keep the nausea in. He'd lied. His Father had watched him buckle under the weight of his heartbreak and he hadn't cared. It was more important to keep Alessandro there, under his control.

To keep the soldier in line, Bernardo had no qualms about breaking his son.

Loyalty went one way only. His Father didn't love him. All this time. All the things Alessandro had done for him, for his love, his approval and all along…he'd never had had it.

Alessandro took the disc out with trembling fingers. He would throw it in his father's face when he called him a liar.

All those years, growing up without his mother, Alessandro had comforted himself with the fact that at least he'd had his father. He felt even more sad for the boy he had been. He'd been so alone, even among friends because he'd known he didn't have families the way they did.

But he had his own family now. He had Brianna and Will and Gianni and the baby that was coming. Gabriella. Oh my darling little baby, I'm so sorry for the thoughts I had towards your mummy. She loves me. Truly.

He thanked God that he had brought Brianna into his life.

The door behind him opened and he forced his tears back, quickly wiping his cheeks.

"How's it going?" Brianna asked popping her head in.

"All done," Alessandro said, turning his chair around and holding up the video tape. He stuck the disc in his pocket.

Brianna's eyebrow's came together in concern. "Are you okay?"

Alessandro forced a smile and nodded. "I was just thinking that this could be the beginning of getting my life back."

The smile she gave him squeezed his heart. Slowly he would pretend to recover and everything would be as it was before. Only now, his wife and children would have his loyalty. Not Bernardo. Not the man who had lied to him and pretended to love him.

He reached up and cupped the back of her neck to draw her face close to his. Her eyes widened in a beat of surprise but she sighed and kissed him back.

"I love you," Alessandro sighed against her mouth. *And I'm sorry. So very sorry I ever doubted you.*

"Do you expect me to apologize?" Bernardo asked sitting behind his desk.

Alessandro fisted his hand against his thigh so that he didn't drive it into his father's face. He loved this man and yet he despised that Bernardo was bringing up these violent feelings in him. He never would have imagined he'd direct these feelings towards his own father.

"I know better than that. A Dardano apologizes for nothing and bows to no one. Isn't that right?" Alessandro asked.

"I'm glad that is clear," Bernardo said.

"I just wanted to see the look on your face. To look at you and have you admit to my face what you've done. I mean, did you think I would never find out the truth?"

"I did what I had to do and I would do it again."

Alessandro took a deep breath and tried to still his shaking hands. "I suppose I have only myself to blame that I didn't have the courage to find out the truth sooner, but I would never fathom that my own father, who spouts off about familial love and loyalty being paramount to all, would try and destroy my marriage and shake my faith in the woman I love. Brianna is my wife, father. At your order, remember?" Alessandro snapped.

"Yes, and her duty was to stay by your side, to fulfill her role as the wife of a Dardano, not to try and make you turn your back on your entire legacy! When I saw that was what she was doing I did what I had to do."

"And never mind that you'd be tearing my heart out in the process. You know how much I adore Brianna and my boys."

"Bah! You're so over dramatic."

"All Brianna wanted was for us to live in peace. You do remember Arturo, right, Father? The reason he is out there is because you turned him into this twisted monster. I can only thank God that Brianna saved me from a similar fate before it was too late."

"So are you saying that you are turning your back on me? After everything I have done for you, the life and power I have handed to you on a silver platter. Do not tell me you are betraying me, Alessandro."

Alessandro stood up, leaned his hand on the desk and glared down at his father. "You gave me power, yes, but only to use it under your order. Like a soldier, not a son. I would gladly give back every penny spent on my prestigious education, every deal made to cement my place in the Dardano empire, every power play, every person we destroyed to have you look at me once as a son, as someone to be cherished just by their very existence, just once."

"Oh for goodness sake, Alessandro. Do you think I would have done all that if I didn't love you?"

"No, all I ever was was an instrument of vengeance against the O'Reileys, someone to lure Brianna away from her family. I mean for God's sake father, Will is not even my blood and I adore that boy as if he came from my own seed, not because I want to groom him to be a soldier but just because he is. Why can't you do the same?"

"So you are choosing them over me, your own Father?"

"YOU LIED TO ME!" Alessandro barked, trembling with such nervousness and rage that his legs buckled and he fell back into the chair.

"I did what I had to do for you, as I always have. If you turn your back on that, you arrogant, self righteous, ingrate, I want nothing more to do with you."

Alessandro swallowed hard, his eyes burning with disappointment. "You never did, Father. I worshipped the ground you walked on, killed for you and you never wanted me just as your son, but for what you could use me for."

"If that is what you believe then you are truly a disappointment to me. I can only hope Gianni can bring pride back to the Dardano legacy. I hope he will be a better example of what it means to be a true Dardano."

"I will raise my son to be a good man. He will have nothing to do with your bloody legacy. My son will not be raised to be a killer."

Bernardo's eyes hardened. "You would keep Gianni from his birthright? Be careful, my boy. Gianni is my blood as well."

"I am his father. I will dictate what his birthright is to be. Don't think to fight me on this." There was no way in hell he was letting Gianni grow up with this feeling of unworthiness in his heart. His son would always know he was loved and wanted.

"I won't have to fight you, Alessandro. I know you will see sense."

"Really? You would do well to remember that you raised me to be a Dardano, Father. So you know full well what would happen if you even attempt to take my son from me."

There was a knock on the door and Brianna popped her head in. "What on earth is going on? I heard yelling."

Alessandro turned and forced himself to smile. "Nothing darling. Just a difference of opinion is all."

"Right, and when Dardanos disagree it's practically World War Three," Brianna said, rolling her eyes.

"Well, it's over now. I believe I've made my point quite clear, haven't I?" Alessandro said. "Darling, if you'd get the boys dressed and get Luke, I'd like to take my family for lunch in the park today. Then, I'd like to pass by our home and see how the renovations are going. I'd like us to move in as soon as possible."

"Really?" Brianna asked looking from Alessandro to Bernardo, who was glowering at them.

"Quite. Now, shall we?" he pointed at the door.

"Alessandro, I just want to remind you that I am your father. I do love you and I will be here for you whenever you need me. And believe me, my boy, you will need me."

Brianna looked down at Alessandro in question but he shook his head, trying to ignore his father's words. He had everything he needed now, Brianna's love and the love of his children.

He didn't need anything else. He would have the family he'd always wanted and nothing was going to stand in the way of that.

He'd destroy anyone who tried. Even if that meant his very own father.

CHAPTER FORTY

"Oh, this is home," Bree whispered looking up at the house as she got out of the car. Morgan, the driver/bodyguard came around and helped Alessandro into his chair. One of the first things installed was a ramp that led up to the door so Alessandro didn't need any help.

"Wow. Is' smaller den da creepy mansion," Will remarked.

And it was. Much smaller and absolutely perfect. Even living in the apartment building for years, having made it a home with Michael, she hadn't had the settled sense of rightness that this house possessed.

She and Michael had always planned to get a house, but they never got the chance.

This house looked like a family could live in it, as opposed to the 'master of the universe'.

Luke, glad not to be cooped up in the car, took off running around the front yard. Bree imagined that the backyard would have considerably less space but they'd get used to that gladly.

She did admit, just to herself, that she would miss the orchard that led to the canopy of apple blossoms by the river.

Maybe they could plant some trees in the back.

Have a garden in the front.

A real honest-to-goodness home!

Bree tried not to squeal in delight as she followed Alessandro into the house. The furniture that had occupied it was gone, giving the living room a wide open feel. Will thought the echo effect of the empty room was hilarious. "Look mommy, I sound really big!"

"Gaaaaah!" Gianni exclaimed from Alessandro's lap, giggling at the effect.

"Howdy Mr. D," the carpenter, a man with a wild mass of dark curly hair and black beard, said from the stairs.

"Who are you?" Will asked coming up to him. "Are you gonna live wif us?"

"Nope, kiddo. Just installing this here lift for your daddy's chair. That way, he can get upstairs."

"Wow," Will exclaimed suitably impressed. "Dat's a good idea." He stuck his hand out. "I'm Misto D too. I'm William Donovan Dardano."

The carpenter smiled over Will's head at Bree and Alessandro. "Nice to meet you." He took Will's tiny hand in his larger one.

"Yep I know," Will said. "Did you put in da fire place yet? We gonna make S'mores!"

"Not yet."

"Dat's okay. We haf a Plan B. Mommy, that's the girl over der. She say we can do a fire in da back like camping. My daddy neber had S'mores. In't dat sad?" Will asked.

The carpenter looked at Alessandro in surprise.

"What?" Alessandro asked.

"I think I might cry," the carpenter admitted shaking his head.

"I don't know if we can save you any 'cause we probably gonna eat dem all," Will explained.

"Will!" Bree scolded. "Leave the poor man alone,"

"No worries, Mrs D. I'm just wrapping up here for the day. I'll leave you guys alone and I'll go home and make some S'mores of my own," he explained. He looked at Alessandro and shook his head. "Dude, seriously. That's sad."

"C' I go pick my room?" Will asked stepping onto the stairs.

"Sure thing. There's no furniture up there anymore but you can have a look around," Bree said.

Gianni looked up at the stairs as Will ran up and he pushed his body towards them. "Up!"

"Oh no you don't," Alessandro said tightening his arm around Gianni's middle and turning away.

"Up, daddy! Me wanned up!" Gianni tugged on Alessandro's pant legs.

"Hey Gianni, remember, Daddy can't take you up yet," Bree

leaned down and smiled at Alessandro. "But he might be able to very, very soon," she dropped a kiss on Alessandro's lips.

Gianni tugged on Alessandro's pant legs stubbornly. "Daddy, up dis!"

Alessandro kissed Gianni's cheek and wheeled him away even further from the stairs.

"Oh would you look at these gorgeous windows. I can imagine baking pies in here and setting them on the window sill like my grandma does."

She heard Alessandro snort behind her and grinned sheepishly at him. "Okay, so my Martha Stewart is getting away from me a bit." She rushed towards him in the doorway. "But I'm so excited, Alessandro. We're finally going to have our own home away from everything and to make our home here where you and I…I love you so much," Bree cupped his stubbled face and kissed him, feeling as if her heart, that was so full of joy, might burst.

The lack of a fireplace had them moving to the backyard with sleeping bags, purchased after their afternoon at the park.

"Now the secret to good S'mores is in the graham cracker, make sure it's the sweet kind. Honey graham crackers if you will," Bree said holding up a rectangle as the warmth from the fire soothed her face.

"Ooooh," Gianni said pointing at the flames from his seat on Bree's lap.

"And melt-able chocolate,"

Alessandro snickered at that. "Melt-able?"

"What? It's a word!" Bree insisted, placing a marshmallow on Will's stick and holding it with him over the fire, turning it around until the flames went out.

Gianni squealed in excitement at the round little ball of fire. "Ooook, mama! Oook dis! Awww. Bye-bye?" he asked when the flames went out.

"Behold, cracker, marshmallow and melt-able chocolate. And smush." The sticky mess oozed out the sides but Bree caught them with her tongue and moaned at the deliciousness.

Alessandro cocked an eyebrow and smiled wickedly at her letting her know he was thinking of the last time she had moaned like that in this very house, and the deliciousness that had caused it.

Bree blushed and threw a marshmallow at him. Then she

proceeded to show him how to roast it over the fire and handed him his own cracker and chocolate. "Now, if you want to be lazy, you could use chocolate syrup but my Grandpa Joe considers that sacrilege. Now, smush,"

"Smush?" Alessandro asked skeptically looking at the mini sandwich he held as if it was a bomb about to go off.

Bree watched him press the two crackers together with such force the cracker crumbled and the marshmallow and chocolate oozed onto his fingers and pants.

"Easy," she warned too late.

"Bloody hell, these are four hundred dollar pants!" Alessandro exclaimed, looking around for a Kleenex.

"Dat's okay, daddy. Is no big deal. Dat's what laundry is fo'," Will explained.

"Oh is that so?" Alessandro asked throwing a marshmallow at him.

Will threw one back.

And the War of the Marshmallows was on.

"So everything looks all right with the baby?" Bree asked, sitting on the examining table.

"Yep, besides being a little underweight, both you and her, I'd say she's progressing along normally," Caroline assured her.

"Pft. Alessandro's been stuffing me with bangers and mash any chance he gets, not that I'm complaining, and he's just discovered the joy of S'mores so barring anymore midnight near burning down of our bedroom, I'd say lack of food is not an issue."

"Burning down…?" her doctor asked.

Bree laughed. "Yeah. He's worse than I am with the cravings so he's taken to using a lighter and a fork in the middle of the night to make impromptu S'mores. But, never mind. So yeah, not eating is not the problem."

"Hmm, well I'd say it's probably stress related then. Though living in the Dardano mansion, I can't really say I'm surprised."

"Oh but we're not going to be living there for much longer!" Bree explained happily. "We're going to be moving into this house outside of town."

"You're leaving New York?"

"Not really. It's literally just outside the city. It's the house we took shelter in when we met."

"Oh that's so romantic," she said smiling.

Bree beamed and wrinkled her nose impishly. "Isn't it? Anyway, it's not ready yet 'cause we're putting in some renovations for Alessandro's wheelchair but he says by the end of the month we should be ready to move in."

"And how is that going? With Alessandro, I mean?"

"Oh, I thought Carlo would have told you. Alessandro's getting some feeling back in his legs. He's getting some twinges and just yesterday he was able to wiggle his toes. Will was playing 'this little piggy' with Gianni's feet and the baby reached over and grabbed Alessandro's feet. Alessandro said he could feel his hand."

Caroline brought her hands together and smiled. "Oh that's wonderful. But I'm surprised Alessandro didn't tell you. Carlo's not his doctor anymore. He's been doing his follow up care with a doctor at Bellevue."

"Oh that's…odd," Bree said, confused. Why wouldn't Alessandro mention that to her? She shook her head, filing it away in her mind to ask him later.

"Hey there. How's my niece doing?" Brian asked, coming out of the hospital elevator. They'd agreed to meet for lunch after her check up

"Just fine. Dr Murdoch suggests I need to eat more," Bree replied, touching her stomach.

"Doctor's orders to stuff your face. Nice," Brian said. "Carrie called me and said that Colin's woken up. You want to take a sec and visit?" He guided her back to the elevators.

"Has he really?" Bree gasped. "That's wonderful. I was going to go sit with him for a while but this is so great that he's awake now. Do you think they'll let us all in at the same time?"

She knocked on Colin's door when they reached his floor and stuck her head in. "Hey you."

Carrie, who had been sitting on his bed stood up and glared at her. "You bitch,"

"Carrie, please," Colin groaned.

"Really, Carrie. Your greetings are really beginning to go downhill," Bree said.

"Let me handle this. Could you leave us alone?" Colin insisted.

"Oh no way in hell am I leaving you alone with Bree after what her husband did to you. She's probably here to help finish the job."

Bree shook her head. "What the hell are you talking about? Alessandro didn't do anything to Colin."

"Yes, he did, Bree," Colin said quietly.

Bree stared at him, twinge of nervousness in her chest. "What are you saying? You don't even remember what happened to—"

"I remember now. Alessandro and his men tied me to a chair and beat me. Then to make sure they did a thorough enough job, they set fire to the warehouse. If it wasn't for Charlie, Alessandro would have killed me."

Bree's legs buckled and she gripped the doorknob to stop herself from falling to the floor. No…no. Trust Alessandro. Don't let them win. Trust Alessandro. "No, I already asked him about it. He told me he had nothing to do with what happened to Colin."

"Oh and we all know Alessandro is such a pillar of honesty," Carrie sneered.

"Oh pots and kettles, you shrew," Bree spat. She turned back to Colin. "Come on, Colin. This is her, right? She's filling your head with this garbage 'cause she hates Alessandro and she hates me."

"You're right. I do hate Alessandro. He's the one who kidnapped me and lorded over me the fact that he could put Beth and Max in prison because of that whole rapist nightmare unless I kept quiet. But you, right now I almost feel sorry for you. In fact, yes, I downright pity you," Carrie sneered.

"Carrie, that's enough!" Brian insisted.

"Kidnapped you? Being quiet about what? Do you even know how ridiculous you sound? Alessandro wants nothing to do with you and has never wanted anything to do with you and you can't stand it, can you?" Bree laughed but it had a hollow sound as waves of fear were building up inside of her.

Carrie was lying. She had to be lying. Alessandro had looked her in the eye and—

"Oh yeah, that's it Bree. I'd rather be you. The woman so stupid that her paralyzed husband has been able to walk for over a month now and she's too moronic to see that he's been pulling the wool over her eyes all this time. I mean how the hell does that even happen?" Carrie taunted.

Bree felt sick. Walk. Able to walk. Her vision blurred and the room swam beneath her feet. She saw the blurry image of Carrie reaching forward to catch her and she shook her head. "What are you talking about?" Bree asked, but her voice sounded far away to her own ears.

"Never mind. Look. Let me just go get the doctor. You're not looking well. Maybe I should have waited—"

"You think!" Brian snapped, holding on to Bree's arms.

"No!" Bree said, but she jumped because the word sounded like a scream in her head. She grabbed her sister. "What do you mean, he's able to walk? He wouldn't keep something like that from me. He wouldn't…He wouldn't…"

"That's what he wanted me to keep quiet about. I came to the house to yell at him about Colin, and I caught him standing." Carrie sounded almost apologetic now.

Bree shook her head. "No, maybe he was just…testing himself to see if he could."

Carrie shook her head. "He was on the stairs, carrying Gianni."

Gianni. Their son. He would never take such a chance on the stairs with their baby unless his legs were strong.

Still her heart was screaming at her to deny the words she was hearing. "You're lying. You're…I have to see Alessandro." She turned the knob and ran out of the room.

Brian followed her toward the elevator. "Let me drive you home 'cause you don't look in any condition to drive."

Bree wasn't listening to him. She was rushing towards the elevator, praying to a God she knew could not exist if what Carrie had said was true.

Please, she thought. *Please.*

"Alessandro!" Bree yelled, fear and fury battling through her veins. She didn't want to believe the man she loved, adored beyond all reason could lie to her and for so long, about something so important.

"Master Dardano is in the backyard playing with the children," Rafe informed her.

He loves our children. He's such a good father. He wouldn't do this. He wouldn't.

Bree stormed through the living room out to the backyard and didn't acknowledge Vanessa who was playing with Will. Alessandro was in the wheelchair, popping wheelies in his chair with Gianni shrieking with delight in his lap as Will bounced a basket ball on the cement walkway Bernardo had laid down so Alessandro could manoeuvre his chair better. All this construction, all of these concessions to help Alessandro get around. Would Bernardo be doing all these things if he knew Alessandro could walk. Or were they in cahoots together to fool her, to deceive her.

"Hello, darling," Alessandro smiled at her.

Oh, that smile. Bree wanted to close her eyes, press her hands against her eyes and keep them shut forever so she wouldn't see that smile.

She must have had the question on her face, the knowledge on her face because as she looked at him now, something flickered in his eyes.

Guilt. Oh God.

"Mommy, look. I make good bouncies. See?" Will said, dribbling the ball. "I gonna be a basset ball player when I gwoed up."

The little boy's voice sounded far away as Bree narrowed in on Alessandro and the look in his eyes. "Brian. I want you and Vanessa to take Will and Gianni out for a little while."

"Oh but we're having a good time out here, aren't we Gianni?" Alessandro asked, tickling Gianni who squealed and curled inward.

"Now," Bree said, her voice tight.

Will stopped bouncing the ball and held it against his chest looking at both of them, picking up on the angry tension that suddenly covered them all.

"Uh oh. I tink mommy's mad."

"I'm not leaving you alone in your condition, Bree. Alessandro, we just came from the hospital. Colin's awake," Brian informed him, his voice tight with anger.

"You spoke to Colin?" Alessandro asked, meeting Bree's eyes.

"I did. And Carrie."

He looks like a cornered animal. And what do Dardanos do when they're cornered? They lie. They cheat. Oh God.

"Fine, then can you just take the boys upstairs?" Bree said, speaking to Brian, but not moving her gaze from her husband.

"Come on, guys. Let's go play upstairs for a while," Vanessa said walking past Bree and taking Gianni from Alessandro's lap.

"Whatever you did, the jig is up, boss," she warned before leaving with Brian.

"Is it true?" Bree asked, holding on to the wall because she was shaking so badly she was afraid she would drop.

"Is what—"

"Don't!" Bree snapped shaking her head vigorously. "Don't. Don't look at me and pretend like you don't know what I'm talking about."

"Brianna, darling. If you could just—"

"Did you kidnap Carrie and lock her in the basement?"

"Is that what she told you? Sweetheart, why on earth would you believe anything that comes out of that woman's mouth?"

Through a blur of tears, Bree shot her hand out and slapped him. "Again. Did you do it?"

Alessandro's hand went to his cheek and he cleared his throat. "All right. Yes."

"Why?" Bree forced the question out begging him silently with all her heart to tell her that this was all a mistake. Bree covered her face and tried to fight the sobs but they broke through anyway. "You looked me in the eye and you lied to me. Colin told me that you were responsible for what happened to him. After you looked at me and swore that you had nothing to do with what happened. That you didn't try to kill him."

"Oh yes and we all know your precious Colin's word is gospel, isn't it?" Alessandro sneered.

"Don't you dare try and turn this around on Colin. Don't you fucking dare!"

Alessandro threw his hands up in apparent frustration. "Well, what do you want me to do, Brianna. Ever since he snapped his fingers and decided he wanted you, you've been at his side."

"I am not the liar here."

"All right, yes. I lied. Fine. But you know what, I didn't tell you because I knew you would get upset and I couldn't bear one more second of that mother fucker trying to get my wife!"

"Carrie agreed to not tell me that you can walk if you keep quiet about the whole Max and Beth nightmare."

There was that flicker of guilt again. Bree felt a numbness settle over her. She recognized the feeling well. The animal inside her was preparing to lash out.

"The woman is delusional—"

"Can you walk, Alessandro?" Bree asked.

Alessandro said nothing.

"Please. I want to hear the words. I want you to look me in the eye and lie. Tell me you're still paralyzed. Tell me you can't walk."

"Brianna, you know that I've been getting some feeling back in my legs. I've shared that with you."

Bree stormed towards his chair and gripped the handles, with a strong shove she pushed the wheelchair backwards, making Alessandro cry out as his head smacked against the ground.

"Are you insane?" he demanded.

"Get up," Bree sneered.

"I can't get up. You know—"

"STAND UP!" she screamed at him. "We both know you can, you son of a bitch. Stop fucking pretending! After everything I've done for you, everything I have given up for you, give me this one thing. If you've ever loved me, give me this one shred of honesty."

Alessandro closed his eyes and pushed himself up into a sitting position.

Bree waited, holding her breath, tears of heartbreak streaming down her face.

Then he moved his legs and placed his hands on the ground for leverage.

Then he stood up.

All six foot four of him, towered over her for the first time in months.

And the happy world Bree knew ceased to exist.

CHAPTER FORTY-ONE

She stared at him and it was like looking at a stranger, or someone she had once known but had hoped to never see again. Alessandro the liar. Alessandro the deceiver. Alessandro the manipulator. Alessandro the Dardano. Gone was Alessandro the man who loved her. Alessandro the man who trusted her. Alessandro the man who would never hurt her. Alessandro the man who put her first.

"Damn you," Bree hissed, pressing herself against the grey stone wall of the house, wanting to dissolve into it. "Damn you for destroying everything."

He reached out a hand to her, pleading. "Brianna, try to underst—"

She slapped away his hand. "No! NO! Don't touch me. Don't ever touch me again." She slapped at his arm, his chest, his face as her fury took over. Good, let the anger in, keep the pain out, just the rage, just the hate. Don't feel the pain, the broken heart, shattered into a million pieces.

Alessandro winced and staggered back, trying to control her flailing arms, her scratching nails. She was drawing blood and she felt a small thrill of satisfaction. If she had a knife she would have stabbed him, cut him up into a million pieces so that he would be broken apart like she was on the inside. She screamed at him, obscenities full of hate, taking comfort in her rage because it gave her strength and kept her from falling apart, or throwing herself into his arms and begging him to make everything okay, even if meant he kept lying to her, as long as everything was the way it was before.

"I hate you! I fucking hate you so much, you bastard! You fucking bastard!" Bree cried, tears streaming down her cheeks and down her neck, into the straps of the summer dress she wore. He said he liked the dress 'cause it looked so pretty on her, she remembered his words. Had that been a lie too? Had he lied when he said she was so beautiful she took his breath away?

"Brianna, for God's sake stop it!" Alessandro yelled finally grabbing her arms and pinning them to her sides. "Listen to me."

"I don't want to listen to you!" Bree filled her mouth with saliva and spit in his face. "You picked him! You'd rather be like your father than love me!"

Alessandro lowered his head and removed one hand and wiped his face, and she realized that along with her spit, there were some raised welts and broken skin and damp that might have been tears if she believed he regretted what he had done.

She didn't.

"You're right to be angry. I understand but I only lied to you because I lo—"

"Don't!" she snapped. "I don't ever want to hear those words come out of your mouth again. Do you hear me?"

He went on, ignoring her. Of course. What did her feelings matter to him? As long as she'd given him the great Dardano heir. That was all he wanted her for. Everything else was just to butter her up to make it easier for him to get what he wanted.

"I thought I was going to lose you. I thought because I couldn't walk that you would leave me," Alessandro insisted.

"Then you never believed I loved you at all. If you could believe that garbage, that I could so easily just walk away from you because of something so out of our control then we never had anything. We have no connection. No bond. Nothing at all," Bree told him, her voice suddenly soft.

"No!" Alessandro said, cupping her face. "I was wrong. Do you hear me? I was wrong to believe that. I was wrong to doubt our love. Just forgive me. I beg you, Brianna. Please, forgive me." He pressed his face against hers, kissing her face fervently.

Bree struggled against his embrace, feeling the weak part of her wanting to give in. No, he would just hurt her again, manipulate her. Never again. She would never allow him to manipulate her heart ever again. "No. I'm done."

He stopped and stared down at her, his dark eyes red rimmed with tears. "What do you mean?"

"I mean I'm done. It's finished. I can't do this anymore. I'm taking Will and Gianni and leaving."

Alessandro grabbed her shoulders. "No!"

Bree pushed against him but he wrapped his arms around her and held her against him. "Don't! Leave me alone. Let me go!" Bree yelled trying to break free but Alessandro wouldn't let her. Both of them fell onto the grass.

"What the hell is going on?" Bernardo asked coming out to the backyard followed by her brother.

"Father! Father, tell her what you did! Tell her about the recording and how you made me think she was going to leave me," Alessandro insisted.

Bree shoved at him and Brian helped her to her feet. "Why the hell would I want to hear anything that Bernardo had to say? And what the hell are you talking about anyway? What recording? You know what? Never mind. It doesn't matter, Alessandro. It doesn't matter because I will never, ever believe another word that comes out of your lying mouth. Not ever."

"Dude, it's fucking true?" Brian asked behind her, obviously surprised to see Alessandro getting to his feet.

"Oh yeah, apparently he's been pulling the wool over all our eyes. Every time you looked at me. Every time you touched me, smiled at me, kissed me, you lied."

"I never lied about how I felt about you. Not once, Brianna."

"You fucker!" Brian yelled and let fly with a fist across Alessandro's face that sent him back to the ground.

"Right, you never lied. You just did everything daddy told you to," Bree turned to Bernardo. "You fucking monster. This is on you too. You couldn't leave us alone, could you? You couldn't let us be happy. You made him into this. You did it!"

Bree lunged for the older man but Brian held her back. "Don't Bree. You need to take it easy, okay? Think about the baby."

"He's right, darling. Please. Just think about our baby and calm yourself."

"My baby, Alessandro. Do you hear me? MINE! Now I am taking my children and getting as far away from you and your screwed up, evil family as I can get. My God, I didn't wanna see it but my family was right about you. They were right. Damn you to hell Alessandro." She called out for Will who came running down the stairs, wide eyed and pale, obviously having heard the commotion. "Get your coat and your shoes. We're leaving."

He looked frantically over at Alessandro who had struggled back into his chair. "Daddy's coming too, right?" He asked, his voice trembling.

"No. Alessandro is not coming with us ever again." She looked back and saw the flash of pain that she had referred to him as 'Alessandro' and not 'daddy' to Will. She felt triumphant at that pain.

Will's lower lip quivered and he shook his head. 'Oh no, mommy. We can't go. We can't leave daddy behin'. Please, mommy. Please we hafta stay or daddy might get sad 'gain." Will threw his arms around Bree's legs and held on tight and Bree's heart, which she thought couldn't possibly break any further, shattered their broken pieces into yet smaller pieces. "Mommy. No. Please. We hafta stay here. You promised. You promised you'd love daddy forever."

Bree forced herself to tear her gaze away from Alessandro who had the decency to look utterly ashamed of himself, but that gave her no relief from the pain in her own soul. She could never trust him again. Ever. What he had done had shown her that the connection of their souls that she had always felt had simply been imagined, wishful thinking on her part.

"Baby, listen to mommy. Daddy did something very bad—"

"Den he can say he sorry!" Will insisted turning to Alessandro and reaching for him, but refusing to let go of his grip on at least one of Bree's legs. "Daddy, please. Jus' say you sorry and it can be okay, right, mommy?"

"I already said I was sorry, little one. So very sorry," Alessandro said, meeting Bree's gaze with his own wet one.

"There are some things that 'sorry' can't fix," Bree snapped feeling a fresh burst of rage. She'd believed him when he told her he loved her, that she was his soul mate. Oh God help me, Bree pleaded, a sharp pain shooting through her abdomen. She squeezed her eyes shut. She had to calm down for her baby's sake. What made him think she'd believe him when he said he was sorry? He was nothing if not an accomplished liar.

"Oh this is ridiculous. Nobody is going anywhere. Brianna, you're staying right here where you belong," Bernardo barked.

Bree grit her teeth and lunged for him but Brian held her back and Will spoke up instead.

"You go away!" Will cried back angrily. "I know you did sumting dat made my mommy mad at my daddy. Is you fault!"

"I suggest you put a muzzle on your brat and get back in the living room," Bernardo ordered.

"Careful, Father. This is none of your concern," Alessandro said.

"Are you kidding me?" Bree asked. "Of course this is his concern because he's the only one you give a damn about. You'll do anything for him. Absolutely anything even if it means betraying me or Will or God forbid Gianni."

"That is not true. I would never—"

"It is true!" Bree yelled. "Everything you've done has proven that."

"Look, every marriage has problems and that is no reason to turn back on the vows you made to each other," Bernardo pointed out. "You made a promise to honor the terms of the O'Reiley/Dardano vendetta. Be careful before you renege on those vows, Mrs. Dardano."

"You and your stupid vendetta!" Bree hissed. "Begun by a man who couldn't handle the fact that he couldn't have what he wanted! God it must be genetic. Well, I guess I shouldn't blame you, Alessandro. Knowing Bernardo and Adriano, at least you come by it honestly."

"Well, I guess that's a bust," Vanessa said coming down the stairs holding Gianni. "I had hoped to try and get him down for his nap but no way he's sleeping through World War Three going on down here."

Bree was alternately annoyed and grateful that Vanessa had brought the baby down. She didn't want Gianni around all this animosity but it would easier for them all to leave now than for her to have to go up to get him.

"You know what you can do with your vendetta Bernardo," Bree snapped. "Let's go Will. Gianni come here." She reached for Gianni but Alessandro stood up out of his chair with a groan and Bree wondered if he was just faking some more, if it was still hard for him to use his legs.

He stepped in front of her. "No. You're not taking Gianni anywhere or Will."

"Excuse me?" Bree asked, stiffening. Oh he couldn't be fucking serious!

"They're my children and you are not taking my sons out of this house. I understand you're upset and rightly so I admit, but that does not give you the right to take my boys away."

"They're MY boys," Bree shot back.

"Gianni is mine by blood and Will is mine by law, or have you forgotten the adoption papers?"

"They are both mine by blood! Do you really think you have a chance in hell?"

"Holy shit, you're standing up!" Vanessa exclaimed then she gasped. "Oh my God is that what this is all about? Boss, don't take this the wrong way but are you an asshole or what?"

"Let me put it another way," Alessandro said ignoring Vanessa's insult. "I'm their father. You're their mother. If you want to continue in that role you will do so in this house."

"Oh you'd like that wouldn't ya?" Bree said. "Then you keep me locked up in here like some prisoner and then what, you think I would just magically fall in love with you again? You're delusional!"

"STOP IT!" Will screamed covering his ears. "Stop it right now! No mo' fighting! Mommy, daddy wan' you to stay. I wanna stay here wif you and daddy and Gianni and 'Nessa and well…why don' HE go?" Will asked glaring at Bernardo.

"Will—" Bree pleaded for understanding but her son shook his head stubbornly.

Gianni began crying and screaming for Bree, affected by all the yelling and tension in the room.

"No! You jus' gonna say tings like I don' unnerstan 'cause I'm little. I'm biggo now and I unnerstan dat you haf to stay or daddy might get sad again and die if we nod here to stop him and show him we love him. We hafta stay and I don wanna hear no mo!" Will screamed jumping up and down.

Bree suddenly clutched her stomach as another spasm of pain seized her.

Will jerked back, wide eyed. "Oh! Oh! Mommy! I sorry. I don' mean to yell. I sorry!" he shrieked.

Bree shook her head as Brian held her and she reached out for Will's arm. "It's okay. It's not your fault. Mommy's just having a little. Owwwww!" she gasped as her legs gave out from under her.

Alessandro kneeled down in front of her, his face white with panic and she almost touched his face to reassure him as well but then she remembered.

"What is it, darling? What's wrong? Is it the baby?" Alessandro asked.

"Mammmaaaaaaaaa!" Gianni screamed trying to reach her.

Bree shoved at Alessandro as another spasm buckled her. "Get away from me, you bastard."

"Come on. I'm taking you to the hospital," Brian said, pulling her to her feet.

"I'll follow you in my car," Alessandro insisted.

Bree shook her head. "No!" Then she looked over at her poor panicked little boys and thought both she and Alessandro had to calm the fuck down for their sakes. "No, you…" she breathed hard as the pain slowly began to ease. "You stay here with the boys…for now. It's okay Will. You can stay with daddy. You and Gianni don't have to leave, okay?"

"But you gonna come back right?" Will asked, his face wet with tears.

She leaned down and kissed his face. "Mommy will see you soon, I promise." She kissed Gianni's face and then looked up at Alessandro and shook her head. "I hope you think all your lies were worth it because if anything happens to this baby, it'll be your fault," she whispered before she left with Brian.

"Do you want to carry this child to term?" Dr Murdoch asked, exasperated.

"Of course I do," Bree groaned. The pain was now gone, thank God. Braxton Hicks contractions caused by the baby being severely agitated.

"When you get upset, that baby inside of you gets upset. Do you need me to tattoo that onto your stomach?" she asked.

"No," Bree sighed, wanting to burrow under the blankets of her hospital bed and make the last twenty-four hours just disappear. "There'll be no more agitation from now on."

"Hmph," Brian remarked, his opinion on that matter clear as the doctor left them alone.

"Trust me. It's so over between me and Alessandro," Bree said, blinking back tears as she stared up at the ceiling.

"And you think he's going to just leave it at that? I know the guy, Bree and I know Bernardo. They're not just going to let you be on your way. You have children."

"Alessandro and I are just going to have to come to some kind of agreement."

"Right, 'cause Alessandro seems like such a reasonable man. I'm sure Colin would agree," he cracked.

"How is Colin by the way?" Bree asked, needing to distract herself from the fact that her heart was no more than a numb organ in her chest.

"He's doing much better. He should be able to go home in a few days. The police were here to question him earlier and should be paying a visit to your hubby any minute now."

"Good," Bree snapped. "I hope he gets into a cell with some big burly guy named Tyrone or Carmine who wants to make Alessandro his bitch. Let's see how that silver spooned jackass deals with prison life." Then she dropped her head in her hands. "God, that is so not what Will needs to see right now, Alessandro carted off to prison. I think we'll be maxing out Dr. Sheri's calendar for the next eighteen years for that kid and who knows what this is doing to Gianni. I mean what was I thinking? Everyone warned me. Literally, everyone warned me not to get involved with Alessandro but did I listen? Noooooooo. I had to follow my heart because we had this magic connection or whatever. Never mind that he's the son of the man I despise. Never mind that we get shot at more times than people change their socks. Forget all the damage that this is doing to my children. What the hell was I thinking?"

"You were thinking with your heart," Brian said sympathetically. "It's not a bad thing…er…usually. But listen, you need to just move forward and do what's best for your children and that means this little one inside too. No stressful situations. Period."

Bree laughed. "So what do you suggest? I move to a tiki hut in Burma?"

"Might not be a bad idea," he said.

Bree was almost disappointed later when she opened the door to leave her room, Andy wasn't standing there blocking it. She felt a sudden beat of nervousness. Arturo was still out there. What was going to happen now? As much as she missed Will and Gianni, a part of her was relieved they were safe behind the Dardano walls.

She caught the contradictory nature of that thought and

groaned inwardly. If it wasn't for the Dardanos in the first place, her children would never be in danger. Maybe she should take Brian's advice and leave the country. She sighed and dismissed that thought, if Arturo didn't come after them, Alessandro certainly would.

No, Bree would just have to stay in New York and depend on the police and her family to protect them. The O'Reileys could certainly close ranks around one of their own when they needed to.

But would they want to? After she had chosen Alessandro over them, would they forgive her and welcome her back? Her grandparents still loved her, she knew that. She only hoped they could influence the other members of the O'Reiley family enough to accept her. It chafed at her to think she would have to lower herself and grovel to the more sanctimonious members of her family like her mom and her aunts, but she would do it, to protect her children.

Caroline wanted to keep her in the hospital overnight and Bree was going stir crazy in her room. It wasn't even ten at night yet so she figured she'd visit with Colin and see how he was doing.

But Vanessa came out of the elevator cutting her off. "Well, that's the end of that," she said coming towards Bree.

"What are you doing here?" Bree asked. "Where are Gianni and Will?"

"They're with your moron of a husband, no offense. I simply informed him that he was being a grade A ass by lying to you about something so important. This is just like that time my uncle Murray took all his winnings from playing Poker with his buddies, which it's not really hard to beat them since one of the group's best players is an ex-Vietnam vet who likes to eat the Jack card , and instead of using the money to help Grandma Jessie fix her trick hip, he—"

"Vanessa!" Bree halted her quickly before she could go any further.

"Oh, I quit," Vanessa explained.

"Why?" Bree asked.

"Your husband informed me that my opinion on matters regarding his marriage were not necessary. I told him if that was what he thought about it he was a bigger idiot than I thought."

"Oh no," Bree groaned.

"I'm not the least bit sorry about it and told him so. Then I told him I was not gonna work for someone who can treat people they claim to love like that and then I walked out of there."

"Oh Vanessa. Why did you do that?" Bree sighed, resting her elbows on the nursing station and dropping her head in her hands.

"Because I'm nothing if not loyal, Mrs. D…er…sorry."

"Well, you have to go back."

Vanessa jerked back. "What? Why?"

"Because, Vanessa. Will and Gianni love you. They've had enough upheaval in their lifetime. They can't stay in that house with just Alessandro and Bernardo until I can get them back. Please, put aside your personal feelings and go back."

"You're even assuming he'd take me back. I gave him pretty good what for."

"Oh trust me, Will is going to raise a big enough stink until you go back. Don't worry."

Vanessa pursed her lips but then shrugged. "Fine. What kind of flowers say, I still think you're an asshole but I can't leave your kids in the lurch so can I please have my job back?"

CHAPTER FORTY-TWO

"Knock, knock?" Bree said, peeking her head into Colin's room.

His face split into a grin when he turned and saw her. "Hey. How are you doing?"

She shrugged. "I've been better. Need some company?"

"From you? Always," Colin insisted bringing the chair by his bed closer.

"So how are you doing? Beth was telling me you're going to be released tomorrow. Isn't that a little soon?"

"Worried about me?" he asked, his brown eyes smiling softly.

She wanted to smile back but an irrational part of her thought that his brown eyes were the wrong color. They weren't his kind of brown, like the deepest caramel color she could lose herself in. Had lost herself in. Well. No more, she told herself firmly. She would never get pulled in by his eyes again. She'd be strong and move on. She had to for her own sanity.

Bree forced herself to smile back. "Of course I am. You're my friend."

Colin's smile wavered.

Bree felt a nervous twinge in her chest. Oh God, please let us not get into THAT now.

"Well, I'm worried about you too. I heard you finally left that son of a bitch."

"Bad news travels fast I guess," Bree said irked by his use of the word finally.

"Did he hurt you?" Colin asked, his face darkening. "Is that what brought you to the hospital?"

"Of course not, Colin!" Bree scowled.

"You can't blame me for asking. I know what he's capable of."

"Alessandro would never—"

"Harm a woman? Would you like me to call your sister and ask her opinion?"

Bree shook her head. "Colin, can we not do this? Let's talk about something else, please."

"Just one more thing."

"Oh," Bree groaned.

"Please tell me you're going to get Will and Gianni away from Alessandro now. You know how dangerous he is."

"What? He's their father! I'm not going to take his sons away from him."

"Gianni is his son."

"Okay, listen to me, Colin. Alessandro is Will's father in every way that counts. As much as I'm hating Alessandro right now, I cannot keep him from his children. I'm not doing the whole custody fight thing. We'll just have to work something out like joint custody or something."

"Right. You actually believe that Alessandro will be happy with joint custody."

"He'll just have to be. Now can we please…I'm trying to stay calm for this baby. I don't want to think about custody fights or even Alessandro right now 'cause when I think of Alessandro I want to take that British head and run it through a meat grinder and those are not what I'd call peaceful thoughts."

"No. Not exactly what that Chopra guy had in mind," Colin agreed.

Bree stared at him and cocked an eyebrow. "Deepak Chopra? Since when do you know him?"

Colin gave a sheepish laugh. "I saw his name on the cover of one of Carrie's CDs. She left it behind when she moved out."

"Ah. Well, anyway. I'm trying to stay calm and that means no fights, no stress, basically, my life will now become a zen Alessandro free zone as much as possible."

He let out a loud snort at that.

"What? You don't think I can do it?" Bree asked.

"I'd put money on it."

Her resolution lasted all of twelve hours.

She woke up the next morning to find Andy outside her hospital room like a watch dog that had returned. "I was beginning to miss your charming face." Bree scowled. "What are you doing here?"

"Boss sent me to look out for you before the police carted him off."

"Police? Why?" Bree asked, catching herself feeling panicked for Alessandro. She pushed the feeling aside with an angry internal shove. He deserved whatever he got and more.

Andy motioned towards Colin's room.

"Oh." Bree cringed. "Right." She went back into her room and gathered her clothes. "Well, just let me get changed and you can drive me to the station." She moved to shut the door but Andy placed a hand on it, halting her.

"Uh, Mr. Dardano didn't say anything about wanting you down there."

"Oh, well, Mr. Dardano has no say in where I go anymore. Either I go alone and Mr. Dardano kills you or you can come with me."

Andy narrowed his blue eyes at her. "You know, my last job was for a Russian mob princess who was a spoiled brat and she did not give me as much trouble as you."

Bree patted his thick muscled arm. "Looks like you're moving on up."

"Darling!" Alessandro exclaimed with a cold sneer as a police guard led him into a holding cell. "What are you doing here? Did you come to tell me that the crazy fog has lifted and you're ready to resume your place by my side?"

"Not in this lifetime. That nut house is not my home, and you really are crazy if you think I'm going anywhere with you."

Alessandro's eyes flickered dangerously. "Careful, sweetheart. You are still my wife. Let's not forget that, eh?"

Bree shook her head. "You are unbelievable. Do you feel any remorse at all for what you did?"

Alessandro clenched his jaw. "I believe I expressed my remorse quite thoroughly if you recall. I begged you to forgive me and I beg for nothing, Brianna. I laid myself bare and pleaded for you to understand but all you had for me were hateful words."

"Oh, was I supposed to believe that little performance?" Bree snapped, forcing herself to block out the image of his hands cupping her face, his tears mingling with her own. "It's hard to know because I believed you when you looked me in the eye and told me you had nothing to do with what happened to Colin,"

"Oh yes, of course, Colin—"

"No. No, we're not doing that," Bree cut him off quickly, feeling herself begin to get worked up again. "I'm not gonna let you make this about him. In fact, I know that this is really about you. Everything is always about you. I mean, since you walked in have you even asked me how my night in the hospital was or how the baby is? No, you're throwing your weight around and making snarky jokes."

"Do you really think I would let you walk out of our home carrying my child and not know how you were doing every single second?"

Bree shook her head and took a deep breath. "Do you get how stalkerish you sound right now?"

"Darling, I don't care. There is a psycho on the loose."

"Oh, I am so sick of hearing about Arturo. You know, I wouldn't be surprised if you killed him already but you just keep waving him over my head to keep me afraid and needing you."

"Needing me. What about loving me? Or has that been completely thrown out the window because of one mistake?" Alessandro asked stepping closer to the bars between them.

"This is not about what I do or don't feel. One mistake." She snorted. "It's not just about making a mistake, Alessandro. I can't trust you anymore. Ever." Her eyes burned with tears. "I can't believe another word that comes out of your mouth. And without trust, we have nothing. I mean, I always believed you loved me. You would look in my eyes and I'd know. Now, I'm always going to be wondering, is he just trying to manipulate me to please his father, to fulfill the terms of the vendetta—"

"Oh, fuck the bloody vendetta, Brianna. You know full well that what I feel for you has nothing to do with Adriano and Francesca."

"But that's just it, Alessandro. I don't know. I don't know what the truth is out of your mouth anymore."

He reached over and covered her hand with his over one of the bars. "Very well, the truth is I didn't have to ask how you spent the night in the hospital because I was there."

Bree blinked in surprise. "Come again."

"That's right. In the middle of the night, I visited you in the hospital. You were asleep and I sneaked into your room and just watched you. You were like this vision laying there. So beautiful and I hated myself for lying to you."

"I don't know what I'm supposed to do with that. I mean, am I supposed to be touched or creeped out? If it wasn't for you, I wouldn't be in the hospital in the first place. That is the real truth, Alessandro. That you're more comfortable lying and listening to daddy, doing what he wants even if you have to sacrifice your own family to do it. I mean I gave up everything for you, everything. The truth is a completely foreign concept to you. You know what, it doesn't matter. I'm done. I just wanted to come here and make sure you get what you deserve. I'm going to get my children out of that nut house and file for divorce. Then maybe we can talk about joint custody or some—"

"Divorce? Custody? You can't possibly be serious," Alessandro said, clenching a fist on his thigh."

"As a heart attack," Bree said, trembling. Everything inside of her recoiled at the words but she had to be strong. She could not allow Alessandro to worm his way back into her heart.

As if he'd ever left.

"Let me explain something to you, my dear. No, please, stay calm. Remember the baby. There will be no divorce. There will be no custody. I'm out on bail and I'm going to beat these ridiculous charges and then sue this department into poverty!" he shouted the last bit out towards the door. "We're going home together and working through this little bump in the road."

"I am perfectly calm. Read my lips. I'm taking my children and leaving. You do not want to fight me on this Alessandro."

"Oh there will be no fight, darling because there is no way in hell I'm letting you walk out on me with our children."

Bree leaned close to him. "You can't stop me, Alessandro. Try and you'll regret it."

Alessandro leaned back and cocked an eyebrow. "That almost sounds like a threat, sweetheart."

"It's a promise, Alessandro. For the sake of the boys, I hope you can see reason here and not just make this about your wounded Dardano pride."

"My pride? Darling this has nothing to do with pride this is about the fact that you are my wife. Not just by law but in every way. Mind, body and soul you are mine."

"Right. Yours to lie to, to manipulate."

"To love, dammit!" Alessandro shouted.

Bree rolled her eyes. "You don't know the meaning of the word. Doesn't really surprise me though considering Bernardo was the one that raised you. I will not let my…our children be raised in the same house as that whack job and that is final. One word from me to the judge and you know I can make it happen, Alessandro."

"And how is that, Brianna?"

"I know what you did, Alessandro. You told me about Carrie, and Colin remembers what you did to him." Bree reminded him.

Alessandro narrowed his eyes at her. "Wow. My father warned me that the O'Reileys knew nothing about true love and real loyalty. Fool I am to think you'd be different, eh? You forget one thing, darling. A wife cannot testify against her husband."

"Hence the divorce," Bree shot back. "Now, I'm going to get my children."

Alessandro shook his head. "Not going to happen, sweetheart."

"I'm their mother, Alessandro," Bree insisted.

"And I'm their father. Now, let's just go home and talk about this rationally and work on getting past this."

"Alessandro, I don't want to get past this because you're just gonna pull something else down the line and I can't live my life wondering if every word out of your mouth is a lie."

"I love you. That is not a lie. That is fact."

Bree covered her face with her hands and resisted the urge to scream. "You don't know the meaning of the word. You don't. Because if you did, you would never ever have lied to me about something so vital. Do you have any idea—"

A knock on the door made them both turn at the same time and Bree was glad to see the guard again before she gave in to the urge to cry.

"Sorry to interrupt but we need to get him processed and then he can go home."

"That's fine. I was leaving anyway," Bree said. "I'm going to the house to pick up Gianni and Will."

"Brianna, wait," Alessandro pleaded.

"No, Alessandro. We're done here."

"Just, please wait for me and I'll come with you."

"I don't want to drive with you," Bree insisted.

"Fine, then wait for me at the house. I need to make you understand why I did what I did. There are things you don't know." He and placed a hand on his chest, his eyes begging her, unnerving her.

She broke her gaze away.

"If you think you're going to take the boys at least wait for me so I can say goodbye," he pleaded.

Bree sighed. "Fine. I won't leave that loony bin until you get there. But that's all I'm giving you." She turned and left wondering why she let the man get under her skin the way she did.

Will let out a squeal of excitement when Bree walked into the living room and Gianni got up from the floor all by himself and took four steps before deciding the effort wasn't worth it and crawled the rest of the way, shrieking in delight. "Mommy! You came back!" Will threw his arms around Bree as she gathered him up in her arms.

"Of course I did."

"Are you okay now? Will asked kissing her cheek. "You forgibbed daddy and now we gonna be okay again?"

Bree sighed and looked over at Vanessa who cringed sympathetically. "I'm sorry kiddo, but…no."

Will's smiled faded. "But he say he was sorry, mommy. He know he did sumting bad and I know he miss you lots 'cause he say so. No matter what stupid Gappy Lector say."

Gianni was pulling on her leg and Bree let Will down and picked him up. He wrapped his arms around her neck tightly. "My dis, mamma. No 'way."

Bree inhaled his sweet baby scent and her eyes burned with the ache of not knowing what the right thing to do was. "And what did Grandpa Lecter say, huh?" she asked running her fingers through Will's hair. He scrambled back towards the couch and she followed.

"He say dat daddy shouldn't love you no mo 'cause you nod a good wife. But I know you is 'cause daddy say he don wan' another wife. He wan' only you."

Bree tried to not be affected by Will's words. She pretended to fiddle with Gianni's pacifier.

"Why can't we be like befo', mommy? Daddy's legs work now

so he know we nod gonna stop loving him."

"Because, Will, daddy lied. He pretended that he couldn't walk when he really could."

Will blinked and stared up at her in surprise. "But...but...dat's so stupid!"

"Yes it was. And it hurts mommy very much to know that he would lie about something so important."

"But he say he was sorry, 'member'? When I do sumting bad, I say sorry and you fogib me. You should fogib daddy too."

Gianni nodded. "Gibbits mamma 'tay."

"Brianna?" Alessandro called out before he came into the living room.

Bree closed her eyes and willed herself to not give in to those damnable puppy dog eyes of his that would try and manipulate her heart into wanting to stay. "In here."

"Mamma, daddy, yay!" Gianni exclaimed bouncing up and down before leaning his head on her chest.

"Thank you for waiting for me," he said.

"Right. I didn't do it for you. I did it for them and for my own peace of mind so I could walk out on you guilt free."

"Daddy, mommy told me what you did. Dat was nod nice!" Will exclaimed. "But 'is okay. I fogib you. See, mommy? Easy. Now you do it."

Alessandro placed his hands on his hips and seemed to fighting for patience. "Was that really necessary, Brianna?"

"Yes. I wasn't going to let my children see me as the villain in this little pathetic tragedy."

"Okay, this is my cue to take the boys upstairs before the shit hits the fan," Vanessa said reaching for Gianni.

" 'Nessa! Dat's a bad word!" Will scolded.

"What word? 'Fan'?" Vanessa teased.

Gianni shook his head and clutched Bree tighter. "Noooo! Mamma 'tay!"

"No you can keep them down here. Brianna, I actually wanted to show you something. Something I hope would make you understand why I did what I did. Would you come with me, please?" Alessandro asked.

"Where?" Bree asked warily.

"My father's office. He's not home so you don't have to worry."

"Peachy," Bree grumbled but she got to her feet and kissed Gianni's face. "Mommy will be right back. I promise."

" 'mis 'tay?" Gianni asked.

"Sure thing." She smiled and nodded at Will who looked worried as well. She turned to Alessandro and motioned down the hall. "All right. Let's get this over with."

She followed him into Bernardo's office and stood against the wall as Alessandro pulled what looked like CD out of the desk drawer and stuck it into the computer. "You know this place even feels like the headquarters of pure evil."

"Just please, listen. Maybe this will explain things more clearly."

"What is—" Bree jumped a little, startled as her own voice filled the room

CHAPTER FORTY-THREE

Bree wiped away the tears that streamed down her face as the audio ended and Alessandro explained he knew it had been doctored.

"By?" she asked, her voice choked.

Alessandro gave her a look that told her she should know very well by whom.

"Right. Who else but your dear old daddy would do something so sick and so cruel?"

"So can you understand now?" he asked moving towards her.

"No," she said shaking her head and giving him a bitter laugh. "Oh, I get it in the technical sense. He lied to you to make you believe I was betraying you. I even get how in the state you were in you could buy that load of garbage. What I don't get is how you could use that as an excuse to be deliberately deceitful, deliberately mean. How you could look me in the eye day in and day out and never once ask me?"

"I think I lacked the courage to hear the words straight out of your mouth. Yes, on the tape it was your voice and that broke me enough but to look into your eyes and watch your lips form those words…I couldn't do it," Alessandro admitted.

Bree leaned against the wall and wiped her face. "So what did you see when you looked in my eyes?"

Alessandro lowered his head. "All my life, I never wavered in my belief that my father loved me."

"I'm not asking about Bernardo—" Bree objected. Just saying that man's name made her want to throw up. To do something so sick and mean…to his own son? He was more of a monster than Bree had imagined.

"Please," Alessandro cut her off and went on. "I believed he loved me. Maybe in some sick way this was yet another way to demonstrate that, I don't know. But for my father, love and control mean the same thing. I thought they were two separate things for him. Yes, he was controlling, domineering, even brutal, but beneath all that I believed there was the seed of that affection I saw lavished on other children when their parents came to pick them up from school. My father wasn't and isn't particularly demonstrative but I thought of course he must feel for me what those other parents show with their hugs and kisses. My father lavished me with praise when I pleased him, when I followed his orders. I thought there was my proof that he felt the same. But when I heard this disc, Brianna, something in me broke. To have him do something like that. I can't reconcile who my father is with who I want him to be."

"I've been trying to tell you that for almost two years."

"But don't you see? Before I knew he had doctored the disc, all I thought was that you had lied. You had been trying to pull me away from my father for months and I was letting you because I wanted that life those children had. I wanted that warmth, that security that you and the boys gave, to know I was loved for me and just me."

"You were!" Bree insisted.

He looked at her with sad eyes. "Were?"

Bree bit back a sob and shook her head. "Don't."

"What I want you to understand is that when I heard your words, it was as if every single second we had spent together up to that point was a lie. Every word, every touch, every kiss. You were looking at me, but you wanted him. I was this…thing to be endured to keep your family safe. You would allow me to touch you, to make love to you all the while wishing for Colin. I thought all that passion we had between us was a complete figment of my imagination and it was a bitter pill to swallow. I hated you. Worse than I'd ever hated anyone in my life. I was determined to make you pay. I'd keep you shackled to me forever as punishment. Keep you away from your true love."

Bree stared at him, unable to fathom such cruelty. Who was this man she loved that was capable of such a thing? "And then?"

He took a deep shaky breath and leaned against the edge of the desk, crossing his arms over his chest. "Then I spent all my energy trying to prove to myself by looking at you that you were lying to me, to justify what I was doing by picking up little gestures or flickers in your eyes that would prove to me that you felt nothing for me."

Bree rolled her eyes and gave a tearful snort. "And did you, after how hard I fought for you, did you get what you wanted? Did you prove to yourself what a lying bitch I am?"

"No. Of course not. So I started to doubt what I heard."

"After living with Bernardo for all your life it had just occurred to you that he just may have tampered with the fucking thing?" Bree bit out, furiously.

"It killed me to think I was wrong about you. I didn't relish even fathoming I could have been wrong about my father. I refused to believe that I had to choose between the two of you."

"Never mind that you made me choose between me and my family."

"You're right," he nodded. "But I did it. I checked the disc again and if you want to gloat and go ahead and rub in that you were right, go ahead Brianna. I don't see how that helps the situation at all but go ahead."

"You're damn right I do!" Bree hissed. "I warned you what he was capable of, over and over, that he was just using you to fulfill his diabolical plans. But you know what, I'm not even that mad at him. Bernardo was just being Bernardo. You, though, YOU I blame for this, for destroying what we had. You know why? Because you believed him. Him over me and you didn't just ASK me."

"Fine, but I learned the truth and after I got the rug pulled out from under me, after I learned that everything I thought my father felt for me was a lie, why would I ask you, Brianna?"

Bree glared at him but he rushed ahead.

"No, honestly, how could I ask you and even fathom you would tell me the truth. I had no fucking clue what the truth was anymore!"

"So what, you just thought it would be better to continue to lie? To fake that you were paralyzed forever?"

"No," he sighed. "I was going to gradually pretend to recover."

Bree shook her head and lifted her arms up in defeat. "Oh my God, I can't do this anymore. It just keeps getting worse.

Alessandro, for God sake. How can you do all this and claim that you love me? That's sick and twisted. Every time I was happy over any small victory over your paralysis, it was never real. Were you even ever paralyzed in the first place?"

"Of course I was," Alessandro scowled at her.

"Oh of course. How could I ever doubt you?" Bree said sarcastically. "Man, I thought I was screwed up, but you. God, Alessandro, you're screwed up times a hundred!"

"Not anymore. Now I see everything clearly. I know that you really do love me and I just want us to leave this place and raise our babies in peace. I want that family we were creating—"

Bree stopped him while she still had the will to do so. "You're not listening to me Alessandro, we can't go back. We just can't."

"Why the bloody hell not?" He burst in frustration, walking towards her.

"Because, you don't love me. You spent all your time doubting if I was being faithful to you and if I meant everything I said when all along you were the one who was proving that you didn't truly love me."

"How can you possibly say that? After everything—"

"Because if you did you never would have doubted me. It never would have happened. It's that simple."

"That simple," Alessandro snorted.

"Yeah. Once again, you chose to believe Bernardo over me. Well that's it. I'm done with this sick competition."

He grabbed her arms. "Don't say that. Don't talk like we're over. We're never going to be over, you and I."

"I'm not living with you wondering if you're going to doubt me again, and I'm not living with you doubting if you're telling me the truth about everything. That's not love Alessandro. We have nothing."

He grabbed her face. "Don't. After everything we've shared, don't say we have nothing. While you're carrying that baby of mine, don't dismiss me, us."

Bree closed her eyes, not wanting to fall into his arms. "We'll work something out with the children and I want to keep this as easy as possible for them but I can't be with you anymore. I just can't." She slid away from him and the wall. "I'm going to get Gianni and Will's things—"

"I said NO!" Alessandro shouted punching the wall. "I already explained to you that those children are not leaving this house. That is not negotiable, Brianna."

"I'm not leaving here without my children!" Bree insisted.

"Then I suppose you're not leaving here," Alessandro told her.

Bree shook her head. "What do you mean?"

"If you want to be a mother to those children, you do so in this house, with me, as my wife."

"Are you insane? I just got through telling you that we're done, over, finished!" Bree cried.

"Brianna, let me explain something to you, when I met you and fell in love with you, I became someone I actually liked to be. I became someone I could actually respect. If you walk out on me now, don't be surprised to see me at my worst. You made me a good man. You walk out of this house and all bets are off. You want to fight me for those children, be prepared to fight dirty." He grabbed her and Bree slapped his face with her free hand.

"You claim to love me and now it's threats? You don't get what you want and so you're threatening to be vicious, to use Will and Gianni as pawns to get back at me?"

"I love those boys."

Bree shook her head. "If you loved them you would try and figure out what is best for them. You would try and work with me on some kind of agreement so that they're not more traumatized than they've already been."

"You want to talk trauma? This is the safest place for them for fuck's sake Brianna. Arturo is still out there waiting like a goddamned snake in the grass. I will not, repeat: not, let him have another shot at my children and if I have to fight their mother to keep them safe, so help me I will," Alessandro insisted, pushing her back against the wall. "And you forget that you also have a child of mine in your body. Even if I were willing to risk your life, I'm not, but for argument's sake, let's say I was willing to let you walk out of here and risk your life, in what universe do you think I would ever let Arturo get a shot at my unborn child." He caressed her stomach and Bree smacked his hand away, afraid not of his words but his touch on her skin.

He must have seen the flicker of arousal in her eyes at his touch because he suddenly smiled at her. Not a genuine smile, a triumphant smile, a smile of cat, playing with a mouse. "You know what I think. I get what you're saying, your trust in me has been compromised—"

"Try destroyed," Bree replied, shakily.

"Shhh," Alessandro said, pressing a long finger to her lips. "I think the reason you want to take those boys is because you're afraid to stay in this house with me."

"Well, that's no secret," Bree snorted, her heart racing as his words were getting to close to the truth. "This house would creep anyone the hell out—"

"Ah," he insisted, tapping her lips. "No, sweetheart. You're afraid to stay in this house because you're afraid you will trust me again. You're afraid to live with me in this house, in my bed, as my wife in every way because you know that you'll forgive me. Because no matter what you say, I'm the only man you'll ever love, the only man you'll ever want. And you miss it. You miss what we are to each other," he whispered, stroking her neck with his fingers, obviously feeling her racing pulse. "You miss this powerful love between us, the passion we had. You know it's only a matter of time before I take you again. It's been so long, Brianna, I doubt we'd even get our clothes off completely. Remember that time in Galway? In the backseat?" His hand reached down to cup her breast, intensely sensitive because of her pregnancy.

"Stop it," she pleaded, her voice, her entire being trembling.

"No. If you want me to believe it's over, prove it."

Bree blinked and stared at him warily.

"I'm going to kiss you and you are going to melt against me because you love me, want me as I much as I love you. If you feel nothing anymore—"

"I never said I didn't love you anymore. But love doesn't fix everything. Sex doesn't fix everything, Alessandro."

"No, not sex, but love does and for us they are one in the same. They always have been from the first time. If I didn't love you with my entire soul, if you didn't feel the same, the sex wouldn't be so good between us. So very good darling, remember? Remember the house? Remember Galway, remember how I felt inside of you on the hood of the car as the rain poured down on us. It wasn't just our bodies fucking, my beloved, it was our souls."

"Alessandro, I beg you, stop it," Bree pleaded, tears filling her eyes as she felt herself weakening, her body warming, growing wet.

"No. I can't stop it, because I can't stop loving you. And you can't stop loving me and you know that we can get past this but you're afraid to give in." His mouth moved along her face, her eyes, down her cheeks, hovering just over her lips.

Her tongue betrayed her and reached out to lick her dry lips in preparation, her body wanted his kiss desperately even as her mind told her nothing would change. Things would be okay just until the next time he decided to lie to her, crush her dreams.

"If you're not afraid to stay in this house with me, then kiss me and tell me it's not fear that's making you walk out, that you're doing it for the boys and not because you're terrified to open your heart to me again, to give us another chance. Kiss me and tell me it's truly over between us."

He didn't give her a chance to stop him. He crushed his mouth over hers and plunged his tongue into her mouth, making her knees buckle with the taste of him.

Bree struggled, or at least her mind did because her mouth was whimpering and kissing him back. Her arms wanted to push him away but they wrapped around him instead.

He groaned and deepened the kiss as if he was trying to devour her completely. His stubble scratched her face and she knew she'd see the redness there later but right now she wanted more. She wanted him to take her right here up against the wall.

"Like this?" he groaned against her mouth, continuing to kiss her as his fingers moved between her legs. "Remember, taking you like this? Up against the wall, that night of the party? In your gold dress? Gold heels wrapped around my waist later, naked on our bed as we fucked?"

"Stop…" she panted, the memories and the fact that he shared them making her even more aroused. "God…just…stop…"

"Wet…so wet, for me…." He pressed his fingers against her center and Bree gasped because she was hovering right on the razor's edge.

She was at war with herself. She had to stop him, had to now or she never would. If he made her come, he'd know that he had won. And she told herself that was what he wanted, to win, because that's what he had always wanted. Victory not love. Because his love for her wasn't real. She'd just wanted him to love her but he didn't. He just wanted her to give in, to break her so that she wouldn't care the next time he hurt her.

"No, no!" Bree cried pushing him away. With trembling legs she covered her mouth that still tasted of him and ran out of the office.

Her mother was knocking on the door. Bree pulled the pillow more firmly over her head. She knew it was Angela because even her knock sounded judgemental. That and every so often she'd hear a "Bree, honey. It's not good for you to be alone right now. Let's talk about this."

Well, screw that, she did so want to be alone. She had no desire to see anyone. Brian had called. Called. He didn't come over. He wasn't banging on her door demanding to fix her, and he'd certainly inherited Angela's 'fix-it' gene. But he understood that Bree needed to just be by herself for a while. She loved her brother. He had asked her if she wanted to watch while he dismembered her soon to be ex-husband.

Bree almost said yes.

He'd promised to come by tomorrow with junk food so they could watch movies and she could bitch and wallow and then he could go dismember Alessandro.

"Bree, come on, baby girl. Open the door. I know you're home because the concierge told me you hadn't left."

She'd gone to the hotel hoping to avoid any of the less palatable O'Reileys, including mommie dearest. Good grief, she should have known better. All of New York was overrun by either O'Reileys or Dardanos.

Maybe she should move to Yemen. If it wasn't for Gianni and Will, she would. Her babies.

A fresh sob burst through her and she grabbed another Kleenex off the night table. Blowing her sore red nose, Bree stared up at the ceiling, which was blurred through her tears.

And now, she could only breathe through one nostril.

Again. "Bree, please let me in. I only want to make sure you're all right."

"Dammit!" Bree screamed in frustration and scrambled off the bed and stormed towards the door. She pulled it open. "What? You wanna see if I'm okay? No. You want to talk to me? No. You want me to open up about my feelings? Not gonna happen. Anything else?"

Angela jerked back, a hand to her chest. "Bree, I am not the enemy here."

"Great. Noted. Bye." She moved to shut the door again but

Angela quickly slid through the opening before Bree could close the door completely.

"Oh for God's sake," Bree groaned, pressing her forehead against the wall.

"Honey, you shouldn't be dealing with this hard time alone," Angela urged, placing a hand on her back.

"You're right, mom. I should be at home with my children. I should be with the man I love. I should be happy. Are you gonna fix any of that? Do you have the ability to magically turn back time?"

"Bree, I know you're broken hearted but don't shut me out. I'm your mother. It kills me to see you in such pain."

"Mmm well if it kills you so much why are you here?" Bree snapped wiping her cheeks as she walked away from her towards the couch.

"I'm here to help you."

"I don't want your help, mom. I'm fine…or…I will be anyway if I could just get some peace." She dropped onto the cushions and didn't have the energy to kick her mother out so she didn't object when Angela took a seat next to her.

"You'll never get that peace until you come to terms with the end of your marriage, with the fact that you made a mistake."

Bree stared at her. She propped her head on her hand, resting the elbow on the backrest of the cushion and just stared at her mother. "Wow."

"Bree—"

"No, you say you're here to help me but what you really want is to…what, gloat? Stupid Bree believed that the big bad Dardano loved her. How dumb huh? Who could possibly want me, right? I'm not Carrie, I'm not even Beth. Stupid me for thinking that my family could actually be sympathetic that my life was going down the toilet."

"I'm not going to apologize for not being upset that Alessandro is out of your life."

"Mom, get out. Just go." Bree opened her door and pointed into the hall.

"Bree, don't do this. You need your family around you right now."

"Right. My family who every time they look at me are gonna gloat over the fact they won me back from the big bad Dardanos. I don't need that. I want you to leave."

"Bree—"

"GET OUT!" Bree shouted.

Slamming the door behind her mother, Bree leaned against it and cried. So much for getting her family's help on anything. She really was alone now. How stupid was she to believe they would welcome her back and shower her with any unconditional love when they didn't know the meaning of the word. It was, ironically, one of the things they had in common with Bernardo. Her family didn't love her. Alessandro didn't love her.

Would anyone ever just accept her for her and love her for her?

Colin. He wanted her. He wanted to be with her. Why not him? Why not be with someone who actually loved her?

That was what she told herself as she drove to his apartment. She pushed aside the voice that told her she would always love Alessandro and that this would simply make things worse. He would never forgive her for this.

Good, her anger answered back. Let him feel what it's like to be betrayed for once. She didn't want him back. What was the point? He'd just lie to her because he didn't really love her or accept her either. She had to move on and what better way to push him away forever and keep her own heart safe than to make sure he never wanted her again.

When Colin came to the door, Bree wrapped her arms around his neck and kissed him.

She swore she thought she heard her very soul cry out against what she was doing. She told her soul to fuck off.

Bree opened her eyes and was immediately aware that something was off in the room. There was an arm draped over her stomach and the body she was pressed against was …different. It didn't smell like Alessandro. Familiar, warm, his sleepy scent usually beckoned her and how many times had they ended up having hot wet morning sex because Alessandro said her scent aroused him as well? He told her there was something to that whole male/female primal scent arousal thing. The hand over her wasn't cupping her breast like Alessandro liked to do in his sleep.

The body was wrong because the man was wrong.

Colin.

Oh God. Oh no. Nonononono!

"You okay?" he asked moving his hand to her shoulder.

Bree squeezed her eyes shut and then forced herself to look back with small smile.

Oh Bree…you stupid, stupid, stupid—

"Look, I don't want you to beat yourself up about this, okay? It happened. I for one am not sorry but I don't want you to think I'm putting any kind of pressure on you. You were going through a rough time, I'm glad I could be here for you."

Oh Colin. You stupid, stupid, stupid… "I just can't believe I…"

His brown eyes flickered with disappointment. "So you do regret it."

Bree looked away guiltily. "I…this is…Colin, I'm still married."

"I know Bree. But Alessandro is…" He closed his mouth and shook his head.

"What?" Bree asked, sitting up, wrapping the blanket around her. Her head spun dizzily for a moment and she felt her stomach lurch.

"He lied to you, repeatedly. He's jealous and controlling and dangerous. I mean, the man tried to have me killed."

"I know," Bree moaned. But I love him. I want this to all go away and for us to go back to being happy. "But this…doesn't fix anything."

Just like 'I love you' doesn't fix anything. Ah, that's right, Bree thought. You love him but he doesn't love you. Isn't that the way it always was with her? She gave everything, always gave her whole heart and she always got slammed for it. She looked at Colin and sighed. She reached over and cupped his face. "I wish…"

But then her stomach savagely demanded attention again and she quickly clamped a hand over her mouth and grabbed the blanket and pulled it off the bed in her haste to get to the bathroom. Over the emptying of her stomach she heard loud banging. Easing back on her knees she grabbed the towel from the wall.

Right. Six months in and the morning sickness decides to make a return appearance. She rubbed her stomach, feeling considerably better and then got up to wash her face. She told herself that it was just the sex. Sometimes mothers get a little nauseous from the movement. She'd read that somewhere.

Though she'd never had that problem with Will.

Or Gianni.

She had a brief flare of paranoia where she thought the baby was piping in with her own opinion of what mommy had done. None too happy that she had betrayed Daddy.

Bree looked into the mirror and a sob rose in her throat at the sadness she saw there in her own eyes. Damn you, Alessandro. Damn you for making me…Ah, who are you kidding, Bree? This is vintage you, she told herself. You wanted to punish him and of course you end up hurting yourself even more, don't you?

Your own worst enemy. She jumped, startled when she heard more banging followed by yelling.

Oh God. That voice.

Before she could think better of it, Bree rushed out of the bathroom just in time to see Alessandro punch Colin, clad only in a sheet, across the face.

Colin fell backwards onto the bed, grabbing the sheet in the nick of time and moved a hand to his face but Alessandro was on top of him.

"I know she's here, you insipid little fuck. And I swear to God I'm gonna finish you off this time!" Alessandro vowed wrapping his hands around Colin's neck and beginning to squeeze.

Colin punched at Alessandro's arms and face but Alessandro had him in a certain death grip and wasn't relinquishing his hold.

"Alessandro, stop!" Bree pleaded.

Rage driven eyes lifted to hers and held.

They both froze and for a second, pain clouded Alessandro's gaze before the rage flickered back and turned those beautiful eyes cold.

He eased back from Colin and stormed towards her. "Why?" Alessandro asked, his voice cracking, belying the coldness in his eyes. "Why him?"

Bree backed away, afraid of the pain radiating off of him. She wanted to feel triumphant, to throw it back in his face that now he knew how she felt but all she could think was I'm sorry. I'm sorry. I wish I had never done this. I wish I could take it back.

He drove his fist so violently into the wall next to her head that chips of paint and plaster smacked against her skin. If it had hurt him, he gave no indication.

"Alessandro, listen," Bree pleaded, reaching for his arm but he jerked away as if she burned him.

"No you don't!" he hissed. "Don't touch me after you let him fuck you."

He turned to the door and all Bree knew was she could not let him leave without explaining.

What? How could she possibly make this right? And why should she have to, Bree thought stubbornly. He hurt her first. Oh what are you, four? She was an adult for God's sake! Now granted, they were over but this…this would make him hate her and something fundamental inside of her screamed against that.

"I didn't mean for this to—" She ran after him towards the door.

He whirled on her. "You lying bitch. All that impassioned garbage about wanting us to be a family and how much you love me and how I broke your heart and then you turn around and sleep with THAT?"

"I was out of my mind, Alessandro. Please. I never meant to do this. I wasn't thinking—"

"I hardly think you're anyone to take any moral high ground here, acting like the injured party when you're the one who betrayed Bree," Colin said coming up behind Bree as she stood in front of Alessandro, tears filling her eyes.

Alessandro didn't even spare Colin a glance. He pointed at Bree. "Well, think about this. There is no way in hell, I'm letting a whore raise my children."

Bree shuddered. "You can't possibly mean to—" Dear God, he couldn't be serious. To keep her away from Will and Gianni? Permanently?

"Oh I do, sweetheart. You'll be hearing from my lawyer."

"Alessandro don't do this. You're angry, I get that but do not drag our children into this."

"You drew the battle lines, darling when you spread your legs for him. Now you're going to reap the fallout."

"Alessandro, you don't want to do this. You don't want to take my children away from me. You're not that man, please," Bree pleaded reaching for his face but he jerked his head away.

Bree blinked her tears back and shook her head. "Wow. Then I guess you really are your father's son, huh?"

"You have no idea," Alessandro snapped before leaving.

Part of her wanted to run after him but a stronger part of her knew he wouldn't listen to anything she had to say while the red haze was still burning inside of him.

He wanted a fight.

She'd give him one.

THE END

ABOUT THE AUTHOR

A self confessed 'city girl' E. Jamie lives in Toronto, Canada and loves roaming the streets of her vibrant city to feed her muse. She loves penning passionate tales that leave the bedroom door wide open! She enjoys writing across all erotic sub genres from contemporary to historicals! In her spare time she wishes she had more time to read, explore her city, watch TV and dish up some delicious creations. Cooking feeds both the culinary and writing muse and she is also going to be working on a non-fiction cookbook soon! She's always thrilled to hear from her readers at her website authorejamie.wordpress.com and you can join her fan page at facebook.com/authorejamie and follow her on twitter @authorejamie.

www.ingramcontent.com/pod-product-compliance
Lightning Source LLC
Chambersburg PA
CBHW060339260626
47160CB00006B/2131
9780992046316